MW01028681

BITTER TEXAS HONEY

BITTER TEXAS HONEY

A Novel

ASHLEY WHITAKER

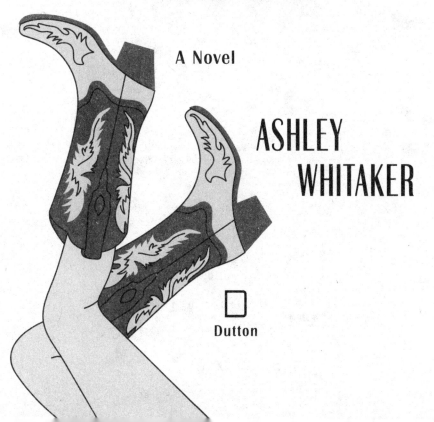

Dutton

DUTTON

An imprint of Penguin Random House LLC
1745 Broadway, New York NY 10019
penguinrandomhouse.com

Copyright © 2025 by Ashley Whitaker
Penguin Random House values and supports copyright. Copyright fuels creativity,
encourages diverse voices, promotes free speech, and creates a vibrant culture. Thank you
for buying an authorized edition of this book and for complying with copyright laws by not
reproducing, scanning, or distributing any part of it in any form without permission. You are
supporting writers and allowing Penguin Random House to continue to publish books for
every reader. Please note that no part of this book may be used or reproduced in any
manner for the purpose of training artificial intelligence technologies or systems.

DUTTON and the D colophon are registered trademarks of Penguin Random House LLC.

Title page art: Cowgirl in boots © CoCoArt_Ua / Shutterstock
Book design by Alison Cnockaert

LIBRARY OF CONGRESS CATALOGING-IN-PUBLICATION DATA
Names: Whitaker, Ashley, author.
Title: Bitter Texas honey: a novel / Ashley Whitaker.
Description: New York : Dutton, 2025.
Identifiers: LCCN 2024036566 | ISBN 9780593476154 (hardcover) |
ISBN 9780593476161 (ebook)
Subjects: LCGFT: Humorous fiction. | Novels.
Classification: LCC PS3623.H56253 B58 2025 | DDC 813/.6—dc23/eng/20240826
LC record available at https://lccn.loc.gov/2024036566

Printed in the United States of America

1st Printing

The authorized representative in the EU for product safety and compliance is
Penguin Random House Ireland, Morrison Chambers, 32 Nassau Street,
Dublin D02 YH68, Ireland, https://eu-contact.penguin.ie.

For my mom and James—the fun ones

BITTER TEXAS HONEY

1.

CANON

Conservative talk radio hosts were the most reliable men in her life. Monday through Friday, no matter what she'd gotten into the night before, they were there, like old friends and confidants, like second fathers, like faithful lovers, their voices booming and authoritative, clever and jovial and worldly, always ready to soothe her mind and silence her thoughts.

Joan listened one morning, in January 2011, while she got dressed for her internship, tucking a button-up blouse into control-top pantyhose, sliding on her black pencil skirt, and dry heaving into her sink. She continued listening as she walked the four blocks uphill to the Texas Capitol, her head throbbing, chugging a sugar-free Red Bull, with two more cans clanking in her purse for later. She listened intermittently throughout her five-hour shift as she tried to piece together the events of the night before, reading through a thread of unsettlingly intimate text messages between her and a man saved in her phone only as "Marine—Dirty 6th." She resumed listening as she packed up her things and left, heading to a coffee shop near campus, where she intended to work on her novel. Because more than anything else, Joan West was still a writer, or at least she hoped to be.

She walked in the harsh cold, earphones in, a lobbyist-gifted scarf wrapped around her neck. Her favorite host, Dennis Prager, was talking again about the inherent differences between men and women. Every Wednesday, Dennis dedicated his entire second hour—called "The Male/Female Hour"—to traditional gender roles and healthy marriages. Even though Dennis was already on his third wife, Joan trusted his advice wholeheartedly. He seemed so wise and confident, often citing his experience counseling young couples as a rabbi. By listening to his show, Joan hoped to uncover the mysterious reason she always failed in love.

Dennis insisted that the Left was working hard to destroy America by downplaying the obvious, natural differences between the sexes. Joan would have thought he was being paranoid if she hadn't experienced it herself. During her first semester of college, at the University of Miami, Joan learned in Sociology 101 that there was no real difference between men and women. Rather, she had been *socialized* by the patriarchy (and her parents) to like pink, to play with dolls, to become clingy after sex, etc. Learning this, Joan tried hard to free herself, to embrace her inner manliness. She went braless in dinosaur T-shirts, stopped shaving, and cut her hair short. She went to drum circles on South Beach, topless, and kissed girls. She had emotionless sex with her platonic guy friends, mostly student musicians in the jazz program. She wrote ultra-minimally, like Ernest Hemingway or Bret Easton Ellis. But instead of making her feel empowered or fulfilled, Joan's behavior only led her to an amphetamine-induced manic episode, a forced year off from college, and an HPV diagnosis.

When Joan reached the Drag, Dennis was explaining that women's denial of their God-given nurturing roles and attempt to enter the man's sphere had led to an entire generation of depressed women and confused men, which, passing by a bus stop full of miserable-looking UT students, Joan felt was a compelling theory. Now that Joan was aware of this omnipresent, nebulous mass called the Left and its nefarious motives, she was on alert for it at all times.

She passed by the iconic "Hi How Are You" frog mural, then the Church of Scientology, where a cluster of redheaded runaways known colloquially as "Drag rats" were gathered with their dogs, playing banjo and fiddle music, wearing dirty army fatigues, probably high on heroin. One of the Drag rats approached Joan, demanding money. She ignored him, turned up Dennis Prager, and walked faster. Dennis was certainly right about one thing: Something was seriously wrong with her generation.

She entered Caffè Medici, her cheeks flushed from the cold, and went to the bar, where her favorite barista, Roberto, was working. She removed her earphones and scarf and set her phone face down, careful to conceal the screen from him, lest he get a glimpse of what she was listening to. She ordered a glass of red wine, pulled Ernest Hemingway's collected stories out of her book bag, and began reading with the cover prominently displayed. Every couple of minutes she used a mechanical pencil to mark passages that felt important or profound.

"What's up, lady? What are you reading?" Roberto asked, setting the wineglass in front of her on top of a napkin. "Oh, I love that book."

Joan had first met Roberto while she was studying for finals the month before, in December, shortly before graduating from UT. They rarely spoke, but he possessed a mysterious, subdued earnestness toward life that intrigued her. He called her "lady," which wasn't anything special. He called all the female patrons "lady."

"You've read this?" Joan asked.

"Of course. The second story is the best one in there. I love the part where the guy bleeds to death after getting impaled by that fake bull."

"I love that part too," Joan said, straightening in her seat. And this was true, from what she could remember of the scene. She hardly remembered much of what she read, perhaps because she was usually high. But she did recall that particular image: the man in Spain dying in a pool of his own blood.

She watched Roberto as he made a latte. He was wearing the same jeans he always wore, and a pearl-snap cowboy shirt that was at least a size too small and barely grazed his belt line. Joan wondered if it was meant to be a woman's shirt. She took a large gulp of bitter wine,

3

hoping her heart would begin to beat more slowly. Joan had chugged all three of her Red Bulls during her shift at the capitol, where she was a legislative intern for one of the most conservative members of the state house, an ex-cop from Houston with tall crispy hair who wore yellow alligator-skin boots every day. The boots had been a personal gift from Governor Rick Perry, she was often reminded.

The job began earlier that week and would last through May. The legislature in Texas only met once every two years. Even though the job was unpaid, it was extremely easy and made her feel that she was one step closer to adulthood. It also greatly appeased and impressed her family, who had agreed to continue paying her exorbitant downtown rent.

Halfway into her first glass of wine, Joan ordered another. After Roberto finished serving his other customers, they continued to talk about literature. To her surprise, it seemed as if Roberto had read every book ever written. There was nothing Joan had read that Roberto hadn't, and she began to feel inadequate. She was on her third glass when she revealed that she was a fiction writer, and Roberto told her that he was too. They exchanged email addresses before she left and vowed to start sending each other stories.

Roberto's first email arrived later that night. Joan was sitting cross-legged in an orange velvet chair, smoking black resin out of her pink pipe, waiting for her dealer to arrive with fresh weed.

The email was short and contained a link to his story "Moshing Towards Bethlehem," which had been published the previous fall in an obscure online journal called *Possum Stinkdom*. Joan felt mildly ashamed that she didn't have anything published to share. She skimmed a few paragraphs before getting distracted, her mind consumed by thoughts of what she should send Roberto in return. She wanted to impress him, to appear as prolific and assured as he was.

"What do you think I should send to this writer guy?" Joan asked her roommate, Claire, who was standing at the window, drinking chardonnay, watching a concert through the blinds. Of Montreal had just started playing on the outdoor stage at Mohawk, one of three music venues next door. The bass was so loud it shook the entire building. The laminate floor vibrated. The dishes rattled in the cabinets.

Claire stood for a moment, considering. "What about something with your dad? That material is always pretty strong."

"That could work, I guess," Joan said. She mostly respected Claire's opinion. They had met at Oxford two summers before, during a Jane Austen study abroad through the UT English Department, where they drank more, and more often, than any of the other girls in the program. Claire was also a writer, working on an epic one-day novel in the style of *Ulysses*.

Claire did a ballerina move into the kitchen, where she picked up her oversized wine bottle sitting half empty on the counter. She filled her glass nearly to the brim, then topped it off with a dash of sparkling water. Claire did this, she often explained, to "pace" herself. She walked back into the den with her glass and examined her profile in Joan's full-length antique mirror.

"I hope I threw up last night," Claire said, sucking in and placing her hand on her lower stomach.

"I'm pretty sure you did," Joan said. She opened her laptop and began searching her chaotic desktop for the latest draft of her coming-of-age novel, *Cowgirls and Indians*, which she'd begun writing in Miami, and from which she would extract an impressive stand-alone piece about her dad. Opening the document increased her heart rate and shortened her breath. The muscles in her chest and neck tensed up. As much as Joan wanted to be a writer, she didn't actually enjoy the process of it, and hadn't since she quit Adderall three years before, at the behest of her parents. Without amphetamines, Joan wasn't sure why she bothered with writing. It was as if she was trying to fill some deep void, the origins of which she chose not to explore.

"Are you coming out tonight?" Claire asked. "Luke's playing at

Cheer Ups." Luke was Claire's on-again/off-again boyfriend of four years.

"Not tonight," Joan said. "I'm pretty tired." The truth was that her dealer would be over any minute, and she didn't want to miss his delivery.

"Fine. Let's at least get a picture," Claire said. The girls took a stoic-faced selfie and posted it to Facebook, with the caption "Great American Novels Coming Soon."

Claire left, her dealer came and went, and Joan remained in her chair with her laptop open, Roberto's story languishing on the screen, unread. Joan smoked a second bowl while looking out her windows, admiring her view. From her corner apartment, she could see so much: the top tip of the capitol, the skyline, the sleek-looking homeless shelter. She zoned out for a few minutes, entranced by Club de Ville's blinking, crown-shaped sign directly across the street. Feeling high and renewed, Joan wrote a quick response to Roberto.

This was amazing, she wrote, even though she hadn't finished reading his story. *Love the homage to Joan Didion. Very subversive.*

Thanks, lady, he replied ten minutes later. *That really means a lot. Hope to see something of yrs soon.*

Joan scrolled through her novel for compelling scenes about her dad, narrowing her choices down to three pieces, weighing them against one another. There was a chapter that chronicled the events of her dad's fourth and most recent marriage, which had ended explosively in 2009, while she was in Oxford with Claire. There was a heart-wrenching vignette about her dad's Chihuahua (the lone remnant of said fourth marriage) ingesting antifreeze and almost dying. Alternatively, she could go with one of her very first pieces, a lyrical dramatization of her dad sinking his houseboat in 1990, on Lake Lewisville, with his fuckup friend Bruce, shortly after her parents' divorce when she was three.

Her dad had always been a major focus of her writing. His life was chaotic and interesting, for better or for worse. He made a compelling character. Joan had never written a word about her mother, though, who she didn't feel had any literary merit.

She decided to send Roberto the chapter about her dad's fourth marriage, which had received a B+ in her intermediate fiction class at UT. It was called "Blond Hair, Big Boobs, Alcoholic, Thief."

She sent the piece without providing any context, making any changes, or checking for any typos and anxiously awaited his reply.

Roberto's response came the following morning while Joan was at work, proofreading a bill that would require proper burials for aborted fetuses. She paused her task immediately to read his note:

> Lady,
>
> Thank you for sharing this piece, which I thoroughly enjoyed. I admired the way this narrator chronicles her dad's relationship from beginning to end with such clarity and precision.
>
> However, I couldn't help but want to see more of her interiority. There is this sense that she is not more than a camera lens, recording her dad's movements. Perhaps you could deepen this character somehow, write a story that reveals more of her inner life—her thoughts, emotions, and desires.
>
> I look forward to reading more. You are a very talented woman with a distinct voice.
>
> Yrs, R

Joan reread the email several times, lingering over the final sentence. She was *a very talented woman with a distinct voice.* She found this line immensely flattering and was pleased to have Roberto taking her work seriously, engaging with her mind and soul in a way that she missed. Ever since graduating in December, Joan lacked an authoritative male mentor to assure her that she had talent, to remind her that her life was worth living, her dreams of being a writer worth pursuing.

Joan started drinking wine at the coffee shop more over the next two weeks, often walking or driving straight over from her internship. The excitement of the Eighty-Second Legislative Session—the Tea Party activists and their causes, along with all the lobbyist-funded buffets, open bars, mariachi bands, petting zoos, and interpretive dances— drained Joan artistically. She retreated to the coffee shop afterward, she told herself, to refill her creative well. Really, she wanted to fill herself with Roberto.

She brought a different book to read each time she visited, to study how famous writers handled "interiority," and to show Roberto how sophisticated and varied her taste was. One Friday, in the last week of January, she brought Flannery O'Connor's *Everything That Rises Must Converge*.

"Ugh. Flannery O'Connor. She's the worst," Roberto said dismissively before loudly grinding a batch of beans.

Joan was noticing a pattern with him. While he'd read every book she brought in, the authors seemed to fall into only two categories: Either they were "the best," or they were "the worst." There was no gray area with Roberto. Joan envied his conviction. If she was being honest, she never knew exactly what to feel about any book she read.

"How can you say that about O'Connor?" Joan asked. "She's canonical." Every anthology of fiction she'd ever seen had contained at least one story by O'Connor. She placed the book face down on the bar, wishing now she hadn't chosen it.

"There is no *canon*," Roberto said in his Tex-Mex accent, shaking his head as if he were explaining a painful truth to a child. "Don't believe that bullshit, lady."

Joan didn't know what to say. She had never given much thought to the word *canon* or considered that the canon might not even exist. She began to feel mainstream and pedestrian.

"When are you going to send me a new story?" Roberto asked, wiping an empty glass with a towel. He had already shared two additional pieces—a story about carnies and a series of three poems about some obscure historical figure he'd made up, both already published in local zines with handmade covers, while she had still sent nothing besides "Blond Hair, Big Boobs, Alcoholic, Thief."

"Very soon," Joan said, feeling a wave of anxiety. She checked the time. It was almost three P.M. She needed to get on the road if she was going to make it to Fort Worth in time. That night, she was going to meet her dad's side of the family at the rodeo, an annual tradition that she seldom missed.

Joan gathered her things while Roberto was cleaning the bathrooms and left the coffee shop abruptly, without saying goodbye. At this point, leaving Roberto in suspense was probably the best way to keep him interested.

2.

SHOULD'VE BEEN A COWGIRL

Joan stopped at a gas station in Waco to change into her rodeo clothes—a skintight black minidress, turquoise earrings with dangling black feathers, and black cowboy boots. On her way out, she bought a bottle of Sprite, which she half emptied onto the pavement, then filled to the brim with vodka that she kept in her trunk.

A little past six, she met her favorite cousin, Wyatt, in the parking lot of his apartment complex. For the past three years, he'd been living here, in his friend's dining room, ever since getting kicked out of her dad's house in Dallas. Before that, Wyatt had lived with various other friends and family members, including with Joan's brother in North Carolina, where Wyatt tried to kill himself. Now he desperately wanted to join the marines.

The air was much colder up in Fort Worth. Joan shivered, her breath visible, walking toward Wyatt's idling car, taking large gulps of her vodka Sprite.

"How much for the night?" Wyatt shouted through the rolled-down passenger window. A radio DJ's voice emanated from the car at an absurd volume.

"Ten thousand," Joan said, and gave him the middle finger.

"Sold!" Wyatt exclaimed. She climbed into his beat-up, pewter-colored Nissan Maxima, which had been gifted to him by his brother-in-law after he totaled their grandfather's pickup truck. The car was dented on every side and looked like it had been in a demolition derby or a hundred hailstorms. Wyatt was underdressed, as usual, wearing a white Smoothie King T-shirt from his previous job, blue jeans, and black high-top sneakers, untied.

"You got your braces off," Joan said.

"Yep," Wyatt said, and smiled big. He had gotten braces voluntarily at twenty-one to fix a minor, hardly noticeable cosmetic issue with his canines, puzzling everyone in the family and making him appear fourteen years old.

"Looking good," Joan said.

Wyatt's front license plate, dangling by a single screw, scraped the pavement as he drove out of the parking lot and turned onto the street. The radio was stuck, playing a country music station at full volume. Earlier that day, he explained, all the buttons had stopped working at once in this unfortunate position. It was this music or nothing at all.

"Quite the dilemma!" Joan yelled.

He swerved and hit a curb on purpose. Joan gripped the handle above her window, her knuckles white. Wyatt threw his head back and erupted in a heavenly cackle, until eventually, Joan relaxed and started laughing too. How could she be afraid in the face of such unbridled joy and destruction?

She jotted the scene down in her notebook the rest of the way, thinking Wyatt's car might be a good symbol to use in the new story she would send Roberto, somehow representing male angst and confusion in contemporary America, like Dennis Prager talked about. She wasn't sure how Wyatt's car would help illuminate her narrator's "inner life." But she could iron that out later.

Wyatt, still giddy from the excitement of the fender bender, sang along to "Born Country" by Alabama as he turned into the parking lot, then backed hard into a cement pole before pulling neatly into a space. Joan's bottle of vodka Sprite spilled all over the floorboard and her cowboy boots. Wyatt turned off the car and a jarring silence overtook them.

"You made me spill my vodka, fuck face," Joan said, wiping off her boots, her ears still ringing from the music.

"Sorry. Guess you'll have to deal with real life a little longer," Wyatt said in his chipper way.

"That sounds terrible," Joan said. She hated "real life." They got out of the car to assess and admire the new body damage.

They walked along the redbrick sidewalk, past the stockyards and boot shops and barbecue restaurants.

"How's your book going?" Wyatt asked. When they briefly lived together at her dad's, the summer after she was pulled out of Miami, they'd talked about writing nearly every day. Together they conceived dozens of ideas for brilliant, edgy films, hilarious skits, and heartbreaking songs. Of course, they had never come close to finishing anything.

Joan explained that she was working on something new, a short story. She told him about Roberto, whom she wanted to impress. "He wants to see something that showcases my narrator's 'inner life' or something," Joan said with a shrug.

"Inner life? That's easy," Wyatt said. "Just write something about love."

Joan scrunched up her face. "I never write about that kind of stuff."

"Why? Isn't love the most universal subject there is?" Wyatt began singing the love medley from *Moulin Rouge*, one of his favorite films. When they lived together, Wyatt had watched the movie all day every day for five days straight, until he had all the lines and lyrics memorized.

"Maybe . . ." Joan said with hesitation. She felt that Wyatt was being naïve. He'd always been a hopeless romantic, obsessed with their grandparents' fifty-year marriage and still hung up on his high school girlfriend. Sure, love was a good subject for musicals and Disney films, but not for literary fiction. She wanted her work to be considered "high art." Besides, love had always been the most embarrassing part of Joan's life. Something to conceal, not showcase.

"What about you?" Joan asked, changing the subject. "You writing anything?"

Wyatt told Joan he'd been working on a new song and asked if she would take a look at the lyrics. He was basically a music prodigy who had taught himself to play the guitar and the piano by the time he was ten, but he had always struggled with words.

"Let's see," Joan said. Wyatt handed her a warm, crumpled-up piece of notebook paper. The title, "Vines," was written at the top in messy, childlike scrawl. As usual, the lyrics appeared to be about his ex-girlfriend from high school, Ruby, a petite girl with a flat affect and an encyclopedic knowledge of the Dallas Cowboys.

Joan stopped walking to read. The page contained several inscrutable words, spelling errors, entire crossed-out lines. Sometimes, when trying to read Wyatt's handwriting, Joan wondered if he had some kind of undiagnosed learning disability. But after a minute, she understood. He'd written a pretty straightforward metaphor about vines growing out of Ruby and following him everywhere. No matter where he went or how many times he severed them, the vines always returned and wrapped themselves around his body, squeezing him like a boa constrictor, so tight he couldn't breathe or move anymore. It read more like a horror story than a love song.

"Try to get more specific," Joan said, handing him the piece of paper. "Like, what kind of vine is this? Poison ivy? Grapes? Something else?"

They passed by an enormous Texas longhorn wearing a saddle, a line of urban Texans in western cosplay waiting to take pictures on its back. Wyatt stopped walking and squinted at the piece of paper, as if the answer to Joan's questions were hidden there. Joan loved the way Wyatt took her feedback so seriously. More than anyone else in the family, he seemed to see her for the great writer she was destined to be. He made her feel wise and authoritative, like a seasoned creative writing professor instead of some loser who couldn't finish her novel.

"Probably something with thorns," Wyatt said. "Roses?"

"Too cliché," Joan said.

"I've got it," he said with a jolt. "Blackberry vines."

"That could work," Joan said.

As children, she and Wyatt and the rest of their cousins had harvested the dark, sweet fruit that grew along the pasture fences in the summer at their grandparents' sprawling West Texas ranch.

"She's sweet, but she's sharp," Wyatt said, excited now. "I like the taste of her, but she hurts me. She makes me bleed. Oh! And her hair and eyes are black."

"That's good. Write that down." Joan handed him her pen, and Wyatt scribbled the word *blackberry* at the top of the page. Joan could do this every day, she thought. With Wyatt, it was the process of creation that she enjoyed, not the end product, which for them never manifested. But that didn't matter. She felt a pang of sadness that they no longer lived under the same roof. Wyatt crumpled the paper back up and shoved it into his pocket as they ascended the stairs of the Cowtown Coliseum.

Inside the arena, the West family took up two rows of green metal chairs. Their grandparents, Wyatt's mother and third stepdad, his siblings and their spouses and children, and their aunt and uncle and cousins were all there. Joan's father was there too, with a woman she had never seen in her life, a brunette he introduced as Jelly Bean. Jelly Bean worked as the receptionist for the California branch of her dad's business—a for-profit career college called Audio Professional Academy (AudioPro) that taught people to record and produce their own music.

"Meet your new mommy," her dad joked when Joan shook the woman's clammy hand. This was the same thing he said about all his new girlfriends.

"Welcome to Texas," Joan said flatly, before squeezing past Jelly Bean to sit near her grandmother, Mama, and Wyatt's mother, who were in the middle of a passionate discussion about Barack Obama and how terrible he was for the country. Mama was confiding in hushed tones that Obama was not only incompetent, he was the literal Antichrist. She was reading a book that explained it in detail. "It's all coming true," Mama said in her soft southern drawl. "Everything in Revelation is happening before our eyes."

"Well, he's definitely not a Christian," Wyatt's mother replied in partial agreement.

Screens around the auditorium lit up with digital American flags, flapping in digital wind while an aggressive post-9/11 song played over the loudspeakers. Joan surveyed the crowd, a sea of Wrangler jeans and sparkling belts, shirts adorned with gaudy crosses, animal prints, and beer logos. Toby Keith's deep, velvety voice filled the arena with quips about bombing the Middle East. As tacky as it all was, there was something oddly comforting about being here, away from the liberal bubble of Austin. Joan loved the familiar smell of soft dirt and manure, the tucked-in shirts and boots and swagger.

"Cap-and-trade's gonna run the economy into the ground," Joan's grandfather, Papa, said with a detached certainty. He was a petroleum geologist who'd begun his career at Texaco in the fifties before being poached by a private oil and gas company. He still collected hefty royalty checks on all the wells he'd discovered—in Midland and Alaska and the North Sea. He was chewing on a toothpick, wearing a suede cowboy hat and an enormous silver belt buckle adorned with the letter W. "That, or we run out of oil altogether. Doesn't matter much to me." Papa shrugged. "I'll be dead here pretty soon. But *you* need to think about it." He winked at Joan and she smiled. She appreciated the calm, easygoing way her grandfather approached everything, including society's imminent collapse.

"Obama's gonna shut me down!" Joan's dad interjected. His trade school was subject to heavy regulation by the Department of Education. When Obama first took power, things got much worse for her dad financially. He'd been forced to hire several administrators just to keep up with all the paperwork. "He wants to throw people like me in jail!"

Joan ignored her dad's comment. Of course, he was exaggerating. But she didn't say so. She didn't want to give him the pleasure of an argument. Besides, she understood the overarching point he was trying to make. The regulations *were* unfair in that they applied only to for-profits, not community colleges or universities. He *was* criminally liable if his school didn't abide by the rules. And big government *was* the enemy of the people. She heard about it on the radio all the time. To keep the conversation flowing, Joan added one of her own gripes with Obama into the family pile-on.

"His healthcare plan is going to destroy the medical profession and turn us into the next Cuba," she declared. "We'll probably all die on waiting lists to see our doctors, who will all suck equally by then, because there will be no incentive to work hard in med school."

Papa smiled with a twinkle in his eye. "Joan's got her head on straight," he said to Mama, then turned to Joan. "Thank god we got you out of Miami when we did."

Mama leaned over and squeezed Joan's hand. She looked glamorous in a sparkling top and bold magenta lipstick. She smelled of fresh, expensive powder.

"It's so nice to have you back home," she said. *"Back to your roots."*

Joan smiled. It felt good to be in sync with her family again. Being a bisexual leftist had made family events awkward and unduly stressful. In Miami, Joan had read the communist manifesto and had been convinced that people like Mama, Papa, and her father were evil oppressors. Now that she was conservative, these gatherings could be relaxing, even fun. Joan ordered a huge beer and a big puff of cotton candy from a man walking around in a red Dickies T-shirt. She chugged her beer as she watched a rodeo clown dancing to "Cotton Eye Joe" in the center of the arena.

Wyatt, uninvested in politics, was in the row beneath her talking with his brother-in-law, troubleshooting his dire financial situation. He really needed to get his ducks in a row, according to the marines recruiter he'd been talking with. Wyatt owed money to pretty much every member of the West family, as well as the IRS, several big-box stores, credit card companies, his orthodontist, and the Duke University Hospital, where he stayed for two weeks after his suicide attempt. He also had two warrants out for his arrest for unpaid parking tickets, which the recruiter was helping him take care of. Wyatt's brother-in-law was emphasizing to Wyatt not to disclose that he'd gone to the hospital at Duke or that he'd gone to rehab afterward.

In the center of the arena, a group of rural junior high students chased a terrified calf around. After a few minutes, a boy tackled the animal, slamming its body into the ground and wrapping its legs rapidly with a rope. The crowd cheered and hooted and hollered. Poor cows, Joan thought, the cotton candy dissolving into sugar on her tongue. The world was so cruel to them.

The lights went down, and the whole coliseum went dark and quiet. "God Bless the USA" began to play. A woman on a white horse rode slowly around the dirt in large circles, her posture upright. She looked elegant in her blue sequined top, but also commanding, holding the reins in one hand, and in the other, a comically large American flag. The woman leaned forward as the horse began to trot, then canter, then gallop. The flag flapped wildly in the air as the song hit an emotional crescendo.

Joan turned to Wyatt, thinking they might share a look, poke fun at the over-the-top song. But Wyatt was swept up in his own universe, standing and singing along with animated passion, tapping out the rhythm on his chest. He looked almost like he did at their grandparents' Baptist tent revivals, where he always had intense spiritual experiences, crying on his knees in front of the traveling evangelists, while Joan would sit as far back in the tent as possible, her arms crossed, feeling numb.

Joan watched the woman on the horse again. The arena was pitch-dark now, a single spotlight following her. She had to admit it was impressive: the horse's speed and the way the woman was so connected to and in command of the animal. The song too was catchy and moving. Joan remembered coming to these rodeos as a child, when a cowgirl was all she wanted to be. Not a writer. Not an artist. Just a woman on a horse, sparkling. It had seemed like such a simple and lovely existence back then. When the song finally ended, before the rodeo officially began, everyone in the arena bowed their heads as the announcer started in prayer. The men removed their hats and placed them over their hearts.

Dear Heavenly Father, the announcer said. *As cowboys, we don't ask for much.*

3.

THE SUBJECT

B ack in Austin, Joan spent most of Sunday pacing around her apartment, drinking Red Bull, and trying to craft a love story about one of her ex-boyfriends. She decided that Wyatt was right. Romance was the best entry point into her narrator's heart and mind. But every time she opened her computer to write, language failed her. She didn't remember her previous relationships in much detail, nor could she recount how exactly any of them began or ended, or who was to blame. She'd been drunk so much of the time. These could hardly be considered "love stories."

By the evening, Joan was feeling jittery and depressed from all the caffeine, and had still written nothing. She smoked several bowls of weed while staring at her computer screen, but instead of feeling more grounded or creative, Joan found herself bored and ravenous, eating an entire package of processed cheddar-flavored snacks, mindlessly watching YouTube videos of rising Republican stars landing zingers— New Jersey governor Chris Christie debating teachers at town halls; Ben Shapiro being bitchy on a college campus; and Scott Brown saying "It's not the Kennedys' seat, it's the people's seat" at a Massachusetts Senate debate—over and over again.

Finally, Joan gave up and went to sleep. If she was going to write believably about her narrator in love, she would need to start over with a new subject entirely. Someone with whom she could generate and gather material in real time.

She met her subject two days later, at Betsy's, a hipster bar on the west side. His name was Vince. He was a thirty-year-old music producer from Long Island and a student at AudioPro. Vince was singing backup vocals for Claire's boyfriend's band, Luke and the Lucky Stars. Luke was a recent graduate of AudioPro. So were Luke's drummer, the guy running sound, the bartender, and even the guy checking IDs at the door. At times, it felt like the entire Austin music scene was littered with students and graduates of her dad's school, a fact that made Joan feel simultaneously glamorous and ashamed.

She sat on a velvet sofa next to Claire during the show, hunched over her notebook and scribbling notes about the night before, when she and other House staffers had gotten hammered and raced office chairs through the hallways of the capitol. After the set, Vince sat on the arm of Joan's chair, leaned into her shoulder, and asked her what she was writing. "Nothing," she said, irritated. She moved her body to shield the notebook from his eyes. Then Vince began telling Joan all the ideas he had that she should write down. Movie ideas, television show ideas, Broadway musical ideas. If only he had the time to write, he said, he would be so rich by now. As Vince explained his ideas in great detail, Joan wrote none of them down, instead taking notes about him.

Exhibits delusional, pathological confidence in mediocrity, she wrote, followed by: *Not as attractive as he thinks he is. Eyes too close together. Butt chin.*

When Vince was finished telling her about his ideas, he leaned back, sighed, and said he felt relieved. That material had been bottled up for some time, and he was glad to have finally gotten it all out. Joan said she was happy to help. Vince admitted he kind of had a thing for writers. He told her about other writers he'd dated in the past, writers who had gone on to big things—*Saturday Night Live, Elle, Veggie-Tales*. He seemed to be framing himself as a launching pad for successful writers. Instead of being put off, Joan was intrigued. She was open to the idea, ready to be launched.

Vince told her he liked the feathers she had clipped in her hair. She'd gotten them done during the fall, at Austin City Limits, and had recently had them refreshed. Vince reached out to touch them, his fingers grazing her left ear.

"Thanks. One of them gets really fluffy sometimes," Joan said, feeling bashful, trying to smooth it back down. He was being incredibly forward with her, for an AudioPro student. Did he know who her father was?

"Is that what it does when it feels threatened?" Vince said, and smiled.

They met up again the following night at a wine bar on Congress, where Vince told her that singing backup wasn't something he normally did. Only as a favor to Luke when he had time in his schedule, which was rare because he was very busy. He claimed he could've gone to one of the top MBA programs in the country, but decided to move to Austin and go to AudioPro instead. Why? He wanted to do something creative with his life. As difficult and frustrating as it was, especially in a stoner, derelict-filled town like Austin, at least it was rewarding on a soul level.

Joan, dumbfounded as to why anyone would choose her dad's school over a place like Booth, the University of Chicago's MBA program, where her brother had started in the fall, lied and told Vince she respected his decision.

Then he told her all about his production company, the Sound Seekers. No matter how many times he explained it, Joan could not understand the company's structure or how it functioned as a business at all. He wore a small silver dream catcher on a chain around his neck. It was their logo, he said. He told her about always loving and collecting dream catchers. He held out his arm and pointed to a place on his forearm where he wanted to get a big tattoo of a dream catcher someday.

"That's going to look cool," Joan lied again. She made a note in her journal about the tattoo. Details like this would make Vince feel authentic and illustrate to Roberto what a giant douchebag he was.

They sampled several wines while Vince told her about his business partner, Monica, also a student at AudioPro, who rented one of Vince's spare bedrooms. Monica was always in a relationship and "loved love," Vince said, rolling his eyes. It seemed to him that all Monica wanted out of life was to get married. He didn't understand why anyone would ever want to get married.

"Me neither," Joan said. "I can't imagine being with anyone forever."

Another lie. Joan, whose parents had each been divorced three times, was low-key obsessed with marriage. She listened to "The Male/Female Hour" religiously. Every week, she saw a therapist—a witchy woman twenty years sober who wore flowy tunic tops and wrote on purple legal pads. Together, they examined all the ways Joan's parents had screwed her up and how Joan might avoid following their example.

However, it was true that Joan couldn't imagine being with *Vince* forever.

She told Vince about her dad owning AudioPro, which didn't appear to faze him, not even when she added that she owned 25 percent of the school herself. She then revealed her politics—telling him first about her internship at the capitol and then admitting to her affiliation with the Young Conservatives of Texas, an organization she had joined last September, during her final semester at UT. Joan revealed this information early and often with suitors she didn't care much about. In the Austin scene, it felt similar to revealing that she had herpes—at worst a deal-breaker, at best a perpetual nuisance. She still hadn't told Roberto she was a conservative, too afraid of what he might think.

Vince shrugged it off. He explained that being older and having worked on Wall Street in his midtwenties, he was more moderate and less idealistic than most of his peers.

"Oh, that's great," Joan said. "I hate idealistic people."

That night, Joan sat on YouTube and watched every video she could find of Vince playing and singing. Most of his songs were about Manhattan and/or girls he'd dated while living in Manhattan. He was nowhere near as talented as Wyatt. He had a nasal, high-pitched singing voice and his wrist went limp when he strummed his guitar. Joan hated his music. Even more than that, she hated him. He had potential, though, as a love interest for her narrator. Perhaps a well-executed story about Vince could communicate something urgent and necessary about her generation at large. He perfectly epitomized the Peter Pan syndrome she so often heard lamented on conservative talk radio. As much as she couldn't stand Vince, she needed him for her career.

4.

HOT MESS

Eleven days later, on Valentine's Day, Vince picked Joan up outside Caffè Medici, where she stood shivering, still in her work clothes. Joan had been sitting at the bar, talking with Roberto about the unique genius of Anton Chekhov's "The Lady with the Dog," when Vince texted her to hang out. He had been at AudioPro all day, he said, with "the biggest producer in Austin," working on his new EP, which was "going to sound fucking amazing."

Joan was surprised to hear from Vince on such a loaded and romantic holiday. Sure, they'd developed a rapport, often ping-ponging jokes back and forth for hours while she was at work, or the coffee shop with Roberto, or out drinking with Claire. But they had only hung out in the flesh a handful of times. And Joan got so drunk on those outings that she hardly remembered them. Had they kissed already? Maybe Vince hadn't checked his calendar that morning, she thought, accepting his invitation. When she left Caffè Medici, she didn't tell Roberto goodbye or where she was going.

"Happy Vagina Day," Vince said as Joan climbed into the passenger seat of his SUV.

"Thanks."

"You look like a Republican."

"Constitutional conservative," she said, correcting him.

"That's the same thing," he said.

"It's actually not," Joan said. Vince rolled his eyes but dropped it. Probably because he knew she was right. There were plenty of so-called Republicans in the government who weren't actually conservative at all, fiscally or otherwise. Once in power, they didn't want to let go. They were known as RINOs, and being a RINO was even worse than being a Democrat. At least Democrats stood for something, as misguided and naïve as their beliefs may have been.

"Here, I got something for you," Vince said. He reached into the back seat, shuffled through a pile of junk mail, and tossed her the latest issue of *American Freedoms*, a magazine devoted entirely to guns and gun laws. It came to his house every month addressed to the previous owner, he complained. On the cover, a bald eagle's head sat alert atop a translucent American flag blowing in the wind.

Joan flipped through the magazine and looked at pictures of rifles while he talked on the phone to Monica. They were discussing their final project for their music business class at AudioPro: a top secret VIP show in a warehouse on the East Side for South by Southwest, which Vince claimed had an amazing lineup and was going to be the biggest thing they'd ever done.

Joan pulled out her notebook and started taking notes. What she appreciated most about Vince was that he didn't ask many questions or care that she wrote down most of what he said and did. She had even told him more than once that her story was the only reason she was spending time with him at all.

"Babe, I know," he said. "I don't give a shit."

If anything, he seemed to enjoy being the subject of her writing. She wasn't sure why. Perhaps it was because it put a certain distance between them, assuring them that the relationship wasn't real.

"Everyone in this town is lazy and stupid," Vince said into the phone. "Nobody has their shit together. Nobody knows what the fuck they're doing. They're all amateurs. I don't have time for this amateur shit."

Doesn't have time for amateur shit, Joan wrote into her notebook before sliding it back into her purse.

The floorboard was littered with event flyers, which featured a black-and-white picture of Vince in a dressy suede hat and a vest, pointer finger held to his lips. Monica peeked out from behind him, covering his eyes with her hands. *The Sound Seekers Present . . .* it said along the bottom. Joan folded one of the flyers up and kept it for reference.

When Vince hung up, he let out an exasperated sigh and started rubbing Joan's neck. She closed her eyes, letting herself indulge. His hands were strong and he knew what he was doing.

"Sorry," he said.

"That's okay."

"This town really isn't what it sells itself to be. It's supposedly the 'Live Music Capital of the World,' but then you get here and it's a bunch of derelicts who don't have their shit together."

He parallel-parked his SUV in a tiny space a few blocks away from the bar and pulled two gifts out of his leather satchel. They were wrapped in vintage maps of Paris and tied together with brown string.

"You didn't have to do this," Joan said. She couldn't remember a time anyone had gotten her anything for Valentine's Day. She hadn't been in an earnest relationship in at least five years, since her freshman year at UM. Her Miami boyfriend had started doing triathlons and then transferred to a school in Boston, explicitly to get away from her. *He must really like me,* Joan had thought when he told her this.

"Yeah, well, I know how pissed girls get about this kind of shit," Vince said as Joan unwrapped the gifts—a Sarah Palin dress-up doll refrigerator magnet set, and a small brown notebook, painted to look old.

"Thank you," she said.

"Don't go crazy on me," Vince said.

"What do you mean?"

"It always happens."

"What?"

"I drive girls crazy."

"I see."

"I'm not the settle-down type," he said. "Sorry."

"I never imagined that you would be," Joan said, typing the conversation into her phone as they walked to Betsy's, where Luke was playing a Valentine's Day show.

Betsy's was cold and had redbrick walls and stained glass windows hanging from the ceiling. There were paper hearts taped up behind the makeshift stage. Vince and Joan stood by the bar and drank whiskey while the opening band, Caterpillar Heaven, played in the corner. One of the three band members lived with Vince; the second was Joan's weed dealer, Thad; and the third member, the one with the neck brace, was at Vince's house "all the fucking time." All three members of Caterpillar Heaven were AudioPro students or graduates.

"See these guys?" Vince said. "They don't know what the fuck they're doing. They think they're going to get discovered, playing shit shows like this, selling their homemade shit shirts for less than they cost to make." He shook his head. "I try to help. I try to give them advice. But they just look at me like I'm the biggest asshole of all time."

"I kind of like them," Joan said, feeling defensive of Thad.

"It's not that I don't like their music," Vince said. "I do. It's good. But what makes someone successful isn't being *good*. You see, being good is worthless if you don't have your shit together."

Joan wrote the line down. Vince was obnoxious, but he spoke the truth. She thought of Wyatt, for instance, struggling to make ends meet in Fort Worth despite being a musical prodigy. His inability to get organized and finish writing any songs meant that he would probably never make a living as a musician. A cosmic injustice.

And then there was Joan's own failure to write anything complete or publishable, despite being told, ever since third grade, by all her teachers, that she was a "good" writer. But what was a good writer, if not a person who could finish things and put them out into the world? Then again, she had grown up in the participation-trophy generation. Her teachers were probably just blowing smoke up her ass out of a sense of liberal obligation.

Feeling depressed, Joan finished her whiskey and ordered more.

Perhaps Vince was right. Just because she and Wyatt had great potential or ideas didn't mean the world or the universe owed them anything.

She sent Wyatt a text: *Come visit Austin. I miss thee.*

Can't, Wyatt replied. *Too many warrants* ☹.

"Everyone in Texas moves around in slow motion," Vince continued. "It's like they're stuck in molasses or something. In New York, people hustle and bust their asses every day. They understand what it takes to make it."

"What about me?" Joan asked. "I'm from Texas. I don't have my shit together. Why do you like to hang out with me?"

"Well, with you, it's a little different," Vince said. "You've got that 'hot mess' thing going on. I can dig a hot mess."

Joan nodded, satisfied with this response. She had never been to New York City and enjoyed hearing about it. Perhaps if she moved there, she would change. Maybe the energy of the city would inject itself into her veins and she would suddenly become prolific, like Joyce Carol Oates or David Foster Wallace. Perhaps it was the city of Austin, not her own shortcomings, that was holding her back.

Caterpillar Heaven finished, and Luke's band started setting up. Vince headed over to the stage to sing, and Joan went out to the patio, where she found Claire, leaning on the wooden railing and smoking a cigarette, staring at the sky.

"You look very professional," she said, offering Joan a drag.

"Didn't have time to change after work," Joan said, taking a deep, painful inhale.

"How was it?"

"It was pretty good," Joan said. She refrained from mentioning the bill she'd been proofreading all morning, which would allow licensed, concealed guns on campus. "They had a bunch of poisonous snakes in the courtyard today."

"So Mesopotamian," Claire said.

"Yeah," said Joan, but she didn't know what Claire was talking about. Joan admitted that Claire was much more educated than her but felt she possessed no common sense. Claire identified as a "Clinton Democrat," whatever that meant. She didn't understand straightforward concepts like American exceptionalism, trickle-down economics, or the invisible hand. The two girls had learned, after several heated arguments about global warming, abortion, and welfare, not to discuss politics. Ever since they had decided to keep their relationship focused on men, drinking, and literature, they'd been doing fine.

"Aren't you cold?" Joan asked.

Claire looked down at her outfit and shrugged. She was wearing a black lace leotard with a mauve tulle skirt. Her thin, pale arms were covered in small bumps.

They went inside, back to the bar. Luke's band had started playing. Vince was standing next to Luke, shaking a tambourine, glowing orange under the stage lights. The girls ordered two gin and tonics. The bartender, who had graduated from AudioPro two years before, held up four fingers. "Four bucks," he said. He had a tattoo of a bird on his neck and a mustache that twisted and curled at the ends. Above the bar behind him, a small television was on mute, playing infomercials. As he made their drinks, Joan wondered if he knew who she was—*the AudioPro heiress*—and if he did know, what he thought about her being out with Vince on Valentine's Day. She enjoyed feeling like she was at the center of rumors, popular in a way she had never been in high school.

Joan sat on a vintage yellow couch near the stage. "I'm so depressed about my thesis," Claire said, sinking into the cushion next to Joan. "It's the worst thing I've ever written."

"I'm sure that's not true," Joan said, relieved to no longer be in school. She was two years older than Claire, had come to UT as a transfer and graduated quietly in December. She set her drink on the floor near a stuffed black bear standing upright, wearing a Native American headdress.

Claire's thesis was about the significance of windows in the works of Virginia Woolf, a modernist Joan had never read. She'd tried to pick up *Mrs. Dalloway* a couple of times, to have deeper conversations with Claire, but she could never make it past the first couple of pages.

28

She vaguely recalled something about flowers being mentioned, and war. All Joan knew for sure about Woolf was that she'd killed herself by stuffing an overcoat with rocks and walking into a river.

"Thank god I never had to write a thesis," Joan said. "I would have probably died." Joan graduated with a regular English major, while Claire was in the highest honors program. Joan thought of the James Joyce paper she'd tried to write during her junior year in Miami, while she was manic, right before her parents pulled her out of school. She had spent weeks trying to analyze *Dubliners*, picking it apart, filling pages upon pages with rambling, incoherent psychobabble about God and the resilience of the human spirit, the true nature of time, the evils of capitalism, etc. She kept asking her psychiatrist for higher doses of everything, thinking a clear thesis statement would come to her, but it didn't. When the semester was almost over and she still hadn't turned in the paper, her Irish literature professor called her into his office. "All I need is something," he said, pleading. "Anything. Don't you have *anything* that I can grade?"

"I have two hundred single-spaced pages of my novel in progress," she offered.

Later, after the dean called her parents and insisted Joan take some time off to figure out her medication situation, a psychiatrist in Dallas said she was surprised Joan didn't have a seizure from the combination of medications she was on. She wouldn't give Joan anything good after that.

Joan sucked on the black straw until the gin was gone and got up to order more. She stood at the bar, watching Vince. She hadn't dated a musician in years. In Miami, she'd fully embraced the groupie lifestyle and exclusively slept with guys in bands. She'd been in bed with a reggae drummer the morning her dad called and told her to pack her shit. She had a flight at three. She'd arrived in Dallas that night, with nothing but the clothes on her back and the drummer's newsboy cap on her head. It had been the most jarring moment of her life. Wyatt had been sitting in the passenger seat when her dad picked her up, his life having fallen apart around the same time. Her dad yelled at her and Wyatt constantly that summer, trying to explain how the world worked and how wrong they both were about everything. Still, she missed those days, the feeling of not being alone in her failure.

Joan returned to the couch, where Claire was alone, falling asleep. Joan sat down, put her hand on Claire's head, and stroked her soft red hair. Claire opened her eyes slowly, then looked around, confused.

"I want you to drag this Vince thing out as long as possible," Claire said. "It's so nice having someone to sit with at Luke's shows."

"I will," Joan said. "For as long as it serves me."

"This is our last song," Luke said into the microphone. "Don't forget there's free CDs up here."

Luke and Vince started singing their crowd-pleaser, "You've Really Got a Hold on Me" by Smokey Robinson and the Miracles. Joan stood up and held out her hand to Claire, who grabbed on to it. She placed a hand on Claire's bony waist, and Claire put her arm around Joan's shoulder while they danced slowly, swaying back and forth and twirling each other around. It was weird hearing Vince sing about love, but he was a skilled performer and sold it well. They sounded good, like the Beach Boys.

Claire twirled Joan around and accidentally kicked over Vince's drink, breaking the glass, but they didn't care. They just kept dancing, shattered glass crunching under their feet until the song was over.

5.

GREATER SACRIFICES HAVE BEEN MADE

A month passed and Joan had still not written her love story. Despite spending countless hours with Vince and gathering plenty of material, she still had not come up with a plot—a clear beginning, middle, or end. She decided to devote the entire week of South by Southwest to finishing a draft. Vince would be busy with Monica and their multiday VIP event, so she could finally focus again. She looked forward to the day she could share the story with Roberto, impress him with her masterful use of interiority, and move on to the next chapter of her life, leaving Vince behind in the dust where he belonged, like the tapped-out resource he was.

It was one of these evenings in mid-March when she found herself back at the coffee shop, sitting at the bar with her laptop open, hoping the change of scenery would help her concentrate. She placed three notebooks next to her laptop, all filled to the brim with details about Vince—his appearance and wardrobe, his quirks, his childhood traumas, his dreams and his goals.

"Hey, lady, long time no see," Roberto said. "You not drinking tonight?"

"Not tonight," said Joan. "I don't feel very well." She was only beginning to come out of an intense hangover. The thought of alcohol made her stomach turn.

"You want some tea or what?"

"Okay, sure," she said. She continued watching the blinking cursor while Roberto brought her a mug filled with piping-hot water and a baggie of dried leaves. She dipped the leaves in the water and watched it turn brown. Tea would be good. She needed to hydrate as much as possible after last night. She'd gone to a lobbyist event for the Cypress Police Department, for which her representative used to work as a hostage negotiator. Joan had only planned to have a few drinks at the event, but the off-duty cops kept handing her little red drink tickets, and she wasn't equipped to say no. The last thing Joan could remember was participating in a mock police training activity, holding a heavy orange plastic gun aimed at an actor wielding a chain, saying: *Don't move! Get on the ground!*

Joan failed the exercise, unable to muster up the courage to shout forcefully. Instead, she'd "shot" the perpetrator almost immediately. The cops joked that she probably wouldn't be hired as a police officer anytime soon, but one of them assured her she had potential. She remembered him also telling her that her shirt was unbuttoned; later he was touching her shoulder, her hair. She wasn't sure how she'd gotten home. She woke up on top of her covers, fully clothed, makeup and jewelry still intact. At least she hadn't slept with any of the cops, she thought, relieved.

It was almost ten o'clock at night, and Joan was the last person at the coffee shop, hanging around and pretending to work while Roberto cleaned up, stacking chairs on top of tables, mopping the tile floor. She had transcribed a few lines of Vince's most memorable dialogue into a document but still wasn't sure where to set the story or what the plot would be.

"Hey, lady, we're about to close," Roberto said.

"Oh, okay," Joan said, feeling rushed. She closed her laptop without saving the document, or giving it a name, and slid it into her large purse, next to a political memoir she'd been slowly reading since Christmas, by former Massachusetts governor Mitt Romney.

"Do you smoke?" Roberto asked.

"Weed?"

"Yes."

"Yeah, sometimes," Joan said, and shrugged. This was a gross understatement, but she didn't like to admit what a stoner she was. It wasn't very feminine, for one, or Republican. Not that Roberto knew about her politics, but still.

Roberto locked up and he and Joan got high in the alley behind the coffee shop, where they started talking about Carlos, her favorite creative writing professor in Austin. Joan had taken three classes with him during her two years at UT. He had gone to the Iowa Writers' Workshop, she bragged. He was from Del Rio and had written an acclaimed collection of short stories called *Del Rio*. He had just released a novel called *The Lone Vaquero*.

"No. That guy sucks. Fuck that guy," Roberto said, taking a hit.

"You know him?" said Joan, feeling a bit deflated.

He told Joan he'd tried to go to Carlos's office once, to get him to read his work, thinking he'd help him out because he was another border writer, but he'd blown Roberto off because he wasn't a student.

"There was only one decent story in all of *Del Rio*," Roberto continued. "About some kid hiding under his mom's bed." He exhaled a large cloud of dense smoke. "And *The Lone Vaquero*"—Roberto shook his head—"that is the worst book anyone has been paid to write."

Joan laughed. She'd never read *Del Rio* or *The Lone Vaquero*, but she loved Carlos. He was jaded and sexy, and he walked the halls of the UT English department like a vampire, tall with his black hair slicked back, carrying the constant weight of what he'd been hired to represent.

After finishing the joint, Roberto invited Joan to a party at one of his friends' houses. When she agreed, he asked her for a ride.

"This is what you drive?" he said, climbing into Joan's white BMW 3 Series, which had been a gift for her twenty-first birthday. Empty cans of Red Bull clanked and crunched beneath his enormous feet.

"Yeah, so?" Joan said, feeling defensive and paranoid. Perhaps she had smoked too much.

"Nothing," Roberto said, but he was beaming from ear to ear. He reached down and picked up a can of Red Bull. "Be careful, lady, this shit will kill you."

"Maybe," Joan said, unsettled that he was seeing this part of her life. Her car was always a complete mess, and so was her apartment, a fact that seemed worse considering how expensive they both were. She was laser-focused on the road, driving less than thirty miles an hour. The lights seemed blurry as they crossed over I-35 to the East Side, a part of town occupied mostly by poor people, artists, and minorities. When they arrived at the house party, she felt a wave of relief to have made it there without incident. She didn't mind driving tipsy, but she hated driving high. Once they got into the kitchen, Joan poured herself a generous screwdriver and drank it quickly as Roberto introduced her to his friends as if they were an item.

Later, standing next to Roberto in the backyard, beneath unseasonal Christmas lights, she drank a tallboy of PBR. She felt herself becoming loose and drunk.

"You're so . . . unique," she said, swaying toward Roberto, letting herself fall into his chest.

"How's that?" he said. He was smiling, his eyes obscured by his glasses.

"Well, for one thing, you're the most well-read Mexican person I've ever met."

"This chick," Roberto said.

"I'm sorry," Joan said, blushing. "Was that racist?"

"Everything is racist," Roberto said.

Joan paused to take in the profundity of this statement. Roberto offered her another shot and she took it.

"You need to milk it more in your work," Joan declared. "Maybe you could sprinkle some Spanish phrases in your stories, like Junot Díaz. Academics love it when people do that."

Roberto smiled all-knowingly and said, "No, fuck that. Junot Díaz is the worst. Academics don't know shit, lady."

Joan mulled this over, unsure of what to say. Junot Díaz was one of her favorite writers. At least, she thought he was. She had read his sophomore collection twice. Which was probably more than she'd read any other book. She didn't say as much to Roberto, out of fear of looking stupid or dull.

"Have you ever thought of getting an MFA?" Joan asked. "I'm thinking of applying in the fall. I need deadlines to function. Otherwise, I'm afraid I'll spin out of orbit."

"No," Roberto said somberly. "Fuck that bullshit."

"Why?"

"I never finished college, and I would need to update my resident alien card. But even if I did all that, I wouldn't get no fucking MFA."

"Really? I'm sure a good one would let you in, though. They love diversity," said Joan. And then, backtracking, "I don't mean that's the *only* reason they'd let you in. I'm just saying."

"It's okay, lady," he said. "I know what I am."

Joan went to the bathroom, feeling mortified about the exchange. Roberto saying he knew what he was begged the question: What was she? Growing up, she'd never felt comfortable in her skin. Her hometown outside of Dallas was around half-white, and during her tween years, she had longed above all things to be Mexican, so that she could fit in with the popular chola girls at her middle school. With their powdery, smooth faces and crispy curls, the cholas posed together in front of jewel-toned, airbrushed backdrops at the local mall on weekends, carrying the photos around in their purses, trading them with each other at school, proving they had friends. They coupled up early; some of them even got pregnant at fifteen or sixteen. One girl she knew left the sixth grade at twelve to have a baby. Joan had been so jealous of her. All the attention her round belly must have gotten, all the love. On weekends, Joan watched with envy as her Mexican peers walked around the mall slowly, the boy behind the girl, his arms wrapped around her waist, simultaneously waltzing and spooning. She was always alone back then. Pudgy around the middle, with pointy, budding breasts—a body like a fat boy's, she thought whenever she looked in the mirror. Who would ever want to spoon-waltz with her? She did what she could to fit in. She wore oversize polo shirts with tight, dark-washed jeans; Adidas Superstars; heavy, pale makeup; penciled-in eyebrows. She drew a brown line around her lips and put large silver hoops in her ears. Only after her mother forced her to move to Houston, to attend an expensive private school for rich screw-up kids, did she realize what she really was, where she really belonged, and how ridiculous it had been putting all that effort into appearing marginalized.

Joan returned to Roberto's side and took a long sip of beer. She looked around at the people at the house party, at all of Roberto's friends. They were a bunch of misfits, like him. Some were pale, some were fat, most were white. All of them were unattractive in their own way, but they possessed a collective beauty. Joan was getting good and drunk, and life was beginning to seem profound again. She watched the bonfire, where his friends were gathered around, smoking cigarettes, nodding along to punk rock playing quietly on an old boom box. Perhaps she could fit in here, in Roberto's world. Here she could create a new life, away from Vince, AudioPro, and the stigma of being an heiress.

Roberto held out his hand to compare its size with Joan's. They both looked at her small, pale hand, doll-like against his big brown palm. He must have liked how different their hands were. So did Joan. The comparison made him feel manly, she supposed, while it made her feel petite, fragile, small.

From the party, Joan drove Roberto back to his place. He invited her inside. He lived in a tiny house resembling a shack on East MLK. Joan sat in an old wooden chair in Roberto's living room, next to a white plastic folding table, upon which a vintage yellow typewriter sat.

"This is where you write? On that thing?"

"Yes," he said. "This is my baby."

"You fucking hipster," Joan said.

Roberto laughed, a wild, sharp laugh. He rolled a joint and sat across from her, on the other side of the tiny room. There were paintings everywhere, all amateur and too colorful. Clearly local artists, she thought. Everyone knew Austin had a terrible art scene. Unless Roberto had painted them himself. Joan didn't ask. She turned her attention to the sad cattle dog pouting in the corner, a bandanna around its neck. "His name is Norman Mailer," Roberto said.

"What are you working on?" Joan asked, fingering a stack of notebooks next to the typewriter, which he appeared to be transcribing.

"Something new. A novella," he said. "I just started it last month."

"What's it called?"

"*Bitter Texas Honey*," Roberto said.

"I like that," Joan said, nodding. She had never read a novella and wasn't sure what one was, exactly, but decided not to ask too many follow-up questions. "I'm working on a love story right now," Joan slurred. "About my narrator going on a date with this unavailable asshole who won't commit." Joan took a hit from the joint that Roberto handed her. "It's going to be a critique of our entire generation," she said, and began coughing.

Until South by Southwest, Joan had been researching Vince nearly every day. She'd accompanied him to bars, restaurants, music venues, and house parties. She'd gone with him to one of his AudioPro classes, a recording session, and a music video shoot. She even went with Vince to his favorite strip club, twice, where he claimed he liked to unwind and relax, and where she overheard him calling her his girlfriend to one of the strippers. Usually, they would end up back at his big brick house in the suburbs, where Joan now had a little designated drawer near his bed with her essentials—a toothbrush, makeup-removing wipes, a change of underwear.

"I can't wait to read it," Roberto said, taking the joint back. She couldn't tell if he was being serious or just polite.

"The guy in the story is actually based on a real person," Joan admitted. "A student at my dad's career college. It's why I haven't been to the coffee shop much lately."

"I see," Roberto said, tossing the joint into his kitchen sink.

"I hate him, but I'm still not done with the story. So I have to keep seeing him until I finish."

"Greater sacrifices have been made for art," Roberto said.

Joan soaked in this wise truth while Roberto retreated to his bedroom. He returned after a minute holding an old Polaroid camera, which Joan didn't mention. Instead of feeling like an idiot for spending so much time with Vince over the past month, Joan felt like a martyr for art, a Method actor dedicating herself entirely to her craft.

"I did come up with a working title the other day. It's called 'Derelicts.'"

"That is a great title," Roberto said.

"Really? You're just saying that."

"No, I'm not. It's very Raymond Carver."

"Really?" Joan said, and blushed. "I love his titles. Titles feel so important to stories, you know? I feel like so many titles these days are boring as fuck. . . ."

Joan kept rambling that way for a while as Roberto watched her, no longer listening. She idolized Carver, she said, his depressing, manly realism. She wanted to be just like him, writing sad suburban dialogue, scowling and holding a cigarette in her black-and-white author photo. Eventually, Roberto stood up and came toward her, bent over, and put his mouth on hers. He thrust his tongue deep into her mouth, nearly licking the back of her throat. Joan was shocked into submission, and they made out like that for what seemed to be an hour but was probably only a few minutes.

"I should go," Joan said finally. She stood up from the chair.

"Wait," he said. "Do you mind if I take your picture?"

"What for?"

"I want to capture this moment."

"I guess that's fine," she said. She turned her head to the side and adjusted her sweaty bangs, hoping to cover as much of her face as she could. The Polaroid flashed before she was ready, and she squeezed her eyes shut, shielding her face with her hand. Roberto shook the photo before setting it on the table near his typewriter.

As he walked her to her car, Roberto told her that he liked her, that he'd even broken an agreement he'd made with himself that night.

"What agreement?"

"I always swore to myself that I'd never kiss a girl wearing a Beatles T-shirt."

Joan didn't know what to make of that. She looked down at her shirt, having forgotten she was wearing it. She had gotten the shirt while thrifting in Houston with her mother, whose love language was shopping, and who loved the Beatles. What was wrong with the Beatles? Weren't they one of the most influential bands of all time? Joan drove home, thinking about the evening and the kiss, feeling embarrassingly unoriginal.

6.

THIS ROOSTER IS HER LIFE

Two weeks later, Joan turned twenty-four. As with her other adult birthdays, she felt old, tired, and disappointed. Another year had passed, and she had yet to achieve any literary fame or anything noteworthy at all. She still hadn't even written her story about Vince.

That morning, she stood at the fridge with Claire, dressed for her internship, playing with the Sarah Palin dress-up doll refrigerator magnet set that Vince had given her for Valentine's Day. Today, they dressed Palin as a revolutionary soldier, holding a teapot in one hand, carrying a Bible in the other. Joan added a tiara and sash.

"Any special plans tonight for your birthday?" Claire asked.

"Not really," Joan said. "Vince wants to hang out, I think."

"I love it. You have a boyfriend."

"He's not my boyfriend."

"Right."

"I'm serious. Once I finish the story, it's over with him."

"Whatever you say."

Joan left for work feeling annoyed. Out of anyone, Claire should have understood that just because she spent most of her free time with Vince didn't mean she liked him. Or that he was her "boyfriend." She was just using him. She felt justified, like she was carrying out some form of cosmic justice. Besides, even if it was all a little morally questionable, *greater sacrifices had been made for art.*

She hadn't heard from Roberto at all in the days since they kissed. He hadn't been at the coffee shop either, which was fine. After all, she wasn't *that* attracted to him. He had a subtle musty smell that reminded her of her father—a mixture of smoke and mothballs. Still, she wondered why he hadn't reached out, wanting to see her again. Was it because she still hadn't sent him another story? Did he not like the kiss? Was it the Beatles T-shirt?

Joan turned onto Twelfth Street, adjusted the top of her pantyhose, and checked her phone. There were missed calls and voicemails from her mother, her father, and her brother. She listened to the messages while trekking up the small hill to the capitol. Her mother, Dolly, sounded overly cheerful, which always gave Joan the creeps. She knew her mother wasn't really happy, and hadn't been for years. Her dad, Randy, sounded typically cavalier, singing the "Happy Birthday" song with an exaggerated southern accent. Her brother, Henry, earnestly explained that he had gotten Joan a yearlong subscription to some great budgeting software he'd discovered while at Booth. He was really enjoying it, he said. He hoped she would too. It allowed him to control his finances in an innovative way. Joan clicked on the link in her email and looked at the program only briefly before closing it. The colorful pie chart was too much for her right now.

She entered the gates of the capitol. The lawn was vibrantly green. Bronze Confederate-era statues gleamed in the bright sunlight, beneath a cloudless blue sky. Spring was by far the most pleasant season in Austin, and was likely the main reason so many hipsters from LA and New York kept flooding into the city after attending South by Southwest, arguably the town's most annoying event.

She walked up the steps and entered the magnificent pink granite building, and ran her bag through a metal detector. Guns were allowed at the capitol, but you needed a license to carry one. Contrary to the childish logic of the Left, this was a fact that made Joan feel secure. From conservative radio, Joan had learned that a "gun-free" zone was actually the most dangerous place a person could be. Criminals would carry a gun anywhere, the hosts explained. They didn't follow the rules.

Her heels click-clacked across the terrazzo floor, across the state seal of Texas. Men in gray suits watched as she walked by. They were sitting on a bench, holding leather folders embossed with the same state seal. It was considered bad form to step directly onto the state's sacred emblem, but today, Joan didn't care. Breaking this rule so publicly and deliberately on her birthday made her feel powerful and reckless.

When Joan arrived at her desk in the basement, Kyle, her chief of staff, warned her that her day might be busier than usual. Yesterday, Wayne Christian's office had filed a controversial bill that would outlaw cockfighting in all forms across the state. Their boss, Allen, had signed on to the legislation at Kyle's direction. Now the capitol was flooded with protestors, lobbying for its rejection.

"Great," said Joan dryly. She had first met Kyle on campus, where he was the chair of the Young Conservatives of Texas, a group Joan had joined out of curiosity and boredom the previous fall. She'd found the group at a table in the Main Mall on campus, where they were holding an Affirmative Action Bake Sale. Each baked good had been priced differently, based on different genders and races. Cookies for Asian males, for instance, were the most expensive, while cookies for Black females were the cheapest. For Native Americans, the cookies were free. A crowd of angry protestors had formed around the table, shouting at the Young Conservatives.

Joan bought a cookie for the white female price and Kyle introduced himself. She found him attractive, in a strange way, and they talked near the table away from the commotion. She told Kyle she thought affirmative action was a complicated issue. He agreed with Joan and nodded back toward the table.

"The younger kids, they like to do this kind of stuff, stir people up on campus, own the libs or whatever. It's silly in my opinion. I'm more interested in making *actual* changes."

Joan had been intrigued. "What kind of changes?" she asked.

"Many changes," he said. For instance, in the upcoming session, they were going to work on getting campus carry legislation through at the capitol.

Joan nodded. She could get behind that, she supposed. She was pro—Second Amendment, after all. She knew how important it was for a nation to have an armed citizenry. Otherwise, there could be tyranny, and who wanted tyranny?

Joan started attending Young Conservatives meetings, mostly just to see Kyle, whom she clicked with. He was overweight and in law school and wrote inflammatory think pieces against gay marriage. Joan wasn't sure why she kept going to the meetings week after week. Perhaps she had a vague hope that she might find some conservative man to marry within the organization, but that soon proved unlikely. Kyle never showed any romantic interest in her, and the other kids were complete dorks who would coordinate days where they all wore Ronald Reagan T-shirts or where they woke up early to decorate the campus with little American flags. They regarded Joan with suspicion at first. Kyle jokingly accused her of being a spy, citing her hipster attire, her Moleskine notebook, and the feathers clipped in her hair. Eventually, though, Joan was welcomed. The Young Conservatives were not very discerning, after all, and needed all the numbers they could get.

When she expressed interest in interning at the capitol after a YCT meeting in December, Kyle had taken care of everything for her, even writing her a résumé from scratch to put on file.

"Get ready," Kyle warned. "These cockfighting people are a special brand of nut job."

"This is not how I wanted to spend my birthday," Joan complained.

"You're a champ," Kyle said, patting her on the back like she was a horse. "Here, this is from the Right to Life people. In case you get stressed." He set a small pink stress ball on her desk and smiled dickishly before retreating to his office, he said, to draft the heartbeat bill for Allen to introduce later that week.

Joan picked up the stress ball, which was the size and shape of a human fetus at fourteen weeks old. *Jesus Christ*, she thought, gently pressing her fingers into the foam. It was so morbid.

Just then, a man and woman entered the office and approached her desk.

"You're taking away our God-given rights," the man said, pointing at her face. "These are *our* roosters. We should be able to do whatever we want with them."

"You Austin bureaucrats have too much power," the woman said. She was wearing a Mickey Mouse T-shirt and hot-pink earrings.

Joan made eye contact with the couple, listening and nodding along while they whined, her eyebrows crinkled with concern. Usually, Kyle explained, this was all these people really wanted. To feel seen, heard, understood. This was her main job. To field angry Tea Party people so Kyle could work unbothered. Joan had already gotten very good at pretending to care, which was an important life skill in itself.

"I'm sorry," Joan said. "I understand your concerns. Personal liberty is very important to Representative Fletcher. But he is working in the best interest of his constituents. Let me take down your names and addresses." She picked up a pen and opened her Moleskine. "Do you live in the district, by chance?"

This left the couple slightly bewildered, as it usually did. Of all the protestors who came in to bother Joan and Kyle, almost none of them lived in Cypress, the town her boss represented. Cypress was just outside of Houston, not far from where her mother and grandmother lived, but Joan had never been to the district herself.

Initially, it had been depressing for Joan to discover that most of the conservative population in Texas didn't seem to actually *understand* representative democracy. Allen's constituents tended to send letters, which Joan would read and respond to herself, without even showing them to Allen, just Kyle, who would tell her, more or less, what to say back.

Her phone buzzed on her desk with a text message. Her heart fluttered, thinking it might be from Roberto. It was from Vince.

Happy birthday, sunshine.

Joan smirked. She hated to admit that she liked Vince's sarcastic sense of humor. Anyone who knew her well would think of her more as a storm cloud, or perhaps a flash flood or tornado. She didn't respond. Perhaps Claire was right. Maybe things with Vince had gotten out of hand. She'd been seeing him too much, letting him grow too attached. The weekend before, they'd gone on a jaunt in the Texas Hill Country, where they stayed at a bed-and-breakfast, hiked to the top of Enchanted Rock, and had sober sex for the first time. After a long night out dancing and drinking, they'd gotten in their first big fight, with Joan calling Vince an asshole, and Vince accusing Joan of only liking him when she was drunk. The next morning, they both acted as if the fight hadn't happened, but something had certainly shifted between them. Joan had agreed to the trip thinking the romantic setting would finally inspire a plot for her love story, but of course, it didn't. She still hadn't decided where the story should take place, what should happen between her two characters, or how it should end.

Just then a large burly man came in holding a poster board with grainy images printed on computer paper. One of the images portrayed a young girl, maybe eight years old at most, holding a rooster in her arms.

"This is my granddaughter," the man said, almost crying. "This is her pet. This is her best friend. You people are going to take that away from her? This rooster is her *life*."

Joan studied the picture, hazy and pixelated from being enlarged. The little girl looked frightened. The rooster looked soulless and predatory, like a dinosaur. Joan wondered if the photograph had simply been lifted from a Google image search and the story made up entirely. She looked at the man again. He didn't appear very grandfatherly at all, confirming her suspicion.

"Well, sir," Joan said, "this bill would not actually ban owning a rooster or keeping one for a pet. It would only make raising the rooster for cockfighting illegal. So, if your granddaughter loves this rooster so much, why don't you just raise him humanely and not attach weapons to his talons?"

The man became inconsolable then, blubbering about government overreach and living in a tyrannical state.

"Sir, I'm so sorry. But if you don't live in the representative's district, I'm going to have to ask you to leave. I have very important work to do on behalf of our constituents."

At this, the man became indignant and left, cursing under his breath.

Joan cracked open a sugar-free Red Bull, took a long sip, and opened her laptop. She perused her notebook, reviewing her notes about their weekend getaway, admiring her favorite scene, in which her narrator two-stepped with a burly ranch hand all night while Vince watched on jealously. The ranch hand had been from Palo Pinto and had blood crusted under his fingernails from delivering a calf that morning. There wasn't much of her narrator's inner life in the scene, though. She figured she would fill in those gaps later. She began to transcribe her notes. But for some reason, something about typing words on her computer felt so terrifying and final. If only she had a few Adderall, she could finish this story easily. Not only would it be effortless, it would be fun. For a few hours, she would be alert, decisive, confident. Her whole life would make sense. This was the delusion that persisted.

In the meantime, Joan filled the void of Adderall with other drugs, drugs that would not derail her life so badly: weed, alcohol, caffeine, the occasional painkiller. And then, on top of all that, she went to her therapist, in whom she regularly confided her inability to stop thinking about Adderall. Just last month, the therapist had challenged Joan to write a goodbye letter to the medication, thinking it would provide closure. The document still sat unfinished on Joan's desktop. *Dear Adderall*, it began. *Even though I don't take you anymore, you continue to haunt me. . . .*

But Joan was only haunted by the good memories. Her brain successfully blocked out the bad parts—the exhausted, sleepless nights staring at her ceiling fan from midnight to five A.M.; her body breaking out in hives; her perpetually upset stomach; the worried stares of strangers when she vomited on campus after class; the dirty looks of her acquaintances at parties when she would try to explain her brilliant James Joyce paper or her novel. Instead, Joan's memories focused on the dozens of notebooks she had filled; the way her body fat had melted off, allowing her to walk around in a bikini unfazed, or stare at herself in the mirror for long periods of time, admiring her beauty. At the peak of her manic episode, Joan had felt so empowered and full of herself that she would begin to weep, driving around campus in her BMW, skipping class to contemplate the profound magnitude of her life. It was as if she were seeing herself for the first time, through heaven's eyes.

Adderall was like a toxic ex-boyfriend Joan would never get over.

Frustrated and unable to focus, she looked down at her phone again. There was another missed call and voicemail from her mother, and another text message from Vince.

Anything special you want to do tonight? Birthday girl's choice.

Joan hesitated. She knew she didn't have an excuse to keep seeing him.

Not tonight, she began to type. *Maybe tomorrow.* Her finger hovered over the send key. As much as she knew she needed to work on her story, she felt drawn to Vince. She enjoyed being swept up in his life, away from her apartment, full of all her problems and filth. Being with Vince was like boarding a quick-moving train on which she could forget about herself entirely.

Just then, she got another text message. Not from Vince, but from her cousin Wyatt.

Hey, I'm at the train station in Austin. Can you pick me up?

Yes! Joan responded immediately, grateful to have the decision made for her.

7.

JOAN'S CAPTIVATING HEART

Joan hurried home from the capitol, sweating through her blouse, and got straight into her BMW without changing. She drove to the Amtrak station, which was on the west side of town, across from the original Whole Foods, BookPeople, and other expensive yuppie shops—Lululemon, West Elm, Anthropologie.

Wyatt stood outside the station, wearing shiny blue basketball shorts and a plain white Hanes T-shirt. He didn't have a suitcase. Just a small plastic shopping bag that read *THANK YOU THANK YOU THANK YOU* and appeared to contain a wad of clothing, a stick of Old Spice, and a small hardcover book.

Wyatt climbed into her passenger seat and tossed his bag into the back, which was full of Joan's dirty clothes, empty Red Bull cans, and fast-food trash.

"Dear lord," Wyatt said, laughing at the mess.

"Shut up," Joan said. "What are you doing here?"

"It's your birthday today," Wyatt said, lowering his voice. "A victory would be nice." It was a line of dialogue from the first level of a PlayStation fighter pilot game they'd played in high school. One summer, after each of their mothers' second divorces, they played the game together every single day for weeks and heard the line so often that it became ingrained in their psyches.

"How long are you staying?" Joan asked.

"Just the night. I'm starting a new job."

"Where?"

"RadioShack. Right across from my apartment. Didn't have much choice, since I don't have a car."

"No more Maxima?"

"I had to sell it," he said, and slumped a little in his seat. "The marines recruiter wants me to get more of my debt paid off before I can enlist."

"That makes sense. It's always good to have a job," she said, wanting to keep the mood light. Although for Joan, this statement was mostly theoretical. Before her capitol internship, she had only ever worked at the Dallas campus of AudioPro, where she sat at the front desk, answering phones for two dollars an hour, during her forced year off from college. During this time, Wyatt was also working at AudioPro and attending classes. It was her dad's way of "keeping them in line" and helping Wyatt get his act together. Mostly, Joan would spend her time flirting with metalhead studio techs, watching documentaries about serial killers on YouTube, or creating experimental artwork in Adobe Photoshop. If she ever complained about her low pay, her dad would yell at her and tell her she should be glad she was getting anything at all. He would then remind her that she was technically part owner and should want to learn her own business. Still, it had never felt like a proper job, not really, because even the campus director and vice president, who were supposedly Joan's superiors, seemed uneasy and almost frightened in her presence.

"What should we do?" she asked. "Do you want to go to Target?" When they lived together, Wyatt used to love going to Target near her dad's house and pretending to work there.

"Can't," he said. His energy seemed low. "Don't have my uniform."

"Don't worry about that," Joan said. "I've got it."

She drove along the river, feeling invigorated. It was an exciting, rare treat to have Wyatt in Austin with her. She turned onto Congress and headed south on the bridge, past crowds of tourists lined up at the railing, waiting for a large cloud of bats to emerge for their nightly hunt for mosquitos.

They arrived at the Target in South Austin, off Highway 71, and made their way to the men's section, where Wyatt picked out a pair of khakis and a plain red polo. Joan purchased the items, removed the tags, and waited as Wyatt took them to the bathroom to change.

When he emerged, he wore the red polo tucked as deep as it would go into the khakis. With his posture rigid and upright, his eyebrows raised, Wyatt walked around the store with his hands clasped in front of him.

Joan followed at a distance, stifling giggles as he distributed boxes of tampons, adult diapers, and douches all over the store. But there was something different this time, something lacking. Perhaps it was just that they'd grown older and the joke had run its course.

Soon, Wyatt was playing salsa music in the stereo section, dancing with a hesitant old woman, who was laughing and blushing as he spun her around, wiggling his hips.

"I really recommend Sony," he said. "Great bass. Very clear. Really gets down into your bones."

Then he put on "Little Bitty" by Alan Jackson, took Joan's hand, and began to lead her in a two-step, reminding her of the moves she always forgot. Wyatt's rhythm was innate, while hers was awful. Joan usually hated dancing, but the two-step took no talent, no skill at all. It was the man's job to keep the rhythm. All she had to do was let go and be led. Eventually, the squeaking of Wyatt's sneakers attracted the attention of a manager, who escorted them both out of the store.

When they arrived at Joan's apartment, Wyatt stood in the doorway and looked awestruck.

"I can't believe this is where you live," he said.

Joan shrugged. "Yeah," she said. "I like the location. I watch someone get arrested almost every weekend."

"It would take me an entire lifetime to be able to afford something like this on my own," he said.

"Technically, same," Joan said. "My parents are splitting the rent."

"Oh yeah," Wyatt laughed. "People in the family still give you money."

"For now," Joan said. She wasn't sure what would happen once her internship ended in two months. What would be her excuse for not supporting herself then? It was a looming problem she mostly avoided thinking about.

Wyatt's phone began ringing. He held up one finger to Joan, answered it, and plopped down on the sofa. Joan went to the kitchen to pour herself whiskey over ice. She listened to Wyatt's conversation.

"This is Wyatt.... Tom? Hey! It's so good to hear from you. How's Angela? And the kids? Ah. Those little rascals. . . . Such a fun age. I'm doing . . . okay. No, I still don't have any money. . . . Literally, nothing at all. . . . I know, I know, I'm sorry. Yes, you'll be the first to know. Okay, I guess I'll talk to you soon? Send my best to Angie!"

"Who the hell was that? The recruiter?" Joan asked. She offered Wyatt a drink, but he refused and requested a shot of apple cider vinegar instead.

"That was a creditor," Wyatt said, taking the shot. "It's the same handful of people that call me all the time."

"And you actually pick up?"

Wyatt shrugged. "Why not?"

Joan laughed, before her own phone started ringing. It was her mother, again.

"There's *my* creditor," Joan said, flashing the screen to Wyatt. Her mother had been calling her multiple times a day since she started researching Vince. Griping at her constantly about being careless with her allowance—forgetting to pay her rent and utility bills, for instance, or eating out too much, spending too much at bars and strip clubs, and never going to the grocery store. Dolly watched Joan's bank account more closely than Joan did. But Joan didn't care what Dolly thought. She was doing important work that her mother couldn't possibly understand.

Joan ignored the call. She knew she would pay for this later, but for now, she wanted to enjoy her night.

"Hey. At least she cares," Wyatt said. "My mom just disowned me for like the third time."

"I wish my mom would disown me," Joan said. She picked up her pipe and began packing it densely with weed.

"You don't mean that," he said. "There's nothing more beautiful in this world than a mother's love."

Joan scoffed, taking a hit and exhaling a large cloud of smoke. She didn't offer Wyatt any weed, and he didn't ask. She'd only seen Wyatt smoke pot once, at their grandparents' ranch in high school, and she didn't like it. His brand of humor got creepy and off-putting. He started crouching in corners and giggling like a devil, then taking nude photographs of himself in the bathroom for an hour. Joan received a notification that her mother had left another voicemail. She put her phone away while Wyatt picked heavenly melodies on her acoustic guitar. He sang her the latest version of "Blackberry Vines," which was actually pretty catchy. Then he played a country song they'd written together during the summer at her dad's, called "Every Once in a While," which made fun of each member of their extended family one by one.

"How's the story about your inner life coming along?" Wyatt asked when he finished playing.

"It's not done. It's been so hard to focus without Adderall. It's basically impossible."

"That's a lie," Wyatt said. "Pills are the devil. Good writing comes from your heart." He tapped his chest for dramatic effect.

"Maybe for some people," Joan said. Adderall was all that had ever worked for her. She found it strange the way her relatives talked about the devil, as if it were a real person rather than an abstract idea, shiny and red with horns, standing on her shoulder, literally whispering in her ear.

Joan changed the subject. She explained her character research and the weird love triangle forming between her, Vince, and Roberto. She hated Vince, she said, but was spending most of her free time with him. She liked Roberto, she thought, but barely saw him lately.

"You need to stop fucking around and find a real man," Wyatt said. "Someone who'll treat you right, take you on a date. Like Randy Travis or Brandon Flowers. Did you know he's a Mormon with three kids?"

"No."

"Such a badass."

Joan found it charming that what made Brandon Flowers a "badass" to Wyatt was being a Mormon with three kids. One of Joan's favorite politicians, Mitt Romney, was also a Mormon. It was early days, but he was favored to be the Republican nominee in 2012, which thrilled her. Ever since she'd been gifted his memoir over Christmas break, Joan had loved Mitt Romney, his stiff, robotic innocence, his sober, sparkling eyes. He was like the father Joan had never had but always wanted.

"You're right," Joan said. She took a hit of weed and looked out the window, at the blinking crown-shaped sign of Club de Ville. "I need to find a real man."

"Well, take my advice with a grain of salt." Wyatt set down the guitar and went into the kitchen, where he opened the fridge, then the pantry. "You'll never guess what's going on in my love life." He returned to the couch with a bag of almonds, which he began eating in small handfuls.

Joan had been so carried away talking about herself that she'd forgotten to ask.

"What?"

"You have to promise not to tell anyone."

"I promise."

"Do you swear?"

"I swear to God."

"I found out Ruby's a stripper now," Wyatt said.

"What? Seriously?" Joan laughed. She loved how singularly devoted Wyatt was to Ruby, for no logical reason.

"I still can't believe it," he said. "She never even liked to dance."

"I'm really sorry," said Joan. "That must be hard."

"I even went to see it for myself. Two nights ago. After I heard, I just had to. And there she was, just hanging on a pole. She doesn't even have rhythm. I don't get why she would want to do that." He shook his head, looking deeply sad. "When she saw me, she got so mad. I tried to get a lap dance from her so we could talk, but she wouldn't do it. I kept asking her why not. I had twenty dollars for her and everything. It was her job now, why wouldn't she give me one? And she had the bouncers throw me out. Literally, they threw me into the parking lot."

He lifted his shirtsleeve to show a large scrape on his shoulder.

"Jesus," Joan said. The scene he described sounded as if it belonged in a movie; it was so dramatic. No matter what was happening in her life, Wyatt's was always more cinematic and interesting. She wondered briefly why she didn't write a story about Wyatt instead of Vince. Probably because Wyatt would be so difficult to capture. Then she had an epiphany. Vince had taken Joan to strip clubs a handful of times during the course of her research. Mostly, she found the establishments repugnant. But hearing Wyatt's story about Ruby was making Joan think about strip clubs in a new light. Perhaps she had overlooked something essential there. Some great truth that could provide insight into her narrator's inner life and deepest desires. She needed to go back. Then she could finally finish her stupid love story, impress Roberto, dump Vince for good, and turn her attention back to her coming-of-age novel.

Joan sent a text message to Vince. *I decided what I want to do for my birthday. I want to go to the strip club.*

Rawr, Vince replied seconds later.

Just before midnight, Joan covered the sofa with a sheet for Wyatt and gave him two of her bed pillows. She folded two blankets at the foot of the couch and set a small table near the head of the bed, where she placed a fresh box of tissues and a bottle of water. She knew from living with Wyatt that he had chronic, mysterious sinus problems, probably some kind of sleep apnea, and would need to blow his nose all night. When he came out of the bathroom, he fawned over the arrangement.

"Oh my god," he said. "You put tissues out. And water? Wow."

"It's not that big of a deal," she said.

He acted like nobody had ever taken care of him. "No, it is a big deal. You're changing. You have maternal energy now."

Joan snorted at how ridiculous he was being. She didn't know what to say. Intellectually, of course, she wanted to be a wife, a mother. She knew from all her conservative talk shows that motherhood was the greatest expression of being a female, and perhaps the only way she might achieve true biological happiness. Sometimes, she wondered if her lack of children explained why she felt so empty, so dissatisfied with her life. Perhaps the conservative hosts were onto something. Beneath everything else, perhaps she was just a mammalian female, looking to reproduce. It seemed so simplistic but possible. But in the practicalities and realities of Joan's day-to-day life, she couldn't have been farther from being maternal. She didn't own a cutting board. When her underwear got dirty, she bought more to avoid doing laundry. She wouldn't know what to do with a husband or a baby. She couldn't even take care of herself.

"Hey," he said before Joan retreated to her bedroom to sleep. "I got you a birthday present."

"You didn't have to do that," Joan said. "You should be saving your money."

"It's not much." He pulled a book out of his grocery sack and handed it to Joan. It was a small, motivational-looking hardcover called *Your Captivating Heart*. On the cover, a woman frolicked freely in a field of flowers, her arms outstretched, holding a piece of sheer fabric floating in the wind. "It's the girl's version of *Wild at Heart*. The guy's wife wrote it. I thought maybe you would like it."

Wild at Heart was a Christian book Wyatt often referenced. Joan was pretty sure it was the only book that Wyatt had ever read. She assumed it informed his deep desire to be a "real man" and take care of a family. Even though she had known about Wyatt's religious convictions, Joan was always surprised and taken aback when he brought them up in conversation. He was so different from the rest of her Bible-thumping family. He was nonjudgmental, irreverent, free. Joan, as a conservative, could intellectually acknowledge the importance of Judeo-Christian values to the fabric of the nation. However, if she was being honest, she found the Jesus story absurd and nonsensical.

"Thank you," Joan said. "That's really sweet of you." She took the book to her room and flipped through its colorful, glossy pages. It was like a children's book for adults. A kind gesture. She knew Wyatt's heart was in the right place, but she had no intention of reading the book that night, or anytime soon.

8.

A FANTASY AND AN ESCAPE

The next afternoon, Joan dropped Wyatt off at the train station and wished him luck in his new job. Wyatt saluted her. "Until next time," he said, before she drove away, back to her apartment to get ready for her birthday date with Vince. Joan's mother called again while Joan was in her bathroom, getting ready. Joan was wearing a skintight red dress from American Apparel, meticulously applying cat eyeliner. She set down her makeup and braced herself before answering. Dealing with her mother was always a balancing act. If Joan ignored her calls for too long, Dolly's repressed rage erupted like a volcano. On the other hand, if Joan answered too many of her mother's calls, it only encouraged her to call more and more. Dolly would call every hour if Joan let her.

"Happy birthday!" Dolly said in a singsong voice.

"Thanks," said Joan.

"I tried calling yesterday, but you didn't pick up."

"I know, I'm sorry. Things got busy."

Dolly asked about her birthday, and Joan talked about her day at work, about the cockfighting bill and all the protestors, and then about Wyatt's visit. But she couldn't help feeling that her mother wasn't really listening. Dolly was just waiting on the other end for Joan to say something specific, though Joan wasn't exactly sure what.

"Did you get my package in the mail?" Dolly asked when Joan was finished talking.

"I can't remember," Joan said. Mail had always been hard for her. She rarely checked it, and when she did, she left it all unopened in big piles around her messy apartment for weeks.

"There was a check inside," Dolly said. "And something else you asked for."

Joan apologized and began fumbling around her room in search of the package, which she eventually found on her desk chair along with some other mail, hidden under a pile of dirty clothes.

"It's impolite to not cash checks in a timely manner," Dolly said. "I want you to become more responsible."

"I know, I'm sorry," Joan said, tearing open the yellow envelope. Inside, there was a birthday card containing a check for a thousand dollars, along with a Skittles bag, which had been opened and re-sealed with Scotch tape. Joan opened the Skittles and dumped them into her hand. There were five Vicodin among the colorful candies. Her mother had a prescription for the painkillers for neuropathy as a result of her mastectomy in the late eighties. She claimed to rarely take the pills anymore. "I don't know why I can't throw them away," she would often say. "I guess it's the addict in me."

"Thanks," Joan said. "These will really help with my headaches."

"You're welcome," Dolly said. "Don't take more than one at once. And don't take them with alcohol."

"I won't," Joan lied.

Dolly asked what Joan's plans were, and Joan told her she was go-ing out with Vince. She didn't say where. Still, her mother grunted in disapproval.

"What?" Joan said, annoyed.

"I don't like him."

"You don't even know him."

"I know his type. All talk."

"Y'all literally haven't even met."

Joan didn't know why she was defending Vince. Of course he was awful. But it felt like her cosmic duty to oppose everything her mother said. It was outrageous that Dolly would try to give her advice about how to choose a man. As if she had any expertise in that area. After all, Dolly had chosen to marry her stepdad, Doug, a literal psychopath who'd made Joan's life hell from the time she was ten to the time she turned fifteen. In the years since their divorce, Dolly had carefully sliced Doug's face out of every family photo and referred to him exclusively as "Satan" if he ever came up in conversation.

"What's his job again?" Dolly asked. "Where does his money even come from?"

"He's an entrepreneur," Joan said.

Dolly grunted again.

"I have to go," Joan lied. "He's here." She hung up, feeling agitated, her entire body abuzz with frustration. She packed a bowl and sat on her bed, smoking, staring at the framed Declaration of Independence she had hung above her dresser. She put in her earphones and turned on Dennis Prager's "Happiness Hour" from the previous Friday. She had subscribed to his show and could access any episode she wanted, on demand, for only a few dollars a month. Dennis talked about happiness on the third hour of every Friday. If more Americans were happy, he theorized, the world would not only be a better place, but there would also be many more conservatives. According to Dennis, happiness was not based on personal circumstances, it was a decision Joan could make for herself, as well as a moral obligation to those around her, like showering or brushing her teeth.

Soon, Vince was standing at her front door smiling, smelling like cologne, with gel in his hair, holding two gifts wrapped in shiny paper and tied with red ribbons. They made a loud clanking noise when he set them on the kitchen counter.

"What are those?"

"Open them," he said, smiling as she opened the first package.

It was a bottle of Kraken rum with an octopus on the label. "Because it's your favorite animal," Vince said. The second was a bottle of whiskey with a picture of Thomas Jefferson. "Because you love America," he said, and kissed her on the forehead. "What better gifts for a little alcoholic like you?"

"I can't think of any," Joan said, and she meant it. She opened the bottle of whiskey and took a sip. Joan felt relieved that he hadn't gotten her any real, enduring gifts, signaling that he wasn't her boyfriend after all. He was only her subject, nothing more.

They walked hand in hand, headed south on Red River Street. They were going to pregame at Pure, where Monica worked as a bartender, because drinks at the strip club were going to be so "goddamn expensive."

"God, I need to make money," Vince complained. "I need to get my own place, downtown."

"It's overrated," Joan said.

"I'm tired of living with bartenders," he said. "That's the main issue with living in a house and renting it out. You get stuck living with a bunch of derelicts. They're messy, they use my studio, they eat my food, they stay up late and make a bunch of noise while I'm trying to sleep."

"It sounds like you have kids," Joan said.

"Exactly," Vince said. "It's like having a bunch of fucking kids."

"Having a kid is kind of my worst nightmare," Joan lied.

"What would suck the most for me is having to hang out with a pregnant chick for nine months," Vince said. "I mean, I'm sure it would be hard for her too, but I just don't know if I could deal with that."

Joan typed the ridiculous line into her phone for her story, which was finally beginning to take shape in her mind. *A quietly brilliant woman goes out with her asshole boyfriend, an unavailable Peter Pan type, and by the end of the night he is left humiliated when she falls in love with a stripper instead of him.*

The closer to Sixth Street they got, the dirtier everything became. The smell of vomit wafted over Joan as they passed by Swan Dive. Someone blew smoke right into her face. A homeless man held out a red rose that he wanted Vince to buy for Joan. They ignored him and walked faster.

When they reached the corner of Red River and Sixth, Joan recognized a tall, slender figure standing in line at a hot dog stand. She stopped abruptly. Vince turned around.

"Roberto?" Joan said.

"Hey, lady, it's good to see you."

Vince approached. Adrenaline pumped through Joan's body. How was she supposed to behave? She was completely unprepared for this moment.

"Vince, this is my friend Roberto. Roberto, this is my friend Vince," Joan said, and the two men shook hands. She wanted to die.

"Working hard on your story, I see," Roberto said.

"Yes," Joan said, mortified. "I am." She turned to Vince. "Let's get going." She was careful not to hold Vince's hand until they were safely out of Roberto's view.

"Who was that guy?" Vince asked. "I didn't realize you were friends with the Mexican Napoleon Dynamite." He laughed at his joke.

"Nobody," Joan said. "He just works at a coffee shop I go to."

Pure looked like a spaceship and smelled like bleach. It was futuristic and loud and reminded Joan of all the clubs in South Beach that she hated, the places her roommate would drag her freshman year, where white northeastern douchebags with rich parents would get bottle service and act like hardened gangsters. Joan could never understand such people, eventually gravitating toward the jazz school hippie crowd, with whom she smoked weed and drank and took LSD from the comfort of house parties.

Joan followed Vince up to the third floor, where Monica was working. She had a thin black band around her bleached blond hair and a large sucker in her mouth swirled with red and white. When she saw them, she removed the sucker and smiled really big. "Happy birthday," she said, almost shouting. Her skin glowed bright blue from the bar as she poured three pink shots. They picked them up and clinked them together. They tasted like candy.

Joan consumed her drink while Vince and Monica had a long,

boring conversation about their event's lackluster performance at South by Southwest. "This town is full of a bunch of losers," Vince was saying. "Nobody wants to spend money, nobody wants to make money. They all want to live in a fantasy world where money doesn't exist."

Monica was nodding along, a solemn expression on her face. Joan interjected with a snide remark about liberals and the nanny state, which Vince and Monica ignored. Joan moved to a blue pleather couch, where she sat alone, taking notes about her story idea.

> A quirky and beautiful Republican woman goes to a strip club with her delusional left-wing boyfriend. Here, she bonds with one of the dancers and tries to rescue her from her life in the darkness. In the end, the women fall in love, while the boyfriend is left alone and heartbroken, eventually realizing the errors of his ways.

It was going to be brilliant, she thought, watching a jumbo screen playing top-twenty music videos. Roberto was going to be so impressed. So were her former writing mentors, Claire, and all the editors at big-time magazines, who would be fighting each other to publish it.

She was still feeling self-conscious about the awkward encounter with Roberto at the hot dog stand. That he saw her with Vince, and that she still hadn't finished her story, made her feel slightly pathetic. Luckily, though, her story and her relationship with Vince would probably be over tonight. In a few days, she would have an impressive story to share, and she and Roberto could resume their flirtation.

Perhaps they would even have a brief fling, which would help her get over Vince. Even though she didn't like Vince, she'd grown used to him, the way he filled silence and touched her constantly. She thought of how tall Roberto was, much taller than Vince. At least six foot two, with a large head of wild, wiry hair atop his lanky, soft, and slender frame. She thought of all the books Roberto had read and all the things he knew, all the literary wisdom he might impart to her.

Vince wasn't dumb by any means, but he wasn't a reader like Roberto, plus he went to her dad's school, which was a huge turnoff. Joan decided that Roberto would be a good distraction. A fantasy and an escape as she continued her search for a conservative, Judeo-Christian husband who appreciated both art *and* fiscal responsibility. A real man who would swoop in, become her "rock," and rescue her from her family's golden shackles.

Deciding it would be wrong to lead Roberto on, Joan sent him a text message, explaining exactly that. *You are a fantasy and an escape.* Followed by: *Do you have any STDs?*

This chick, Roberto replied almost immediately. *No, I don't.*

Vince came over to the couch with two more drinks and sat down. He sighed and started rubbing her neck. "Sorry about that," he said.

"That's okay," Joan said.

"God, this place is fucking annoying," he said. "Let's go. Hurry up and finish your drink."

9.

CONQUISTADOR

The Yellow Rose was a large, windowless building off North Lamar, with a red-carpeted entrance and cement lion statues flanking the front door. Joan sat with Vince at a table near the center stage. A waitress came by, and Vince ordered a second round of Jack and Cokes to fulfill their two-drink minimum.

"I love strip clubs," Vince said, leaning back in his chair. "It's nothing sexual or anything. They're just chill, relaxing places to hang out."

"Yeah, totally," Joan said, swallowing the last of her drink. She looked around the club. Women's bare bodies were flawless under the flashing purple lights. Loud bass buzzed through her bones. She tried to suppress any feelings of insecurity or jealousy and instead mustered empathy for the girls. She'd listened to enough Dr. Drew in high school to know that each one of them had probably been traumatized in some way as a child. And now they probably all despised men. How could they not? Seeing them at their worst and most pathetic, day after day. Joan wondered what Dennis Prager would have to say about such a place.

"That girl kind of reminds me of my first stepmom," Joan joked, pointing to a blonde in a silver thong across the room. She was straddling the leg of a balding man in a suit. He stared at her with his hands by his sides.

Joan's first stepmom had worked at a strip club when her dad met her. Her dad was forty, she was twenty-three, and Joan was seven. Her stepmom wore red lipstick and smelled like Neiman Marcus, and Joan loved her because she always drove her around in a tan Lexus her dad bought her.

"She's got a hot ass," Vince said.

Joan, wanting to keep the mood light, didn't say who the stripper also reminded her of, which was her mother, Dolly. During the four years her mother was married to Doug, Dolly looked like she'd walked straight out of the pages of *Playboy*. Her pale skin got as bronze as a penny, her dishwater hair became platinum, her breasts became the size and shape of cantaloupes. Every day Dolly dressed like she was the sixth member of the Spice Girls, wearing crop tops, tiny mini-dresses, and thigh-high boots or enormous chunky platform heels. Around the house, Doug referred to Dolly exclusively as "Kitty," and her mother would reply, "Meowwww." Once, Joan had walked in on Dolly, topless in a Santa hat, giving Doug a lap dance in their kitchen. Joan was ten or eleven. It was a memory Joan's therapist consistently wanted to revisit, despite Joan's resistance. It was all so disgusting. She shuddered thinking about it and finished her whiskey.

The waitress came back with more drinks and set them down on the metal table. Joan watched her return to the bar and count her tips. She had red hair and was wearing fishnet hose. She looked tired.

"I made the mistake of calling my father for financial advice today," Vince said, removing the straw from his drink and putting it on the table. "All he does is yell at me for quitting Goldman Sachs and going to AudioPro. He said I'll wake up one day and be forty-five and broke and no woman will ever love me."

"Jesus," Joan said, feeling vaguely guilty knowing that Vince had spent at least twenty thousand dollars for the AudioPro certificate he would earn in May.

Vince rolled his eyes and took a sip. "He just doesn't get it. He's almost seventy and he just doesn't understand the entertainment industry and how it all works. It takes a long time for a website to make a profit."

"How does a website make a profit? Ads?"

"It's complicated."

"I see," Joan said. She looked around for the waitress, ready for another drink.

"I could have had a million dollars saved up by now," Vince said. "I was making six figures a year at Goldman Sachs. *At least*. Like, that was the bare minimum."

"What exactly did you do there?" He talked about his old life all the time, but Joan always forgot. It was so boring.

"Commercial mortgage-backed security trading."

"What's that?"

"We would give lots of money to people who were buying or refinancing commercial properties, then we would take the income from the monthly payments and mortgages and pool it together into a bundle and then sell the bundle on the bond market. We were incentivized to lend out as much money as possible, no matter what, then turn around and sell the right to collect the mortgage payments immediately. So there was zero risk for us if the loans defaulted. It was a total fucking scam, and it was legal."

"Good thing you got out when you did, right? Before the crash and everything."

"Morally, yes. Financially, I could have stayed a couple more years and made more money."

"Oh."

"I wish I could just be an explorer or something," Vince said. "That's all I've ever really wanted to do." He looked wistfully at a blond dancer swaying around half-heartedly on the stage.

Joan laughed. "An explorer?"

"Yeah. I just want to use maps and compasses, discover land and stuff like that. I just want to hold a sword and yell."

"Like a conquistador?"

"Yes! Exactly like a conquistador. Except for all the religious shit."

Joan was going to write this down once she was sober. Vince, complicated by his role in the financial crisis of 2008, was the perfect tragic literary figure. A soul born into the wrong era. In the wrong place at the wrong time. Kind of like Wyatt, she thought, who had always wished he lived in Sparta.

Joan got up and went to the bathroom, which had a bench and lockers and was awkwardly filled with strippers who were doing their makeup and counting their tips. They hardly looked at Joan as she slipped into a bathroom stall, feeling uncomfortable and out of place. In the stall, she dug through her purse, broke off a piece of painkiller, and swallowed it dry, to take the edge off.

Joan saw the pills as a peace offering from her mother, to make up for all the suffering she'd caused Joan by marrying Doug. Dolly never said outright that she was sorry. Once, after Joan started therapy, she tried to bring up the effect Doug had on her psyche. "That's my pain," Dolly had barked at her, shutting down the conversation immediately. The pills were of course insufficient to make up for it all, but Joan appreciated them nonetheless.

When she sat on the toilet, her phone fell into the bowl, and when she pulled it out, the screen went black, and she figured that it was dead. She set the phone on the floor. She was starting to feel dizzy, and when she sat down on the toilet again she nearly fell over. She stared at the stall door for a while. It was covered in bumper stickers and graffiti. Strippers had written all over the door with permanent markers. Some wrote that they were there, and what day they were there. Some wrote "Fuck You," some wrote "Fuck Me." Some wrote phone numbers to call for a good time or a bad time or drugs or blow jobs. Some wrote warnings—names of men in town who were assholes or pussies or had small penises or herpes. Some drew genitals, some drew hearts. Near the bottom of the door, Joan spotted a small orange and black sticker with Vince's name on it, and she wondered who may have put it there.

She returned to the table and sat down. Now she just needed to decide which stripper she would try to fictionally fall in love with and rescue. She wanted to evoke the heartbreaking scene that Wyatt had described with Ruby. However, she hoped she wouldn't get thrown into the parking lot.

Joan watched a new dancer emerge on the center stage—a girl with short brown hair who climbed up the pole with grace and ease. She looked like Winona Ryder and didn't shave her underarms, but the hair was light and scarce, and it actually didn't look too bad. Entranced, Joan watched as she spun slowly down the pole, reminding her of a ballerina music box she had as a child. It had been one of her favorite items before Doug had broken it in a drunken rage. According to her therapist, Doug was the source of most of her ills. When the stripper reached the bottom of the pole, she landed in the splits and began gently dry-humping the stage.

"I want a lap dance from her," Joan said.

"From who?"

"That girl with the short hair."

"She's pretty hot."

"How do I make that happen? I've never gotten one before."

"You go ask her."

"But I don't know what to say."

"You say you want a lap dance, you fucking idiot. Tell her it's your birthday."

"Give me a dollar," Joan said. "I want to put it in her thong."

Vince pulled out his wallet and handed Joan a dollar bill. She went up to the stage and stood there, holding it out. When the stripper saw Joan, she smiled and moved toward her, low and long like a spider crawling toward its prey. "Hey, gorgeous," she said. Joan slid the dollar beneath the string of her hot-pink thong; her skin was smooth and warm.

"I want to save you," Joan said. The stripper stroked Joan's hair and smiled. Joan asked her for a lap dance and the stripper seemed happy that she'd asked. She said she'd come over after her set was finished.

She led them to a couch on the other side of the club. When Joan sat down, the stripper crouched on the carpet in front of her and looked at her with big brown eyes. She placed her hands on Joan's knees and opened her legs. As she slowly moved her hands up Joan's inner thighs, she felt a tingle of pleasure threatening to awaken her from her drunken robotic state.

The stripper stood up and turned around and put her arms together and started shaking her ass really fast. It made Joan laugh, the abrupt shift of tone, how fast the flesh moved. She watched it for a while, and when she got bored, she slapped it, and it made a loud clapping noise. The stripper didn't get mad, she just turned around and smiled and kept shaking it, so Joan slapped it again.

Soon she was back on top of Joan, grinding on her lower stomach and rubbing her boobs in her face. They were small but soft and nice to look at, and when Joan put her hand on one, she didn't say anything. She just smiled, and for the first time, Joan noticed a tiny gap between her front teeth that made her look Eastern European. Joan slouched farther and farther into her seat and her dress kept sliding up her thighs. Vince kept reaching over and pulling it back down again.

"Can I touch you?" she whispered into Joan's ear.

"Sure," Joan muttered. "Do whatever you want."

"Darling, everyone can see your ass," Vince said, looking around.

His voice sounded muffled and echoey to Joan, like it was coming from another dimension.

The first song ended, and Joan told the stripper to keep going. It was her birthday and she deserved more. Vince handed the stripper another twenty, rolled his eyes, and went to the bar. She put her hand down the front of Joan's dress, slid it under her bra, and rubbed her nipple, sending a tingling sensation throughout Joan's lifeless body. Vince returned from the bar with another drink, sat down, and pulled Joan's dress down again.

"Hey," he said, "as the one paying for all these fucking lap dances, can I at least get *something*?"

The stripper glanced over at him and put one of her feet in his lap.

"Great. Thanks a lot," he said. He kept his hand around the stripper's ankle throughout the entire song, sipping his Jack and Coke.

When the fourth song ended, she stood up and looked at Joan, then Vince.

"It's last call. If you want, I could go back to your place. I've got some coke."

"I don't think that's a good idea," Vince said.

"It is a good idea," Joan said defiantly. "I'm rescuing her. That's why we're here."

She didn't want her story with the stripper to end. She felt there was more to unpack with her. But only Vince heard Joan, and so the stripper left. Flat on her back with one leg dangling off the couch, Joan began moaning incoherently for her to come back. Vince closed his eyes and started rubbing his temples, before escorting Joan out of the club and heaving her into the front seat of his car. "It was a good idea," Joan repeated as he buckled her seat belt. "You're keeping me from good things. I hate you so much."

They were headed south on MoPac, toward Vince's big brick house in the suburbs, which he'd purchased in 2008 with the help of his father. Joan's face was pressed into the cold car window, her head too heavy for her neck to support. They were listening to Jeremiah Stone, a local singer-songwriter who Vince said could make it big if he quit doing heroin and got his shit together. He was singing a pretty song about missing his dead cat.

"There's too many goddamn high-rises in all the wrong places," Vince said, looking at the skyline in the distance. "I swear. This town was designed by a bunch of fucking idiots."

Joan said nothing but assumed the leftist, moronic Austin city council was to blame.

"It'd be really easy to nip it in the bud too," Vince continued. "But they'd have to do it soon. The problem is that more and more people are coming in and this city is just not equipped to handle the traffic. It's going to be a disaster. I know exactly how it happened too. When I was working at Goldman Sachs, I saw it happen all the time. My bosses would always take advantage of dumb southern people who didn't know what the fuck they were doing."

Joan's skull skidded across the glass as he turned onto Brodie Lane and lurched forward when he stopped abruptly at a red light. Even though she could hardly think, she felt so happy to have completed her story, at least in her mind. She knew exactly what it was about. She knew where it took place, how it began, and how it ended. Now she would just have to write it.

"See?" Vince said. "Everything here is fucked. The lights aren't even synchronized. That's the first thing you do in a big city. You synchronize the fucking lights."

10.

DEAR ADDERALL

The next morning, Joan woke up in Vince's bed, her head throbbing. She had a vague recollection of the night before. She remembered getting several lap dances in a row while Vince grew increasingly irritated, perhaps even jealous, which delighted her. She remembered the stripper, with the gap in her teeth and the hairy armpits, offering to come back to Vince's house with them, but it was clear that she hadn't. If she had, she'd already left. Joan couldn't remember the ride home at all. There was a lot she would need to piece together or fictionalize to finish her story. Vince was awake, packing a small suitcase on his bed. He was flying to Long Island that afternoon to see his family. Something about a birthday party and his niece getting baptized. He would be gone for over a week. He was singing hymns in a loud, dramatic way.

"Did we have sex last night?" Joan asked, searching for her phone, which wouldn't turn on.

"You seriously don't remember that?" Vince let out an exasperated sigh. "God, you're an alcoholic."

"So, we did?"

"Yes, we did."

"Hmm," Joan said. "Interesting."

"It was awesome. You even let me lick your asshole."

"Disgusting!" Joan said.

"It was *your* idea."

Joan got out of bed, appalled and refusing to believe him, and went to the bathroom. Perhaps this was an April Fool's joke. But her skin was raw from the friction, and when she peed it burned. Sitting on the toilet, she rummaged through Vince's toiletry bag, looking for his Adderall, but couldn't find any. From previous conversations, Joan knew Vince had a prescription, but he was adept at hiding the medication. He seemed to rarely take any himself. Which Joan found unfathomable. Whenever she had her own prescription in Miami, the bottles would never last more than two weeks. Sometimes they would disappear even faster.

"I wish you would stop doing that," Vince said when Joan emerged.

"Doing what?"

"Blacking out. It's really creepy for me."

"I know," Joan said. "I'm sorry."

"Look, when I get back from my trip, I'm not going to have as much time to fuck around like we have been," he said.

"Oh. Okay."

"I'm thirty. I need to get my shit together and meet with investors. I'm just not at a place in my life where I can spend four, five nights a week with somebody."

"Fine, whatever. I'm going to get something to drink. My head is killing me." Joan put on a T-shirt from Vince's failed clothing company and a pair of boxer shorts. She discreetly grabbed one of her mother's painkillers, hid it in her palm, and walked down the hall. At the top of the stairs, Monica's bedroom door was wide open, and she was asleep on top of the covers, wearing a red bra and black panties. Joan went downstairs, into the kitchen, and made herself some hot tea. At the sink, while she filled up a mug with tap water, she looked at the windowsill and noticed that Vince's other roommate's dead bug collection had grown. There were beetles and crickets and cockroaches and cicadas, spray-painted gold and silver and copper, holding miniature swords and shields, arranged in battle poses to look like they were at war. It had clearly taken a lot of time to build, Joan thought, impressed. And nobody besides a few would ever even see it. Perhaps this was the truest version of art there was.

Joan took the tea into the control room of the recording studio that Vince had built in his garage the previous summer, during his second semester at AudioPro. She swallowed her pill, sat on the brown sofa, and scanned the room for possible hiding spots for his Adderall. She picked up a black leather book she found sitting next to her on the couch. Maybe it was a journal containing new insights into Vince's character. But as she flipped through the pages, she was disappointed to realize the book was filled only with his terrible song lyrics, about girls from all different places. There was one about a blond yoga instructor from Chattanooga, one about a girl from San Antonio whose eyes had stars in them, one about a tattoo artist in Brooklyn who floated around like a butterfly and smelled like cherry ChapStick. There was even a song about a girl from Argentina named Esmeralda who moved her hips so well that when she danced, the whole world shook until the earth's crust cracked open.

As she neared the end of the pages, her hopes began to rise. Would she find something about herself? Had Vince written any lyrics in her honor? Ever since she could remember, Joan had always wanted to inspire a song. To move a man's heart and soul and be firmly immortalized in music, like that blond model who'd inspired both Eric Clapton and George Harrison, whatever her name was. In Miami, she had dated several musicians with this objective in mind, to no avail. But now it seemed possible. She could tell Vince had become smitten. He called her pet names unironically. He got upset when she blacked out. He had even invited her to attend his AudioPro graduation ceremony in May, which she'd declined, horrified. Still, it seemed like evidence that he was serious about her. But when Joan reached the end of Vince's notebook, she was dismayed. There was nothing she could even pretend was inspired by her. After all this time together. Was she too boring to inspire him? Her headache became sharper, more acute. She put his journal back exactly how she'd found it. She drank her tea, shut her eyes, and squeezed her temples, feeling jealous of Esmeralda. She wondered if she was a real person, and if she was, where she was, what she was doing, and if she knew she had her very own song.

Joan went back upstairs, where Vince was still packing for his trip.

"Hey, do you think I could borrow some Adderall before you go?" Joan asked casually, like it was no big deal.

"No way," Vince said. "I'm not giving you any."

"Come on."

"Don't 'come on' me."

"Think of all I've done for you," Joan said. Two weeks earlier, Joan had convinced her dad to sponsor Vince and Monica's South by Southwest event for three thousand dollars. Other than that, she hadn't done much for him.

"That's exactly why I'm not giving you any," he said.

"Why?"

"I'm not going to help you relapse."

Joan instantly regretted telling him the story of her drug-induced euphoric mania in Miami. She took note not to open up so much in future relationships. The more someone knew about her, it seemed, the more problems it would cause for her.

"But I've got to finish this story," she whined. "I need help."

"Fine," he said. "You can have one pill. If that's what you need."

He briefly left the room and returned with the pill. It was twenty milligrams, instant release. She knew by the color and texture. He'd broken the orange chalky pill into four tiny pieces and put them in a small plastic baggie. "Here. You're only allowed to take five milligrams at a time. You have to agree to that."

"But that's nothing."

"Babe, it's not supposed to be like a drug, it's just supposed to make you a little more focused."

"But I like to be a lot more focused," she said.

Vince shook his head and withheld the baggie.

"Okay, okay," she said. "I promise I won't take more than five milligrams."

He handed her the bag and she placed it in her purse.

"Thanks," she said.

Once he dropped her off and left for the airport, Joan took all four pieces at once, turning the baggie inside out and licking up any remnants. Before beginning the story, she started calling around, looking for more. Using Facebook Messenger, she was able to convince a kid from YCT to sell her half his bottle. Her car sat idling outside his apartment for an hour while she began outlining the story on her phone, her teeth clenched.

She hardly left the apartment that weekend or talked to anyone besides Claire. When she was hungry, which was rare, she went no farther than the panini stand across the street, where she would climb inside and smoke weed with the owner, Teddy, from Florida.

For the first time in years, she wanted nothing but to be alone with her writing. She wrote and rewrote scenes dozens of times. She read passages out loud and toiled over the structures of sentences until they were perfect. She looked up the definition of any questionable word, using an online thesaurus to make sure every word she chose was the best, most concise possible word. She bought a pack of different-colored highlighters, which she used to organize her backstory.

It was hard work, but Joan felt excited and capable. As she wrote, she took frequent breaks to imagine what the story would look like published, the way the pages would feel between her fingertips, the satisfaction of seeing her name printed in a fancy yet understated font, on the clean white pages of some prestigious journal.

Each time she finished a new draft, she sat on the floor of her apartment and used a pair of scissors to cut her story apart and reorganize it once more. It was like assembling a jigsaw puzzle. She needed to make sure all the information about Vince was relayed in the correct order, that the flashbacks blended effortlessly with the present action. Revising the story became easier the harder she focused.

With so much focus, she realized she could accomplish anything. This story was only the beginning. From here, she could write an entire collection of stories, about all the disappointing men in her life, which would be her literary debut and win several prestigious awards. She would be branded the anti–Pam Houston. Her short-story collection would pave the way for her to finally finish her coming-of-age novel, *Cowgirls and Indians*, an impressive sophomore effort that would be hailed as a triumph. After that was released, she could write six or seven more novels, some poetry, and possibly even an experimental poetic memoir. Other writers she knew, like Roberto, would watch her career in awe, wondering how she could produce such brilliance time and time again. Now that Joan had Adderall back in her system, she could do anything she wanted; she could have it all and nothing would stop her.

11.

HOW WRITERS ARE

When the pills ran out, Joan's crash into ennui and despair came hard and fast, but at least she had something to show for it. She had titled her story "Conquistador" and was convinced it was the best thing she'd ever written. She wondered why she'd avoided the subject of love for so long. Clearly, it was a strength of hers. Writing about Vince and the stripper was much easier and less painful than writing about her dysfunctional family. Before she submitted the story for publication, however, she would need to gather constructive feedback and revise. But mostly, she just wanted assurance that the story was amazing. She sent "Conquistador" to her two former writing mentors from college—Carlos at UT and Paul at UM—as well as to Claire and Roberto.

Paul responded first. Joan was at work, proofreading a bill that would allow widows of veterans not to pay property taxes. Most of Allen's bills revolved around law enforcement and veterans' affairs. Easy wins, Kyle explained. The main goal of being a representative seemed to be cranking out as many bills as possible. It didn't really matter what they were, as long as they passed. With her pills now gone, Joan was feeling bored, sad, and empty. Seeing Paul's name in her inbox gave her a needed jolt of excitement. She opened it immediately.

It's nice to see you writing at such a high level, Paul wrote. *Vince is a nearly perfect loser. I especially love the part in which he mansplains his role in the debt crisis. I wish there were more of these intrusions of "real life" into the weirdly hermetic world in which Vince and your narrator reside.*

Joan looked up the definition of *hermetic,* then read Paul's email over and over again. She missed him intensely, his wit and his passion and his authority. His greasy blond hair, tan skin, and strange teeth. Paul was a young, stylish adjunct who wrote articles for *Esquire.* She'd taken his Intro to Creative Writing class during her sophomore year at UM. He made his students put their work on an overhead and read it out loud, while he sat in the back of the room, slouched, insulting their shitty lines like he was Gordon Lish. Joan had found it all incredibly sexy and motivating. That was when she began writing in earnest. She changed her major from studio art to English, and it became her sole purpose in life to impress Paul. She read every book he recommended, and they became her favorite books—works by Bret Easton Ellis, Denis Johnson, John Kennedy Toole. Every week, Joan took Adderall, cranked out pages about her dad at the library, and brought them directly to Paul's office hours to show him. He would read her work in front of her, smirking. "You could make a lot of money in Hollywood, writing scenes like these," he'd said once.

I'm going to make a lot of money in Hollywood, Joan would think to herself, walking around the alligator-infested, palm-tree-lined campus. For the first time in her life, it felt like all her childhood suffering might actually pay off. Paul had been disappointed when Joan took so much Adderall that she had to leave school. He had hoped she would finish her novel under his mentorship, he said when she broke the news. "Why do you care so much if I finish my novel?" she asked, genuinely baffled. "So my daughter has something cool to read when she's older," Paul had said. His daughter was a tiny, lucky little baby, Joan thought. She was sad to leave Paul but grateful that he was willing to stay in touch.

Later in the day, during an oil-and-gas-lobbyist-funded lunch buffet, Joan received Carlos's reply. She held her breath in anticipation, opening his email. She and Carlos weren't as close as she and Paul had been. Carlos was much more serious and demanding. When she would send him long, sloppy excerpts of her novel in progress, he'd always remind her that being a writer was like being a surgeon. It was about cutting, toiling, revising. Joan still hadn't internalized the advice, but she was glad to have him in her corner.

Finally! Carlos wrote. *Finally, you've written the story I knew you were capable of writing. The antagonistic love interest illuminates your narrator in new ways. She is somewhat more present here than in the family material. Nice work.*

Carlos followed his praise with some suggestions for revision, which Joan glossed over, disinterested. She took a screenshot of both the men's emails, so she could read them whenever she wanted. The praise buoyed her spirits for the rest of her shift at the capitol. She was relieved to know that her Adderall relapse, and all her present physical suffering, had been worth it.

After work, Joan went to Cain & Abel's with Claire, where they talked about her story, their novels, and their future writing careers while drinking enormous Texas Teas—mixed drinks so strong they could only legally order two. The girls discussed the probability that literary critics would someday study their novels side by side, looking for connections and overlapping symbols or themes. Perhaps there would be a college class, somewhere, devoted entirely to the topic of Joan's and Claire's writing. They chain-smoked cigarettes on the patio, talking about themselves as fratty-looking college boys approached them, and they shooed them away like flies.

Just then, Joan received an email from Roberto in response to "Conquistador."

Wow, Roberto wrote. *I really fucking hate that guy. You were extremely successful in producing a lot of hatred within me, toward that guy. I really liked the strip club scene, though.*

Joan didn't know how to take his feedback, which was much briefer than she would have expected. Instilling hatred for Vince wasn't exactly what she was going for with the story. Well, of course it was a part of it. But the other, larger part was that she wanted to showcase how damaged, desirable, and sharply intelligent her protagonist was. She read over Roberto's email again and began having doubts about the quality of her story. She didn't reply to Roberto, unsure what to say.

An hour later, while she was still at the bar with Claire, she received a text from him.

What's up, lady. Do you want to go get some tacos tomorrow or what?

Joan showed the text to Claire, who raised her eyebrows. Joan was a bit surprised by the invitation. It had been so long since they'd hung out, and he'd had such a lukewarm reaction to "Conquistador." Was it something in her story that drew him back in? Was he asking her out on a date? She thought of what Wyatt had told her. A real man will ask you out on a date.

"What about Vince?" Claire asked.

"What about him?" said Joan.

The following evening, Joan drank whiskey on ice as she paced the apartment, talking to Claire about her plans. Vince was still on Long Island. Joan was starting to feel guilty for going on a date behind his back.

"Should I talk to Vince first?" Joan said, panicking.

"Why not?" Claire said.

"He probably wouldn't want to see me anymore."

"But if your story about him is done, why does that matter?" Claire asked.

Joan thought about it. Technically, she wasn't 100 percent done with her story. She still had to revise. What if she needed to collect a few more details or lines of dialogue? It felt unwise to cut off her subject until she felt absolutely certain she didn't need him anymore. She decided not to tell Vince about her date with Roberto.

She put on a short black cotton dress with white polka dots and red flowers with her red cardigan sweater. Roberto showed up at her apartment at eight, wearing his usual clothes, but he seemed clean and freshly shaven.

They went to a Mexican restaurant on East Sixth, where they drank tequila and ate.

"I haven't heard from you in a while," Joan said. "You haven't been at work either."

"I'm sorry," he said. "Part of that time I was in Brownsville for an art show. I showed some of my Polaroids."

"Oh?" said Joan, intrigued. "I didn't know you were serious about photographs."

"Yes, I showed mostly a series of abandoned kitchen appliances on the street. But there were some others. I used your portrait too. I hope you don't mind."

"You used that in a show?" Joan was shocked, but she didn't feel violated. Instead, she felt extremely full of herself, even though she had never seen the photo. That Roberto would find her picture so moving that he would stand behind it as an artist, placing his name underneath it on a blank white wall, filled her with immense pleasure. She imagined clusters of random hipsters in Brownsville standing in front of her image, taken by Roberto Rosa. She imagined them tilting their heads, considering her mystery. Joan felt glamorous all of a sudden, and her entire physical presence became more meaningful and beautiful.

"I've been writing for four days straight," Joan bragged. "I've hardly slept or eaten, and I think I even pinched a nerve in my neck from working so hard."

"Damn, lady, it's time for you to take a break."

When they finished eating, Roberto paid for the meal, which took her by surprise. Was he trying to woo her?

"I like your short dress," Roberto said as they walked along Red River Street, back in the direction of her apartment. He placed his hand on her lower back, moving it down toward her ass. Joan, suddenly terrified of where the night was headed, took Roberto's hand and pulled him into Headhunters, a metal bar that had devils and flames painted on the walls. She felt flooded and confused. Should she text Vince and end things now? But since they weren't a couple, who cared? Why did she feel so guilty and tethered to him? She needed to drink more to help her process her feelings on the subject. They sat at the bar and Joan ordered more tequila. There were girls in bikinis walking on the bar tops. Joan usually avoided tequila, but since she'd broken her Adderall fast, she figured what the hell. Soon, they were both very drunk.

Feeling loose and reckless, she began acting out, putting dollar bills in the girls' bikinis, making lewd comments like "Nice ass," "Sit on my face," and "Give it to me, baby." She wasn't sure if she was trying to repel Roberto or recapture the magic of the night at the strip club, or some combination of the two. But she quickly realized none of the girls possessed the same captivating aura that her hairy gap-toothed stripper had. When Joan grew bored of trying to manufacture chemistry with the lame bikini-clad girls on the bar, she turned her attention back to Roberto. It felt like the perfect moment to let the cat out of the bag and reveal her politics. Surely, that would nip whatever romantic momentum was building in the bud.

"I'm reading a book by Mitt Romney right now," Joan said. "It's called *No Apology: The Case for American Greatness*. I'm a registered Republican. I'm pro-gun, pro-life, and anti–illegal immigration. Though I would like to see a more streamlined, straightforward path to citizenship."

Joan sat and waited for Roberto's reply. She imagined he might end their date right then and there, now that he knew the truth. Then she could go home, perhaps stop at the sandwich stand before, and enjoy a meatball panini in bed alone before passing out.

But Roberto laughed as if Joan had said the funniest thing in the world.

"I don't give a shit about that, lady," he said. He rubbed her knee with his gigantic hand.

"Really?"

"I'm apolitical," he said. "But that was ballsy as hell. I like it."

Just then, the tequila hit Joan hard. Her body went numb, her mind went blank, and her guilt melted away along with any other emotions. They left the bar and walked together to her apartment. She wrapped her arm around Roberto's midsection, steadying herself, feeling his soft middle through his thin button-down shirt.

They sat in the living room, where Joan smoked herself further into oblivion. Roberto looked around her apartment but didn't ask her how expensive it was, which was a relief. That was one of Joan's pet peeves when people came over for the first time. Instead, he complimented her selection of throw pillows and played with the fringe of one of her lampshades, all purchased with her mother while antiquing in Houston. "If I lived here, this is what I'd do all day," he said.

He wants to live here, Joan thought.

He scooted in close and told her that he'd known she was different from other girls the moment he met her. Why? Because she hadn't even smiled. Most girls smile when you meet them, he said, and she didn't. That way, when she finally did smile for him, he felt like he'd achieved something.

He accepts me for me, Joan thought optimistically, before they started making out.

Soon, Joan was naked on top of her covers, her calves resting on Roberto's shoulders. He was looking into her eyes through his thick lenses, a pained expression on his face, his lip curled in a way that slightly disgusted her. Joan began her perfunctory moaning, even though she could barely feel a thing. Not that he was particularly small; she was simply too drunk, too numb; it felt like she was being fucked in a dentist chair, high on laughing gas, shot up all over with novocaine.

"You are a very beautiful woman," he said. "You have a beautiful body."

Joan reached forward and dug her nails into his chest, which was impossibly soft and covered with deep craters, even deeper than the ones that covered his face. His body had been ravaged by acne.

"Please don't talk to me," she said.

"I love you," Roberto said, and Joan slapped him across the face, so hard that it shocked them both. He kept his head turned to the side as if to accentuate the drama of the slap.

"No, you fucking don't," Joan said, so angry she could have cried.

"But I do, in this moment."

"Don't tell me that shit," she said. "That's not how it works." She knew from conservative radio, Dr. Drew, and therapy that love was not a feeling but a series of actions and a vow of commitment. It wasn't just a passive emotional response but a decision. She closed her eyes and turned her head away from Roberto, refusing to look at him for the rest of the night.

The next morning, Roberto was gone, but his spiral notebook sat on the floor by her bed, apparently forgotten. Hungover, Joan smoked a joint and read the notebook out loud to Claire in the living room. One of the pages was autobiographical and began "My name is Roberto Rosa and I was born in Matamoros, Mexico. . . ." He went on to talk about his hometown, how there were no bookstores, and how he learned to read on his own. He wrote that he had virtually no friends growing up and nobody liked him because of his terrible skin. He said that books were the only thing he had to turn to as a child and teen. He didn't lose his virginity until he was in his midtwenties, after the acne cleared up, leaving behind "terrible battle scars." He talked about making love to women; he liked to tell them how beautiful they were and whisper in their ears. He talked about his mother, still in Mexico, with a mysterious, debilitating illness. He seemed to resent her for it. Reading the notebook, Joan was struck by Roberto's self-assured tone, his ability to define himself, to view himself through such a clear and objective lens. She had never even thought to open a notebook and begin a piece "My name is Joan West and I was born in Lewisville, Texas," but perhaps she should. Perhaps that was the way she should begin her novel.

"He kind of sounds like a narcissist," Claire said after Joan finished reading.

"No," said Joan, feeling defensive. "He's just a writer. That's how they are."

Joan and Roberto became inseparable for the next week. While Vince was on Long Island, Joan went out drinking almost every night with Roberto, returning to his house to smoke tons of weed and have sex. It was theatrical, brutal, and passionate, like Joan had never experienced. It almost felt like they were actors in a play. He would tell her the whole time that she was beautiful, grabbing her neck as if to choke her, pulling her hair. One night, when Joan forgot a G-string at his house, Roberto wore it to work the next day. He sent her dirty text messages that she would receive at her desk in the capitol, telling her that he was wearing her underwear, that last night she shook like a freight train or cried like a little baby lamb. He wasn't always sexual in his texts. Sometimes, he quoted Dickens or Faulkner or Bukowski or Miller to her, whatever he was reading that day, and she'd wonder how the fuck he could read so many books so fast. She was still trudging her way through Hemingway's story collection and was only halfway through Mitt Romney's book.

She asked him over texts why he liked Charles Dickens so much.

Because, lady. I can relate to a guy like that. He came from nothing, like me, and literature saved him.

That's so beautiful, Joan replied, but she never read any Dickens, or any of the other authors Roberto recommended.

When Vince returned from Long Island, he texted Joan to hang out again, but she ignored him. She was having too much fun with Roberto.

One night, while they were having sex, Joan started her period and bled, thick and heavy, all over Roberto's erection and his gold palm tree bedding, cheap and wiry, sent from his ailing mother in Matamoros.

"I'm sorry," she said. "I'm so sorry."

"That's okay, lady," he said. "I like having your blood on me, it's more operatic that way."

He didn't wash the sheets after that, and the deep red stain stayed there for days and turned dark brown, like a crime scene. Each time she saw it, Joan was filled with pride.

"He loves even the most repulsive parts of me," she bragged to Claire. "He sleeps on my discharge."

Over the next two weeks, in the mornings, Roberto woke up, smoked a big bowl, and typed for thirty minutes while Joan lay on the stain and stared at the ceiling. Without Adderall, the discipline she needed to revise "Conquistador" and send it out had all but vanished. Roberto tried to help her by sharing his own method. He had gotten to the point where he wrote one scene a day, he explained. It sounded so unsatisfying to Joan, making progress slowly, little by little. "I know," he said. But it was the only way he'd ever get this shit done. He was still working on his novella, *Bitter Texas Honey*, which Joan had read parts of and was now convinced was about her. It was a love story. The girl was pale, like her, and it opened with her having sex on her period, like she had. The idea of appearing in Roberto's novella made Joan feel important, as if she was contributing in some way to the world of literature, not as a writer herself yet, but as a muse. Unlike Roberto, who had a handful of stories and poems in online journals, and collections of Polaroids on display, Joan still had nothing to show for herself as an artist. At least in this small way, by inspiring Roberto, she was accomplishing something.

12.

YOUNG AND CONSERVATIVE
IN THE AGE OF OBAMA

The last weekend of April, Joan packed a bag and drove to Dallas to attend the annual Young Conservatives of Texas convention, where chapters from colleges all over the state would be gathered. She had initially been on the fence about going, but Roberto told her he needed some time to focus and be alone with his writing, so she decided to use the convention to distract herself and to make it appear that she had a rich life of her own.

Joan checked into the DoubleTree hotel, where she discovered she would be sharing a room with Faith, a freshman who was five years younger than her and had been homeschooled before college. Other than being members of the same organization, Joan and Faith had nothing in common, and she wished she had just splurged on her own bedroom. Joan picked up her name tag and went to the first event of the convention, where Kyle introduced an up-and-coming Senate candidate named Ted Cruz, who was supposed to represent the future of the Republican Party. Joan had not seen Kyle so excited about someone.

"This guy is such a genius," he whispered into her ear when he sat down. "He memorized the US Constitution by the time he was *twelve.*"

"Why would anybody do that?" Joan asked. She was briefly reminded of a memoir she'd found and read at her grandparents' ranch house, written by a former Islamic terrorist, now a born-again Christian, who had memorized the Quran at the same age. Kyle didn't answer. He was too focused on Cruz, who was speaking about government overreach and the pitfalls of Obamacare. Ted Cruz had pointy elf ears, a boyish face, and a nasal voice that Joan didn't envision getting very far in national politics. But she conceded that there was something different about him. His energy seemed boundless and young. He had a Hispanic last name, which was always helpful. Ted closed his speech by praising YCT, telling everyone in the room how brave and courageous they were. It was not easy being young and conservative in the "Age of Obama," he said. The kids in the conference room all seemed to puff up with pride. The boys, in their khaki pants, white button-downs, and navy blazers, all seemed to go to great lengths not to distinguish themselves from one another. They were defiantly dull, as if being young and conservative was some new version of being punk rock and countercultural. A new way to stick it to the man, perhaps. Joan wrote this observation down in her notebook as the room erupted in applause.

She skipped the rest of the speeches and lay in her room, trying to nap before dinner. She texted Roberto, who asked what she was doing. She told him for the first time about the convention.

Disgusting. Politics are the worst, Roberto replied, following it with a quote from Charles Bukowski.

She didn't reply to Roberto right away, wishing to appear busy and unbothered. Instead she began texting with Wyatt, who revealed that he'd been officially disqualified from the Marine Corps. The recruiter had broken the news to him earlier that week. *Oh no,* Joan wrote. *I'm so sorry.* She told him she was in town and wanted to see him. They made plans to meet the following day at his apartment before she returned to Austin.

That evening, Joan dressed up in a black shift dress and pearls and attended Rand Paul's keynote, in which he discussed the deficit at length. He seemed smart and thoughtful, potentially more broadly palatable than his quirky dad, Ron, who was inexplicably polling second to Mitt Romney in the Gallup polls. Rand's background as a physician was impressive, giving him good authority on how terrible Obamacare was for the country. But she was dismayed to discover how tiny Rand was physically. He looked like a little doll, and for that reason, she knew that he would never be a serious presidential contender. Voters liked height. The room was filled with old people along with the YCT kids, because the Texas Republican Party had piggybacked onto the event for a fundraiser. Joan wondered how much money these donors had shelled out just to meet Rand Paul. After his speech, Joan stood in line for twenty minutes for a chance to take a photograph with Rand, which Faith ruined by inserting herself. Faith, at five foot nine, towered over Rand, and his tiny head made both Joan's and Faith's heads appear massive. Joan refrained from posting the photograph to social media for this reason.

The after-party was at a bar on the rooftop of the hotel. It was dark, and all the boys were letting loose, drinking tumblers of whiskey, chomping and puffing on cigars. A few wore cowboy hats and boots, to signal their rowdiness. These types usually flaunted their firearms and told off-color racist and sexist jokes that made even Joan uncomfortable. When she brought these concerns to Kyle, however, he explained that racism existed on a spectrum like anything else, and that every person was at least a little bit racist. Even, or perhaps *especially*, the Democrats, who had literally invented slavery. Kyle made a good point there. Despite the few bad apples, it felt good to be in the party of Lincoln.

She missed being around Roberto, though, and having someone to talk with about literature. Joan found that the Republicans she encountered totally lacked an appreciation for the arts. They all seemed to misunderstand nuance, depth, and complexity, things that were very important to Joan. Kyle was a slight exception to this rule. He liked to read classic novels and old Anglo-Saxon poetry. He also liked to listen to Adam Carolla, like Joan. But even Kyle could not compete intellectually with Roberto, a true original and artist.

She spent the remainder of the evening trying to avoid Faith, who kept following her around from group to group, stroking her hair and trying to kiss her. Faith was drunk for the first time in her life. Instead of feeling flattered, Joan felt turned off by her inexperience and some-what offended by the attention. Why was Faith after Joan and not any of the other girls in YCT? Did Faith see Joan as some kind of loose whore who would just make out with anybody? Was she looking for a lesson in kissing? Joan wasn't interested in being anyone's teacher. She'd gone through that phase of her life in eighth grade. She was twenty-four, a seasoned veteran now, a grown woman drinking ex-pensive whiskey.

Having not left the hotel in over twenty-four hours, she was be-ginning to experience cabin fever. Joan felt so out of place at the DoubleTree. She found Kyle and sat in his lap, soft and khaki. She often cuddled with Kyle at these dumb parties, and he never seemed to mind or even notice. It felt good to sink into him, to bury her face in his neck while he discussed Ted Cruz's political strategy with some members of the Texas A&M chapter. He was telling them he was considering quitting his job at the capitol to work on Ted's campaign. He was so *driven*, Joan thought, looking at his face while he talked. From the right angles, he was attractive, like a pudgy version of Ryan Phillippe.

"Save me," she said to him. She followed Kyle to his room, com-plaining about her roommate. "I can't go back to my room. I might get assaulted."

They lay beside each other in the bed, talking. "I'm too old for this. I'm not used to being around such sheltered people," Joan said.

"I know what you mean," Kyle said.

"Then why do you come? How can you stand it?"

Joan, tired and drunk, rested her head on his chest and watched his soft belly move up and down. Their lower halves were several inches apart.

Kyle sighed. "Because. I am interested in *winning*. YCT is a very powerful organization. This is part of our base. Things like this are the only way to mobilize people and win."

"That makes sense, I guess," she said.

Joan snuggled deeper into Kyle's cushion. Her thoughts drifted around in a disorganized manner. The room seemed to spin.

"I miss Roberto," she whined.

"Oh, for Christ's sake. You've been dating that guy for like two weeks."

"Linear time is an illusion," Joan said, unsure of what she meant. She'd read it in a self-help book her therapist had recommended and it felt true.

"Okay, Gandhi."

"We're in love. He told me he loved me on our first date."

"Get over the barista," Kyle said.

"He's a *writer*," Joan muttered, drifting off. "He's going to write very important things."

"Of course he is."

"He's writing a book about me."

"That sounds so important."

Joan decided she didn't care what Kyle thought about her relationship with Roberto. What did he know? He was only focused on attaining power and influence. She and Roberto, on the other hand, existed on another plane. They lived to serve art.

13.

CRUSHING IT

Joan woke up in Kyle's bed at six in the morning, on top of the covers, still wearing her black dress and jewelry. She checked her phone. Roberto hadn't texted her again. Anxious to get back to Austin and see him, she decided to skip breakfast and the morning's events. She wiped the black smudges from beneath her eyes and returned to her room, where she quietly gathered her belongings, careful not to wake Faith, her tormenter. After she checked out of the hotel and retrieved her BMW from the valet, she drove to Wyatt's apartment complex in Fort Worth.

The apartment was dark and quiet when she entered through the unlocked door. Wyatt's roommate's bedroom door was closed, and Wyatt was standing in the middle of the living room, slightly hunched toward the television, entranced by a game of *Call of Duty.* Joan felt sad for him. All he'd ever wanted, since they were children, was to be a soldier. To join the marines or the SEALs and fight on the front lines of battle. "First ones in, last ones out," he would say with intensity as a child, chasing imaginary enemies around Papa's sprawling ranch, holding a toy walkie-talkie. But now even the military wouldn't take him.

Wyatt jumped when a grenade landed near his avatar. He looked pale and tired, with subtle dark circles under his eyes.

"Your room looks nice," Joan said. Wyatt slept in the dining nook off the kitchen. Since she'd last been over, the dining table had been removed and Wyatt had settled in more. Now there was a twin-sized mattress against one wall, a Casio keyboard against another, and all his personal belongings—clothing and paperwork and photographs—in clear plastic bins stacked in the corner. On top of the stack of bins, there was a reading lamp and a copy of *Wild at Heart*, the companion to *Your Captivating Heart*, for men.

"Thanks," he laughed. "It's been quite impressive with the ladies."

On-screen, Wyatt's soldier moved with agility, shooting Arab terrorists with an AK-47 and ducking behind a crate.

Beside the television, a larger-than-life-size decal of Tony Romo was adhered to the wall. On the coffee table and the floor beside her, motivational self-help books were scattered in small piles, with folded pages and Post-it notes sticking out of them. Books like: *The 4-Hour Workweek*, *Think and Grow Rich*, and *Crushing It!*. Joan assumed these books belonged to his roommate, Chet, who had always been full of shit.

Wyatt's body tensed up as he threw several grenades at a group of terrorists to no avail. His avatar was dead.

"So, what exactly happened with the marines?" Joan asked. "Did they find out about North Carolina?"

"No," Wyatt said, his head hung in shame. "They said I have scoliosis."

"Whoa. I didn't know that."

"Yeah . . . It sucks because there's nothing I can do about it. I got disqualified on Thursday, and I've just been playing this all weekend," he admitted.

"Really? Don't you have to be at RadioShack?"

"No, I got fired," he said, sitting down on the floor, pausing his game.

"What happened?"

"I kind of yelled at my boss," Wyatt said.

"Why?" Joan asked. It didn't seem like him to yell. He rarely became angry.

"He kept harassing me. He was touching me all the time. I couldn't take it anymore." Wyatt seemed viscerally disturbed by the incident, as if it had done irreparable damage to his psyche.

"Well, that's not good."

"I think he was spying on me too. On social media. That's why I deleted Facebook."

"Interesting," she said. Wyatt wasn't making a lot of sense to her, and she didn't know how to respond.

"Doesn't it freak you out? Facebook? All those strangers watching your every move?"

"Honestly, I don't give it much thought," she said. "Everyone else is on it too, so it doesn't seem like a big deal."

Perhaps he just needed sleep, she thought, noting the circles beneath his eyes. He never seemed to get enough sleep. When they lived together, he would fall asleep sitting up sometimes, at a restaurant, in the middle of the day, because he was so tired. Once, he'd fallen asleep in the shower with the door locked, and she'd banged on the door for an hour thinking he was dead. She thought of offering him something, to help him relax, but she knew how much he hated pills. He wouldn't even take them when he went to the psych ward at Duke. Wyatt would hold the pills under his tongue before spitting them out, he had confided.

Joan remembered when her brother had called and told her what Wyatt had done—that he'd tried to stab himself in the neck in the kitchen. Henry had been forced to hold Wyatt down for hours, wrestling knives out of his hands all night, while Wyatt cried about his dad not loving him, about seeing demons in the corners of the apartment. Eventually, Henry forced Wyatt into the back of his SUV and took him to the emergency room, because he had to take two final exams that morning. Despite not sleeping, not studying, and being traumatized, Henry had still gotten A's on both tests. Joan would never understand her brother. She'd been a freshman in Miami at the time, and she dealt with the news by getting blackout drunk and crying in the elevator of her dorm all night. She wanted everyone in the entire building to witness her agony.

The next day, Joan started writing a letter to Wyatt from her dorm room. She told him he was like a brother to her and that she couldn't picture life without him. But she never made it past the first couple of sentences and never sent the letter. For some reason, it embarrassed her. She still had it somewhere in her files.

The doctors at Duke kept Wyatt in the hospital for two weeks after that, until his mom, Charlene, drove the seventeen hours up from Dallas to get him.

When Joan spoke with Wyatt afterward, he told her that he was afraid of electronics—TVs, computers, car stereos, cell phones, anything that had a screen. He wondered if Joan felt the same way, and she didn't. He never brought it up again, and neither did she. Soon enough, he bounced back, returning to his old self, constantly making everyone around him laugh with his creative stunts and characters and jokes. He seemed happy again, so the entire family, except her brother, Henry, swept the whole Durham incident under the rug, collectively deciding it had been some kind of anomaly.

Just then, Chet emerged from his bedroom, shirtless in baggy gray sweatpants.

"Whoa," he said, with a look of surprise at the sight of Joan. "Hey."

"Hello," Joan said flatly. She'd hated Chet ever since they were fifteen. He'd come on one of their family trips to Padre Island, with her dad, her best friend, and Wyatt. The first night, Chet hooked up with Joan, while Wyatt hooked up with her best friend. Chet asked Wyatt if they could "trade girls" the next day, in front of her. She'd never forgotten about it, but he clearly had.

Chet sat down on the sofa beside Joan and began rolling a blunt. "How's your book coming along?" he asked. He licked the paper and sealed the blunt. Every time anyone asked her this question, Joan felt attacked.

"Oh, it's coming along," she said. "I've turned my focus to short stories, though. I'm going to put out a collection first, to get my name out there and build hype."

Chet lit the blunt and took a hit. "Nice," he said. He passed the blunt to her. She assumed Chet had never read a short-story collection in his life.

Joan inhaled deeply. "I just finished a story about going to a strip club with a guy I dated," she said. "It's a social commentary about how men don't want to grow up anymore. It's an epidemic of this generation."

"That sounds deep," Wyatt said. "Can I see it?"

"Sure," Joan said, looking for a place to set the blunt. Wyatt held his hand out.

"You're smoking?" Joan asked.

Wyatt shrugged. "Doesn't matter anymore. I'm not joining the military."

Joan passed him the blunt, even though it made her uneasy. How could she be such a hypocrite? She smoked constantly, and she was doing fine.

She found the story draft in her email, opened it, and handed the phone to Wyatt. He squinted and looked at the screen for a while.

"Ah," Wyatt said. "I see what you're doing here. *You're capturing time.*"

"Exactly," Joan said. She was feeling higher than she'd been in a long time. Blunts always hit harder. "That's exactly what I'm doing. Capturing time." She loved Wyatt. He made such simple, childlike observations, which still managed to carry immense depth and weight. What was art, she thought, but capturing time? Wasn't time the most valuable commodity of all? What more precious thing could a human possess? She took another hit when the blunt was passed to her. She wished she could bring Wyatt back with her, that he could be her sidekick and make her feel this important every day.

"Can you email it to me?" Wyatt asked. "I'd like to read the whole thing."

"Of course. So, what's next for you, Wyatt? Back to Smoothie King?"

Chet answered for Wyatt. "No, no," he said. "We're choosing to look at this situation as an opportunity. RadioShack, Smoothie King,

Pita Pit, all that crap is holding Wyatt back from his full potential. Now we can finally focus full-time on Wyatt's music career."

"Is that what you want, Wyatt?" Joan asked. "To pursue music professionally?" When they lived together at her dad's, Wyatt always claimed he didn't want to do music as a job. That it would ruin it for him somehow. Money, he would often say back then, ruined everything. And Joan, being a vehement communist at the time, had agreed with him wholeheartedly.

Wyatt shrugged. "I guess so. What else am I going to do?"

"Look," Chet continued. "Someone with Wyatt's talent doesn't come around every day. We'd be idiots not to try to cultivate that. While he's young and in his literal prime."

"And what's your role in all this, Chet?"

"I'm his manager."

"I see."

"First, we have to get him exposure." Chet motioned toward the Casio. "We're going to get some batteries in that thing and bring it out to the people. I know the busiest street corner in town. Once the public sees what Wyatt has, it'll just be up from there."

The idea was absurd. But Joan bottled her doubts and looked around on the carpet, at the piles of motivational business books. She began to feel sick to her stomach from the tobacco in the blunt.

"I'd better get going," she said, feeling the sudden urge to be back in Austin, in Roberto's shack, surrounded by books, lying in his bed, on the stain, while he typed.

"Another one for the road?" Chet said, rolling a second small blunt.

Driving home, she tried not to worry about Wyatt, but she was concerned for his well-being. Chet was clearly a negative influence on his life. Encouraging him to use drugs, putting grandiose ideas in his head about his music career. She hated the way Wyatt deferred to Chet. He was so impressionable. She wished they lived closer together so that her influence could combat Chet's. Wyatt was going to be okay, she assured herself, turning her attention instead to conservative talk radio. The host's nasal drone comforted her, like a lullaby. He was interviewing Bjorn Lomborg, a gay scientist from Denmark and pre-eminent climate change skeptic, who said that Obama's policies would crush the free market, hurt the poor, and threaten individual liberty. By the time she hit Waco, Joan's concern had moved from Wyatt to the state of the country at large, to the imminent threat of government tyranny masked as "climate justice." Mitt Romney was uniquely situated to steer them out of this mess, Joan thought. He could get the government back to its proper role—protecting the free market and the American Dream. Approaching Austin, Joan felt so alone in her views. Like she was one of the only people in the whole town who understood the truth.

14.

FEELING ALIVE

Over the first three weeks of May, as the legislative session was nearing its end, Joan came to the slow but convincing realization that she was in love with Roberto, and that she needed to claim him as her own. For so long, she'd been wasting her time, searching in vain for some nonexistent conservative man who would understand her as an artist. Now it was obvious the answer had been in front of her all along, working behind the bar at the coffee shop. She belonged with Roberto. The realization made her giddy. They would be an iconic literary power couple for the ages. She could be the Zelda to his Fitzgerald, the Didion to his Dunne. They would conduct interviews together from his shack, Roberto's sad dog resting by their feet, talking about how they became more empathetic writers just by being around each other.

On Monday morning, after a long night of drinking together, during the last week of her internship, Joan finally built up the courage to talk him into the idea. "I've been up all night thinking about this," she said, shaking Roberto awake in his gold sheets with manic urgency. She was dressed for work already, wearing her pencil skirt and blouse. "I just don't think I can do it anymore. I can't have sex with you anymore if there's no commitment."

Joan knew from conservative talk radio how bad it was to keep a

relationship undefined. Men were rudderless, sexually motivated crea-
tures who needed to be tamed by women. Deep down, it was what
they wanted. They were kind of like dogs that way. She imagined he
wouldn't want to lose their beautiful sex life and was fairly certain he
would comply with her ultimatum.

But instead of agreeing to a commitment, Roberto became visibly
agitated. A look of panic came across his face. He stood up, left the
bedroom, and began pacing around his house, grabbing his hair in
frustration. Joan followed him into the living room and sat next to his
typewriter. "Can you at least say something?" she pleaded. But he kept
pacing. "No, no, no," he said. "Look around you, lady. Can't you see?
Look at where I live."

"What about it?" Joan said, confused. She liked his shack. It was
cute and comfortable.

"I can't even pay my bills!" Roberto said. "They are going to turn
my electricity off any day. I can't even put food in my fridge!" He
opened his refrigerator to show her. There was nothing but a foam
container and some condiments.

"What does that have to do with anything?" Joan asked. "What
does that have to do with being with me?"

"You can't do it anymore," he said, flattening his tone. "I understand, lady. I can respect that."

"What? No, I—"

"It's almost eight. You don't want to be late for your job."

"It doesn't matter if I'm late," Joan said, her face hot. "It's my last
week. I already won an award for being the best intern."

Roberto ignored this. He stood in front of Joan and gestured to
help her stand up. She took his hand, and before she could finish her
thoughts, Roberto escorted her quickly out the back door, onto the
porch, his hand on the small of her back. It reminded her of the time
when a bouncer kicked her out of a bar on Sixth Street for accidentally
dropping a drink on somebody's head from the balcony. They walked
through Roberto's backyard this way, past all the eclectic, rusted
sculptures, the stolen road signs, his fence covered with graffiti.

"Let go of me," Joan said, jerking herself away from him.

"You are a beautiful and talented woman," he said. "I will miss you."

"Fuck you," said Joan. "I don't need you to walk me any farther."

"Okay," said Roberto. He stood by the fence and watched her as she approached her white BMW, dead grass crunching beneath her feet. She didn't turn around. As she opened the car door and climbed in, she heard the flash of his Polaroid camera. *That motherfucker.* She slammed the door and drove away. Once she reached the first stop sign, safely out of Roberto and his Polaroid's view, she began sobbing desperately, gasping for air. Crying like this made Joan hate herself with the same intensity with which she hated her own mother, who had cried in this same pathetic way, like a toddler, sitting on the floor of Joan's bedroom, after Doug finally moved out when Joan was fifteen. It was another memory her therapist was hung up on, despite Joan never wanting to talk about it.

How could she have misread the situation with Roberto so completely? If she hadn't confronted him, they would still be together right now. It was possible that she would have grown on him. After a bit more time, he might have decided on his own that he couldn't live without her. But no, she'd been overly confident, impatient, naïve. She looked in the rearview mirror, at her makeup smeared all over her face. She would need to stop at CVS to buy some wipes on the way to the capitol. She was already late, but it didn't matter. Nothing did.

Driving to CVS, she called Wyatt and blathered on about Roberto while he listened patiently. He was at Guitar Center, he said, playing one of their display acoustic guitars because he'd been forced to sell his own. "It just hurts so bad," she said. "I thought he was the one."

"I understand," he said. "But try to embrace it. At least you met someone who makes you feel alive."

"How do you embrace it?" she asked. She didn't like feeling "alive."

"What I've been doing is just listening to Hans Zimmer a lot," he said. "It makes me feel a little better, for some reason."

"That's a good idea," Joan said. "I'll try that."

She wandered the aisles of CVS in a daze, earphones in, listening to the *Gladiator* soundtrack. Wyatt was right. The music made her search for makeup-removing wipes feel like an epic mission of spiritual redemption.

She stood in front of the wipes. There were dozens of brands to choose from, in all different colored packaging. Natural, chemical, cucumber scented or grapefruit, oil free, oil filled. This was what was so great about America, Joan thought as the song hit an emotional crescendo. *Abundance. Competition. Choices.* In all the other countries she'd visited, in Central America and Europe, there had been so little to choose from. Sometimes, there was only one choice. She was so glad to be out of that state of scarcity and lack. Joan left the store with her new product and wiped the mascara off her cheeks in the car. Driving toward the capitol, despite her sadness, she felt grateful to at least live in the best country. The land of opportunity.

15.

THE VOW

Joan spent her entire shift at the capitol listening to the *Gladiator* soundtrack on repeat and crafting a long, desperate text message to Roberto, who hadn't responded to a single one of her messages since their breakup that morning. Perhaps she could write something so beautiful that he would welcome her back into his life. She wrote a few words and paused, considering. Maybe she would say that she just wanted his friendship, that he had inspired her artistically, and she just wanted to be around him, no strings attached. This wasn't true, of course. She wanted much more, but she saw friendship as a possible entry point.

She was typing words and deleting them, then retyping them, then deleting. Now that she knew unequivocally that Roberto didn't want to be with her, he had grown in both magnitude and importance. His unattainability transformed him into the most bewitching person she'd ever encountered. She had to have him back. The challenge invigorated her.

Her therapist had warned her about this phenomenon—that having sex with men too early would make Joan see them through rose-colored glasses. The therapist insisted that Joan should be very careful in her choice of mate. "Especially with your family-of-origin issues," she said. She had suggested Joan spend *at least a year* getting to know someone before having sex with him. A length of time so unrealistic Joan had laughed in her office, thinking it was a joke.

What Joan eventually wrote was a rambling, desperate plea asking if Roberto would please just talk to her.

Finally satisfied with the contents of her text, she read it over once more. She added in a few lines that she hoped would make him feel guilty. Surely, guilt would reel him back in. Didn't it always? Then she had what felt like a clever idea: She would translate the entire text message into Spanish before sending it. What could reveal the depth of her passion more than communicating with Roberto in his mother tongue?

Joan spent the next half hour on Google Translate, going over every word of her text, meticulously conjugating each verb. She had taken three semesters of Spanish in college and had been speaking the language casually since she was sixteen. In Miami, one of her roommates had been half-Cuban. Once, on a trip to Costa Rica, she had spent all evening with a local, talking about her hobbies. In high school, her best friend's family was Mexican and owned a tamale factory, where Joan worked as a Hot Tamale Girl one summer. Because of these experiences, Joan was confident in her ability to write something poetic and meaningful to Roberto. When she finally finished her translation, she held her breath, hit send, and began anxiously waiting for his response, which she expected to come soon, but it never did.

Three days later, when Joan arrived home after her last day at work, she found a tattered, yellowing book lying on her welcome mat. She picked up the book and examined the powder-blue cover. It was *One Hundred Years of Solitude* by Gabriel García Márquez, an author Joan had never heard of.

She brought the novel to her bedroom, flopped down onto her bed, and opened it. On the inside cover, she found a note from Roberto, scrawled in felt-tip pen.

Lady Joan,

Before we broke up, I had been wanting to give you this book, which has meant so much to me and my craft. I hope it means something to you too. I'm sorry that I've been out of touch. It is nothing personal. I simply cannot engage with you right now. I thought you should be aware that I've taken a vow of celibacy until I finish my book. Therefore, I will not be talking to you, or any other women during this time. It's not going to be easy, of course, but much greater sacrifices have been made for art. As for the future of our relationship, I've decided to leave it up to fate whether we see each other again.

Yrs, R

PS—I really hate it when girls try to talk to me in Spanish. Please don't do that again.

Joan reread Roberto's note a few times, trying to decipher its meaning and decide how it made her feel. She wasn't sure if she was offended, flattered, or some twisted mixture of the two. After all, Roberto had gone to the trouble of bringing her a personal gift and leaving it by her doorstep. There was something undeniably romantic about that, she supposed. She appreciated that he was not speaking to other women while working on *Bitter Texas Honey*. Surely, this was a signal that he was still carrying a torch for her. However, that he didn't want to give her the gift in person, and that he asked her never to speak to him in Spanish again, made her stomach queasy. The more she read and absorbed the note, the more confused she became. What did Roberto mean by "fate," anyway? If he never wanted to see her again, he should have the courage to just say that. Like a *real man*, she thought self-righteously.

In this moment, Joan resolved to beat Roberto to publication. She would take her own vow of celibacy and really put her nose to the grindstone. Her novel, *Cowgirls and Indians,* was going to be an un-disputed masterpiece once it was finished, much better, longer, and weightier than Roberto's pathetic novella. *Bitter Texas Honey* (if it found a publisher at all) would only hold any commercial value be-cause it was about her, Joan West, the best writer to emerge from Austin in an entire generation.

16.

A NEW, EXCITING PHASE OF HER LIFE

Ten days later, Joan stood at FedEx on Cesar Chavez, watching the pages of "Conquistador" shoot out of the printer with great satisfaction, her heart beating rapidly. Her Adderall prescription had been surprisingly easy to obtain. The previous week, she had simply explained to a psychiatrist that she couldn't focus and that she'd taken the drug before to "satisfactory" results. Joan had the pills in her possession later that very day. Looking at the bottle full of the big orange capsules, with her own name printed on the label, Joan had felt a sense of awe and possibility.

She was certain that the best way to launch her writing career and humiliate Roberto in the short term would be to publish "Conquistador" somewhere respectable, like *The Paris Review*. Joan had never read *The Paris Review*, or any other literary magazine, but had seen Roberto bring several issues to the coffee shop, and she recalled him lamenting being rejected by them one evening, so she knew it must be good.

After she finished printing, Joan paper-clipped the manuscript together and slid it into a large envelope, which she addressed to the editor, Lorin Stein, directly. Even though she hadn't ended up implementing any of Carlos's suggested revisions, Joan was pretty confident that Stein would be so blown away by her crisp sentences and well-chosen details that it wouldn't matter. He would see her potential and probably want to mentor Joan and nurture her into the literary star she was destined to be. Perhaps they would even fall in love. She had looked up his photograph online and he appeared young enough, attractive but bald. They could sit in bed together, rejecting Roberto's stories. That would really show him. She took the envelope to the counter and paid for rush delivery.

As she left the store, the hot air engulfed her. It felt like walking into an oven. It was early June, and the summer heat had begun to descend upon the city like a plague.

Driving home, her AC cranked high, Joan felt extremely hopeful and took a second pill. It was such a relief to have "Conquistador" off her plate. She was entering a new, exciting phase of her life. With no more internship or boyfriends to distract her, and the laser focus her bountiful supply of Adderall would provide, she could finally be a writer full-time. After "Conquistador" made a splash in *The Paris Review*, her novel would come out to great acclaim, and Roberto would still be struggling with his little scenes, tapping one out each day, obsessing about her.

Arriving home, she got an email from her dad's secretary, who had forwarded her an itinerary for the following day. Joan had reluctantly agreed to go visit him for Father's Day. He was in Encinitas, California, living out of his RV while he built his fifth AudioPro campus, the first out-of-state location. The idea of trying to take Adderall and finish her book in her dad's presence felt terrifying and risky. If he ever caught wind of Joan being on amphetamines again, there could be dire consequences. She might be cut off financially, or worse, sent to rehab. Still, Joan had no choice but to go, seeing as her dad was paying half her allowance and she didn't have a job anymore.

Reading over the itinerary, Joan called her dad. "This is a one-way ticket," she complained, somewhat panicked. "And it leaves out of Dallas, not Austin."

"So?" he said. "What's the problem?"

"When am I going to get home?"

"Who cares? You've got nothing going on there," he said. Joan felt annoyed and condescended to but didn't argue with his point.

"You got me first class?" she said.

"Yep. That's how I roll now. No more coach for me. Coach is for losers."

"Wow. The school must be doing well."

"Shit yeah," he said. "We just got veterans funding."

She quickly packed her things and drove to Dallas, arriving at her dad's big empty house as the sun was setting. His house stood out from all the others on the block. With its red Spanish tile roof, stucco columns, and tropical landscaping, it resembled the home of a Colombian drug lord. It was unlocked, as always, so she walked through the entire house, checking all the bedroom closets for squatters or murderers, before settling into her dad's recliner in the living room, where she could unwind with a joint. Joan lit the joint and smoked the whole thing, trying to take the edge off from her Adderall comedown, which would now be her nightly reality. On Adderall, Joan's days were split into two antithetical but necessary parts: the morning high and the evening crash.

Stoned, she opened her laptop and began reading through *Cowgirls and Indians*, but quickly became dismayed with how aimless and meandering it was. What was the point of it? Why had she felt so proud of it before? Mostly, it was comprised of scenes about her and Randy talking on the phone spliced with scenes about her and her freshman-year roommate, Nazma, doing drugs together and then driving to Taco Bell. Joan grew overwhelmed and agitated after skimming the first forty pages. She closed the laptop.

She called Wyatt, thinking maybe he could join her on the trip to California. When they were children, and throughout high school, he would often join in on Joan's family vacations, making them a hundred times more tolerable for her. She would buy him a ticket herself if she had to.

"I'm sorry, I can't," Wyatt said. "I just got another job."

In May, he had been discovered playing his Casio on the street downtown and hired at Rick's Dueling Piano Bar. Again, it sounded like a scene from a movie. Joan couldn't believe that Chet's idiotic plan had worked.

"That's exciting," Joan said. "You're getting paid to play music?"

"Yeah. You should come out. I work tonight."

"Okay," Joan said. "Totally."

It was unclear whether he was genuinely excited or was just taking the job out of obligation. Wyatt's whole life, everyone in the family had been pressuring him to make a living as a musician. He was so naturally talented. What else was he going to do? Become a stand-up comedian? There was no money in that. When they lived together, Joan's dad had tried to help Wyatt the only way he knew how, by enrolling him in AudioPro, building him a state-of-the-art rehearsal space (the "jam room"), and yelling at him constantly. "You need to memorize songs!" her dad would yell every time they left the jam room. "You're worthless as a professional musician unless you can memorize a bunch of songs!"

But Wyatt could never do it. He'd bounce aimlessly from one idea to another, unable to focus, and after around six months, her dad kicked him out for not holding up "his end of the bargain." That was when Wyatt moved into Chet's dining room. Shortly after, Joan applied to UT as a transfer. She found the DFW metroplex intolerable without Wyatt by her side to make fun of it.

"How did you do it?" Joan asked. "How did you memorize all the songs?"

"Well, I started out bussing tables, and the manager would train me in the daytime. I'm not sure what changed. But I have the songs memorized now enough to play them. They're actually all pretty easy. I don't know what was so hard about it before."

"Wow," she said. It was amazing. Wyatt was finally coming into his own, growing up, kind of like she was.

Late that night, she drove to Rick's piano bar to see Wyatt in his new element. Rick's was located among a small cluster of bars in downtown Fort Worth, where TCU students went out drinking. She climbed a tall, narrow staircase and squeezed through a crowd of drunken students. All the tables and chairs were taken, so she stood against the back wall, on her tiptoes, and watched Wyatt playing.

He had a fresh haircut and was wearing a dark V-neck and black jeans. There was gel in his hair, and was that eyeliner? He was sweating and pounding the keys, his hands outstretched, singing the theme of *Footloose*. His left hand played heavy and legato, while his right hand tapped staccato. His piano was facing another piano where an older, bald man played along with him. Behind them, two other men played drums and a bass. They didn't seem to be dueling at all. It was really more of a duet. They were trying to rile up the crowd and instigate drunken sing-along behavior.

It was unlike watching him play at the studio, or the jam room, or at home. The intimacy and spontaneity weren't there. A large fishbowl sat between the pianos, overflowing with tips. A drink sat on Wyatt's piano, and he drank from it periodically. She could tell by the way he sipped that it was something strong, probably straight whiskey.

Behind the piano, a deer head hung on the wall, covered in colorful lacy bras. At a table nearby, a bachelorette threw her own bra and the group squealed when it hit Wyatt on the side of the head. The girls, and the entire crowd, seemed excited to have a new, young piano player at one of the only bars on the TCU strip.

Wyatt sounded great, of course, but Joan couldn't help but feel that something was off. He hadn't been a big drinker when she lived with him, and here he was, surrounded by hundreds of drunks who were sending him drink after drink, which he accepted. And the music. She'd never heard him play "Footloose," or "Don't Stop Believin'," or "Sweet Caroline" before. The songs all seemed beneath him somehow. They reminded her of all the fratty bars she hated in Coral Gables. And the clothes. He looked strange in all black. She was used to his basketball shorts and Hanes undershirts. She was used to him singing sentimental country songs or romantic ballads from musicals and Disney movies.

Chet approached Joan, beaming. He was with a girl wearing a crop top. He gave Joan a side hug and handed her a mixed drink.

"This is Mabel," Chet said. "Wyatt's friend."

"Nice to meet you," Joan said, and shook the girl's hand, which was so limp and bony that Joan decided immediately that she didn't trust her. Perhaps she was to blame for Wyatt's douchey new wardrobe.

"Wyatt tells me so much about you," Mabel said. "He says you are really close."

"Yeah, for sure," Joan said, no longer making eye contact, hoping the girl would go away. Mabel turned, made her way back into the sea of people, and began dancing alone, her eyes on Wyatt, her movements jerky and intense. Joan wondered if she was on cocaine.

"Who is that?" Joan asked Chet. "Wyatt already has groupies?"

Chet laughed. "They've just been hanging out," he said.

Joan grunted and took a long sip of her mixed drink. Chet watched Wyatt, nodding along. "He is *so good* at this," he said, shaking his head in awe. It was as if Chet was bragging about his own accomplishment, which, to be fair, it partially was. After all, the insane Casio ploy had been his idea. "I've honestly never seen him so happy," Chet said.

Joan watched Wyatt. She wasn't sure she agreed. Did he look happy? To her, he looked slightly tense, somewhat nervous. The happiest she could remember seeing him was probably when they were kids. Every Christmas, Papa would give them all a thousand dollars cash in an envelope. Joan, her brother, and all their cousins would put the money into savings accounts, while Wyatt would go to Walmart the following day, filled with joy, and spend every bit of it, coming back to the ranch with piles of toys, weapons, survival equipment, CDs. He also seemed happy on their family vacations, to the Bahamas or Costa Rica or Colorado, where their days were sprawling and structureless like blank canvases. He had even seemed happy working at Smoothie King, putting ice and fruit into a blender all day while making up stupid rap or country songs and joking with the rest of the staff. He thrived in low-stakes jobs like that. He was a people person, not a rock star. But she didn't say anything about any of this. Instead, she said, "I'm happy that it all worked out. It's really great." Because wasn't it? Wasn't Wyatt born to play music? Who was she to judge? If anything, he was way ahead of her already career-wise. She was nowhere near becoming a self-sustaining artist.

"Now that he has this exposure and financial backing, we'll be able to find him a good band, and he can start working on his own music," Chet continued. "We'll get him into the studio, record an EP. Of course, we'll have to make sure your dad's on board."

"That sounds awesome," Joan said. She loved Wyatt's original songs and felt genuinely hopeful about the prospect of his finally making an album. She understood Chet's manic optimism. If she were Chet, she would probably feel the same. In fact, she realized she was jealous of Chet, of his proximity to Wyatt and his access to Wyatt's genius, as well as his influence over him.

She thought of all the nights she spent in her dad's jam room, when she'd lie on the sofa watching him play. Randy claimed to have spent four hundred thousand dollars at Guitar Center setting it all up. He built a stage, hung a professional lighting grid, installed a live sound console, a disco ball, a fog machine. He bought every guitar pedal and vocal effect available. To Joan, it seemed like her dad built the place more for himself than for Wyatt, but she never said that. Instead, she'd lie on the green felt couch, drinking clear tequila, while Wyatt and her dad played, enjoying the music and the lights. They tried in vain to teach Joan to play the bass, but she had no stamina, no natural rhythm.

Before Joan left the bar, she squeezed through the crowd to Wyatt, handing him a handwritten request on a napkin, along with a dollar bill. It simply read *Phantom*. One of their favorite pastimes had been singing the *Phantom of the Opera* duet together. When Wyatt read the paper, his eyes lit up, and then dimmed.

"I can't play this here," he said. "I wish!"

Joan shrugged. She told him she would see him when she got back from the trip in a few days. They could sing it together then.

"Sounds good. Godspeed!" Wyatt yelled, before the manager gave him a look, and he pounded out the opening chords to "Baby Got Back" by Sir Mix-a-Lot.

17.

LOVE ADDICTS

The next day, at the airport, Joan was tweaking on Adderall, tinkering with the title page of *Cowgirls and Indians*. She was cycling through different fonts and font sizes when her dad called. There would be a slight change of plans, he said. He'd broken up with his latest girlfriend, Jelly Bean, the receptionist at his California campus, again, and wanted to get away for a while. Instead of spending Father's Day in Encinitas, they would take the RV up to see Joan's brother, Henry, in Seattle, where he was interning at Microsoft for the summer, as part of his international business program at Booth.

"How long is the drive?" Joan asked, anxious and flustered. She didn't appreciate sudden change. She wished she could just stay home so she could focus on her novel and take Adderall in peace. She felt cold, but her armpits were sweating through her T-shirt due to the amphetamines.

"About twenty hours," her dad said. "But it depends on how many stops we make."

On the plane, Joan took her second pill, and once it kicked in, she tried to soothe herself by imagining the trip was destined. She could use this road trip as an opportunity, she thought, feeling the powerful rush of inspiration. She would pivot away from *Cowgirls and Indians*, which was frustrating her, and start working on a new book, about a beautiful and intelligent girl traveling up the West Coast with her insane father in his stupid RV. She envisioned it as a Kerouac-esque, countercultural road novel that would redefine the genre, get published before *Bitter Texas Honey*, and become a cult classic. As much as Joan wanted to finish *Cowgirls and Indians*, mostly because she liked the title, starting fresh seemed like it would be easier, faster, and less painful. Then *Cowgirls and Indians* could be her second or third book, firmly establishing her career. She began taking notes about the new concept in her Moleskine. She had the idea to insert Wyatt into the novel fictionally. He could serve as a "Dean"-type character. It was no problem that Wyatt wasn't there with her. Normally, she was terrible at making things up. But now that she had her Adderall prescription, there was no limit to what her mind could invent.

She drank red wine from a plastic cup and made a long, bulleted list of possible scenes. Having an outline was always good for something so long. Even if she didn't end up using the outline, she liked the way writing it made her feel. She looked at the list and highlighted each bullet point in pink.

The bitter taste of the wine brought a familiar warmth to Joan's chest and limbs. It was nearing four P.M., time to start winding herself down. She had come up with a strict set of rules for her Adderall use this time around:

1) Never take a pill past four P.M.
2) Never take more than two pills in a day.
3) Go to sleep every night, no matter what.
4) Never open a pill, crush it, dissolve it into a drink, or snort it.

If she followed these simple guidelines, there was no way she could go off the rails as she had before in Miami. Her father would never notice that anything was different with her.

Outside of baggage claim, Randy pulled up in a bright yellow Jeep Wrangler that Joan had never seen before in her life. Skipper, his Chihuahua, was in the front seat punching his paws against the window, excited and frantic to see her. When Joan climbed into the Jeep, Skipper hopped into her lap, and she rested her hand on his tiny, quivering back. He resembled a small fox, wearing a sleeveless blue hoodie.

"New car?" Joan asked.

"Yep. Check out my data center."

There were two brand-new iPads velcroed to the dashboard, one screen showing their position on a three-dimensional GPS map, and the other tuned in to Fox News. The GOP primary was heating up. They were airing footage from two weeks ago, when Mitt Romney had officially announced his candidacy at Bittersweet Farm in New Hampshire. Mitt looked dapper and eager in a checkered buttondown tucked into his slacks, smiling adoringly at his wife, who had multiple sclerosis and wore a red cardigan. Joan hoped Romney would win the nomination. He was the only candidate capable of defeating Obama. But she didn't bring this up to her dad, who she figured was probably a birther and would prefer a much more obnoxious candidate. Skipper licked Joan's hand obsessively; his breath smelled strongly of fish.

"Gross, Dad, Skipper won't stop licking me."

"Skipper! Quit bothering your sister. Don't make me pull over."

Once they merged onto the highway, the canvas top of the Jeep began flapping wildly in the wind, creating a constant, loud beating noise.

"Did I tell you I got a new therapist?" he shouted over the sound.

"No," she shouted back. Ever since her dad got sober when she was seventeen, he treated her like a close confidante.

"Yeah, know what she said? She said I'm a love addict."

"Gross," Joan said. She put her feet on the dashboard and turned toward the window.

"No, no, not like that." He took one hand off the wheel, holding it in the air as if he were preparing to do a karate chop. "It's not that I'm a *sex* addict. It's not about sex. . . . Well, of course, that's part of it. But it's not the whole deal. You see, there are love addicts and love avoidants. I'm a love addict, and Sandra was a love avoidant. Bonnie's another example of a love avoidant." Bonnie had been a receptionist at AudioPro's Dallas campus and was only four years older than her brother, Henry. "Basically, every woman I've ever wanted is a love avoidant. Love avoidants attract love addicts. Like magnets."

"That sounds like a bunch of crap," Joan said.

"It's not! My therapist says it's my primary addiction. Alcohol was just my secondary addiction. Think about it. I went to rehab because of Bonnie, not because of alcohol."

"What does alcohol have to do with love?" Joan asked, annoyed.

"Everything," her dad said confidently. "Absolutely everything."

All the talk about alcohol was making Joan want some herself. Her mouth was dry from her comedown, her forehead burned, and she was starting to feel miserable and hopeless. She couldn't believe she was going to be trapped with her dad in such a small space for God knew how long.

When they arrived in Encinitas, which Randy called "the armpit of California," it was starting to get dark. They passed a long stretch of trashy shopping centers, full of car-stereo shops and surfboard shops, before he pulled the Jeep into the parking lot of his school, which was surrounded by a tall chain-link fence. He parked the Jeep next to his RV, which was newly "wrapped," plastered with advertisements for the school. It looked like a billboard on wheels. There were pictures of hipster guys in their twenties, twisting knobs and pushing faders on soundboards, staring intently at screens. *Jump-Start Your Audio Career Now*, it read in big white letters, next to an 800 number. A large rectangular strip of Astroturf sat on the cement in front of the RV; two rainbow-colored lawn chairs were situated atop the plastic grass.

A lump formed in Joan's throat when she realized that one of the people printed on the RV was Vince, wearing his stupid vest and fedora, singing into a microphone.

"When did you get these pictures?" she asked.

"No idea," her dad said. "Tanya would know, she did it." Tanya was the vice president of AudioPro and ran most of the day-to-day, face-to-face operations of the school, while her dad remained behind the curtain as the enigmatic creative force and risk-taker.

Joan opened the door of the RV, which was flesh-colored and pixelated, and walked through Vince's face into the living room, where she found a deflated twin-sized air mattress in the middle of the floor. There were white sheets and a floral blanket wadded into a ball on top.

"There's your bed," her dad said. "You'll have to share a closet with Skipper."

He opened the small cabinet to show her. On the rod, all of Skipper's outfits were hanging on tiny plastic hangers—a red polo shirt, a Santa suit, a Hawaiian shirt, a Harley-Davidson jacket, and yellow duck footy pajamas. Joan slid the outfits over to one side of the closet and began to hang up her clothes. She thought the trip would be only a few days, and hadn't brought much, only a couple plaid button-downs, graphic tees, and jeans full of holes.

Her mattress rumbled and hummed while it filled with air. She watched Skipper as he rose slowly off the ground. He was curled up in a ball in the blankets, and he looked around, confused and curious, but was too tired to move. After sneaking three large sips of NyQuil in her dad's bathroom, Joan checked Vince's Facebook page. He was relentlessly promoting his CD release party in July. A show Joan wouldn't attend, now that he had officially broken up with her, a fact that was hard for her to accept, considering she didn't even like him and they were never dating to begin with.

"I don't want to stop seeing you completely. I just need to take a step back," Vince had said. He'd taken her kayaking on Lady Bird Lake to talk. It was the third day of June. Shortly after her breakup with Roberto, Joan began texting Vince again, trying to flirt and wanting to see him. Setting aside her vow of celibacy, she told herself she needed to research Vince further, and write a sequel to "Conquistador."

But after only a few days, Vince nipped it in the bud. "I can't be in an emotional relationship right now," he said, gently stroking her thigh. "I told you this from the beginning. It was fine when you didn't care, but it's beginning to seem like you do."

"I'm such an idiot," Joan said, watching the cars driving across the Congress bridge.

"You aren't an idiot," Vince said.

"This isn't how it was supposed to end," she said, beginning to cry.

"Don't cry, baby," he said.

"Don't call me that," Joan snapped.

"Okay, fine, big girl."

She began paddling away from him, trying to reach the dock, but she moved very slowly in her bright red kayak.

"You look like Pocahontas," Vince said. "But paler. A lot paler!"

"Leave me alone," Joan said. "I hate you."

Feeling sad and tired, Joan closed Facebook. She found it difficult to admit that she missed him, or at least, she missed the way it felt when Vince cradled her from behind on the sofa while they watched documentaries. The way he massaged her in all the right places. The way he filled silence, making loud animal noises unexpectedly if there was nothing to say. Oh well. It was all for the best. Vince was wasting her time, slowing down her writing progress. Now she could be focused and celibate again, like Roberto, and write her novel quickly and without distraction. She lay down with the book Roberto had given her and reread his note for perhaps the hundredth time, then stared at the first page of *One Hundred Years of Solitude*. She read the first sentence a few times before setting the book down and resting her eyes, which were beginning to hurt from her Adderall comedown. No matter how hard she tried, Joan could not muster any interest in this man—this Colonel Aureliano Buendía. She could not care about his life or about the events that had led him to this moment—standing before a firing squad—all these years later. Joan drifted off to sleep to the sound of homeless crackheads screaming at each other outside of the beach club next door.

18.

WOMB ON WHEELS

The next morning, her dad gave Joan a tour of the new campus, which he'd built from the ground up over the past two years. The receptionist who'd broken up with him wasn't there, but Joan met the sales guy and the financial aid representative and toured their offices before checking out the studios. As they walked through the building, Randy went on and on about the physics of soundproofing. The school was built directly next to a train track, but you couldn't hear a thing from any of the studios, he bragged. "You see, it's all about mass," he said, almost shouting. "The more mass you have, the more you can block sound. That's the only thing that actually works. Nothing else matters. Just mass." Randy had named each of the three studios after a type of wave, an homage to his surfing days, and he showed off hand-painted signs he'd made for each room. He'd found pieces of wood on the beach, he told her, and painted waves on each of them before coating them with epoxy. Joan told him everything looked great. She was impressed. He'd done a wonderful job with it all, really.

Her dad had been in the music business since the seventies as a recording studio owner. In the eighties, his studio in Dallas had been the most famous in the state and had produced albums by several A-list musical acts out of Texas. In the late nineties, however, technology pushed more and more albums to be recorded at home, and Randy had to pivot to continue making a profit, so he turned his recording studio into a school to teach people how to record themselves. At first, the school had been a small, cash-only operation with just a handful of students, all with wealthy parents. Back then, the business had felt personal and manageable. However, in recent years, under Tanya's leadership, AudioPro had been granted state and federal accreditation and had quickly ballooned. With the infusion of government money came regulatory bodies upon regulatory bodies, and the need for more and more administrators to handle the meticulous recordkeeping. Her dad complained about this constantly. He now had five campuses and over a hundred employees, he would lament, as if it were a burden he hadn't invited on himself.

After the tour, Joan rode her dad's bike in circles around the parking lot while she waited for her Adderall to kick in. She made sure not to appear too focused or energized, and tried to present as her usual bored and depressed self. Her dad folded up the lawn chairs and rolled up the strip of Astroturf like a carpet. "What do you think, should we bring the front yard on the road?" He leaned the roll against the RV.

"If there's space, why not?" Joan said.

"Yeah, it'll be nice to have a yard. I'll have to make some room in here."

He opened the undercarriage compartment and pulled out a large pink ride-on Barbie jeep, which he said belonged to Jelly Bean's five-year-old daughter.

"Guess I won't need this anymore," he said passive-aggressively, and heaved the jeep into the dumpster. It crashed into the metal, echoing like a gong. He put the rolled-up Astroturf and lawn chairs into the compartment and closed the door.

While her dad drove north on the coastal highway, Joan sat hunched over in the front seat, wholly focused on her iPhone, reading an interview with Lorin Stein, in which he described what compelled him to reject most stories. "Not enough stakes," he said was the most common and fatal flaw. Joan thought about the plot of "Conquistador." Did the story have stakes? What did "stakes" even mean? She looked up the definition on her phone.

> *Stakes: a sum of money or something else of value gambled on the outcome of a risky game or venture.*

She put her phone under her thigh and sat thinking about the definition. For the story to have stakes, her narrator would have to have something of value to lose. Did she? What was it? The stripper, perhaps? Or her dignity? She became confused, thinking about stakes.

She thought of Roberto, alone, celibate, typing *Bitter Texas Honey* on his stupid typewriter, high as a kite. He probably didn't worry about things like "stakes" when he wrote. She wondered how far he had gotten in his own project, what memories he might be mining from their brief but intense romance. Perhaps he was writing about the morning they got breakfast tacos and slow-danced to World War II propaganda music. Or perhaps he was writing about how beautiful and ethereal Joan was, looking at the Polaroid of her often, regretting letting her go. Joan liked to imagine Roberto obsessing over her, immortalizing her in a written form. In this way, they were still connected, linked by the invisible, unbreakable chain of art.

As tempted as she was to reach out to Roberto again, Joan decided to keep her ego intact by not contacting him until she had something published. She felt that proving herself as a writer was the only path forward, and the only thing that might change Roberto's mind. She had deleted his phone number to help control herself.

Randy scrolled through pictures of women on his iPhone, swerving in and out of his lane, periodically hitting the little ridges at the edge of the road, which created a loud, rumbling growl beneath them.

"My new therapist said I'm not allowed on dating sites anymore. She said every time I log on to a dating site should be considered a relapse. Look, Skipper, I'm relapsing," he said.

Skipper was sitting on Joan's lap, staring at her dad in earnest with his glassy brown eyes.

"Quit looking at me, Skipper! Why do you always do that? What's your problem?"

Skipper cocked his head to the side.

"Look at the way he just stares. He's obsessed with me. Skipper, you're codependent. You need to go to Al-Anon."

"You're not on Sugar Daddy again, are you?" Joan asked.

"No, MillionaireMatch."

"Isn't that where you met Sandra?" Sandra was Randy's latest ex-wife, the subject of Joan's story "Blond Hair, Big Boobs, Alcoholic, Thief."

"Nope, met Sandra on Sugar Daddy. She cyber-winked at me the other day. Isn't that somethin'? Here, wanna see her profile? She's using a picture I took of her. Can you believe that? Some nerve, huh?" He handed his phone to Joan, and she looked at the picture of her most recent stepmom. Sandra stood in front of her dad's Harley, wearing oversized sunglasses and a tight white shirt that said *Everything's Bigger in Texas* in black letters, which stretched across her ample chest. Behind her, the ocean and sky were bright blue.

"Did you respond to her?" Joan asked.

"Nope," he said. "Haven't talked to her since I got out of jail. My lawyer told me not to."

Joan opened her notebook and grabbed one of her fountain pens, suddenly ready to work on her new book. The Adderall was hitting her hard, and the world felt open and vast. The rumbling of the tires beneath her gave her the sensation of being on a boat or a plane or a roller coaster. She took in the coastal scenery, ready to document everything. She had so much hope.

"My therapist wants me to write my life story," Joan's dad said, putting his phone away. "From age zero to eighteen. How am I supposed to remember when I was zero?"

"Don't ask me," said Joan, annoyed. Randy was disrupting her flow.

"Go get your computer."

"Why?"

"You're gonna write it for me."

"No way. Write your own."

"Yes! I paid for your degree, now you're gonna do something for me. Go get your computer."

Joan sighed. "Fine." There was no use arguing with him. He always won.

She stood up and walked toward the kitchen table, holding her arms out to keep from falling over. Everything around her rattled. Items that hadn't been fastened to the counter with Velcro were rolling around on the floor. She unplugged her laptop and returned to the passenger seat, where she opened a blank Word document and watched the blinking cursor.

"Okay, go," she said.

"How do I tell the story of my life?" he said. "What should I call it?"

"I don't know."

"Oh, come on. You're the *writer*. You're the one who went to college for *writing*."

"So? That doesn't mean I can write the story of *your* life."

Joan usually loved titles, but the idea of wasting her creative energy, not to mention her Adderall high, on someone else's story made her agitated.

"Okay," her dad said. "Here we go. I was born in 1953. Wasn't even a color TV. Should it rhyme? What if I made it rhyme?"

He slapped her on the arm, his eyes twinkling. She looked at him blankly, not wanting to encourage him.

"Let's see, what do I remember about being a kid? I remember always wanting the best, newest toys. Whenever something new came out, I *had* to have it. I mean I absolutely had to, or I would have died. That's how it felt at least. My dad was in the oil business, and he was never around, so when I wanted a toy, I'd make my mom's life a total living hell until I got it. I remember lying on the kitchen floor screaming and crying until she'd buy whatever it was."

"Kind of like how you are with women now," Joan observed.

"What?"

"Never mind. Keep going."

Skipper sat on the floorboard next to Joan's feet, watching her while she typed furiously. She was peaking on her Adderall now, and having been given a task, she was overcome with the need to complete it perfectly. The quality of the prose was secondary to the visual satisfaction Joan received from filling the white space with symmetrical black letters.

Randy blathered on about his life, veering quickly into his high school water polo years and then the mess of his twenties, when he discovered horse tranquilizers and flunked out of college in Lubbock, then flew to Hawaii with only twenty dollars in his pocket. There, he dedicated his life to surfing and ate a single five-cent burrito per day. If he needed more food, he said, he would go to Mexican restaurants, say he was meeting a friend, and eat baskets of free chips before leaving. He claimed he slept in the sand traps of golf courses until he found a home in an old woman's garage. Eventually he got his life together, returning to Texas and opening his first recording studio in his thirties with the financial backing of his father. These stories were all familiar to Joan. He told them over and over. Still, she liked hearing them, in a way. They'd become like fairy tales or bedtime stories, predictable and comforting.

"You've gone too far. The therapist wanted age zero to eighteen," Joan reminded him.

"Oh right. Let's see . . . When I was young, I remember we moved all the time," Randy said. "I moved four times before I was in the third grade. Fort Worth, Mississippi, Canada, Houston . . . Isn't that fucked up?"

"Yeah," Joan said. "That's probably why you are the way you are."

"What do you mean the way I am?"

"You can't stay still. You're never content with anything."

Her dad sat quietly, mulling this over. He didn't disagree, that was clear. Joan used the silence as an opportunity to change the subject to something more useful for her road novel. If she was going to write anybody's life story on this trip, it was going to be her own.

"When did you meet Mom?" she asked. This felt like the most practical way to get started. Her inception. To find out where it all began. She thought of Roberto's journal, in which he'd been so unafraid to explore his own origins.

"Dolly? She was living with a meth dealer when I met her," he said.

"What?" Joan said. She had never heard this story from her mother.

"Yep. Tinfoil in the windows and everything. You'd walk in and the whole house stunk like meth. Did you know that meth stinks like that when you cook it?"

"No, I've never cooked meth."

"Worst smell in the world. Anyway, she was living with this dealer. . . . What a catch, huh?" He laughed to himself. "I really know how to pick 'em."

"You sure do." Joan typed robotically, no time to process her shock. She'd had no idea her mother lived with a meth head. Until Dolly married Doug, Joan's life had been relatively stable. Dolly, albeit a little anxious and controlling, had been mostly a responsible, doting mother, filling their house to the brim with delicious snacks, going to great lengths to entertain Joan and get her whatever she needed to thrive—books, art supplies, toys, piano lessons, horseback riding lessons. Of course, Joan had been to AA and NA meetings with her mother over the years, where Dolly referred vaguely to her "cocaine days," but she was always laughing about it. Joan also remembered all the dumb prayers and recovery slogans taped around their house, which Dolly claimed she needed to stay sober. Joan assumed she was exaggerating for attention. This new information, while a little disturbing, excited Joan. It would ensure that her road novel would be much deeper and more interesting than Roberto's debut. She noted the way her dad seemed to light up discussing his and Dolly's seedy past. She loved this about him. He was an open book, unlike her mother.

"She loved speed. Loved it more than anything. She'd be on all fours looking for pieces of it in the carpet whenever we were done smoking it. She just couldn't stop. She had it bad, man. I didn't have it bad like she did. I never really even liked meth that much. Wasn't my thing. Quaaludes, LSD, pot, sure, but speed was her thing. Cocaine too. Uppers, man."

Joan conjured the image of Dolly digging in the carpet for remnants of meth. It was so unbelievable. Her mother always seemed to have so much natural energy. In this way, she'd always felt like Joan's opposite. Dolly could accomplish in a single weekend what Joan couldn't do in months. About once per quarter, Dolly would invite herself over to Joan's apartment on a Friday, swoop in, and do every load of Joan's laundry, including sheets and towels; get all her bills opened and paid; fill her fridge; vacuum; and mop Joan's floors before going back to Houston on Sunday. Joan couldn't imagine having as much energy as Dolly, or why Dolly would have ever been so desperate for more.

"I always liked to go to sleep before the sun came up," her dad continued. "That was my rule. I didn't care what I had to do. Shit, I'd drink a bottle of rubbing alcohol if I had to. Anything to get to bed by the time the sun came up. There's nothing more depressing than watching the sunrise while you're coming down off meth. Nothing more depressing than that."

Joan couldn't have agreed more. She'd taken meth once in high school, by accident. It had been cut in with some ecstasy, and she remembered the comedown being so bad that she had seriously considered suicide. It was like coming down off Adderall times ten. She noted that she and her dad had a similar set of rules.

"Wow," Joan said. "I didn't know that's how y'all met. Mom said you met in high school."

"Oh yeah. I guess we did, technically. But we didn't get together until later, when she was living with that meth dealer. He ended up getting busted by the feds. There were helicopters flying around his house. It was really something."

"That's so intense," Joan said. She watched the palm trees and hills fly by as they drove through Los Angeles. When her autobiographical road novel came out, it would probably be adapted into a screenplay and become a hit movie. Then she could live in those hills, among the stars, beneath the hazy fog. She imagined herself attending the film premiere, having her picture taken on the red carpet next to whatever A-list actress had been cast as her. She would never need to deal with her family again.

"She was bad, man," Randy continued. "The worst of the worst. Even breast cancer couldn't slow her down. I remember one time, she was recovering from surgery, and she just disappeared in the middle of the night. That's what she always did. Vanish. Like a ghost. I'd wake up and she'd just be gone. I couldn't find her anywhere. She came back hours later, totally blacked out, with her new fake boob just ripped completely open. She'd gotten in a fight—she was such a mean drunk, probably harassing some poor girl—and the girl, trying to get away from her probably, had run her over with a car. I instantly knew that whatever happened, it was Dolly's fault. I'll never forget the way she looked standing there in the bathroom, all bloody with her chest hanging open."

"Dear lord," Joan said. She knew her mother had a problem with drugs, but she had never heard these stories. Aside from one six-month relapse when Joan was fourteen, when Dolly found out Doug was secretly sleeping with hookers throughout their whole marriage, Dolly had been sober for most of Joan's life.

"She even drank and used all through her pregnancy with Henry," Randy said. "I tried to tell her, you know, people usually stop for things like this, pregnancy. She wouldn't hear it. So I just went along. I didn't have control over it either. We were both high on coke the night she went into labor. It was my birthday, the day before Halloween, so we were up all night, partying. Her water broke and when we got to the hospital all the doctors and nurses were dressed up in costumes— devil horns, pumpkins. The doctor who delivered Henry was wearing a clown suit. Isn't that ridiculous? It was trippy, man. Then Henry came out with a cone head. I was like, *Uh-oh,* but the doctor said it was normal, he just smashed it back down with his hand right there."

"Did she use when she was pregnant with me?" Joan asked. She stopped typing and waited for his response, her heart racing. Her forehead burned. Her armpits were warm and wet.

"No," he said. "She went to rehab before she had you."

Joan felt surprisingly disappointed learning this. It could have explained so much.

"She relapsed when you were a baby, though," he said. "Started drinking beer again first. We were at the ranch and she said she wanted to have a beer and make a fire. Then one thing led to another, and she was taking pills after we broke up. Sometimes, when I'd come to pick y'all up, she'd be stumbling around in the yard, completely out of it. I considered fighting for custody, but I didn't have my own shit together enough to raise y'all. I was an alcoholic too, after all; I wasn't perfect. I was waking up in my front yard, I totaled my Porsche. Did I ever tell you that story? I hit a median going around eighty. Popped all the tires, even the spare in the trunk. I'm lucky to be alive."

Joan knew the Porsche story well. She'd heard it half a dozen times since Randy got sober. Afterward, he told her, he'd bought another Porsche, same model, year, and color, to avoid telling anyone about the accident.

"What happened between you and Mom? When did you break up?"

"She's never told you about that?"

"No, she doesn't talk about anything bad," Joan said.

"I'll never forget the day we broke up for good. You wouldn't believe what she did. Henry was four years old, and she sent him to kick me out. He came out from our bedroom and said, 'Daddy, Mommy says you have to leave.' Can you believe that? A four-year-old kid kicking his own dad out of the house? She was somethin' else, man."

"That's pretty fucked up."

"Yeah, and you know the story of how you were conceived?"

"No, I was just going to ask—"

"She pretended she missed me and wanted to get back together with me. Invited me on this camping trip to reignite our love or whatever. So I rented an RV and went out to Big Bend. Then she got pregnant. Afterward, she said never mind. It had all been a setup. She said she wanted a second child and wanted Henry to have a full sibling, not a half sibling. Can you believe that shit? She totally used me."

"Wait, I was conceived in an RV?" Joan asked. She assumed the story was missing some key elements, that her mother might have another side to share. But this fact stood out to her.

"Yeah." Her dad chuckled.

Suddenly the RV felt womblike. Joan let it sink in that she'd been spawned in a fake house on wheels, not out of love or affection, but out of an act of manipulation on her mother's part and willful ignorance on her father's. Everything about her life and disposition made sense in this light. She felt cursed. She wrote the observation down, thinking it could thematically tie together her road novel, which perhaps she would title *Fake House* or *Womb on Wheels*. But instead of feeling hopeful about the project, she felt a wave of depression settle. Her comedown was hitting.

They passed through San Francisco as the sun began to set. She put away her laptop, feeling like she might throw up. She took a photo of her dad driving in front of Alcatraz and posted it to Facebook. The picture garnered several likes and comments from AudioPro employees, from all the different locations.

It was dark by the time they reached the RV park in Bodega Bay. "Hey, I probably shouldn't have said all that stuff about Dolly," her dad said as he pulled into the parking spot. "Everyone's fucked up. We've all got our demons. Doesn't mean we need to dwell on the past. Try to get over everything I just said by the time we see her in Seattle, okay?"

"Wait, Mom's going to Seattle too?" Joan felt like she'd been punched.

"She's coming to meet us, yeah. She wanted to see Henry too. Didn't I tell you that?"

"No," Joan said. "You did not." The walls of the RV felt like they were closing in on her. It was just like Dolly to insert herself into their Father's Day trip.

"Well, all that stuff I told you . . . you can't be mad at her for it. She had a fucked-up childhood. Way worse than mine. Her dad was Eastern European, and he was the meanest, drunkest man I ever met."

A sense of dread crept over Joan as she anticipated her mother's arrival. It would be much more difficult to hide her Adderall use from Dolly, who watched Joan like a hawk, and who, Joan now realized, had been just as much of an upper-lover as Joan now was.

While her dad dealt with all the RV hookups, Joan took Skipper for a walk around the park, trying to unwind. The breeze was cool and crisp and probably should have felt spiritually cleansing but didn't at all. Having fully come down, she was too trapped inside her horrid flesh prison to appreciate the outdoors.

Skipper stopped every five feet to sniff another bush and mark it with urine. Even after his bladder was long empty, he kept stopping and lifting his leg anyway. Like he didn't even notice he wasn't peeing anymore. Some of the trailers in the park were up on cinder blocks, and by the amount of junk that had accumulated outside of them, Joan could tell they'd been there awhile and weren't going anywhere soon. While Skipper sniffed around a trash can, Joan stood and observed a woman through a small window, watching TV alone. What was her story? How did she end up here, like this? She thought of Dolly, who had slept on their living room floor with the TV on for two years after Doug moved out, unable to be alone with her thoughts, too traumatized for the silence and darkness of her bedroom. In high school, Joan would have to sneak her friends awkwardly past her mother, asleep on the carpet. Now Dolly still fell asleep in front of the TV most nights, on Joan's grandmother's couch, before sauntering into her bedroom in the middle of the night.

Back in the RV, Randy had already fallen asleep. Joan snuck past him and dug through his medicine cabinet. She grabbed a bottle of Tylenol PM, went to the kitchen table, and skimmed the twenty pages of notes she'd taken that day. The writing life wasn't easy. But at least her book was already better than *Bitter Texas Honey*. She just needed to finish it. Once it was published and Roberto read it, he would probably want her back. How could he not? Her life was so tragic, so profound, and so beautiful. She swallowed three Tylenol PMs. She would knock herself unconscious and do this all over again tomorrow, hopefully doubling her page count. She planned to have a first draft finished by the time she returned to Austin. This was what discipline looked like. She was living in moderation, rationing her pills successfully and taking them at appropriate times. She would never get caught if she kept up this regimen.

19.

THE LONE VAQUERA

The next morning, Joan and her dad went sightseeing in Bodega Bay, a town made famous by Alfred Hitchcock's *The Birds*. In the Jeep, Randy was griping about how rude everyone in California was, and how much more friendly Texans were. He theorized it was due to the weather and scenery being so nice. Something about it spoiled people. Joan nodded along, pretending to pay attention. But she was distracted, still reflecting on everything she'd learned the day before, about her mother, about her father. Her dark origins. Her rotten roots. She wondered how she would shape it all into something beautiful and worthy of acclaim. She felt a profound pity for herself, a sadness that she hoped would diminish once she could share it with the world.

She checked the clock. It was almost noon, which meant she could take her second Adderall. Using Skipper as a shield, she picked up her purse from the floorboard and placed it on her lap next to the dog. As Randy complained, she slowly and delicately reached into her purse, slipping a single Adderall out of the side pocket. She turned toward the window and placed the pill quickly into her mouth, then swallowed it with a large gulp of coffee.

They stopped to have lunch on the edge of a cliff, sitting on a wooden bench, watching deep-blue waves crash into jagged, menacing rocks. Her dad ate smoked salmon from a plastic package and Joan picked at a few pre-sliced strawberries. She was uninterested in food but forced herself to eat anyway. She wrote a brief description of the cliff in her notebook, but not so many notes that her dad might suspect anything unusual. She tried to look coy and uninterested, sliding the notebook casually back into her purse, her heart pounding.

When Joan was twenty-one, after her dad pulled her out of Miami and forced her back to Texas, they fought so much they had to go to a family therapist to mediate. During the session, her dad said he didn't know what to do anymore. He told the therapist about Joan's prescription drug abuse, as well as her claims of being a communist and a bisexual. He said he thought Joan was going to hell.

"I want to go to hell," Joan had said. "I'd rather be in hell than here, with him."

"Wow," the therapist kept saying. "There's a lot going on here."

Her dad had looked at Joan like she was poison. He told her she was just like her mother.

"I don't know if that's a helpful comparison," the therapist offered.

After the appointment, while her dad was writing the therapist a check, Joan overheard her say: "You aren't alone. It's an epidemic. Twenty-one is the new two."

Now that Joan was older, conservative, and (he thought) no longer abusing prescription pills, her dad was much more tolerable to be around. He didn't yell at her in the same way. Mostly, he just talked about himself and didn't ask many questions, which was fine for her purposes as a writer.

They drove the Jeep through the town, visiting landmarks where famous scenes from *The Birds* had been shot. Joan hadn't seen the film, but having just taken her Adderall, she enjoyed seeing the white chapel on the hill, striking against the blue sky, and she took several photos of the church on her iPhone. She posted one of the pictures to Instagram— a new app she'd joined only because Roberto was on it—along with some hashtags: #thebirds, #alfredhitchcock, #unfiltered. Joan hoped that Roberto would see the photo and be impressed, wishing he could take part once again in Joan's exciting and unconventional life. At the gift shop afterward, Joan walked through each aisle with purpose, inspecting every item, eventually picking up a portrait of a beautiful blond woman looking up at a menacing black crow. *I need this picture*, she thought, and brought it to the counter, where her dad paid for it absentmindedly along with a small pile of items he'd gotten for himself—T-shirts, mugs, a hat.

Later that afternoon they drove up to the redwoods before heading inland to Mount Shasta, where they were spending the night with an old friend of her dad's. "Don't talk about politics," her dad warned. "He's a total liberal. Been living on disability checks the last fifteen years. Kind of like Skipper. Skipper's a Democrat too, you know."

"You've told me," she said, walking toward the bathroom. Joan took one of her mother's painkillers from her toiletry bag and lay in the master bedroom, on the hideous floral comforter that matched the rest of the upholstery throughout the RV. She opened her laptop and stared at the road trip document on her screen. Skipper lay curled up in a ball against her hip.

Feeling uninspired, she logged on to the internet and began G-chatting with Claire, telling her about her new novel. As usual, Joan found the actual writing of the project very difficult, but talking about it to Claire was a breeze.

> JOAN: It's going to be like a Texan Jack Kerouac, but also, unapologetically female. Like the beatnik generation meets Sex and the City, or something.
>
> CLAIRE: I like it.
>
> JOAN: I'm going to have to get into my parents too, obviously. As backstory. And Wyatt is going to be a Dean-like character, adding that kooky, wild-guy element and everything. He's not actually here, he

had to work, but I'll add him into the trip fictionally later. Nbd.

CLAIRE: Good idea. It's always good to insert chaos where there is none.

Unlike Joan, Claire had actually finished reading *On the Road*, and had even gone to see the original Kerouac scrolls at the Harry Ransom Center. Joan felt pleased with herself for getting Claire's approval on her road novel.

JOAN: How's your book going? Any developments?

CLAIRE: I'm actually taking a break from that right now. I decided to apply to literature PhDs for next fall.

JOAN: What? You can't stop writing your novel. Our novels were supposed to be in conversation. We were supposed to be building the contemporary Austin canon.

CLAIRE: I'm just being realistic with my time. I need to focus on what I'm good at, you know?

Joan felt so overcome with emotion that she didn't respond. She closed her laptop and flopped onto her back, watching the enormous trees rush by out the bedroom window. She tried to read Carlos's novel *The Lone Vaquero*, which was about an old Mexican man grieving his wife, but could not get past the first paragraph. She kept feeling carsick. She couldn't believe Claire was being such a coward, giving up on her novel, settling instead for being a lowly critic. Had all their conversations meant nothing to her?

Joan closed Carlos's book and looked out the window again, hating Claire, missing Roberto but hating him too. She looked forward to the day they would speak again, perhaps after she published her story in *The Paris Review*. She imagined Roberto casually finding "Conquistador" in the journal and rereading it at the coffee shop.

Afterward, perhaps he would write or call to congratulate her. Things would progress from there, naturally. Over dinner or drinks he would confess that he'd made a terrible mistake, rejecting her. He would then compliment her story about Vince. "I'm sorry you had to deal with such a jerk for so long," he might say. "Greater sacrifices have been made for art," Joan would reply, a smile creeping across her face. Then they would make out passionately.

They arrived at Bruce's house in Mount Shasta late that evening. He stood in the front yard with his wife, a large, cute redheaded woman who was smiling big, squinting, and waving. When she saw Skipper, she squealed with delight. It was cold at night, so Joan put on a Harley-Davidson fleece pullover that her dad had bought for her in the redwoods. She also got Skipper's blue sweater from the closet, and he sat still and complacent as she squeezed his little head through the neck hole and his two front legs through two tiny armholes. He was like her little baby.

Bruce's house was small and charming, painted a deep forest green with bright colorful flowers all around its perimeter. They went inside and all sat down in the living room, where Joan eagerly accepted a beer from Bruce while her dad declined. He hadn't had a drink in six years, he told Bruce. Bruce and Joan's dad started catching up. It had been years and years, and Randy seemed invigorated by the attention and the reminiscing. Bruce and Randy had been buddies since their twenties. Bruce had worked for her dad's studio all through the seventies and eighties, and in the late nineties, he became the first director of AudioPro's Austin campus, before it had ever been accredited. He had been fired after Randy caught him using expensive brochures as kindling for his fireplace, and for going on dates with students, which they were now able to laugh about. They made up after Randy got out of rehab and made amends with Bruce. Joan didn't care about any of this; she focused on drinking the beer as quickly as possible, scanning the room for something stronger to blot out the physical misery of her comedown.

Bruce's wife brought out bowls of dip, which Joan devoured greed-ily along with another beer as they asked her dad all about his life, about the success of the career college, how it'd blown up since earn-ing accreditation, how he had over a hundred employees. Forgetting his rule about not mentioning politics, Randy began to complain about the left-wing government constantly trying to shut him down and put him out of business. Then the conversation moved, naturally, to his love life and he looked at Joan with some hesitation. "Should I tell them about Sandra?"

Joan shrugged. "If you want to," she said. After all, it was a good story, and the inspiration for "Blond Hair, Big Boobs, Alcoholic, Thief."

"Well, I met this girl online," Randy said. "We started talking on the phone. I'd had a string of fucked-up, bad relationships. Just one after the other. I figured it couldn't get any worse. So I got on like ten dating sites."

Bruce started chuckling. "If you've got ten fishing rods in the wa-ter, you're bound to catch at least one fish, right?"

"Exactly," Joan's dad said. "That was my theory."

Bruce's wife playfully touched her husband's shoulder. "Don't get any ideas, Bruce."

He smiled at her and put his hand on her knee and kept it there.

"So, anyways, I met this girl online and we started talking on the phone. We talked on the phone every night for two weeks. I told her if I liked her, I was just gonna bring her back to Texas, and she said okay, fine. She lived in Reno with her parents. She was forty-one. Well, she said she was thirty-seven, but she ended up being forty-one."

"There's a red flag," Bruce's wife chimed in. "If she's lying about her age, what else is she lying about?"

"Everything," Joan's dad said. "Just wait."

Joan remembered the two weeks her dad had been on the phone with Sandra. She and Wyatt had been living with him, and they hid under his balcony at night, eavesdropping on their conversations, sit-ting on his Astroturf putting green, stifling giggles. Her dad had sounded so different talking to her, they joked. Like a little baby man.

"Anyways," Randy continued, "she seemed like this very sweet girl;

if you met her, you'd think she was the sweetest girl in the world. She had this real sweet face and talked in this real sweet voice. . . . Just sweet all around."

Joan, realizing the scene might be useful for her road novel, took out her phone and began recording under the table. Perhaps her dad would reveal a detail she had missed before. Perhaps she would write entire sections from her dad's perspective. Maybe she would even write a chapter from Skipper's point of view. Maybe the novel could take the form of William Faulkner's *As I Lay Dying*.

"So I went out there and she picked me up and we went to this real fancy resort, and everything went fine. It was great, actually, so she came back to Texas with me. Everything was amazing. My family loved her. Joan and Wyatt loved her. She even fooled my parents. She went to church with them, she got baptized with Joan at my dad's ranch. We got married after three months."

"Two and a half months," Joan said, correcting him.

"Fine, two and a half. Whatever."

"I just think that's an important detail," Joan said. "Because you've always told me that it takes three months to really know somebody." She realized that was about the length of her relationships with Vince and Roberto. Once they got to know her, they each decided to take a step back. She tried not to dwell on this or think about what it meant. She focused on her beer and her recording.

Her dad was glossing over all the warnings he'd received—from her; from her brother, Henry; from Dolly. Even from Wyatt, who could trust anybody. Pretty much everyone had told Randy not to marry Sandra, a virtual stranger, that soon.

"Oh okay, whatever," her dad said. "Anyway, one day after we were married, I came home and she was bouncing off the walls, acting real crazy, and I said, 'What'd you take?' She said, 'I didn't take anything.' She swore up and down that she hadn't taken anything, so I just let it go. But it kept getting worse. Things would seem normal, and then, every once in a while, she'd get so fucked up she couldn't walk or talk. The next day she'd deny taking anything at all. So I told her we should take her to a neurologist, because she had some sort of brain damage. I was starting to wonder if *I* was the one going crazy."

Joan was pleased watching the minutes tick by on her phone. Her novel was writing itself. She got up to get another beer and left her phone face down on the table.

"Then one day she was in a mode I'd never seen before. She was yelling, 'What happened to us?!' and crying. Going freaking nuts. She was tearing our condo up, throwing stuff at me. She threw a paperweight at my head and almost killed me. She said, 'I'm takin' Skipper.' I took my chance and got out of there before she murdered me. I ran to the school and locked myself inside. Then I heard a loud banging on the door, and it was the police. They kept shouting 'OPEN THE DOOR!' at me through the glass with their guns up and pointed at me. I couldn't open the door without getting the key from the back office. I tried to tell them that, but they wouldn't listen. They just kept screaming 'OPEN THE DOOR!' and I kept yelling back with my hands up 'I CAN'T!'"

"Oh my god," said Bruce's wife.

"What did you do?" asked Bruce.

"Eventually, after enough of that yelling back and forth, they let me go back and get the key. When I opened the door for them, they immediately tackled me and put me in handcuffs and took me to jail. I had to spend the night there. I was charged with a felony. Assault. Turns out after I left, she'd hit herself in the forehead and called the cops to tell 'em I did it."

Bruce and his wife stared in awe at Randy. Joan remembered when she'd learned about the incident. When her dad called her from jail, she was in London, standing outside the Globe Theatre with Claire, waiting to see *Romeo and Juliet*, as part of the study abroad.

"Tanya bailed me out of jail," her dad continued. "When I got back to the condo the next day, I saw that Sandra had cleaned me out of everything. Wasn't even a toothbrush left in there. The only reason I have Skipper now is that he ran away from wherever she took him. He was microchipped in my name."

"Aw, thank god," Bruce's wife cooed. She was holding Skipper on her lap now, in love.

"And that isn't even the whole story," Randy said. "I'm pretty sure she'd been drugging me the whole time too."

"Oh my god," Bruce's wife said again.

"Not the whole time," Joan said.

"Okay, not the whole time, but for a while there. She was making me spaghetti every day and I'd feel real lightheaded and dizzy after I ate it; I was sleeping all the time, horrible constipation. Had no idea why. Now I think she was putting opiates in the sauce."

"I can't believe it," Bruce's wife said.

"Is she in prison or jail or anything?" Bruce asked.

"Nope, nothing."

"How can someone do something like that and get away with it?"

Joan's dad shrugged and shook his head. "California's fucked up, man. Everything's backward. No matter what happens, it's always the man's fault. Fucking liberals."

"Wow, what a hell of an experience," Bruce said.

"Do you all like avocado?" asked his wife from the kitchen.

At the dinner table, Bruce shook his head and said, "Wow, you just never know. I've been following you on Facebook all this time, and you just seemed to be doing so well, with your business and all, but this just goes to show that you never know what a person is actually going through behind the scenes."

Randy shrugged, unsure how to respond.

After everyone had gone to bed, Joan stayed up, drinking and researching literary journal response times. How long could she endure this torturous waiting? The Google results said three to six months for *The Paris Review*. And even if the story was accepted, it could take many more months to appear in print. What a joke. She couldn't wait that long to speak to Roberto.

She didn't have his phone number but considered writing him an email. Something nonchalant. *Hey, just checking in*, she might say. No, she could not email him now. She needed to maintain discipline.

She texted Vince instead, using him as her emotional whipping boy. Who cared if Vince thought she was desperate?

You never talk to me, Joan wrote.

Vince didn't respond.

Twenty minutes later, she was in bed, drafting an email to Roberto on her phone. It was just a draft. Nothing she would send. She wanted to express her truth and let it go, like her therapist often encouraged. *What happened to us?* she wrote. *Why don't you want to be with me? You said you loved me.* Without allowing herself to think about it anymore, she hit send, dropped her phone next to her pillow, and went to sleep.

20.

A GRAVE TACTICAL ERROR

The next morning, Joan woke up and checked her email. There was no response from Roberto. Remorseful, she walked into the living room, where Bruce's wife told them they were welcome to stay another night, but Joan's dad declined.

"That's okay," he said. "We're ramblers. We live for the road. We don't stay anywhere too long or the moss starts growing. In fact, I can feel it growing right now. Joan, can you feel the moss growing?"

"Yeah," Joan said. She liked Bruce and his wife well enough, but she couldn't imagine spending another day with them. Her Adderall was kicking in and she was anxious to keep moving. The more they moved, the sooner the trip would be over.

"So, is that what it's like to be normal?" Joan's dad asked her when they pulled out of Bruce's neighborhood and headed toward the highway again. He sounded angry. "Is that what I'm supposed to do to be happy? Just find some gross woman and stay at home with her all day?"

Joan remained silent, unwilling to dignify his question with a response. Bruce's wife was not even unattractive. On her phone, she played a zoo game to keep herself busy. She refreshed her email at five-minute intervals, hoping for a reply from Roberto, but there was nothing.

"Huh?" her dad said, louder this time, almost shouting. "Get off your phone! Is that what I have to do to be happy? Get with some gross chick?"

"How should I know?" Joan asked. "Do I look happy?"

Once her Adderall went into full effect, she became laser-focused on expanding and cleaning her miniature digital zoo. She watched visitors walk from exhibit to exhibit as she picked up their trash and built pathways and planted trees. She hoped they were enjoying themselves.

"Doesn't he get bored? What do they talk about all day?"

"I don't know!"

Joan got up and went into the living room to escape. She plopped down on the couch, where she could enjoy some peace and quiet with her zoo. She was desperate to save enough money to purchase a tiger. Randy put music on and cranked up the volume. "Ramblin' Man" by the Allman Brothers blared through the speakers. Skipper came and buried his head between her hip and the couch. Like her, he hated loud noise.

"I know, Skipper," Joan said, stroking his soft fur. "I know, it's painful."

Nine hours later, they arrived at an RV park in Seattle and Joan's dad went to bed early. It was seven P.M., and Joan sat outside, still playing her zoo game. She felt completely drained and was disappointed in herself for wasting the entire day's Adderall on playing a phone game. She must have been building up a tolerance to her dose. She tried not to think about the coming days, when the four of them would be gathered as a family.

Finally, a ding from her phone notified her that she'd received an email. Her heart skipped when she saw that it was from Roberto. That he'd responded within twenty-four hours gave her some hope that the content might be positive. She opened the message, ready to relish every word. The email read:

Lady Joan,

Since you said in your email that you deleted my phone number, I've gone ahead and deleted yours too. You asked where things went wrong and why I didn't want a relationship with you. You might recall that several times throughout our courtship you emphasized that you didn't see me in that way. You told me often that I was just a "fantasy and an escape" to you. Being attracted to you, and enjoying your company, I was completely fine with the arrangement. But that's not something you say to a person you want to date seriously. As I said before, I've decided to leave it up to fate whether I see you again.

Yrs, R

The email hit Joan in the chest like a brick. She didn't remember saying Roberto was a "fantasy and an escape" multiple times. Did she? Her mind raced through the trajectory of their relationship, glossing over the parts that made her uncomfortable. Even if she had said something like that, why would he take her literally? Couldn't he see she had been joking? Even if she hadn't been joking at the time, couldn't she change her mind? People changed their minds all the time!

Contacting Roberto so soon had been a grave tactical error. She should have waited until she had accomplished something, anything. Getting her story published, finishing her road novel, getting into an MFA. Anything that might have impressed him enough to lure him back. Instead, she'd bombarded Roberto with vulnerability and desperation. Never in her life had Joan felt like more of a loser.

She called Wyatt. No answer. Probably playing at Rick's or hanging out with Mabel. She scrolled through her contacts and decided to call Kyle. He always made her problems feel important.

"Talk to me," Kyle said, sounding breathless and rushed. She hadn't seen him since the last day of session. He had quit Allen's office to work on the Ted Cruz campaign, which Joan thought was crazy. Ted Cruz had no chance against the wealthy incumbent, Dewhurst.

"Where are you?" she asked. There was a lot of noise in the background.

"The middle of nowhere, East Texas," he said. "A fundraiser."

"How's it going?"

"Oh, it's exhausting," he said. "All I do is drive him around from town to town. I've never spent this much time with anyone in my life. Not even my own mother."

"Do you think y'all might actually win?"

"It's a long shot. We're running against some very rich people. Still polling in single digits, but people are responding. Also, we are getting some big endorsements. We got Sarah Palin the other day."

"Wow, that's a big deal!" Joan said.

"You betcha."

"Hey, I wanted to ask you something. I'm thinking of doing this thing that I shouldn't tonight, and I want to get your opinion."

"Don't do it," he said.

"You don't even know what it is."

"Well, that's my opinion. Hey, I gotta go. Ted's here."

"Tell him I said hi."

"I'll talk to you soon."

She had planned on trying to get Kyle to talk her out of breaking her rules and taking more Adderall. She realized now that he'd been a stabilizing force in her life, often giving her sage advice on how to behave like an adult. Oh well, at least she tried. She went inside the RV, found her pills, and counted them. She had ten remaining. She swallowed two with a Diet Coke. She would stay up all night, writing. She would have a first draft by the time she got home. She was beholden to nothing now, besides her art.

She opened a Word document and stared at the blinking cursor. When nothing came to her after ten minutes, she took two more pills out of her bottle, broke them open, and poured the beads into her

Diet Coke. Doing this transformed the time-release medication into instant release, which was what she needed.

Then, finally, the rush of inspiration arrived. Shaking and sweating and guzzling her drugged Diet Coke, Joan began typing stream-of-consciousness memories about the road trip thus far. She wrote about Encinitas, LA, Bodega Bay. She wrote about the redwoods, about Bruce's house in Mount Shasta. She described the way the trees looked, the way the RV felt, sounded, smelled, moving along the highway. Every detail felt sad and beautiful and funny at once. She recorded what she could remember of her dad's endless rantings. She wrote down all the things he'd said about her mother again. She wrote about his motocross phase, all the parrots he used to own, his surfing and LSD stories. The way they called him the Lude Dude in high school because he took so many quaaludes. She wrote about when he sank his houseboat and when his yacht melted in Miami, after her twenty-first birthday party. Another boat at the marina had caught fire and the fire had spread to other boats, toasting her dad's like a marshmallow, until the infrastructure collapsed. Wyatt had been there, serving as her dad's skipper, shirtless and panicked, trying to put out the massive fire with a tiny water hose. He'd made all the local news the next day. All these things seemed thematically connected somehow.

There was no break in her writing. One thought, one memory, one observation, led seamlessly and effortlessly into another. Something had finally been cracked open. Perhaps this was how Roberto felt when he sat at his typewriter. It wasn't that the medication wasn't working, she realized. She had just been taking the wrong dose.

By morning, Joan had written fifty straight pages, single-spaced. A good start. It read kind of like a prose poem that captured the essence of her beautiful and tragic life. The thought that it wasn't good didn't cross her mind. With her new dose of Adderall, doubt was a foreign concept. Times like these, she wondered why she was so depressed and why things were so hard for her. Things didn't need to be hard. Her life was good. She had so much to look forward to.

Joan saved the document as "womb_on_wheels.docx" and emailed it to Paul and Carlos. She cleaned up all her clothes, folding each piece carefully and stacking them neatly in the closet. If only she could be this organized, this confident, every day, her whole life would fall into place. When she heard her dad begin to stir, she climbed into bed and pretended to sleep. She gripped the sheets in her hands, her teeth chattering.

21.

SHELF PANDAS

Later that morning, Joan dissolved two more pills into a cup of coffee, then took the Jeep to pick up her mother from the airport, her hands shaking. She kept her pill bottle hidden in her purse. She only had four pills remaining. When she pulled up to the gate, Dolly was smoking a long Marlboro and talking on her outdated blue flip phone. She wore dark sunglasses, and her hair was tied in a scrunchie on the very top of her head, so far up that it fell toward her face. She did this because she was short and claimed it "gave her height." Joan thought the hairstyle made her mother look three years old.

"Tell those assholes we're not taking any less than fifty thousand," she said into the phone as she entered the car. "Make them think we'll take them to trial. I know we can't afford it. I said make them *think* we can."

The smell of cigarette-smoke-tainted clothing filled the Jeep.

"This is the third pipeline they've put through our land. We should rename it Duncan Pipeline Junction instead of Duncan Ranch. That's basically what it is now."

Joan's mother spent most of her time managing a crumbling set of real estate assets she'd inherited from her father. Duncan Ranch was among them.

"My darling daughter!" She hung up the phone and turned to Joan, who forced a smile. Her entire body ached. The front of her neck and jaw felt clinched together. She tried to appear as normal as possible.

"Are you tired?" her mother asked. "Have you been getting enough sleep? You have bags under your eyes."

"I'm fine," Joan said. Her dad would have never noticed such a thing, which was part of the reason she preferred his company to Dolly's. It felt like Dolly cared more about Joan than about herself, which was a lot of pressure.

"How much sleep are you getting? You know, you've always needed ten hours."

"I'm not a baby anymore."

"Not just when you were a baby."

Already, Joan was being overanalyzed. She locked up like a walnut. Her mother reached over and held Joan's hand.

"Mom, please," she said, pulling her hand away.

"What? I'm just trying to show affection. I miss you."

"I don't like it."

Then Dolly was distracted by another phone call, thank god. She put it on speaker. One of her tenants—the Chinese restaurant—was calling about a leak. Dolly promised to fix everything better than new, and the panic in her tenant's voice subsided.

"I'm selling everything off," her mother said after hanging up. She was smoking another long cigarette and blowing it out the cracked window. "All the properties. Every last one."

"Great," Joan said. "Then you can finally do something else."

"Exactly. I'm ready to move on with my life."

"Good," said Joan, participating in her mother's perpetual fantasy of beginning anew: of moving out of Joan's grandmother's and getting a house of her own, then getting hobbies of her own, maybe even starting her own small business. Then she would care about the way she looked again, start dating again, maybe even get married again. Ever since the divorce from Doug, her mother had let herself go and instead thrown herself into caretaking and managing, anything to avoid looking at her own life. To Joan, it seemed like Dolly was determined to be stuck in Houston forever, wasting away alongside Joan's grand-mother. It was depressing.

Now, knowing all she knew about her mother's past, she wondered if Dolly might have legitimate brain damage.

They listened to Rush Limbaugh together on the way back to the RV park. Rush wasn't Joan's cup of tea, but she didn't mind listening to him occasionally. He was skilled and, in his own way, entertaining. Listening to Rush blather about liberty was better than listening to Dolly. They picked up Joan's dad and Skipper and drove straight to the Microsoft campus, Rush still blaring from the stereo. Henry was standing outside one of the entrances, looking sharp in a gray suit, his hair wet and slicked back. He didn't look anything like someone who had fetal alcohol syndrome, Joan thought.

He was working on the Microsoft Word team, which was interest-ing to Joan as it was the only Microsoft product she ever really used. Joan's dad, on the other hand, as a music industry veteran, hated Microsoft and had always boycotted anything they ever created in loyalty to Steve Jobs.

"Look," her dad said. "We're pretending to be a family."

"Stop it, Randy. We are a family. We're not pretending."

Joan's dad laughed at his joke and ignored Dolly. Joan felt sick and dizzy, carrying Skipper around, hidden in her oversized purse. There were manicured lawns, napping pods, and floor-to-ceiling windows. "This is ridiculous," her dad said at the sight of the napping pods. "You can't let people nap at work!"

"Naps are good for health," Henry said. "Microsoft cares about its employees."

They headed toward the cafeteria, where there was a reggae/ska band playing cover songs. The music was so loud and stimulating that Joan felt as if she might faint or vomit. She reached into her purse to comfort Skipper, as well as check for the presence of her prescription bottle.

"A live band? Oh, come on, that is crazy," Joan's dad said.

"Yeah, it's pretty nice here," Henry said.

"Don't they care about people working?"

"People do a lot of work here."

"With reggae music playing?" Randy got up and stood closer to the band and inspected all the equipment, scowling.

At lunch, Joan barely picked at her food while her mother peppered Henry with questions about his internship. He answered them in a chipper and upbeat manner. He seemed to love everything about his life, Joan thought, perplexed. He'd always been like that. Hopeful and optimistic, driven and organized and consistent. Joan, an unremarkable child, had grown up in Henry's shadow. While he'd written his own math formulas, been first chair in the orchestra, become fluent in Chinese, and taken practice standardized tests for fun, Joan made B's and C's and spent most of her spare time sitting on the couch, watching *Saved by the Bell* or *Boy Meets World* while eating Cheetos.

When the conversation turned to Joan and what she would be doing with her life now that she had graduated and her internship had ended, she panicked.

"Uh, I don't know," she said. "I submitted a story to *The Paris Review*. And I'm working on a novel. I wrote fifty single-spaced pages last night."

"When will you hear back?" Dolly asked, trying to be supportive. "About the story?"

"I don't know. A few months."

"Don't you need some kind of backup plan?" Henry asked. "Something to pay the bills while you write?"

"I can't think of what else I could do," Joan said. "I'm not qualified for anything."

"Of course you are," Henry said. "A lot of companies need people with strong writing skills."

"Not the kind of writing I do," she said. As much as she hated disappointing Henry, she knew that no company in its right mind would find her to be an asset. Henry was just deluding himself, as usual. It was his way of coping.

"Joan, quit thinking about that kind of stuff," her dad said. "Who cares?"

"This is a normal thing for someone her age to think about," Dolly said.

"I don't want to do anything corporate," Joan said. "Maybe I could work at a grocery store." She was feeling so uncomfortable that she would have cried if she weren't so hyped up on Adderall. They were here to visit Henry; why was everyone talking about her?

"I could help you write a résumé," Henry said. "You worked at the capitol, right? That's a nice bullet point."

"Yeah, and I was the best intern," Joan said. "They gave me a plaque that says so." She didn't mention that there had been only three other interns to choose from, and the competition wasn't stiff. One intern had simply quit showing up after a few weeks. Another showed up but was consistently high on synthetic marijuana. Even so, Joan had hung the plaque on the wall by her desk and stared at it often. It made her feel good. She'd never been the best at anything.

"Nice," Henry said, nodding. "Include that. Even better if you can give a numerical value, though. Like, 'increased office productivity by X percent.'"

"What?" said Joan. "How would I ever know that?"

"You can come work for me," her dad said, perking up. "My Austin campus needs a spy."

"A spy for what?"

"To find out why Craig isn't getting more programs going. I want to start a video program and an app program."

"Okay, I'll consider that option," Joan said. She had worked for her dad on and off over the years and hated the idea of going back. But she had to appear open-minded and willing, with her whole family jumping down her throat.

"Well, that was easy," Henry said. "I guess you'll never have to enter the real workforce."

"What are you saying, my company isn't real?" Randy said, raising his voice. "AudioPro is more real than any school you've gone to. It teaches real skills for the real world. None of that liberal brainwashing bullshit."

"Randy, don't be so sensitive. That's not what he meant," Dolly said.

"What did he mean, then?"

Henry shrugged and smugly took a bite of his sandwich. Henry had worked for AudioPro too, after graduating from Duke, before going to Booth. During that brief time, Randy and Henry fought constantly. Joan's dad had been convinced, despite Henry's genius-level standardized test scores, that he possessed no "common sense." Common sense, her dad thought, ever since becoming an avid Glenn Beck fan, was more important than anything else. For that reason, he believed Joan was the smarter of the two siblings, and he didn't hide his feelings about this.

After lunch, they walked from the cafeteria toward the wing where Henry worked. Outside, employees were playing soccer on a sprawling green field.

"Oh, come on. You can't tell me those people are working," said Randy.

"Microsoft likes to keep their employees happy," Henry said. "They have to compete for top talent in the tech world."

"I have to compete for employees too!"

"Yeah? How is it working for you?" Henry said.

"It's working fine," Randy growled. "Enrollment's up and we're expanding. I just opened a new campus."

"It's true," Joan said. "I just saw it, it's really nice."

From the Microsoft campus, they drove to Henry's spotless high-rise apartment, where he'd set up the guest bedroom for Dolly. She went straight to the room and began unpacking carefully, placing her clothes into the empty dresser, arranging her jewelry and makeup in the bathroom. Nesting. Joan's dad began inspecting the kitchen. Joan searched the fridge for something to drink. Her tongue was so dry it kept sticking to her lips and the roof of her mouth.

"What the fuck! Look how clean this place is!" Randy was opening and closing every drawer and kitchen cabinet. "Look how organized the pantry is! Oh my god, do you alphabetize your cereal?! What is wrong with you?"

Joan went over to inspect the pantry. Her dad was right. Every box was perfectly lined up and straight; every can seemed arranged as if in a store for sale, in sensible categories, meticulously placed for maximum visibility.

"It saves time," Henry said.

"How could that possibly save time?"

Henry shrugged. "It makes me more efficient."

Her dad shook his head in awe.

"Randy, stop being so judgmental," Joan's mother said. "You've been complaining all day and I'm sick of it. Not everybody has to be a slob like you."

Joan's dad disregarded the comment and disappeared into her brother's bedroom.

"Oh my god," Randy exclaimed. "Look at his closet! The shirts are color coded!"

Joan followed her dad into Henry's bedroom, where she was immediately drawn to her brother's desk. This was the center of his life. While Joan's desk was just another surface to throw her things on, Henry had always used his desk. He sat there every night, working, reading, expanding his mind, and developing character. It was as if his brain were infused with Adderall organically. It wasn't fair.

"What is this?" Joan motioned toward a whiteboard hanging on the wall. It was separated into hand-drawn boxes, outlining yearly, monthly, weekly, and daily goals. One of his daily goals was to read an article in the *Economist*. Weekly, he was supposed to have read an entire book.

"That's my goal board."

"No, but I mean what is this?" She pointed directly at a line under the daily goals category, which read: *SHELF PANDAS*.

"Oh, SHELF PANDAS? That's just a little acronym I came up with to make sure I'm always mindful of health."

"What does it stand for?"

"'Sleep, H$_2$0, exercise, leafy greens, fats, protein, and no drugs, alcohol, or sugar.'"

"You have to remind yourself to sleep?" their dad said, emerging from the closet. "Really?"

"Randy, that's enough," said their mother. "Let's get out of here."

When everyone had cleared out of the bedroom, Joan went to the bathroom and splashed her face with water. She looked at herself in the mirror. Her dark circles were pronounced and purple. Her skin was pale and translucent as paper. She was so tired. Her neck was hot and burning up, and when she lifted her shirt, she saw that her midsection was beginning to break out in hideous, bulbous stress hives. What if they spread? Then her parents might catch on that something was wrong. She dug through Henry's medicine cabinet, looking for Benadryl, and swallowed one. She took one more Adderall out of her purse to counter the Benadryl. She needed it to hit quickly, though. She carefully untwisted the capsule and sprinkled some of the beads onto Henry's bathroom counter. Using the end of Henry's toothbrush, she began crushing the beads into a fine powder, then snorted some off her finger.

"What are you doing?" Henry said from the doorway.

Joan froze. Her heart stopped.

"What are you taking?" he asked. "Mom and Dad are waiting downstairs."

"Nothing," she said, wiping away the dust and discarding the opened capsule. But the prescription bottle was still sitting on the counter.

Henry picked up the bottle and read the label. "This shit again? Seriously?"

"I need it," she said, sounding more desperate than she'd intended. She was worried he might flush the remainder down the toilet. "Or else I can't do anything."

"I don't understand why you think you need to *take* something to *do* something," he said gently, and to her surprise handed her the bottle, which she slipped into her purse, relieved.

"I don't know why," she said, and she didn't. She hated disappointing her brother. Since she had no constant father figure at home,

Henry had filled the void. He had been the most stable man in her life. He'd left for college right after Dolly's divorce from Doug, and Joan had never forgiven him for abandoning her there, in that hell-hole.

"Please don't tell them," Joan said. "If our parents find out, things could get really bad for me."

Henry stayed silent. Joan became frantic.

"Don't blame me. It's genetic. I got it from Mom. Did you know she was a speed head? Dad told me everything on the way here."

"That was a long time ago," Henry said. "She's clean now."

"Sure, it was a long time ago. But not that long. Did you know she used all through her pregnancy with you?"

"What?"

"Don't tell her I told you."

"What was she using when she was pregnant?"

"Everything. Drugs, alcohol, probably cigarettes too."

"Come on, we need to go."

Henry drove the family to see where Bill Gates lived, and they looked at the lush, tree-filled estate while Randy went on a long, heated diatribe about how Gates had allegedly stolen all his ideas from Apple. Henry then drove the four of them downtown, where they walked the streets of Seattle. The sky was deep gray and overcast.

"God, this place is depressing," said Randy.

Henry gave a statistic on how many days a year it rained in Seattle.

"No wonder Microsoft has to have live music and free drinks," said her dad. "Not to keep people working there, but to keep them from killing themselves."

They went to a marketplace and watched men throw fish at each other over rows and rows of giant crabs on ice. Henry then took them to the very first Starbucks ever, where a crowd was gathered around a group of Black men clapping and singing a cappella. It started raining, so they went back to the car. As soon as they started driving, Joan's mother asked Henry to stop at a gas station.

"No," he said. "I'm not helping you kill yourself."

"Stop the car. I'm serious."

"No way."

"You need to respect me. I'm your mother."

"Why? You didn't respect me enough to tell me I was a crack baby."

"Oh god," Joan said.

"What?" Dolly looked at their dad in horror. "I don't know what he's been telling you, but you are not a crack baby."

"Yes, I am," Henry said.

"She wasn't on crack," Randy said. "It was just regular cocaine."

"Oh, so that's better?" Henry said.

"A little," Randy said.

"That's racist, Dad," Joan said. When she was liberal in Miami, she'd learned all about the so-called War on Drugs.

"Times were different back then!" Dolly said. "People weren't so uptight about pregnancy like they are now. You turned out completely healthy!"

"Yeah, well, who really knows? Maybe I could have been taller."

Joan held her breath. Henry was being so bold and loose-lipped, she figured he was about to rat her out.

"Please stop at a gas station right now," Dolly said.

Henry still refused, and at the next stoplight, their mom opened the door of the car, got out, and scampered across the street to a Chevron. When the light turned green, Henry drove away.

"I'm not going back for her," he said. "She needs to learn a lesson."

"She's going to get so mad," said Joan, feeling a little guilty.

"Do you ever think she's subconsciously trying to kill herself by smoking? So that she never becomes a burden on us, like Grandmother is on her?"

"Wouldn't it be a burden on us if she got lung cancer?" Joan asked.

"No, I'm pretty sure lung cancer patients die pretty quickly."

"Oh, come on, you've gotta go get her," said Randy.

When they returned to the gas station, Dolly was standing outside against the wall, visibly upset. Upon entering the car, she said nothing and looked at nobody. She just stared out the window until they arrived at a highly rated seafood restaurant.

Once they were seated in the crowded café, Joan tried to lighten the atmosphere by showing everyone a video she'd taken of Wyatt playing at Rick's piano bar.

Dolly watched the video with curiosity but said nothing.

"Wow," Randy said. "He's really doing it. He's playing a whole song, beginning, middle, and end."

"That's actually pretty amazing," Henry said, a hint of bitterness in his voice. "I never thought he'd get his act together."

Henry had given up on Wyatt years ago. They'd once been as close as brothers. When Wyatt was failing in high school, Henry had attempted to tutor him, to no avail. He'd tried to explain the concept of credit, which Wyatt couldn't grasp. In Durham, Henry had helped Wyatt form a band, finding players, arranging rehearsals and gigs. But Wyatt could never harness his energy. Any time something started to feel like work, he shut down. It had all been massively frustrating for Henry, and he had seemed to take Wyatt's suicide attempt as a personal affront, the last straw.

After Joan put her phone away, Dolly spoke, slowly and carefully, as if she had been crafting the speech in her mind while waiting at the Chevron.

"Listen," she said, deadly serious. "My new therapist said that I need to learn to set boundaries, so I'm going to set a boundary right now. No more picking on me."

"We're not picking on you," Henry said. "We love you and we don't want you to die."

"That's not how that works," said Randy. He set down his phone on the table.

"Randy," she hissed. "I said to stop picking on me. I don't deserve it and I'm not going to take it anymore."

"But that's not how a boundary works."

"End. Of. Discussion."

"You've got it all wrong," he said, raising his voice. "You can't *do* that."

"Boundary, Randy." Her voice was low, almost a whisper, and shaking.

"No! That's not a boundary! A boundary is something you're supposed to set for yourself, not other people." He was shouting now, and Joan and her brother shared looks of torment as the people around them began to stare.

"Can y'all please keep it down?" Henry said.

"Are you finished?" Joan's mom asked her dad. "Is everyone finished using me as their piñata?" She went silent, her eyes wet.

"Mom," Joan said. "Don't get so touchy about everything."

Dolly shook her head and continued to stare beyond them into the kitchen.

"Boundary," she said finally. She held up her hand, as if to protect herself from the three of them. "I've had it with this. I can't take it anymore. I'm going outside."

"You just want a cigarette," said Henry. "Don't pretend it's anything more than that."

"Leave me alone, Henry," she said. "Every time we're all together you three gang up on me, and I'm sick of it. I'm not going to be the punching bag, not anymore."

"If you keep smoking, you'll get lung cancer and die. How do you not get that? How am I the bad guy in this situation?"

"Please." She put her hand up again. "Respect my boundaries."

"You can't do that!" Randy shouted. "You can't use your boundaries to change other people's behavior! It's about changing *your* behavior!"

"I'm so tired of this." Dolly stood up and walked quickly out the front door. The three of them watched her as she walked by the window, around the side of the restaurant, out of view.

"Every single time the four of us hang out this happens," Henry said.

"She's got it all wrong, she's still trying to change people," Randy said, shaking his head. "Hey, I think I can feel the moss growing. What about you, Joan?"

"Yeah, moss is definitely growing." Her teeth were clenched and she was jotting down notes on a napkin about the trip. She was un-sure what any of it meant, or if it was a good story. But it was comfort-ing for her to record the details; it felt like an escape.

The food came, Joan's mother came back to the table, and they ate as if nothing were wrong. Joan moved food around on her plate in-stead of eating.

"Has anybody checked in on Facebook yet?" Joan's dad said. "I'm gonna check in. What's this place called? I'll tag everyone."

22.

PLENTY OF TIME

On Sunday, Henry took them all to the Space Needle before saying goodbye. Joan and her dad dropped Dolly off at the airport before leaving Seattle. Randy decided they would stop at Yellowstone National Park on the way back to Texas. Joan swallowed her last three pills at once, a bittersweet moment. She wouldn't be able to fill her next prescription for two weeks. Still, she was relieved to at least be getting high for now, to be free of Dolly's watchful eye, and to be on the second leg of the journey. "Family time" was always so exhausting.

"What the hell is wrong with Henry?" Randy said. "Did you see his apartment? He can't be my blood."

"I don't know," Joan said.

"Dolly must've slept with someone else. He's one hundred percent Dolly."

"Well, he has to be part *somebody* else," Joan said.

Randy was chewing gum while he drove and suddenly put his hand up to his cheek.

"One of my teeth just fell out!" He'd just gotten cosmetic veneers; his real teeth had been sawed down to nubs and the new ones glued on. They were as white and shiny as a movie star's. "Shit! Go look in the back for something to put it in."

Joan unbuckled and dug through the kitchen drawer until she found a plastic bag, which he dropped the tooth into.

"Is this what it's going to be like from now on? Are my teeth just going to keep falling out?"

At Yellowstone, it took them a few hours to find an open campsite. When Randy parked the RV, he went outside and built a fire in a small pit, and they sat in the lawn chairs on the strip of Astroturf staring at the flame as it crackled and moved in the breeze. Joan, coming down, hated herself for wasting all of her Adderall already. She was starting to feel dirty and hadn't washed her clothes. She despised showering in the RV. The water smelled and seemed to leave a residue on her hair.

"This place sucks," her dad said. "All I wanted was to find a campsite on a river. Somewhere I could fish, have a fire, DirecTV, Wi-Fi, water, electricity, sewage, a bunch of tall trees, no bugs, and a picnic table. Is that too much to ask?"

Yellowstone seemed to be infested with giant horseflies, which she kept swatting. Skipper sat on her lap and whined.

"I remember I found a campsite like that one time in Big Bear when I was with Sandra," her dad continued. "It was the best RV park in the world. Like heaven. That's when we found out she was pregnant. It was the day after we got married. She was sick to her stomach, and we went to the doctor and he said congratulations."

"Sandra was pregnant? What a nightmare."

"She decided to have an abortion. I was kinda like, 'Yeah, that's probably smart, we're too old,' so I took her down to the abortion clinic and there was a lady out there showing us pictures of fetuses, protesting. I went in there and there were a bunch of hoodlum guys hanging around and they all knew each other, they were talking to each other as if they were in there every other day. I said, 'This is wrong. Fuck it, we're having a baby.' She was already in her appointment, but I got her outta there. Fifty-five freakin' years old and I was just gonna have a baby. Then a few days later she was bleeding and

164

stuff, little clumps were coming out. The doctor told her to put the clumps in a baggie and bring it into the office. She'd had a miscarriage. She was so mad 'cause I wouldn't go with her. Later she used it against me, saying I made her put our baby in a plastic baggie and take it to the doctor and didn't go with her. . . . Just think if we'd had it. It would be two or three now, probably retarded, sitting over there in a car seat. We'd have to buy diapers every time we stopped for gas. She'd have probably left by now, left me to take care of the retard baby."

The smoke from the fire was blowing into his face and he kept getting up and moving his lawn chair.

"Everywhere I move it follows me!" he said.

The next morning, they went to a small diner in West Yellowstone and sat at a table with a red-and-white-checkered tablecloth. Joan traced the little squares with the tips of her fingers. The smell of grease and eggs turned her stomach.

"So," her dad said. "Have you thought about the job?"

"What job?"

"Working for me. As a spy at my school."

"Oh, yeah," Joan said. "I think I could do that." She hesitated, thinking of her forced year off college, when she'd shown up to the Dallas campus in a blackout and cussed out all her dad's night employees. They'd been forced to lock Joan in the microphone closet until Wyatt came and picked her up. Nobody ever told Randy about the incident, but she was pretty sure the vice president knew. If she worked for her dad again, she was putting herself at risk. Randy would have a larger window into her life and might discover her drug use.

"Would you keep paying my allowance?" Joan asked, hopeful.

"I guess so."

Joan, feeling like she had the upper hand, continued to negotiate her salary. "Could you pay all of my rent instead of half? So I don't need to get money from Mom anymore?"

"Why?"

"That way, she wouldn't have any power over my life," Joan said.

"We'll see," Randy said.

"Okay, then."

"You know, someday, I'm going to die, and you'll have to take over. You're a part owner, you know."

"I know," Joan said. Over the previous Christmas break, she had sat at a conference table with her dad, her grandfather, and Henry, where she had signed dozens of documents as lawyers had explained her new status. She didn't understand the purpose of the arrangement, and neither did Henry.

"Will we inherit your debt too?" Henry had asked. "What happens if you go bankrupt?"

Joan, unconcerned with these types of questions, had felt a new sense of importance and responsibility in the world, as a business owner.

"What's the matter with you, why are you so quiet?" Randy said. Joan stiffened.

"I don't know," she said. "I'm just thinking."

"Are you depressed?"

"Yeah."

"Why? What happened? Some guy dump you or something?"

"Yeah," Joan admitted, relieved. "Two guys, actually."

Randy sighed. "Look, I know all about that. I'm an expert. I've been through it a thousand times, and I've learned that the only way to get over somebody is to get under somebody else."

"Thanks a lot."

"It's true."

"I know."

"Whoever it is . . . whoever *they* are. They're not the right person, not the right people. That's the only answer. And maybe there is no right person. You have to accept that. You've just gotta cruise along and be free. You can't make anything happen. That's what I always tried to do. Force things. It doesn't work, just makes it all worse."

When the waitress brought their plates, Joan began shoveling food into her mouth. Without the pills, her appetite had returned.

From the diner they drove through the park, spotting elk, buffalo, a grizzly bear, a bald eagle. Skipper stood in her lap and barked at all of the animals wildly. That afternoon, they sat on a bench with a view of Old Faithful, surrounded by a crowd of tourists. Joan slumped on the bench typing long messages to Roberto and deleting them.

"All right, that's enough," Randy said gruffly, lightly elbowing her. "Quit being depressed. What about me? What if you were fifty-seven and didn't have a boyfriend?"

"I guess I'd be even more depressed then," Joan said.

"Exactly! Think of how I feel! At least you have your youth. That's more than I can say. How old are you again?"

"Twenty-four."

"Twenty-four, let's see . . . You've got twenty—no, thirty . . . how many years until you're forty-five?"

"Twenty-one."

"Twenty-one. You've still got twenty-one years until you start looking old. After forty-five, it's over for women."

"Well, at least I've got some time, then," Joan said.

"Plenty of time."

They sat in silence, waiting for the geyser to erupt so that they could acknowledge its beauty and move on to something else.

23.

FATE STEPS IN

After Joan got home from the road trip, she reinstated a new, more lenient set of rules in which she was allowed to take up to three pills per day, but only if she was writing her novel. In her downtime, she focused on her new job, working for her dad's Austin campus as a spy. What this meant was that she showed up two or three times a week and walked around, talking to students and employees. The campus was in a touristy area off South Congress, in a recording studio her dad rented from Willie Nelson's cokehead cousin. Each week, Joan would call her dad with observations.

"The building is too small for the number of students. There are no hallways. It's awkward how everyone has to walk through everyone's classes or sessions to get to the next room."

"Find more space to rent, then," her dad said, so she began looking around.

"The library is sad and outdated," Joan said. "It's more like a storage closet. There are hardly any books."

"Then fix it," he said, and Joan spent thousands of dollars on IKEA desks and shelves and new Apple computers. She filled the shelves with new hardcover books and created a magazine archive and even bought a little globe for some added charm.

"Everyone hates the director," Joan told him. "They say he's a micromanager."

"Normal. Everyone hates the boss. If they liked him, that would worry me more."

Soon, when people began asking what exactly Joan was doing at the school, her title was changed to marketing director. Tanya shipped her a large box of business cards and assigned her a company email. Not knowing what to do in her new role, Joan placed AudioPro magnets on her BMW and drove aimlessly around the city. She attended concerts and visited recording studios wearing AudioPro T-shirts. She put AudioPro stickers inside bathroom stalls at bars and coffee shops. Beyond this, she had no idea what marketing even was.

The job was only a paycheck, she reminded herself often. Her main focus was still her writing career—her road novel, her coming-of-age novel, her story collection. Working for her dad didn't have to mean that she was giving up on art. A lot of successful writers had day jobs. If Roberto could finish his novel working as a barista, then Joan could finish her novel while being a marketing director at AudioPro. As long as she remained disciplined and celibate.

Most days, Joan would sit in the lobby of the school, tweaking and working on her road novel. She got skinny again, attractive in the way she had been in Miami, with a visible jawline and thin, waifish arms that photographed well from every angle. Things were looking up for her.

Paul had been encouraging about her "Womb on Wheels" draft, though in a somewhat backhanded way. He'd said in his email that there was something pure and beautiful and true about bad writing, and that she should keep following this work until it took shape. Carlos, on the other hand, still hadn't replied.

Paul's feedback wasn't what she wanted to hear, exactly, but she took his advice. She now had over one hundred pages of childhood memories and observations about her homelife, about all her parents' marriages and all the stepparents and siblings who had come in and out of her life, as if through a revolving door, and were, according to her therapist, a large part of her problem with commitment. She typed her memories robotically, without stopping to understand the meaning or emotional significance of any scene. Instead, Joan focused on sights, smells, colors, words. Her narrator was not more than a lens, recording. She didn't want to feel. She just wanted to fill pages. Joan planned to have a long, weighty book that angsty boys like Roberto would like to read and could be used as a doorstop, like *Infinite Jest* or *My Struggle*.

Still, despite her productivity, in the evenings, during her comedowns, her thoughts regularly drifted toward Roberto and how much she hated him. They hadn't spoken since the terrible email exchange in Seattle, but sometimes she would reread the note he'd left on her doorstep, which began to feel more like a challenge, or an invitation, than anything else. Joan was desperate to know what kind of progress he was making on his book, so she could compare it to her own. She also wanted to rub her own progress in his face. "Fate" was taking a long time to intervene and bring them together. One day, after work, Joan couldn't take it anymore. She decided to take fate into her own hands.

She went to the coffee shop with her laptop. She wore a floral halter dress with no bra that she thought made her look feminine and tragic. She adhered Icy Hot patches to her arms and neck, which had started hurting from all the time she'd spent in the RV, typing on her laptop with all muscles clenched.

"What's up, lady? It's good to see you," Roberto said casually when she sat down at the bar.

"Oh, hey." He seemed completely unaffected, so she feigned the same.

"Why do you have tape on your arms?"

"It's Icy Hot. I hurt myself from working on my book so hard," Joan said before ordering the most tedious drink to make on the menu—a chai latte frappé.

"How is celibacy going? Are you still writing a scene a day?" she asked while he gathered the ingredients.

"Yes. It's going very well," he said, and laughed. "Sometimes I even write more than one."

"Do you think you're close to finishing *Bitter Texas Honey*?"

"What?"

"*Bitter Texas Honey*? The novella you were writing in the spring, about that young couple. It opened with the girl having her period."

"Oh, yes, of course. I actually set that one aside."

"Why?"

Roberto shrugged. "It no longer felt true to me. I'm working on something much better now."

"Really?" Joan said. Her chest felt tight.

"A new voice came to me. About a week after our breakup. She's so vivid, I just can't ignore her," Roberto explained.

"Who is she?" Joan asked, feeling threatened by the imaginary voice.

"She's this really old woman in Mexico, and she's talking to me in Spanish. She's telling me stories, about the cartels and shit. It's crazy."

He shook his head and looked toward the window, in awe of his own muse and artistic process. Joan was irritated and jealous. She had always wanted to be one of those writers "haunted" by voices that simply "came to them," and "followed them around," and "told them what to write." Voices never came to Joan. For her, writing fiction was more like pulling out her own guts and smearing them around on the page, it was so unpleasant.

"You always said you didn't want to write in Spanish," Joan said, almost crying. "That's what you told me."

"I know. I did say that. It's funny how things can change."

"Yes, so funny." Joan began to pack her things. She had to get out of there before she broke down.

"What about you, lady? You working on anything?"

"Yes, actually," Joan said. "I'm working on something very lyrical and deep about my family. It's going to be long. I'll be using an excerpt from it to apply to MFAs."

"Sounds good."

"Carlos is helping me with it all," Joan lied.

"As long as it's not about a road trip," Roberto said, and laughed.

"What do you mean?" Joan was shocked. Had he been stalking her? Had he installed spyware on her computer?

"Isn't that the old joke about MFAs? That it's just a bunch of rich white people writing about road trips?"

"I have to go," Joan said, her face hot.

"Good luck with the applications."

"Thanks. Good luck with your old-lady book."

Joan got off the barstool and moved toward the door. His polite demeanor made her incredibly angry, and she felt like she would explode if she didn't say something more. She needed to hurt his feelings, the way he was always hurting hers.

"You know," she said, her hand on the door, "you are starting to sound very arrogant when you talk about your writing. Maybe you should try to be humble, for once." Saying this to Roberto felt good. Like she was finally being honest and winning the conversation.

But Roberto only looked at Joan flatly through his thick lenses, a serious expression on his face.

"Can I explain something to you, lady? If you really want to be a writer, you need to know this."

"What?"

"You've gotta be arrogant. Or else it's over."

24.

A GOOD, SOLID TITLE

Joan cried in her BMW on the way home, unable to handle all the feelings she was having. That Roberto had abandoned their love story so soon, that it no longer felt true to him, stung to her core. And worse, he said a road trip novel was some kind of cliché. She had no idea it was a trope. Her whole project felt pointless. Her whole life, in fact. Once home, she stood at the window in a daze, her eyes swollen, watching a concert at Stubb's.

"I'm so glad I'm here and not there," Joan said to Claire, who poured herself a glass of cheap chardonnay before joining Joan at the window.

"Me too. The line to the bar looks a fucking mile long. Are you okay?"

Joan shrugged. "I will be." She pulled a pair of sunglasses over her eyes. She picked up her pipe—small with pink swirls—and started packing it densely with her almost-empty baggie of weed. Joan needed to wind down. Her Adderall prescription had her running on empty, not hungry but starving at the same time. Not sleepy but exhausted. Perhaps she would flush the rest of the pills later, to give herself a break.

She sent a text message to her dealer, Thad. Joan knew she shouldn't buy drugs from AudioPro students, especially now that she worked there, but Thad had become her favorite drug dealer of all time. He delivered on demand, so there was no risk of going to jail for her and no risk of having to wait days for her fix. He was also willing to do odd jobs around her apartment—like hanging artwork and cleaning the bathrooms—for a reasonable hourly rate. Joan respected Thad's work ethic and felt he would make it far in life. He was so industrious. The American Dream was well within his grasp. Thad said he could be over by midnight.

Claire did a ballerina move across the laminate floor into the kitchen, where she refilled her glass. She sat down across from Joan and complained about a tall German girl who went to all of Luke's shows. Joan picked up a notebook and pencil and began drawing Claire, curled up on the love seat with her wine. She used a light touch and swirls to first capture her shape—the angles of her limbs, the relative sizes of her head and torso.

"There's no way she likes his music that much," Claire was saying. "There's just no way. There has to be something else." Claire took a long sip of wine and looked at Joan, her big brown eyes lined heavily with jet-black eyeliner and glitter. "Right?"

"I don't know," Joan said, splitting Claire's head into four quadrants, using small lines to mark where her eyes, nose, and mouth would go. "Maybe she does."

Joan had majored in figure drawing at UM. Before she ever wanted to be a writer, before she had ever met Paul and changed her major to English, she wanted to become a courtroom sketch artist. She simply wanted to take what she saw in front of her and re-create it, no emotion, no exploration of her "inner life" necessary. Maybe this had been her real purpose. Maybe writing had derailed her from her true calling.

"And she never even talks to me. I've seen her a million fucking times and she never says a goddamn word to me."

"Have you tried talking to her?" Joan asked. She used long, elegant strokes to depict Claire's hair, which went down to her rib cage.

"No," Claire scoffed. "What could she and I possibly have to talk about?"

"What about Kafka?"

"Please. Like she has anything interesting to say about Franz Kafka."

"Maybe she does. She is German."

"So? That doesn't mean she knows anything about anything."

There was a loud knock on the front door before it swung open. Claire's friend from the English honors program, Bianca, a Chaucerian, walked in carrying a large leather bag covered in gold spikes, which made a loud clanking noise when she tossed it on the kitchen counter.

"'Sup, sluts?" Bianca said. "Who's ready for some Loko?" She pulled two large purple cans of Four Loko from her bag.

"I thought they made that stuff illegal," Joan said.

"They did, but I saved some for tonight, baby. It's Loko Night." She cracked open one of the cans and held it in the air. "Woo!"

Claire held out her empty glass and Bianca filled it with the purple fizzy liquid. "Want some, Joanie?"

"No, thanks."

"What's wrong?"

"Nothing. I just have a lot of work to do."

"Oh yeah. How is your writing going?"

"It's good. I'm still waiting to hear back from *The Paris Review*."

"Where should we go tonight?" Claire said.

"We could go to Barbarella," Bianca said. "It's eighties dance night. And the bartender is in love with me."

"Is he the one who kept making us those shots last time?" Claire asked. "Those pink ones with the cranberry? What were those called again?"

"Bloody abortions?"

"Yes!" Claire cackled. "Those were so good."

"I fucking love bloody abortions," Bianca said, and Joan grimaced. Were they trying to annoy her? How could people be so cavalier about the sacred miracle of human life? Her entire generation was cursed. "Are you coming out, Joanie?" she asked.

"I'm too old to go to Sixth Street."

"You are not old."

"I am too," she said. She was two years older than Claire and Bianca.

"Fine. Text me if you change your mind," Claire said. She emptied the remainder of the Four Loko into a flask, then wobbled out of the apartment in stilettos with Bianca, their arms linked.

"I will," Joan said. But she knew she wasn't going to change her mind. What was the point of going out? Until she finished her novel, she was as good as worthless.

Thad showed up at midnight, as promised. With her weed now abundant, Joan stayed up, smoking bowl after bowl. She began to feel slightly more at ease, high, imagining what her book launch would be like when her novel was finally published. She imagined Roberto and Vince sitting sheepishly in the audience while she answered questions about her artistic process, about how she balanced being a genius with her family life, which would be flourishing by then. Both men would then wait an hour in line for her to sign their copies. *What was your name again?* she would say to each of them. *How is it spelled?*

Her phone rang, disrupting her daze. It was Wyatt.

"Hey. Remember that story you emailed me? About that asshole guy?" He sounded breathless, urgent, like a detective who'd figured out something important.

"'Conquistador,'" Joan said.

"Yeah. I wasn't sure how to pronounce it."

"Of course I remember it. I wrote it."

"Well, I made it into a song. Do you want to hear it?"

"Okay."

He set the phone down and put it on speaker. She heard him play a few notes on the Casio. "Can you hear me?" he said.

"Loud and clear." Joan closed her eyes. She heard his fingers spread wide across the keys, hitting a broad range of notes that seemed random and scattered, then became an orderly cacophony, which eventually condensed into a sweet melody—obvious in its simplicity, yet unique in its sound. It was like it had been written a hundred years before, in the cosmos, but no human had the courage or will to muster it up, until now. It was magnificent.

Wyatt began to sing:

Yellow rose of Texas
Pure, like bleach
A spaceship, on the street

On the pole, the dancer slides
She moves toward you, on the stage
A spider, toward its prey

A conquistador
Took you to a body bar
A gap-toothed dancer
Took you by the heart

You knew not to fall from the start
But you fell anyway, and say
Greater sacrifices have been made for art
Greater sacrifices have been made for art
Greater sacrifices have been made for art

After he finished playing, Joan sat impressed. Wyatt's voice had matured since she last saw him. Perhaps from all the practice at the piano bar. It seemed to come from a place of depth and vision. Sure, the lyrics were silly. But the song was catchy. She wanted to hear it again and again. She wanted to twirl around while it blared through her speakers. Wyatt was a genius.

Best of all, the song was about *her*. About her pain. Her love. She had inspired it. Finally, after all this time and patience, a song existed in the world that was dedicated to *her*.

"When did you write that?" she asked.

"Oh, I just made it up."

"On the spot?"

"Sort of. I kind of thought of it when I read your story. And then forgot about it. But I just remembered it again before I called."

"You can just come up with songs like that?"

"I guess so."

Her mind played tapes of crowded concerts of screaming fans. She and Wyatt could be like Elton John and that other guy, his lyricist, whatever his name was. A team. An artistic force. They could tour the world together. Joan would stand backstage proudly, while Wyatt would share her words with the masses. Roberto would be so jealous. His old-lady story would never have that level of reach.

"I love it," Joan said. "We have to get it recorded as soon as possible."

"Yeah, that's what I was thinking. Maybe you could talk to your dad?"

"Yeah, for sure. I have some sway. I'm the marketing director now."

"Wow," Wyatt said.

"I know," she said.

"Hey," he said. "There's something else I wanted to talk to you about."

"What is it?"

"I don't think it's been good for me, living here with Chet."

"Really? I'm so glad you are saying that. I don't think it's a good thing either."

Her heart raced; she was feeling manic, ready to solve all of Wyatt's problems.

"I was doing some research," he said, "and it turns out that there's a dueling piano bar in Austin too."

"There is! It's on Sixth Street. I walk by it all the time."

"If I could transfer to that location in the next few months, maybe I could stay with you?"

"Of course you can. That would be great. My roommate is moving in with her boyfriend in September. The timing is perfect."

"Thank you," Wyatt said. "I need your wisdom in my life."

"And we could keep writing songs together," she said. "I have a ton of scenes that I could show you. I have hundreds of pages about my childhood. Maybe you would get inspired again."

"Yeah," he said. He was just rolling along with her. She felt like she had everything under control. Things were going to be so much better soon.

"You know, I was having the worst day. But now everything just makes so much sense," she said. "I think I can feel God's presence in my heart. The way you do at the tent revivals."

"Ah, yes. Enjoy that feeling," he said, sounding a little sad. "It comes and goes."

Joan felt giddy at the prospect of having Wyatt as a roommate. It would be like old times. He would perk back up, and so would she. She would have a constant source of energy and inspiration with him living in her apartment. He saw the world differently than other people. He could make a trip to the grocery store interesting and significant. He made her feel alive. She would never feel alone anymore.

She looked out the window and watched a homeless man digging through the dumpster by Mohawk, collecting cans in a trash bag. If Wyatt were here, he would probably go out and jump in the dumpster with him to help. He was so beautiful and pure. The music from Stubb's had subsided; all she could hear was drunken voices shouting, sirens, laughter. Club de Ville's crown-shaped sign was on. She watched the red and white lights blinking on and off, from the bottom of the yellow crown to the top, creating an illusion of upward motion, over and over again.

"I feel like that sign is going to be a symbol in your book," Henry had said when he helped Joan move into her apartment. "Definitely," Joan had said, sensing that it was a good idea. But she still had never written about the sign or her apartment, nor did she understand what the sign could be a symbol of, if anything. Excess? Alcoholism? The American Dream? Perhaps she and Wyatt could write a song about it when he got here. Perhaps it would be the cover of their EP.

She wrote Wyatt a text message.

I just thought of a possible title for our first EP. Bitter Texas Honey. What do u think?

It's perfect, Wyatt replied. *Like, it doesn't really make any sense. But at the same time, I can FEEL it, you know?*

Exactly, Joan wrote. *I agree 100%.*

She didn't want Roberto's title to go to waste. It had been such a good, solid title. Now it would be infused with a new life.

25.

NAKED MAN, BILLBOARD, FORT WORTH

n late September, Joan went to Dallas for Wyatt's birthday. She wanted to surprise him at the piano bar that night. Hopefully, after his set they could talk about his moving to Austin and finally recording their song. Wyatt had become distant since their call about recording an EP, and he'd been unreachable for days. Joan worried that maybe he had changed his mind about it all. Now, when she called, it went straight to his voicemail.

"It's my half birthday today," Joan said into his voicemail. "A victory would be nice."

She lay on her dad's living room floor with a notebook, hoping to write some lyrics before heading to Fort Worth. She wanted to have something new to inspire Wyatt. The house was empty and quiet. Her dad was in Virginia in his RV, attending some kind of work conference. Joan swallowed a cocktail of pills and stared at the blank page.

She was on several medications now. Her thirty-milligram time-release Adderall prescription had led to another, second prescription of ten-milligram instant release, to alleviate her midday crashes. With so much Adderall, however, her life had quickly tipped out of balance. Joan had typed so much in the past few months, with such bad posture, that she'd pinched her brachial nerve with tight neck and pectoral muscles. Now Joan had a pain management doctor and prescriptions for muscle relaxants, nerve relaxants, and opioids, to counter the activating forces of all the Adderall.

Her road novel had stalled out, and so had her coming-of-age novel and story collection. It seemed that she only had the attention span to write haikus lately. She'd written dozens, primarily about her resentment toward Roberto. Today, she wrote one about her dad's house.

> *My Spanish-style McMansion,*
> *Quiet and empty,*
> *Wyatt is not calling me.*

One night at a party, Claire told Joan that her haikus weren't even real haikus. She'd gotten the syllables all wrong. "It's five-seven-five," Claire had said smugly. "Not seven-five-seven." Joan felt embarrassed. Claire had been getting more curt with her lately, often asking questions like "Are you high?" At which Joan would shrug, annoyed, and mutter under her breath. Of course she was high. She was always high. Why would Claire even ask her that?

"I know that," Joan had lied. "These are western haikus, I invented my own form."

Exhausted, Joan dozed off on her dad's shag rug, watching a show about serial killers. On-screen, a woman was bloody, bound, and gagged on blue carpet. Yellow plastic numbers sat scattered around her, marking areas of interest.

She woke up to her phone ringing. It was her cousin Grace, Wyatt's older sister. She was crying.

"Have you heard about Wyatt?" Grace asked, a note of panic in her voice. Grace was ten years older than Joan and Wyatt, a high school softball coach, electric harp player, and mother of two. Joan sat up and muted the television.

"No," Joan said. "I've been trying to call him, but he won't pick up."

"He's naked on a billboard right now. I'm on my way there."

"You mean there's a picture of him naked?" Knowing Wyatt, this seemed plausible.

"No. He's standing on top of it and saying he's going to jump. It's all over the news."

"Oh no," Joan said. Her stomach leapt into her throat. She stood up and began to pace around the living room, circling the kitchen island, barefoot on the tile.

Grace choked on her words, as if she couldn't believe she was saying them. Her voice, usually strong and commanding, was meek and afraid. "Please," Grace said. "Please get on your knees right now and pray to God and ask Him to get Wyatt off the billboard."

Joan promised Grace that she would pray.

When Grace hung up, Joan went into her dad's office and typed "naked man billboard fort worth" into Google. It felt weird, thinking of Wyatt as a man, but he was twenty-five now, so she guessed he technically was one. By that logic, she was a grown woman, which was also hard to accept. She was still leeching off her parents, no prospects in love or vocation. She looked at a picture of Wyatt on CNN. The billboard was bright yellow with a cartoon caveman. "We buy ugly houses," it said. Wyatt was standing upright, looking at the sky. His arms were outstretched like he was worshipping something. His groin was blurred out.

Joan felt obligated to pray because she'd told Grace that she would. She decided to make it quick. She opened the blinds and looked at her dad's swimming pool, tranquil and blue and glistening in the sun. She and Wyatt had wasted hours by that pool, talking about their ideas—their dreams and their beliefs and their gripes with the world. Joan kneeled on the Persian rug in front of the window.

She wasn't sure how to pray; she felt so far from God. She just looked around the room and paid attention to her breathing. She looked at the framed pictures on the wall. Her dad with his arm around Elton John, holding him in a headlock. Her dad laughing with Stevie Ray Vaughan. Her dad's yacht, white on the glistening blue sea, before it had been totaled on her twenty-first birthday, in Miami.

She squeezed her eyes shut and thought hard about what she wanted. Wasn't that what prayer was? She envisioned Wyatt coming back to his senses, coming down from the billboard, slowly and safely, staying alive another day. Until the next episode struck, which seemed more certain now. Then she was bombarded with horrific images of what it would look like if Wyatt jumped or fell. Would he flail through the air? Would he die on impact or would he jerk around on the ground, bleeding out? Either way, Joan would be fucked up for life. She would have to start going to therapy two or three times a week, instead of just once. It would cost a fortune. She would have nightmares, imagining what Wyatt's body looked like in various stages of decomposition, rotting in the ground. She would wake up every morning having forgotten, thinking Wyatt was still alive. Then she would experience the loss all over again. Like a bad breakup, but gory. Joan began to cry, right there on the carpet, which made her feel embarrassed even though she was alone. She let herself indulge in her pain for a few minutes before she stood up and left the house as quickly as she could. She would drive to the billboard and talk to him, she decided. And then he would come down.

The drive from her dad's gated community to Fort Worth, where the billboard was, would take forty minutes, according to Google Maps. The sign was across the street from Chet's apartment. A big red line showed the gridlock that awaited her in Fort Worth. Presumably because of Wyatt's charade. Joan didn't care. She drove her BMW recklessly, weaving through cars to get into the left lane. On the freeway, Joan called Chet, to find out how this had happened.

"Well, he'd been crying all morning, you know, having one of his *mood swings*," Chet said.

"Right," Joan said.

"He was stressing out about work, you know. They've been asking him to play more and more, and he said he couldn't handle it. He couldn't memorize any more songs. I kept trying to get him to relax and play *Call of Duty* with me, but he just kept getting worse."

Joan found it both irritating and mystifying that Chet would try to calm Wyatt down with a violent video game, but she said nothing.

"The first thing he did was start stabbing his cell phone with an army knife and screaming at it," Chet continued. "He stabbed it until it was in a million pieces, then he put the knife against his throat. He kept saying they were coming for him, that they'd killed his family. He said he wanted to kill himself before they got to him."

"Who was coming for him? Or who did he think was coming?"

"The people at the piano bar, I guess."

"What did you do then? What did you say?" It was her first instinct to blame Chet. But some part of her knew, deep down, that something was seriously wrong with Wyatt. Chet wasn't to blame. Even if Wyatt had lived with her, the same thing probably would have happened.

"I got on my knees in front of him and started crying and begging him not to do it. I told him I didn't want to watch him die. I tried to tell him that no one was coming for him, but he didn't believe me. He just kept pressing the knife up to his skin. I thought blood would start spurting everywhere at any second. I had to act fast. So I tackled him. Then he really freaked out. He started screaming, 'You're one of them! Don't kill me!'"

Chet's story sounded almost identical to what had happened in North Carolina with her brother, and her brother had never been the same. It had traumatized him, and he'd never been close to Wyatt again. Joan, on the other hand, had been able to erase the incident from her mind, for the most part.

"I tried to tell him that I wasn't going to kill him, that I loved him," Chet said. "Then he started crying and kissing me on the neck and ears. I know it sounds a little weird, but I started kissing him back, you know, just to see if that would calm him down. It seemed to work. So I just held him there. I thought everything was going to be fine. Then when I let up on him just a little, he got out from under me and ran onto the balcony with the knife. He jumped over the railing like it was nothing and ran away. You can still see the imprint in the bush where he landed."

"Shit," Joan said, in shock. "I can't believe it."

"Yeah, I was honestly afraid that he was going to go kill somebody. I think it worked out for the best. He's gonna come down for sure. This is just Wyatt being Wyatt."

"How do you know that?" Joan said. "How do you know he'll come down?"

"Look, Wyatt is going to be fine." Chet's tone changed abruptly, as if he were trying to pep her up. "He's a genius. He's an entertainer. He was put on this earth to entertain the masses. That's just what he does. You know how geniuses are. I don't know, he may have some kind of mental problem or something, but I know he's gonna come out on top. He'll be the winner in this situation. I just know it."

"I hope you're right," Joan said. She didn't feel so certain. She could almost smell the blunt Chet was smoking and could see the piles of inspirational self-help books in front of him on his coffee table.

Joan hung up with Chet and called Henry, who was in Chicago, back at Booth, where the fall semester had just started.

"Jesus," he said. "It's like Wyatt's whole life has been nothing but a desperate plea for attention."

"It's online. You can look it up. There are pictures and everything."

"Oh my god. Look at how he's straddling those two billboards. Have you thought about the physics of all this? How did he even get up that high?"

"I have no idea," Joan said.

"It's honestly impressive. Think about it. This article says the bottom of the ladder is twelve feet off the ground. Seriously, how did he get up that high?"

Next, Joan called her dad, who was in Virginia for a two-week seminar on how to develop iPhone apps.

"That is too much," her dad said. "Ah. That is just too much."

"It's all over the internet," Joan said. "Just type 'naked man billboard Fort Worth.'"

"Oh my god. There he is! I can tell that's him," he said. "Oh my god. What is *wrong* with him?"

"I don't know."

"That's just too much, man . . . ," he said again. "What do you think about this, Skipper?" he asked the dog. "Skipper can't believe it. I showed him the pictures and everything."

"He must be in denial," Joan said, unable to resist the joke. Her dad laughed.

"Hey. Guess what," he said. "I made my first app today. It's a fraction calculator. It calculates fractions."

"I'm impressed," Joan said, but what impressed her most was the speed with which he redirected the conversation to himself.

"After I'm done with this thing, I'm gonna drive across the entire country, right through the middle this time. Back to California. From sea to shining sea, like in that song. What's that song? How does it go again?"

When she reached Fort Worth, Joan exited the freeway a mile early. Traffic was completely stopped, as the entire street had been closed off. She parked her BMW illegally on the side of the feeder and headed on foot toward the billboard, which was on the 2300 block of Seventh Street, right next to a bar called 7th Haven, where Joan and Wyatt had gone drinking together a couple of times when he was happy, or perhaps, she realized now, when he was manic. He'd introduced her to everyone as his little brother. Those nights, they always made inappropriate, offensive jokes, and often ended up singing romantic duets together—usually songs from Disney cartoons or *Moulin Rouge*, or the *Phantom of the Opera* theme. Joan wasn't the singing type, but being around Wyatt was like being on a drug; it transported her into another realm, where she was free from her usual limitations. Approaching the billboard, Joan remembered the way he'd laughed out loud those nights, his braces gleaming in the darkness, white rubber bands struggling to hold his jaws together.

Approaching the billboard, Joan looked up at Wyatt, tiny compared to the large sign he was standing on. The side facing her was all black with a bright green iguana. *Visit a museum where the art looks at you*, it read. An ad for the Fort Worth Zoo. She watched his naked, lean body pace back and forth across the top of the sign. He seemed to be totally in control, walking it masterfully like it was a tightrope. There was something off about the way he moved. As if he were possessed. The warm wind blew gently against Joan's skin, and she wondered if it was stronger up there, if it would be enough to make Wyatt fall. As she got closer, she noticed that he'd shaved his head since the last time she saw him. She could barely make out the small tattoo around his upper biceps, a tattoo he got while living in Durham that he always said he regretted—a black strand of geometric birdlike shapes.

Police cars and fire trucks were scattered on the grass below with twinkling red and blue lights. There were cops on horses wearing cowboy hats. The SWAT team was also there, but Joan didn't understand why. She thought their main purpose was busting through metal doors. They all stood around their boxy van, wearing bulletproof vests, talking to each other and pointing at Wyatt, as if they were at a garden party and Wyatt was an avant-garde statue they were debating the meaning of.

She joined a crowd of bystanders gathered behind yellow police tape, mostly people in the service industry, it appeared, wearing all black, or polo shirts with khakis, taking time out of their dull shifts to witness the spectacle. Several had their phones out, aiming them at Wyatt like guns. "How is he keeping his balance up there?" one guy said. Someone made a dick joke, which prompted laughter. Joan stiffened with rage.

"Hey, assholes," she said. "What if that was your brother up there? What if he were your son?"

The guy looked at Joan confused and she made her way closer to the billboard, where a polished woman in a suit stood in front of a news van with a microphone. Joan watched the professional videographer scampering around, capturing Wyatt from different angles, getting his B-roll for tonight's evening news.

A suicide negotiator stood behind the opened door of a police car. She was speaking into a megaphone, telling Wyatt that she really

wanted him to come down. She warned Wyatt that he could be getting dehydrated up there, that she didn't want to see him stumble and
fall. It had been a few hours in the sun with no water. He ignored her,
moving back and forth on the sign with purpose, like he was trying
to burn calories. She continued to plead with him, and eventually he
stopped pacing, standing in the middle of the sign, facing the woman.

"Fuck you!" he yelled, bent over with his hands cupped around his
mouth. "My name is Wyatt Marshall! I was born in Breckenridge,
Texas! My entire family is dead!"

What was he talking about? Joan wondered, feeling unreasonably
offended. Did he think she was dead too? She had been calling him
all day. He then raised his arms as if he was preparing to do a swan
dive. Joan froze, held her breath. *Don't*, she thought. *Please don't.* He
stood like that for several moments, but then he crouched down and
crawled quickly on all fours toward the other end of the billboard,
where he vomited off the side.

Then Joan spotted Wyatt's new girlfriend, whatever her name was,
that she'd met at the piano bar, talking with the suicide negotiator.
She was wearing bright pink hospital scrubs. She must've been a nurse
or something. It looked as if she was being briefed by the negotiator.
They were going to let her talk to Wyatt? Joan couldn't believe it.
They'd literally just started dating.

She found a cop. "Excuse me. Can I try talking to him instead?
He's my brother," she lied. "He hardly knows that girl in the scrubs
over there."

The cop eyed Joan with skepticism, but to her surprise he led her
around the yellow police tape and over to a sweaty blond woman
wearing a light gray shirt that said *Fort Worth Emergency Response
Team* in shiny black letters. Joan's mind began to race, thinking of
what she would say when she had the megaphone. Perhaps she would
start singing the *Phantom of the Opera* theme.

"Another relative. His sister," the cop said to the woman, who
looked at Joan, put her hand on her back, and hurried her away
toward an unmarked trailer. "We're keeping all relatives out of his

sight," she said in a harsh smoker's voice. "We're not sure how he will react to seeing family. It doesn't always turn out pretty."

"This has happened before?" Joan said.

"I've been doing this a long time," she replied, opening the door of the trailer, which Joan reluctantly entered.

26.

WE CAN NEVER LAUGH ABOUT THIS

nside, the trailer was beige and clean and reminded her a little bit of her dad's RV, but less homey. Wyatt's mom, stepdad, sister, and brother-in-law were all sitting in there on the little upholstered couches, and they each hugged Joan gravely when she entered. She sat down next to Grace. They'd been there two hours already, Grace said. Joan could tell that her aunt Charlene wanted a glass of chardonnay more than anything in the world. "What did I do wrong?" Charlene cried, burying her blond head in her third husband's shoulder. He looked down at her and said, "Shhhh. This isn't your fault."

Grace's husband, Steve, had a yellow legal pad out and was scribbling notes. Joan asked him what he was writing. He told her the notes were just in case Wyatt needed to be represented in court. Joan thought that was probably a good idea. She took out her Moleskine and began doing the same, for different reasons. She wrote a quick haiku.

> Forty feet up in the air.
> You are naked, and
> I'm in a trailer, waiting.

"You can't joke about this later," Steve said sternly, pointing at Joan with his pen. She closed her notebook. "We can *never* laugh about this. Wyatt has to know how serious this is."

"Okay," Joan said. But she hoped above all things that someday she and Wyatt would laugh about this. That it was a big joke. Another stunt motivated by the same force that had led Wyatt to Rollerblade around her dad's gated community in her cutoff denim shorts while holding a boom box on his shoulder, or dive into the mall fountain, splash around, and then scream, "I found my penny!" triumphantly at the top of his lungs.

But she knew that something about this was different. She'd seen him up there, the way he was moving; he wasn't having fun. He wasn't there. She asked Grace how long he'd been on the billboard.

"Since noon," she said. "He keeps saying that his family's dead and everyone's gone and that he's not coming down alive. He told the cops to shoot him." Her voice broke again, and her face crinkled up. Tears ran down her cheeks. Steve handed her a Kleenex and she dabbed her eyes.

Joan picked up her phone and got on the internet. She typed "naked man billboard fort worth" and browsed the latest results. Threads of comments had formed at the bottoms of news articles. People were mad about the traffic jam, about the street being closed, about all their tax dollars being wasted on something like this. About the whole city being shut down because of one single nutcase. Someone wondered whether the worst punishment would be to ignore him, since it was obvious that he only wanted attention. A few people were 100 percent sure he was on acid. Others were 1,000 percent sure he was on meth. "Gots to love white people," someone wrote. Some wished he would just jump already. One person asked why they didn't set up a big net around the billboard, then shoot him down with a tranquilizer gun. Another person told that person that they were an idiot.

Aunt Charlene announced that it was time for the family to pray again. Joan slid her phone into her pocket, and they arranged themselves in a circle and held hands. Joan's palms immediately began to sweat as Charlene started talking about Wyatt's soul being lost and needing redemption. "Amen," everyone said. Charlene asked God to come down from heaven and put His hand upon Wyatt, to show him the light of His way. She asked God to pour His holy and righteous blood all over the family, and all over Wyatt. "Amen," everyone said again. Joan opened her eyes and looked around. She must have been the only one spooked by the image. She imagined them all dripping in blood, like Carrie at prom. Grace chimed in, asking Jesus to expel the demons that had infected Wyatt's heart and to deliver him from the evil darkness. "Praise Jesus," everyone said.

Joan felt like she should say something too, but she was too embarrassed. She'd never addressed Jesus or God in public and didn't want to start now. She figured it was all a waste of time. A way for her relatives to pretend they were in control. God had nothing to do with the situation. If Wyatt really wanted to jump, he'd jump.

When they lived together in Dallas, Joan and Wyatt used to stay up late watching televangelists. One night, they were sitting on her dad's living room rug at three A.M., watching their favorite, Mike Simons. He was asking for money in a room full of fake plants, sitting next to his wife, Hazel, who had sky-high bangs and nodded the entire time, saying "Amen" and "Praise Jesus" after everything her husband said. Joan had come down off all the medications by then and was feeling spiritually empty and cynical. She told Wyatt she thought the Jesus story was a load of bullshit. She had expected commiseration. Certainly, someone as smart and talented as Wyatt couldn't be a Bible-thumping moron.

However, Wyatt seemed saddened by her disbelief. Like she had disappointed him. He asked her if she'd ever thought, *really* thought, about what happened to Jesus—if she'd ever really thought about the nails physically being driven into his skin. He held up his arm while he spoke, for dramatic effect, his eyes bright and excited and blue. At that moment, she envied him, in a way. His earnest belief in an admittedly beautiful fairy tale.

She told him she hadn't given it much thought, honestly. Not since she was a kid.

"Imagine," Wyatt said. "Just imagine having something hammered through your wrists and ankles, and doing it for the good of all of humanity." Joan said she couldn't imagine it.

Maybe that was what he was doing up there on the billboard, she thought now, praying with his family. In his deluded state, maybe he thought he was trying to save humanity.

They waited in the trailer for two more hours until an officer came in with an update. Wyatt had come down from the billboard, he said, of his own accord. It was about to rain. Storm clouds had rolled in and must've scared him off. "Praise God," everyone said. The prayers had worked. "Hallelujah, Lord," said Charlene, gripping her husband's hand.

For Joan, it was all too convenient. When something her family wanted to happen happened, it was God; when something they didn't want to happen happened, it was the devil. You couldn't have it both ways, she thought. Moments like this, Joan longed to be Jewish, like Dennis Prager and her other two favorite conservative hosts. Jews were allowed, even encouraged, to "struggle with God." That was literally what *Israel* translated to in Hebrew, Dennis often explained. The most appealing part of Judaism for her, though, was that it was the only religion that didn't want her to join.

The family filed out of the trailer, stepping out onto the grass. The sky had turned dark gray, and the air had grown thick. Joan could hear thunder in the distance. They'd already cuffed Wyatt and made him put on pants. They were escorting him into the back of a squad car. He wouldn't face any criminal charges, the officer said, consoling Charlene. He'd be taken straight to the hospital instead of jail. Charlene nodded along, in a daze. The officer wanted the family to be standing outside when they drove Wyatt by so that he could see them and know that they weren't actually dead. Maybe it would help ground him in reality.

"Here he comes," the cop said, and as the police car slowly drove by, Joan saw Wyatt through the window. They made eye contact, but there was no spark of recognition. He was like a caged animal, looking at her as if she were a demon. Grace started crying again. Joan watched the car until it disappeared.

27.

WHAT WE DESERVE

From the billboard, they took Wyatt to a local hospital, where the drug tests all came back negative, except for marijuana. He ended up staying longer than the standard seventy-two-hour hold, because the doctor said he was still exhibiting psychotic behavior. He told one of the nurses that the TV was talking to him and sending him messages about his family, saying they weren't his relatives but imposters plotting his murder. After a week, Wyatt was transferred to the state hospital in Wichita Falls, two hours away, for further evaluation and care.

Joan looked the hospital up online a few times. It resembled a college campus, but more depressing. She didn't visit. She rationalized that she was too busy to go; she was trying to finish her book, trying to do her job, trying to maintain her adult life in Austin. Every week was peppered with appointments with doctors and gurus and yoga instructors, to ease her chronic pain. But really, Joan was terrified of seeing Wyatt in a place like that. If she saw him in a mental hospital, what would she say? Wouldn't he just accuse her of being an imposter? She told herself that, just like last time, Wyatt would emerge unscathed. They would sweep this incident under the rug the same way they had with his previous suicide attempt. This would all go away if she waited it out.

He'd been in the state hospital for nearly a month when Joan returned to Dallas in October for her dad's Halloween-themed birthday party. She still hadn't called Wyatt, but she had been keeping up with his progress through a family Facebook Messenger thread created by Grace called "Wyatt's Healing Journey." At this point, Wyatt had finally stopped having delusions (or at least stopped talking to his doctors about them). He blamed the entire billboard incident on a bad batch of mushrooms and a lack of sleep. He was allegedly desperate to get out of the hospital and work at Rick's piano bar again. Pretty much everyone besides Chet agreed that wasn't a good idea. Henry had written a single, long message early on in the thread, detailing the events in Durham, North Carolina, when Wyatt had tried to do exactly the same thing, and had eerily similar paranoid hallucinations. He reiterated that Wyatt hadn't been drinking or doing any drugs back then. When Wyatt was in the hospital, Henry had searched through his entire apartment, through all of Wyatt's things, and didn't find any drugs, but he did find a notebook where Wyatt had been writing an intricate plan to purchase a gun, bring it to downtown Durham, and shoot himself in the head at the busiest intersection he could find. Unfortunately, Henry wrote, Wyatt had a mental problem, not a drug or alcohol problem. Everyone thanked Henry for the information, then kept talking about the mushroom theory as if it were true, and Henry stopped chiming in.

Tonight, her dad's house was decorated extravagantly. Rubber corpses lay scattered around his front yard and driveway, clothing shredded and torn, dried fake blood splattered around the cement. Foam tombstones dotted the yard and flower bed. Zombielike hands emerged from the grass. A decapitated head hung from one of his palm trees, wide-eyed and open-mouthed. Next to the front door stood a seven-foot-tall, robed monstrosity. The Grim Reaper. When Joan stepped on the front porch, the reaper moved and laughed—a horrific evil laugh. The eyes lit up red. She jumped. Jesus Christ, it all looked so real.

Inside, the house was dark and quiet. Joan took two painkillers and watched TV in the living room—something about rat hoarding. On the screen, a man was crying about all his rats being taken away. They were like his children, and they needed him. Joan, softened by the pills, was starting to feel a little sorry for the man and rats when a woman she had never seen before came downstairs wearing a hot-pink bathrobe. Her oily, dyed red hair was pulled back into a large black claw clip, with her dark brown roots showing. On her ankle, she had a tattoo of a cherry with the word *Wild* scrawled underneath in cursive. She looked trashy and straight out of the nineties. Kind of like Tai from *Clueless* but several years older. She introduced herself to Joan with a casual warmth. Too casual. Her name was Amber, she said. Suddenly, Joan recalled her dad mentioning Amber once, over the phone during one of their spy calls. He met her at an AA meeting. She had been sixty days sober.

"She's a lesbian," he'd said. "But now she wants to go back."

"Back to what?" Joan asked.

"I dunno. Back to bein' straight, I guess."

Amber yawned and stretched her arms over her head. "I can't sleep," she said. "I'm not used to going to bed as early as your dad."

"I don't blame you," said Joan, familiar with her dad's deranged sleep schedule. Usually, he fell asleep at sunset, rising around three in the morning. He was like an infant. Joan eyed Amber suspiciously and remained seated in her chair.

"I'm going to have a cigarette," Amber said. "Do you want one?"

Joan followed Amber out back and sat across from her on the upholstered patio furniture by the fire pit. By now, Joan was accustomed to these kinds of encounters. A new girlfriend trying to build intimacy through a shared vice. Joan was determined not to get sucked into another one of these twisted friendships. Not again. She'd take the cigarette and run.

"I don't want my dad to know I smoke," Joan said.

"Don't worry. I swear I won't tell him."

"Thanks."

The backyard looked like a tropical oasis next to the barren golf course beyond the wrought iron fence. The bean-shaped saltwater pool changed colors every ten seconds, from pink to green to purple, over and over again.

Amber got two cigarettes out of her pack and handed one to Joan along with a lighter. They were Marlboros, Joan's mother's favorite. As she sucked in and felt the chemicals rush into her throat, she tasted her childhood.

"I've been so excited about meeting you," Amber said. "Your dad talks about you all the time. He says y'all are just alike."

"We are in some ways, I guess," Joan said.

"He's so nice to let me stay here," Amber said. "I'm in a really bad situation with my roommate. She's very controlling."

"He's a generous man," Joan said, taking a deep inhale from her cigarette. But she knew that if Amber were any older, or less busty, her dad wouldn't have bothered helping her at all.

"At first, I was intimidated by him. I've never dated anyone with a lot of money before. I'm not used to places like this." Amber gestured toward the house, which suddenly felt like an ominous presence, looming over their conversation.

"I've never dated anyone with a lot of money either," Joan said.

Amber laughed, but Joan wasn't kidding. Because of her financial situation, Joan gravitated toward men who struggled with funds, a trait she seemed to have inherited from her mother. She told herself it was because she didn't like to feel owned, but perhaps it was something else. That was why she found Roberto's reason for not being with her—that he was too poor—thin and meritless. She could have paid her way, and probably his as well, using her allowance. It was just an excuse he had used. There had to be something else about her that he couldn't tolerate, something he wouldn't say. What was it about her that was so impossible to love?

"It's hard for me," Amber said. "I'm not used to having a guy buy me things. I feel like I don't deserve it."

"I understand that," Joan said, ashing her cigarette into a potted plant. "It's hard to know what we deserve."

"Lately I've been staying here almost every night," Amber said.

"Sometimes I worry that things are moving too fast. I plan on getting my own apartment soon. Your dad's just helping me out until I get back on my feet. I can't wait until I have my own place, where I can just be by myself."

Joan wasn't sure whom Amber was trying to impress. It didn't matter to Joan what Amber wanted to do with her life—whether she was moving forward or backward, whether she was building something or destroying it.

"I get that," Joan said. She understood the appeal of being alone. Claire had recently moved out, leaving her spare room vacant. Joan held on to the deluded hope that Wyatt would come move in after he got better, but she knew it probably wasn't happening. While she missed having Claire to talk to, it was nice not having anyone around to witness her debauchery and judge her for being so messy.

Amber seemed satisfied by Joan's clipped, emotionless responses. Which was good, because that was all Joan would be giving her. She wasn't going to tell Amber anything about any of her problems. She wouldn't talk about Wyatt, or Roberto, or her unfinished novels, or her story languishing at *The Paris Review*. She wouldn't complain about being marketing director of a company and not knowing what marketing was. She wouldn't give Amber anything. Knowledge was power, after all.

Amber didn't go back upstairs after her cigarette. Instead, she sat with Joan in the living room, cross-legged on the shaggy carpet, and kept talking about herself. Joan put her rat-hoarding show on mute and tried to keep up with the subtitles while Amber blathered on. She was very open, she said. You could ask her anything and she'd tell you straight up. That was the type of person she was. She was forty-one. She had low self-esteem (this was something she'd always struggled with). She had tried killing herself twice. She had an eighteen-year-old son whom she worried about constantly. She had lost custody of him when he was thirteen. She felt terrible about that, obviously. Now her son lived in Boston with his best friend, a DJ that Amber was not sure about. They went to raves all the time, and Amber suspected they did ecstasy together.

"That's unfortunate," Joan said. "About the DJ, I mean. You seriously can't trust those people."

That night, Grace posted in "Wyatt's Healing Journey." It was not an update but a link to a Christian music video that she said had been helping her deal with the Wyatt situation. Joan opened the video and closed it after less than a minute. She didn't mind hymns, but modern church music had always initiated a trauma response within Joan. She wasn't sure why, but she assumed she associated the awful music with her stepdad. Her mother met Doug in a Bible study for singles and started dragging her and Henry to church twice a week after that. Doug had been horrible, forcing her to sit at a table with him every night while he read the Bible out loud to her. He'd posted notes on her bedroom door, outlining everything she'd done wrong every day and how she needed to repent. He'd gone through her drawers and her closet, trying to find things she was hiding. He'd derided her for being sarcastic. For being shy. For not calling him Dad or telling him she loved him (she didn't). He'd confiscated all Joan and Henry's music and movies and games, calling them works of the devil. The list went on and on. At the same time, he was sleeping with all kinds of prostitutes on the side. He was the worst person she'd ever met.

The next day, Joan woke up at one in the afternoon and went downstairs, where her dad sat in his red leather recliner, eating a turkey sandwich and watching God TV in high definition. The refrigerator doors were wide open, and the fridge was beeping periodically. All the food he'd used to make the sandwich sat all over the kitchen counter, the packages still open. Joan sat on the couch and put her feet on the coffee table.

"Hey," he said. "You ready to party?"

"I was born ready," said Joan.

"Did you meet Amber?"

"Yeah, last night."

"What do you think?" He looked at Joan expectantly, waiting for a specific answer of which she wasn't sure.

"She seems nice, I guess." Joan shrugged.

Her dad grunted and set his half-eaten sandwich on his lap, indicating trouble was already brewing between them. She didn't ask what was wrong, which was obviously what he wanted.

"I'm just home on my lunch break. Did I tell you I've got a new job? I'm a chauffeur now."

"What do you mean?" Joan said.

"I'm a professional chauffeur. All I do now is drive Amber around. Took her to work this morning, and now I gotta go pick her up."

"She doesn't have a car?"

"Nope," he said. "No car, no driver's license." He shoved the rest of the sandwich into his mouth.

"Why not?"

"She's too poor."

"Too poor to get a license?" Joan said. This was the common argument from the Left for why voter ID laws were "oppressive." She was surprised to learn there might be any real validity to that claim.

"I dunno," he said. "She's got a phobia or something."

"A phobia of driving?" A phobia of driving in DFW was like a fish having a phobia of swimming. Everything was spread miles and miles apart, and public transportation wasn't a real option.

"Weird, isn't it?" He stood up and wiped crumbs off his shirt and shorts and onto the shag rug.

"What did she do before?" Joan asked.

"Before what?"

"Before she met you. Like, the entire rest of her life leading up to now."

"Oh, I dunno. I guess she always found someone with a car to take her places."

"Weird."

"At least it keeps her out of trouble, right? She can't get into any trouble if she can't go anywhere. Right?" He was standing by the door, about to leave.

"Sure," Joan said. "Whatever you say."

On God TV, Joan watched a sermon by Joel Osteen, a pastor from

Houston whom she'd despised when she was a teenager. She recalled throwing a copy of *Your Best Life Now* gifted by her dad down the trash chute of her dorm in Miami. Watching him now, she tried to be open-minded. He was different from the pastors she was used to growing up. He seemed more eccentric, more mystical. Like a forest creature. She wanted what he had, or what he seemed to have. He said it was important to live life happily. God didn't create us to endure life but to enjoy life. He smiled so much and blinked like crazy. Could he be telling the truth? Joan took some nerve relaxants and a painkiller. She listened to his words. Jesus came so our joy could be full. You have everything you need to be happy. Where you are is not an accident; it's all a part of God's plan. Today is a gift from God. Do not waste His gift by being unhappy.

Joan turned off the TV. She went upstairs and walked past Skipper, who sat moping at the top of the staircase, watching the front door the entire time Randy was gone, his pathetic face resting on his pathetic paws.

She went into her bedroom, a new addition to the house, and closed the door. She took a few more pills and played a conservative podcast on her phone while she tried to read her new book, *Marketing for Dummies*. The host was talking about the new front-runner, Herman Cain, a Tea Partier who'd recently surpassed Rick Perry and Mitt Romney in the polls. Joan didn't mind Herman Cain. He had an awesome name, for one thing. He also had spunk, and she liked that he had experience as a business owner. As much as she loved Mitt Romney, she would hop on the Cain Train if necessary. She would take great pleasure in seeing him go head-to-head with Obama, who knew nothing about how to run a business, whose knowledge was all theoretical.

She tried once more to muster interest in her marketing book, but her neck started hurting. The pain radiated down her right arm, into her wrist and hand. It was like being stung by a jellyfish from the inside. She flinched, turned her head from side to side. She'd done enough work for the day. Exhausted, she lay down on the bed and fell asleep, still listening to her podcast, thinking about Herman Cain.

When Joan's dad returned with Amber, he sent the two of them out together to buy some things for the party. The house needed more fake cobwebs and Skipper needed a costume. Her dad couldn't go. He had a professional makeup artist coming over at four to make him look dead.

In the car, Amber kept yawning and stretching and saying how tired she was. Amber's incessant yawning made Joan pretty tired herself. That, and all the downer medication she had taken earlier. Joan drove through a Starbucks and ordered two coffees with shots of espresso and pumps of caramel syrup.

"This should help wake us up," Joan said. She paid for the drinks and handed one to Amber, who thanked her too sincerely, as if she'd been handed an award. They walked through PetSmart together, sipping the coffee, and stood in front of a rack of dog costumes. Joan couldn't decide, and Amber had no opinion, which was not surprising. She didn't even care about her own clothes, Joan thought, noting the ill-fitting pale pink sweatpants Amber was wearing. Overwhelmed, Joan bought three dog costumes with her company credit card—a butterfly, a football player, a pirate. She'd let her dad decide. It was his dog after all.

When they got back to the house, there was a valet stand set up by the mailbox, with two attendants ready in their uniforms. Joan left her car running and let one of the men park it somewhere nearby, for no reason. There was no shortage of parking in her dad's gated community. A catering van was parked in his driveway. People in white scurried in and out of the house carrying large silver platters of food. The front door was wide open, and Skipper was running around the foam graveyard in circles, barking and nipping at the gray cloud emanating from the fog machine.

Joan drank beer alone in her room while she got dressed for the party. She appreciated the way her pills enhanced alcohol's effects so that drinking one beer was more like drinking three. Listening to music, she put on a black minidress and a tiara and painted her eyelids

203

thick and heavy. She put on long silk gloves, a string of thick white pearls, and oversized sunglasses. She would be Holly Golightly again, her favorite costume. It was so easy.

Beneath her buzz, Joan was sad that Wyatt wasn't coming. Last year, he'd come dressed as a Spartan, and they'd had fun walking around and pretending to do battle. She began to feel guilty about not calling him in the hospital or driving to Wichita Falls to visit him. To blot out the feeling, she chugged another beer.

She was already tipsy when the house started filling up with people. Some of the guests were from AA, Joan guessed from their sparkling waters and irritating senses of humor. They smiled and laughed at every little thing, no matter how prosaic. Joan avoided the AAs like the plague. The rest of the party guests were all right, mostly her dad's Dallas employees—administrative staff, faculty, studio techs, and some student interns. Each city had a distinct subset of students, and the Dallas campus students and employees had a heavy metal flair that the Austin and Houston campuses lacked.

Joan talked to Tanya about marketing initiatives for the school, to make it seem like she was doing something in her new role. She suggested they revamp the website, which looked dated to her. Tanya agreed enthusiastically and encouraged Joan to start working on a blog for the school. It would be perfect for her, since she was a writer. She could write articles about former student success stories, for instance. Joan pretended to be excited about this idea. Then they discussed the possibility of Joan going to the annual ACCSC conference later that fall, where she could learn all about government compliance and get acquainted with their federal regulatory body. It sounded horrible, but Joan agreed to go; it seemed important for her to do, as part owner and marketing director.

Brave Combo, a marginally famous local polka band that had appeared on *The Simpsons* in cartoon form, could barely fit its ten-piece band into the dining room, where her dad had a professional lighting grid and sound system set up. This was where she and Wyatt had spent countless hours singing duets, trying to write songs about their family, about Ruby. She missed him terribly. She should really call him. What was she so afraid of? She decided she would try tomorrow.

When the band started playing, the horns were so loud and distracting that Joan spent most of the night in the garage drinking and flirting with the student interns and studio technicians, mostly heavy metal heads in their twenties and thirties whom her dad paid minimum wage. He often called them dispensable, but Joan got a rush out of hanging out with the techs and students. They made her feel like a celebrity—important and desirable, but unattainable; like Paris Hilton but smart.

Joan went to the kitchen and refilled her red Solo cup with wine. Amber was standing in there wearing a long pink sheer robe covered in feathers. Joan couldn't tell what she was supposed to be. Maybe some sort of prostitute? She didn't ask. Amber smiled at Joan, and Joan smiled back, tight-lipped. She didn't want to talk to Amber, not when there were so many better options. Instead, she reached past her and grabbed a fresh beer for later. Leaving the kitchen, Joan overheard a woman dressed as a scarecrow ask Amber if they would need help cleaning up after the party.

"Oh, no," Amber said. "We have people for that."

She was getting comfortable here, Joan thought, returning to the garage to flirt with the techs. Too comfortable.

28.

~~MARKETING~~ DIRECTOR

Joan called Wyatt the next morning, hungover, packing her stuff to go back home. Wyatt answered and said that he never expected to talk to her from a mental hospital. He sounded embarrassed. Joan told him about the Halloween party, said she missed him, and asked him if he was bored in there. He said that he was, that the pills they gave him blurred his vision and made him constipated.

"So you're taking your pills?" Joan asked. She remembered after he'd gotten out of the psych ward at Duke, he told her he hid them under his tongue and spit them out.

"Yes, it's been horrible. They won't even let me have a guitar," he said. "I can't even play music."

"That's so sad. . . . I guess it's probably considered a weapon," Joan said. "You might try to hang yourself with the strings."

"Probably."

"Do they let you have shoelaces?"

"Yeah. They let me keep my shoes."

"That's good. Don't hang yourself with those."

"I won't," he said. He didn't laugh.

She told him that she'd gotten a new roommate. Claire's friend from the English honors program, Bianca, had moved in for now. But once Wyatt was back on his feet, the room was his. If he still wanted it.

"For sure," Wyatt said.

She told him that the bar by his apartment—7th Haven—had changed the lettering under its sign. It now said: *Position Available. Now Hiring. Crazy naked person to stand on our sign. No experience req'd. Apply within.*

Wyatt laughed, finally, but not the way that he used to. It sounded forced and stale. Joan figured it was the medication. She told him about developments with her job. She was going to a government compliance conference in California soon. She was rapidly climbing the corporate ladder, she quipped. But he took her seriously.

"That's great," he said. "I wish I had been smart enough to finish the audio program when I had the chance."

"You are smart," she said. "In your own way."

"No, I'm not smart. I got naked and climbed a billboard. What smart person does that? Who will ever hire me now? Who will ever want to marry me?"

Joan tried to tell him not to dwell so much on the past, or the future, but to stay in the present moment. This was something she often heard happy people say about how to live, something she still hadn't mastered.

He told her about a class he'd been taking at the mental hospital called Social Interactions, and another one called Life Management. He sounded exhausted. He told her he just wanted to get out of there. All he really wanted out of life, more than anything else, was to be normal.

"I think you can get there," Joan said. "I think that's a good thing to want."

Joan drove back to Austin with Icy Hot patches all over her right arm, secured to her skin with duct tape. Approaching her apartment, she got stuck in traffic for half an hour behind a horde of Occupy Austin protestors. The movement had entered its fifth week, and Joan had read somewhere that the losers had already cost taxpayers upwards of a million dollars. She felt smug and contemptuous toward the protestors as she pulled her BMW into her parking garage. Setting up tents all over the sidewalks like idiots.

Joan spent her next few mornings on Adderall trying to draft her first blog post for the school. Using the theme of graduate success stories that Tanya had suggested, she decided to write about Vince and Monica and their dumb South by Southwest event. Joan didn't want to think about Vince, whom she'd saved in her phone as "Please Don't Do This to Yourself," but since she already had so many notes about him, she thought writing the article would be easy. She was wrong.

She pivoted to Claire's boyfriend, Luke, another graduate of the school, who had released a couple of albums and was now running sound at a megachurch.

But in the end, she found the task of writing a blog impossible. She could not muster the correct tone. True, she was technically a writer. But she realized her authentic voice shined only when it was highlighting the negative aspects of life, not putting positive spins on things. Marketing, promotion, sales—they all ran counter to who she was, as a person and artist. She would need a new position in the company, effective immediately, so she could stop working on the blog. She called her dad to discuss.

"I can't be marketing director anymore," she whined. "It's just not my strength."

"Why not?"

"It's hard. I've never studied it. I don't understand it."

"Okay. What about just director?"

"What do you mean?"

"Do you want to do Craig's job?"

"Seriously?" Joan said.

"Seriously. We've been wanting to get rid of Craig anyway. He's weird. And he's dragging his feet on getting the other programs started."

"But I don't have any managerial experience," she said.

"You'll figure it out. It's easy."

"Would I at least get a pay raise?" Joan asked. Her dad was paying her twenty-five thousand dollars a year in addition to covering her rent.

"Nope," he said. "You're lucky to be getting anything."

Joan sighed.

"The school's your entire inheritance. That should be motivation enough. When I die, it's all yours."

Joan thought about it. She didn't have any other job prospects. She had never worked anywhere besides AudioPro and the capitol, and the capitol wouldn't be hiring interns for another year. If she had to work at AudioPro, any role would be better than marketing director. Besides, she didn't like Craig either. He was a dorky know-it-all who made her transcribe long, boring meetings for his compliance reports to the government. Everyone complained about him. How difficult could his job be?

"Okay," Joan said. "I'll do it."

"All right," Randy said proudly. "Go tell Craig."

"What?"

"Go fire Craig."

"You and Tanya aren't going to do it?"

"Why us? You're the boss now. Firing people is your job."

Joan got dressed in her nicest T-shirt and jeans and drove to the school, her hands shaking. She started to cry in the car from anticipation and spent a half hour in the bathroom in the lobby of the school before she splashed water on her face, trying to mask that she'd been crying. But it didn't work. Embarrassed, she wore floral-print sunglasses into Craig's office to deliver the news.

"Today is your last day as an AudioPro employee," she said meekly. "I'm so sorry."

Craig sat stunned at his desk. He was wearing a red polo shirt and khakis. He'd worked there for over ten years.

"They sent you to tell me? Why?"

"Because I'm your replacement," she said, mortified for him.

Joan watched as he packed up his things into boxes, something she'd been instructed to do. The minutes felt like hours, with neither of them speaking. Finally, when he finished, Joan escorted Craig out the front door, the staff and students staring in disbelief as she returned to his office and took her place in his worn leather chair, behind a large mahogany desk, surrounded by beige file cabinets.

Later that evening, she was decompressing with her new roommate, Bianca, who'd just gotten a job at a solar panel company, in sales. They were talking about the thrills of the corporate world when Joan received a text message from Amber.

> I heard about your new job. Congrats. Your dad is so
> proud. Your going to do great. I miss u. Can't wait for u
> to come back and see my new apt:)

Joan didn't respond.

29.

RED FLAGS

Joan returned to Dallas the Tuesday before Thanksgiving. When she arrived, her dad was sitting on the back porch, watching golf on his flat-screen TV, eating lunch meat out of a plastic bag. They briefly caught up about AudioPro. Two weeks before, she'd gone to San Diego for the annual conference held by their regulatory body, ACCSC (Accrediting Commission of Career Schools and Colleges). Joan had spent two days in a hotel attending long, boring seminars, taking notes about government compliance. The main theme of the conference that year was the new gainful employment regulations being imposed by the Obama administration, which many of the conference attendees found confusing, unfair, and impossible to comply with. Joan assumed the new rules were simply Obama's sneaky way of getting rid of for-profit colleges without looking like a tyrant. Her dad listened to her talk about the conference for a few minutes, then changed the subject.

"Did you hear about Wyatt?" he asked.

"No."

"He's leaving the hospital."

"Really?"

"Yep. Going to a halfway house downtown."

"For alcoholics?"

"Yep. Charlene got power of attorney over his healthcare."

"Isn't that what they did last time, though? When he had his first episode, they put him in rehab, and then he got kicked out?"

"Oh, yeah."

"When does he get out of the hospital?"

"I'm not sure. Hey, I gotta go pick Amber up from work now," he said. "Did I tell you she moved out?"

"She mentioned she had an apartment."

"Did she tell you I'm paying for it?"

"She didn't say who was paying."

"Of course she didn't," he said. He placed the bag of meat on the table and sat up. "Guess where I'm taking her now. You'll never guess where."

"Where?"

"To pick up her social security check. She gets six hundred dollars from the government. Can you believe that? Isn't that something?"

"Because she's poor?"

"I don't know. I think it's because she's retarded," he said. He turned off the TV with one remote, then used another remote to lower the screen back into the kitchen counter behind the barbecue pit. He then put both remotes into a Tupperware container, sealed it, and set it on the glass coffee table.

That night, Joan went to Barnes & Noble and perused the business section. She purchased half a dozen books on management and took them to the café, where she sat at a table and began to read. Joan wanted to be good at her new job, and she was trying. Back in Austin, to boost morale, she had begun holding weekly staff and faculty meetings, where employees could voice their concerns, openly and without judgment. However, she couldn't help but feel that nobody took her seriously as director. In the management books, they emphasized that Joan, as leader, created the culture of the entire campus. Whatever she did, however she acted, would trickle down to even the lowest employee. It was an overwhelming amount of pressure. She took the stack of books and left the store.

When she got home, her dad was lying next to Amber on the shag rug in the living room, watching a romantic comedy and holding her hand. A fire flickered in the fireplace.

"I brought you home a cupcake from work," Amber said to Joan. "It's in the fridge."

"Thanks," said Joan. She went to the refrigerator and found the cupcake, which was in a clear plastic container, decorated with a cartoon turkey.

"I thought maybe we could get mani-pedis tomorrow," Amber said. "I want my nails to look good for Thanksgiving dinner with your family."

"Okay," Joan said, unsure why Amber would be worried about her nails rather than something more pressing, such as her hair, wardrobe, or personality.

"And afterward I could show you my new apartment. Does that sound good?"

"Yeah, okay," Joan said. She opened the plastic container and took the first bite of cupcake as she walked upstairs to her room. It was pumpkin spice flavored, dry, and with less frosting than she would have liked. She shut herself in her room and lay in bed, listening to a conservative show while she devoured it. Herman Cain had plummeted in the polls after revelations of a sex scandal came out, and now Newt Gingrich was surging above Mitt Romney. Joan did not like Newt Gingrich at all and did not understand his appeal. *Why is the GOP so resistant to Romney?* she thought, frustrated. If Newt ended up being the nominee, she would seriously consider not voting.

The next day, Joan sat at the Hawaiian Nail Bar near her dad's house and drank a complimentary margarita as she waited for Amber, her feet soaking in lukewarm bubbling water. Amber was already twenty minutes late, and Joan was getting annoyed. This was valuable time when she could have been reading her management books. To ease her boredom, she typed a new haiku in her phone.

Students, staff, and faculty,
Filing cabinets,
Everything depends on me.

Eventually, Joan hoped to publish an entire book of her western haikus, but she realized that would take time. She would need to establish herself first with another, more commercially appealing book. She'd first learned the importance of poetry from Roberto, whom she often saw reading slim poetry collections at the coffee shop. When Joan told him she found poems boring and confusing, Roberto said he understood, but reading them was essential if she wanted to write good fiction. It was like eating her literary vegetables. She still hadn't read any poetry collections he recommended, but she was enjoying writing her own.

Amber finally showed up, and Joan watched through the window as she chained her bike to a sign in the parking lot. Amber looked around, worried and frazzled.

"I don't know if I can get my nails done," Amber said when she sat next to Joan. "I don't have the money."

"My dad didn't give you any?"

"It's just a really bad time. Rent is due and they're charging me more than they said they were going to."

"Don't worry about it," Joan said. "I'll pay for it."

"Are you sure?"

"Yeah. It's no problem."

"That's so sweet of you. Okay, well, I owe you. I'll get yours next time."

"That sounds good," said Joan, knowing she and Amber would probably never get pedicures together again in her entire life, and even if they did, Amber would never be able to pay.

A man dumped a scoop of blue crystals into the water and started scrubbing Joan's feet. A woman kneeled in front of Amber and did the same.

Afterward, Amber insisted that Joan come over and see her new apartment. They left her bike chained in the parking lot of the nail place and drove in Joan's BMW across the street to Park Place Apartments, where Joan parked in Amber's designated space.

"This is such a nice car," Amber said, stroking the leather gently, like it was a cat.

"Thanks," Joan said. "My dad bought it for me. It's really fast."

"I don't drive," said Amber. "But I want to someday."

"It's good to have goals," Joan said.

She followed Amber up three flights of stairs, which made her feel winded and breathless. Amber apologized for the stairs. She had to get the top floor because it was the cheapest, she said. She showed Joan into the small apartment, which looked like any other crappy apartment Joan had seen, boxy and plain, with white walls, white plastic vertical blinds, no hardware on the kitchen cabinets. Many of her Lewisville friends lived in apartments just like this one. But Amber seemed proud, so Joan went along on the tour as if she cared.

In Amber's bedroom, there was an antique rolltop desk that originally belonged to Joan's grandmother. It had been in Joan's bedroom at her dad's house when she was a kid. Joan had sat at that desk for hours, drawing pictures of horses, unicorns, dolphins, and whales, during weekends she spent with her dad, per their custody arrangement. Joan also recognized Amber's canopy bed, which had been in her room at her dad's old Padre Island beach house. He bought the beach house when Joan was seventeen, right after he got out of rehab, because he thought his Higher Power was the ocean. Amber had wrapped the canopy bed with white curtains and fake plastic vines.

"I like what you've done with the place," Joan lied, feeling the silk leaves with her fingers.

"Thanks," she said. "I love decorating."

In the bathroom, gaudy blue towels hung in layers with inspirational words sewn into them, like *love*, *faith*, and *serenity*.

"I love stuff like that," said Amber, watching as Joan ran her fingers along the threaded words.

"Yeah, me too," Joan lied. "Nice toilet seat."

"Thanks." Amber laughed as if she had picked it out herself.

The seat of the toilet was painted like the body of an acoustic guitar. Joan recognized it from her dad's old jam room. Joan thought briefly of the way Wyatt looked onstage in the jam room, performing for her under the spotlight. She thought about his brilliant musical rendition of "Conquistador" and how it would probably never be recorded, now that he was mental and on antipsychotic medication. She wondered if he would even write another song or play anything again. She became filled with grief but tried to push her thoughts away.

Amber made a pot of coffee, and they sat on the balcony at a small table, also from her dad's old beach house on Padre Island.

"I want to get real plants," Amber said. "But I don't know what kind to get. I can never keep plants. I try, but they always die."

"I can't keep plants alive either," Joan said. "It's hard. Finding the balance between overwatering and underwatering, too much light or too little. Who has time for it?"

Amber took out a cigarette and offered one to Joan, who accepted.

"I wrote something the other day," said Amber. "I wanna show it to you because you're a writer."

"I'm not really a writer," Joan said, hanging her head. "I barely have time anymore with the school. And I've never had anything published." She thought of her story, gathering dust at *The Paris Review*. Were they ever going to respond?

"You don't have anything published *yet*," Amber said, correcting her.

Joan wondered where Amber's confidence in her imminent success came from, and if it was authentic or just an act. Amber set her lit cigarette on the edge of the ashtray and went inside. Joan took a deep, painful inhale of her cigarette and watched the smoke rising from Amber's.

Amber returned holding a crumpled, torn-out piece of notebook paper and wearing reading glasses, which made her appear intelligent.

"I like those glasses on you," Joan said.

"Thank you," Amber said, smiling, and sat down. She said she'd written a poem about her son, and she thought Joan would appreciate it. Joan's entire body tensed up with dread. Amber read for a minute or two before it was finished.

The poem was awful. It rhymed, and was full of generic terms like *angel*, *god*, *baby*, and *love*. There was not a single interesting image or turn of phrase. Amber used the obvious metaphor of a baby bird flying out of its nest to describe her son leaving her to live first with his grandparents and then with the DJ in Boston. After Amber was finished reading, Joan felt deeply embarrassed for Amber, and for herself for being on the same balcony as her, on her dad's old beach house furniture, with her hair and fingertips reeking of cigarette. She was feeling lightheaded and dizzy and nauseated from the smoke.

"That was really good," said Joan.

"Thank you," Amber said.

Joan wanted to make Amber feel better, for some reason. She wanted her to think the poem was worthy of discussion. So she kept talking. "I can relate to a lot of the feelings in there. The guilt."

"Yeah?"

"Yeah, you know, my cousin Wyatt has been in a psychiatric hospital for two months, and I've only called him once. He's suicidal, and I don't know what to say or how to help him. He seems like a different person."

"You should be easier on yourself," Amber said. "Just being there for him is enough."

"But I haven't been there for him."

"You can start anytime. It's not too late. At least that's what my sponsor says. It's what I have to tell myself to get through the day."

Joan put her cigarette out in the ashtray and started rubbing her temples. She'd said too much.

"I'm so tired," Amber said, and yawned.

"Me too."

"I have to meet with my sponsor soon. I wish I had time to nap before."

They went inside and Amber lay on the couch and turned on the TV. "I hate watching the news," she said, but didn't change the channel. Joan sat in the recliner and stared at the screen. Pundits on CNN were analyzing the Republican national security debate from the night before, focusing on Newt Gingrich's performance since he was the front-runner. He'd made a major flub by admitting he believed in amnesty for illegal immigrants. Joan looked around for a place to put her coffee, eventually setting it down on the carpet.

"That's what I need," Amber said, her voice groggy and fatigued. "I need a little table to go next to that chair."

Joan was stopped at the entrance gate into her dad's neighborhood. The sticker on her windshield was expired, the woman explained, and she didn't have her ID. Joan waited for the woman to reach her dad by phone so he could confirm her identity. When Joan finally arrived at the house, he emerged from his office, where he claimed to have been coding nonstop, all day. He was building software that would organize the school, tracking student attendance and grades and employment status, basically documenting their every move, he said. Forever until they died.

"That sounds awesome," Joan said. "That will really help us with compliance."

"You see Amber's apartment? Nice, isn't it? That's all my shit in there."

"Yeah. I recognized a lot of it."

"I told her if we break up, I get it all back. I'm pretty stupid for giving her all that shit, huh?"

"Yeah," Joan said. "You're totally stupid." Her head was still aching from the cigarette.

"Did you know she's already relapsed twice since I met her? Did I tell you that?"

"No."

"Yeah. Once in Texarkana on vanilla and lemon extract. Can you believe that? I took her there in the RV. We went to an AA meeting, and she was stumbling around, smelling like muffins. I found the empty bottles in the trash can."

"That's fucked up," said Joan.

"You wanna hear something *really* crazy? I probably shouldn't even be showing you this." He took his phone out of his pocket.

"What is it?"

"Her son sent me a Facebook message yesterday. Wanna hear it?"

"Sure."

He read the message out loud. "So, I hear you're taking care of my mom," it began. "I just want to warn you what kind of person she is." The note went on to talk about all the lies that Amber had told her son over the years, all the things she'd stolen, all the drugs she'd done while the son was around.

"Pretty bad, huh," Joan's dad said after he'd finished reading.

"That's quite the Facebook message," Joan said.

"Lotsa red flags."

"Yes," said Joan. "A lot of red flags." She closed her eyes and squeezed her skull as hard as she could, temporarily relieving the throbbing ache.

"If she relapses a third time, that's it. I told her, three strikes and you're out." Randy stood by the front door, about to leave.

"Good plan," Joan said.

He let out an exasperated sigh. "But who knows? Maybe this'll become something beautiful."

"You never know," Joan said. "Anything's possible, I guess."

30.

WHO WANTS TO BE ALONE ON
A SATURDAY NIGHT?

The next morning, on Thanksgiving, Joan and Randy drove to Aunt Charlene's house, where the family was gathered. Amber didn't come after all. She was sick, Randy said. So the nail salon had been a complete waste of time, Joan thought, irritated all over again.

"What illness does she have?" Joan asked.

"The flu," he said. "That's what she said this morning."

"Sure," Joan said.

Charlene's house was loud and full of people—Joan's cousins and other aunt and uncle and grandparents, along with some poor people from Charlene's church. While Charlene and Grace prepared the food, Randy bragged to his parents about Joan's new role in the company, explaining his "sink or swim" approach to teaching her what she needed to know. He seemed genuinely pleased with the chaotic nature of the transition. The entire staff had been shocked, he said with glee. Joan was then cornered by one of her uncles, a sports recruiting executive and motivational speaker who had recently been on the cover of *Texas CEO*. He started asking her about her novel, his eyes sparkling, and talking about his own experience with the publishing industry. He had recently debuted with a networking book called *You've Got What It Takes to Win*. As intense as he was, Joan always felt a little pumped up after talking to him, like her life was going to pan out the way she wanted it to, as long as she continued to believe.

When the food was ready, everyone gathered in a large circle around the kitchen, while Joan's grandfather led them in prayer.

Joan sat next to Grace at the table and asked about Wyatt. Grace explained that he was still in Wichita Falls, but not for long. He was ready for the next chapter of care.

"What makes you think he's ready?" Joan asked.

"That hospital is awful," Aunt Charlene said, and crinkled her nose. "It's more like a prison."

"Worse than a prison," Grace said.

"Oh, really?" Joan wasn't surprised. She knew from working at the capitol that the legislature loved to slash funding for mental health services wherever possible. The state was ranked fiftieth in this area, and the work was outsourced mostly to jails and homeless shelters instead.

"It's horrible," Charlene said. "He's walking around like a zombie all day. Nobody could recover from anything in there."

"So, where's he going?" Joan asked. She tried to feign interest in her plate of food, but she had taken an Adderall right before, so she couldn't eat much.

"It's a great place," Charlene said. "Grace, tell her about the place."

"It's a men's sober living facility run by Christians," Grace explained. "These guys are the real deal. They're well-grounded, sensible Christians. I went and talked with them, and they are really walking with God. I think they can help Wyatt."

Joan wondered what that meant. To be well-grounded, sensible.

"He needs good, strong men in his life," said Charlene. "He's never had that." Joan assumed Charlene was alluding to Wyatt's father, whom she had divorced when Wyatt was a baby and who was in prison for being a con artist, running an oil and gas Ponzi scheme for over ten years. Joan had never even met the man.

"But it's a place for alcoholics?" Joan was confused. "What about mental illness? Do they know how to deal with that?" It didn't make sense to her, but she felt the need to tread lightly. Wyatt wasn't her brother or her son. He was only her cousin.

"He needs spiritual guidance and sobriety," Charlene said. "Whatever he has, he's not going to get better without first learning to put the *plug in the jug*."

Joan poured herself a generous glass of chardonnay from the bottle being passed around the table. She nodded in agreement. It was true. Wyatt's demise had seemed to align with his increase in drinking. Sobriety couldn't hurt.

"They're living in scripture," Mama, who had been mostly silent, added.

"It's unclear what illness he has, if any," Grace said. "He says he was on mushrooms when he climbed the billboard. He was drinking and doing drugs every day at Chet's. He wasn't thinking straight. He needs to sober up if we're ever going to get to the bottom of it."

"But Henry said he was sober in North Carolina, when he had that episode. He wasn't drinking or doing drugs or anything up there. They searched the whole apartment afterward."

They nodded as if they understood and agreed but didn't engage with this line of thought. Perhaps they didn't believe Henry.

Joan didn't say anything more about Wyatt. His mother and Grace seemed so confident in their plan, like they'd been thinking about the issue a lot harder than Joan had. Maybe they had been. Joan didn't exactly have any brilliant ideas about how to help him.

"It'll be good to have him closer to home," Mama said.

"Yeah, it will," Joan conceded. She was feeling woozy from her Adderall, painkillers, and wine. She didn't know what the truth was. Who was she to say that Wyatt's problem was purely physical? What if they were right? What if it was spiritual? She wanted Wyatt out of that hospital as much as anyone.

Two days later, Amber came over and ate dinner with Joan and her dad.

"Looks like you're feeling better," Joan said. "I heard you got the flu. That sucks."

"Yeah," Amber said. "It was really rough."

"I bet," said Joan.

Afterward, Amber and Randy got into the hot tub, listening to jazz playing from a rock-shaped speaker.

Joan, grossed out and wanting nothing to do with them, went upstairs to her bedroom and took her eighth painkiller of the day. The last one, she promised herself. Back in Austin, she had finally found a doctor to help her treat her chronic pain with opiates. She lay in bed, zoning out and playing her zoo game, until her dad started shouting her name from downstairs, loudly, as if there was some kind of emergency. She rushed downstairs. When she got to the kitchen, he was pacing around the island, visibly upset.

"Where's Amber?"

"She wanted me to take her home. Back to 'her apartment.' Can you believe that? She won't even let me up there."

"So? She's allowed to have space."

"She never stays here anymore. She keeps saying that she wants to be independent. I don't get it, man."

"What does she mean by 'independent'?"

"She's always saying she wants to relax and be by herself. Why does she want to be by herself? Isn't that the whole point of dating someone? So you don't have to be alone?" He was shouting now.

"I guess so," said Joan.

"It's Saturday night! This is when people are supposed to want to be together. Who wants to be alone on a Saturday night?!"

Joan shrugged.

"What could she possibly be doing over there?" he asked.

"I don't know," said Joan. "She's your girlfriend. Ask her."

"You know what else is weird about her? She's always talking about how spontaneous she is, about how she just likes to get out and go do things, like go to museums and shit like that. But when? How? How would she ever get to a museum?"

"Don't ask me," Joan said, exhausted, wishing she were alone at her own apartment like Amber. "I need to go lie down. I have a long drive tomorrow."

One week later, Joan got a phone call from her dad. She was at work, slogging through an online training course about government compliance for the Texas Workforce Commission. Not only did Joan have to worry about federal regulations, she had to worry about the State of Texas as well. Randy told Joan that he and Amber had broken up for good this time (apparently, they'd broken up before). Amber had officially crossed the line, he explained. How? She invited her *husband* over to her apartment. The apartment that *he* was paying for. Could Joan believe that?

"Wait. Amber's married?" Joan said.

"Well, technically, yeah. I never told you that? I thought you knew that."

"You said she was a lesbian."

"She is. She claims she invited him over to talk about getting a divorce. But I don't believe that for a second. That's something you can talk about over the phone, right? Why would he need to come over to talk about divorce in person?"

"I don't know, I've never been divorced," Joan said. "You're the expert there."

She listened to her dad gripe for a while and wondered if he was serious about the breakup. She hoped so. She was tired of receiving awkward text messages from Amber, who seemed to believe they were becoming close for some reason. After Joan hung up, a sharp pain jolted up her right arm, and she had to stop to stretch on a yoga ball she kept in her office. She checked her phone throughout the rest of the day, in case Amber wanted to offer her side of the story. But there was nothing.

31.

THE SNEAKY WHORE

Joan returned to Dallas two days before Christmas, stopping first at the Miracle House to see Wyatt before going to her dad's. It had been two months since they last spoke, and she didn't know what to expect. They wouldn't let her inside, so Joan sat with Wyatt in the backyard in mismatched lawn chairs, surrounded by dead brown oak leaves and acorns, while Wyatt chain-smoked cigarettes. He looked gaunt and pale, as though he'd been through a war.

"It's so weird to see you smoking," Joan said.

"I know, it's gross. But it's pretty much all there is to do here," he said.

"Remember when you were like seven or eight and you wanted to smoke cigarettes so bad? You used to follow my dad around, picking up his butts and smoking them." Joan laughed. When he was little, Wyatt mimicked everything he saw in movies. He had some nineties action movies memorized beginning to end.

"Yes, I remember. He would start yelling at me and chasing me around while I smoked them." Wyatt laughed. "Anyway, what's new with you?"

She told him about her new job. She was the campus director now. She had eighteen employees reporting to her.

"Wow. That's amazing. You've sure come a long way since *the*

Incident," he said, referring to the time she'd gone to the Dallas campus in a blackout, cussed out the night staff, interrupted a student recording session, and ridden around on a scooter until she was finally restrained and locked in the microphone closet.

"Right? I've come so far," Joan said, and laughed.

She asked him about the recovery program. It was twelve-step based, he said, but with a religious slant. Meaning they studied the Bible as well as the Big Book. He was working at a Starbucks down the street. Part of the program was you had to have a job. He went to AA every day. Another requirement. Sometimes, Randy would pick him up and take him to meetings. He'd even met Amber a few times, a fact that distressed her. She didn't like the idea of Amber hanging out with Wyatt more than she did.

"How do you like Starbucks?" she asked.

"I hate it. I have to walk there every day and it's in a really bad part of town, and prostitutes yell at me every time."

"You mean you haven't fallen for any of them?" Joan quipped. She began singing the romantic ballad from *Moulin Rouge*, but he didn't seem very amused, so she stopped.

"When I get there, I can't even count people's change," Wyatt continued. "It's the weirdest thing. I can see the number on the cash register, but I can't figure out how to create that number with coins."

He hung his head, baffled.

"It's okay. This is just temporary. A lot of people struggle with math."

"And I'm going to these AA meetings every day, and everyone seems so happy in there, and I don't understand. I feel so different from them."

"Do you really think you're an alcoholic?"

"I was spending every dime I made on weed and alcohol. I definitely have a problem with it."

"I know, but do you think you might have something more? Like schizophrenia or something?" Joan almost whispered the word *schizophrenia*. It felt so confrontational, so unwelcome. The family had stopped using it months ago. Nobody wanted to hear it. Especially now that he was in a halfway house, for which that diagnosis would make him ineligible to receive insurance money.

"Oh, no," he said. Almost brushing it off. "Yeah, they used to think I might have that, but they don't think so anymore."

"They don't?" Joan asked, wondering who *they* referred to.

"I just have a bad drug problem. All the symptoms I had could have been from drugs too. Like the billboard thing. That could have been from mushrooms."

"Were you on mushrooms, though?" Joan asked. Wyatt didn't answer, he just looked down, flicked his cigarette on the ground, and stubbed it out with his shoe before lighting another.

Joan didn't press. She didn't want to spook Wyatt and make him think she was an imposter again. She felt like she was walking on eggshells. She felt like the old Wyatt was already gone and had been replaced by someone cowardly, dishonest, and afraid.

"Do you have any instruments here?"

At this, he seemed to lighten up a bit. "Yeah," he said. "I have my keyboard."

"Do you remember the song you wrote? 'Conquistador'?"

"Yeah, of course," he said.

"Maybe we could make another song soon. I've been experimenting with poetry. I've got a ton of haikus. Maybe some of them would inspire you again."

"I'd like that," he said unconvincingly. He didn't ask to read any.

The wind picked up. Dead leaves blew around. Joan shivered, wrapped her jacket tight around herself. A counselor from the Miracle House peeked out onto the porch and warned Wyatt that it was almost time for a house meeting.

"Please. Whatever you do, don't kill yourself. Okay?" Joan said before leaving. She didn't know why, but she felt compelled to say this.

"I won't," he said.

"Things will get better, I swear they will. But you have to stay here on earth. You have to promise me."

"Okay," he said. "I promise."

227

That night, Joan went to a Dr. Seuss—themed ice sculpture exhibit with her dad and Amber. They'd gotten back together, apparently. She wasn't sure when and didn't ask. Randy bought them all VIP wristbands, because, as he put it, money was "no object." The wristbands earned them unlimited rides down an ice slide, professional pictures together in front of the Cat in the Hat, and a cup of hot cocoa at the end. The event was a complete bore, but Amber appeared to enjoy it immensely, and Randy pretended to enjoy it as well.

On Christmas morning, Joan sat in the living room with her dad and Amber, exchanging gifts, and still acting as if their breakup had never happened. Amber wore her reading glasses, a bathrobe, and snowflake-print pajama pants while she watched Joan open the gifts she'd bought her—a hot-pink G-string from Victoria's Secret, a small motivational journal called *Beautifully You*, and an ugly white purse. Joan's dad gave her a wrapped shoebox with four hundred dollars cash inside.

Joan thanked them for the gifts but realized how immensely sad the scene was. In years past, the entire extended West family, including Wyatt and Henry, would have all gathered at Mama and Papa's ranch in West Texas. But things were changing and fracturing. The Wyatt situation, among other things, had disrupted the family's ecosystem.

Joan packed the gifts into her trunk before driving to her second Christmas, with her mom's side of the family, at their ranch in Central Texas.

Henry would be flying into College Station that night. He had spent Christmas Eve with his girlfriend's family, in order to spend the least possible time with theirs. Joan felt jealous that Henry had a partner and a new family he could insert himself into. She was desperate to do the same.

She picked up Henry and drove in the darkness. The stars were bright in the sky, and at times like these, she wished she could live out in the country. There were no Occupy protestors out here. There were no prostitutes screaming at you on the way to Starbucks. There wasn't even a Starbucks. Joan told Henry all about the madness between their dad and Amber.

"God," Henry said. "Why does he always make such bad decisions with his love life?"

"Beats me," she said.

"Why can't he just find one nice girl and then stick with her? That's what I'm doing. It seems so obvious to me."

"I don't know," said Joan. She didn't want to think about her own awful decisions in love. After all, she was still struggling to get over Vince and Roberto. The weekend before, she'd accidentally had sex with her neighbor in a blackout, breaking her vow of celibacy. She didn't even like him, but his dad owned *The Onion*, which she thought was impressive. It was so much easier to talk about how bad her parents were at life and love. Henry didn't need to know the sad truth about her own failures.

She told Henry about her job, about how stressful it was and how nobody respected her.

Then she told Henry about Wyatt. About how the family was all in denial about his illness.

"I don't know what to do," she said. "All I can think is that I need to quit AudioPro so I can go to medical school to become a psychiatrist, then I can study the brain and try to solve Wyatt's problem myself."

Joan had had this idea while she was high a few weeks before but hadn't shared it with anybody yet. It seemed too far-fetched.

"That's a great idea," Henry said. "Med schools are always looking to diversify with other majors like English."

"Really?"

"Yeah, there'll be more hoops to jump through, and you'll need a good MCAT score, but I could help you study for that."

Henry had been a lead teacher at the Princeton Review in Durham and knew how to ace every standardized test. It was one of his life's passions.

"You quit taking those pills, right?" he asked. "I don't think you'd do well in med school on crack."

"Oh yeah," Joan said. "Of course."

"Good. I didn't want to have to stage an intervention." Henry patted her on the shoulder and smiled like they were in on a joke.

They arrived at the ranch, a squatty, decrepit house designed and built in the seventies by Dolly's late father, an alcoholic real estate mogul who immigrated to the United States from Czechoslovakia. He'd changed his last name to Duncan to sound more American. He died when Joan was a baby, from drinking. The patio was littered with tacky décor—frog statues, rusted wagon wheels, and metal signs that said things like *Eat, Drink, and Remarry*; *Texas ain't no place for amateurs*; and *Life is too short to live in Houston*.

Joan and Henry sat in the living room with Dolly and the rest of the Duncan family, around a bushy cedar tree decorated with tinsel and lights and mismatched ornaments collected over the years. Dolly had gotten Joan an entirely new wardrobe from Nordstrom. Clothes fit for a school director. Colorful and patterned skirts, silk blouses, shift dresses, trousers, all modest yet spunky, emanating cool-teacher vibes.

"I spent over four hours at the store picking them all out," Dolly said, invigorated. "If you don't like any of it, they have a really good return policy. We could go back together sometime and get more."

"Thanks so much," Joan said. She hoped the new outfits would help the faculty, staff, and students take her more seriously as the director. But that was doubtful.

She was interrupted by a phone call from her dad and went outside to take it, under a vast black sky peppered with bright white stars. Randy was just wondering if she'd taken Henry's Christmas money with her. He'd withdrawn four hundred for Joan and four hundred for Henry. He'd meant to put Henry's shoebox in Joan's trunk but forgot, and now it was missing. Joan told him no, she only had her own cash and shoebox.

"Are you sure?" Randy said.

"Yes," Joan said. And then, "Did you ask Amber about it?"

"Yeah, she said she hasn't seen it."

"Hmmm."

"She wouldn't sink that low. No, no, she couldn't. There's just no way she'd do that."

After Joan hung up the phone, she went immediately into her bedroom and closed the door. She turned on a cowboy-boot-shaped lamp and emptied her suitcase onto the bed. She opened her bottle of Adderall and emptied it onto the patchwork quilt, counting the orange pills slowly and carefully, one by one. She checked the date on the bottle and counted the pills again. And then again. Seven pills were missing. *Bitch*, Joan thought. Amber, the sneaky whore, had taken the one thing that was irreplaceable to Joan. She'd robbed her of three days' worth of motivation. It was official: Joan hated Amber.

32.

A BLANK SLATE

Shortly after Christmas, when Joan returned to Austin, the roof of the AudioPro campus caught on fire. Joan arrived to work one morning and there was a fire truck in the parking lot, and all the staff were standing outside. Leaves had piled up on the roof, a firefighter explained to her, over many years of maintenance neglect. One spark had set them off, and dense gray smoke came billowing through every vent, ruining all the expensive audio equipment almost instantly.

Even though the incident hadn't technically been Joan's fault, she felt like the faculty and staff blamed her anyway. How was she supposed to know the roof needed to be cleaned? She just got there! She hated Craig for making her look so negligent.

With the semester starting up again in mid-January, Joan had only two weeks to:

a) find a new building for the school and move all the files there
b) furnish the new building with all new office furniture and audio equipment
c) record every purchase meticulously in a spreadsheet, against previous equipment, to try to recoup insurance money later.

Randy, Tanya, and the insurance adjustor emphasized that Joan had to purchase the new items as quickly as possible, to prove to the insurance company that they absolutely needed them. The longer she delayed a purchase, the easier for the insurance company to argue that they could operate the business without it. She spent days ordering soundboards, speakers, microphones, desks, office chairs, and filing cabinets. It was a million-dollar game of chicken, and Joan was at the wheel. The pressure she felt was immense. It was like the time she'd revamped the school library, times one hundred. She hardly slept for two weeks. She was on the phone with her dad constantly, which usually ended with him yelling and her crying and hanging up. Her chronic pain became worse and worse as she took more and more pills to manage herself. Some nights, she slept on the floor of her office at the new campus to maximize her productivity. She had so little time. Being a campus director was even harder and more mentally taxing than being a writer. Her job was a never-ending and nebulous cloud of stress that followed her constantly, even in her dreams. She felt sorry for herself and the tremendous weight she was forced to carry. Still, despite everything, the school was put together and ready for the students in mid-January. She spent most of her days afterward meeting with unhappy students, who complained that they'd signed up for the old location, not this location. The old location had character and history. This one felt like an office. This wasn't what they'd thought they were getting. Joan had to sit and nod and say she understood their concerns but her hands were tied. In this way, it was similar to her job at the capitol.

She returned to Dallas in February. Her dad was having surgery to replace his shoulder and needed someone to take care of him. He and Amber were seriously over this time, so she definitely couldn't do it. Amber couldn't be trusted to take care of anything, he said. Randy had found out she *had* stolen Henry's Christmas money after all. Could Joan believe that? Her former girlfriend, the controlling lesbian/roommate, had sent him a text message confirming the theft.

"Unbelievable," Joan said, even though it had been obvious to her all along.

When she got to her dad's house, he told her that while he was in surgery, he needed her to do him a small favor. She needed to go with Tanya to clean out Amber's apartment. He'd hired movers to get his furniture back. Since his name was on the lease, and he'd paid the rent in full, the apartment manager said he'd unlock the door for them, as long as Joan showed her ID.

"What? Why would you schedule the movers at the same time as your surgery?" Joan panicked.

"Why not?"

"Don't you think you should be there?"

"Why would I need to be there? You and Tanya can handle it."

Joan came to the grim realization that it was part of her job as campus director to execute the task. She had to follow the orders of her CEO. She dropped him off at the outpatient hospital and met Tanya at the leasing office of Amber's apartment complex. The apartment manager seemed invigorated and excited by the task, almost forgetting to ask for Joan's ID. They all rode together in a golf cart to building number three, where the big white moving truck sat hissing and wheezing and ready to go. The three of them, followed by the two movers, walked up the three flights of stairs to Amber's front door. They knocked and waited. There was no answer. The manager knocked again.

"Must not be home," he said. He inserted the key and swung the door open.

"Hello?" Tanya barked. "Knock knock!"

Joan followed Tanya into the apartment. It looked pretty much the same as Joan remembered, only a lot messier. Along the walls were several white trash bags filled with empty tallboy cans, liquor bottles, and cigarette butts. There were a couple of new stains on the carpet. Tanya directed the movers, who began hauling the largest pieces of furniture away, which bobbed through the air like dark brown clouds.

Joan dug around through Amber's drawers and cabinets, looking for pill bottles and finding dozens. She wanted to take her revenge and steal seven pills back from Amber. But the good ones—painkillers, antianxiety, uppers—were all empty. The rest were useless antidepressants and antipsychotics.

In Amber's bedroom, she started shuffling through plastic bins under the bed, hoping to find better pills, but all she found were papers and photographs. In one box, Joan found a framed picture of the two of them together from December. They were at the Dr. Seuss–themed ice sculpture exhibit, wearing heavy blue coats, hoods pulled over their heads. The frame was silver, with etched flowers. "Best Friends," it said. Her dad had taken the photo. She ripped it in half, placing Amber's side of the picture back into the frame, and returned it to the bin. She folded the picture of herself and shoved it into her pocket.

In another bin, she found photos of Amber with her infant son and a stash of notebooks and journals. Joan sat on the floor, flipping through the notebooks, devouring the entries as quickly as possible. They were full of regrets, complaints, despair, suicidal thoughts, and delusions. Wow, Joan thought. She'd had no idea how screwed up Amber was. She almost felt bad for her.

Tanya was on the phone with Randy, updating him. All the furniture was out. They were about to leave.

Joan felt rushed, confused, and in danger of losing something important. She wasn't sure what. Perhaps she could write a short story about Amber someday called "Red Hair, Big Boobs, Alcoholic, Thief." Perhaps she would get it published somewhere extra flashy like *The New Yorker*. Before they locked the apartment back up for good, Joan looked one more time at the empty space, at all the trash bags full of cans and bottles and cigarette butts. Amber still had what mattered most—her bins, her photos, her notebooks, her soul. Joan imagined what it might feel like to be Amber, coming home to find her apartment like this—nearly empty. A blank slate. From here, Amber would be forced to begin life anew. Perhaps, in this way, she was receiving a gift from Joan and her father and Tanya. The gift of minimalism. This was all she had now.

33.

BLOODSUCKING VULTURE

Joan stayed in Dallas for several more days while her dad recovered from surgery. During this time, he and Tanya updated her that firing Craig and moving locations had triggered an emergency ACCSC audit of the Austin campus. Agents of the accrediting body would visit her school in only a month and would have free rein. They could interview whomever they wanted and look through every nook and cranny for something, anything, Joan had done wrong. "If you screw this up, they could shut the whole school down and put me in jail," Randy reminded her, lying in bed with bandages wrapped all around his new shoulder. "Your inheritance is at stake." Joan spent her free time sneaking her dad's Oxy and writing haikus about how stressed out she was.

Tanya recommended Joan go to the Houston branch of the school, to meet with the campus director there, who could help prepare her for the audit. Joan spent an entire morning with the woman, going over everything the auditors might be looking for. The Houston director explained that the ACCSC would be especially hard on Joan, now that a new regulating body, NACIQI, had been created by the Department of Education to oversee their audits and ensure they weren't getting too buddy-buddy with career colleges. It really was unbelievable. What would happen when NACIQI was accused of cozying up to the ACCSC? Joan asked. Would a new regulatory body be formed to audit them? Would every honest small business be closed and every person end up working for some regulatory body someday? Mitt Romney couldn't take power soon enough.

After her training, Joan drove across town to visit her mother, who had been calling and wanting to see her since Christmas.

When she arrived, her mother greeted her cheerfully, Joan's black cat following behind her. Dolly had been living at Joan's grandmother's house for the past nine years. After the divorce from Doug, she sold Joan's childhood home in Lewisville, claiming PTSD, and came to Houston to help with the family business.

"Catwoman, your mommy is here," Dolly chimed. "She misses her mommy," she reminded Joan.

It had been almost two years since Joan had left her cat with her mother. Whenever Dolly complained about the burden on the phone, Joan would tell her to just take Catwoman to the pound if she didn't want her. Joan was done with pet ownership. She couldn't handle the guilt she felt listening to the cat's unhappy yowls. She was a terrible cat mother. "You don't mean that," Dolly would say. "I'm not taking your cat to the pound, Joan."

Joan reached down and stroked the cat, who quivered with pleasure at the feel of her fingernails against her spine. Joan sat down in a miniature pink chair next to a massive lamp; the cat jumped on her lap and purred. Her mother sat at the fireplace, smoking and craning her neck to blow the smoke up the chimney. This was something she'd done Joan's whole life. Remarkably, the trick worked, and there was no lingering cigarette smell on any fabrics in the home.

Dolly updated Joan on things she already knew. Over the past several months, she had sold all the family's commercial properties for a modest but considerable sum. Joan's grandmother had been moved to Arizona to live with Joan's aunt, who Dolly felt wasn't stimulating

Grandmother enough. While Dolly used to take Grandmother on field trips—to museums and gardens and movies—she worried that Joan's aunt was keeping her in front of the TV too much. Dolly reiterated to Joan that she had chosen not to take any salary or commission for the extra work she'd done on her siblings' behalf to sell the properties. She wouldn't dream of it. Instead, she chose to move through life perpetually stewing in resentment toward her siblings for taking advantage of her. Dolly then reminded Joan of the exact amount of money the family now had, and while it seemed like a lot, it would be divided into three, and then divided again between her and Henry. So it would not be enough for Joan to live on. Joan would need to find a dependable source of income, or at least get married to somebody who had one. But Dolly warned Joan against thinking a man would swoop in and take care of her. She really wanted Joan to have her own money, she said. She then told Joan that she'd updated her will again and started explaining the changes.

It had only been fifteen minutes, and Joan was already on the verge of an anxiety attack.

"Mom," Joan said. "You talk about your will every time we're together. If you die, your lawyers will explain it to me."

Her mother asked about Wyatt and listened while Joan relayed that Charlene had put him in a Christian halfway house for alcoholics, even though he probably had paranoid schizophrenia and/or bipolar disorder.

"She gave up on him too early," Dolly said, shaking her head. Joan had heard this before. Dolly didn't approve of Charlene's decision to move away while Wyatt was still in high school, apparently missing the irony that she'd done the same thing to Joan after her divorce from Doug. Joan had spent a whole summer unsupervised at her house in Lewisville when she was sixteen, playing video games and Ping-Pong with her friends late into the morning hours.

Dolly began peppering Joan with questions about Amber. *What was her name? How old was she? How long was she sober? Why would Randy date her if she had so little sober time? Didn't he know you're not supposed to "thirteenth step"?*

"Imagine what the people in his home group say about him," Dolly said, and shook her head, thinking about how superior she was to her ex-husband.

"I have no idea why he liked her, she was so boring," Joan said.

"He always needs something to stick it in," her mother said.

"Disgusting!"

"I'm sorry!"

"Why did you marry him, anyway? Why did you choose to have kids with him?" Joan was tired of her mother trying to pit her against her father, as if it were somehow Joan's fault that he was the way he was. As if Dolly had nothing to do with bringing him into her life.

Dolly sighed like this was something she'd often wondered. "He was fun," she said.

Joan got a Fudgsicle from the fridge and lay on the sofa, ready to relax. Her mother, on the other hand, had finished her cigarette and was becoming restless.

"Do you want to go look at antiques?" she asked.

"Not really," Joan said.

"Why not?"

"Look around. We are already surrounded by antiques. We should be getting rid of them, not shopping for more."

"Okay. . . . You can come with me to my storage unit. I've consolidated two into one. Aren't you proud? I only have this one now. No more stuff in Lewisville. I'm making *progress*."

Dolly smiled, working hard to counter Joan's stormy mood with her manufactured sunshine.

"That's great," said Joan. "But I would rather not. I'm actually really tired."

"I need help going through it," her mother said. "You're never here. It's mostly your stuff in there."

"Oh. Really?" Joan said. The cat lay purring on her uterus. "In that case, just burn it."

"You don't mean that. You don't want me to burn all your childhood things."

What in a past life have I done to deserve this? Joan wondered as her mother drove through the tree-lined streets of her grandmother's neighborhood, swerving in and out of the correct lane while also re-filling her plastic cup from a two-liter of Diet Coke and smoking a cigarette. Joan gripped the handle above her window tightly. Dolly saw herself as a master of multitasking, but her distracted driving had required her to hire a personal traffic lawyer to deal with all the tickets she received, which was at least one per month for her entire adult life.

"We used to own that house," Dolly said, stopping in front of a white mansion on the corner of Memorial and Voss. "Grandmother sold it for almost nothing in 1990. It wasn't even listed. She just accepted the first offer. That's how bad she was at negotiating. She was nothing like Dad." Dolly shook her head. "Guess how much it's worth now."

"Please, don't tell me," said Joan. And she meant it. She didn't want to know. But her mother told her the number anyway, which was in the seven figures.

"Mom! I said I didn't want to know." Her mother never seemed to hear a word she said, and if she did hear, she never took anything Joan said seriously. It had always been like this. Ever since she'd developed the ability to speak.

Joan felt genuinely heartbroken, knowing how rich they could have been if they still had the mansion in their portfolio. If her grand-father hadn't drunk himself to death so early, and if her grandmother hadn't been so foolish with his assets. Now that she had a dollar amount, she had one more reason to resent her poor grandmother. That mansion was worth more than all their shitty strip malls com-bined. If they would have just kept it, Joan wouldn't have to worry about getting a job or getting married to someone who had one. She wouldn't have to work at AudioPro and listen to students complain to her all day. She wouldn't have to oversee the big audit coming up. She wouldn't have to worry about anything at all.

Dolly pulled into Public Storage on San Felipe. The bright orange door slid open to reveal towers of boxes and plastic bins and trunks, neatly stacked to the ceiling. The mere sight of the unit gave Joan a wave of anxiety. Her mother was a hoarder.

"Oh my god," said Joan.

"Quit it. Just help me."

Together they began heaving some of the bins aside, loading them onto a rolling cart. Despite never stepping foot in a gym, her mother was freakishly strong, much stronger than Joan. Joan watched her mother's agile but toneless body as she bent down. Her shorts were ill fitting, hanging down and revealing the top of her lavender panties. Her shirt, bandana printed, was too short and exposed a sliver of pale belly. Together, they filled the back of the Expedition with a dozen random containers to bring back home and sort through. Joan wanted nothing to do with the task and slumped in the passenger seat. Her mother, however, seemed invigorated by Joan's presence.

"Once we go through all this, I'm going to start looking at houses in Austin," she said, before hitting a curb. "I lived there first, you know. In college."

"Congratulations," Joan said.

"I'm just saying, I wanted to live in Austin before you moved there. I'm not just moving there because of you."

"Okay," Joan said.

"I want something by the water, I've decided. . . . Also, I think I'm going to get a job. It's always good to be refilling the tank, not just depleting it. I want you to learn that."

"I know," Joan said.

When they got home her mother began unloading the boxes and bins, arranging them all over the yellowing carpet of the formal living room.

"I'm taking a break," Joan said, and she walked up and down the street, listening to a conservative podcast to drown out the sound of traffic and the feeling of being inside her own body. Dennis Prager was talking about the danger of godlessness and leftism. When people look to the government to fulfill their basic needs, he said, society loses its sense of community, churches and charities lose their power. The bigger the government, the smaller the citizen, he said.

A ding from her phone alerted her that she'd received an email. She basically gasped when she saw that it was from *The Paris Review*. The subject line read: "Your Submission." She opened it immediately and held her breath. This was her moment of redemption.

> Dear Joan West,
>
> Thank you for submitting your manuscript. We regret that we are unable to publish it, but we appreciate your interest in The Paris Review.
>
> Yours sincerely,
>
> The Editors

It seemed like the standard form rejection, but at the bottom of the email was another note, which read:

> PS—We'd like to pass along a note from our editor regarding your submission:
>
> "This sure is lively, but no stakes."

Joan closed the email. It was official: She was a total and complete failure. She had sent out her best work, and it had been cast aside, discarded. No stakes. Perhaps her entire life had no stakes. Maybe she wasn't really an artist at all and was destined for a bland career in vocational school management. She would never be a famous writer. She'd only been deluding herself this whole time. Depressed, she hurried along the shaded sidewalk back to the house.

Inside, her mother was still emptying the bins onto the floor. "I have a headache," Joan said. "I need to lie down." Joan escaped to her bedroom. She plopped down on her creaky four-poster bed and read over her submission to *The Paris Review*. In this light, the story seemed awful. Why had she ever thought it would be published?

She pushed her laptop away and opened an MCAT study guide she'd brought with her. Henry had sent the book to her in the mail, and she'd signed up to take the test in the spring. She tried to study, but it was so boring that she closed the book after five minutes. She didn't know what to do with herself. She pulled her laptop back onto her legs and opened cowgirlsandindians.docx. Surely, there was something good in there. Something in her writing had convinced Paul that she was worth mentoring. Surely, it hadn't all been a complete waste of time and energy.

Her cat jumped onto the bed and attempted to crawl on top of Joan. She swatted the cat away. "I'm working, Catwoman."

But fifteen pages in, Joan was already frozen, unable to proceed. Every paragraph, every sentence, every word, was infused with an embarrassing mixture of third-wave feminism, nihilism, and narcissism. Now that Joan was older, wiser, and Republican, she couldn't identify with the girl, the voice telling this "story," which seemed not like a story at all but a string of miserable moments recounted by a narrator who thought she was the next Bret Easton Ellis. Aside from a few memorable scenes—her narrator and her roommate, Nazma, going to South Beach for Halloween, dressed as a Sexy Islamic Terrorist and Sexy Jeff Gordon, respectively, and backing her BMW into a palm tree while tripping on LSD—Joan knew the novel was absolute trash. She couldn't read any further. She closed her laptop again, her face flushed.

She would never make it as a writer. She would probably never make it as a psychiatrist either. She would be stuck in the nepotistic hell-web of her dad's career college forever. Perhaps she could go to law school and become a political commentator, like Ann Coulter, but prettier and more nuanced. No, she could never do that. She wasn't sure enough of her own opinions to broadcast them publicly.

Joan's head was spinning; her muscles ached and burned. Her

pain pills never seemed to be working. She would venture to the kitchen looking for chocolate. Something to numb herself. Something to enjoy.

When Joan emerged, she saw that her mother had arranged all her childhood toys around the family room. Power Rangers stood guard in front of the fireplace, whale stuffed animals swam about the carpet, dolls in dresses holding Beanie Babies lined the sofa. A Furby, a Tamagotchi, and Polly Pockets were displayed on the coffee table.

Had she gotten rid of anything?

"Come sit," her mother said, sitting on the fireplace hearth. "Help me go through this stuff."

Joan sighed, "I don't want to right now."

"If not now, then when? You're never here."

"I already said I don't want it. Just donate it all."

Joan's mother ignored this comment.

"Do you remember this?" Her mother held a stuffed orca that Joan had gotten at SeaWorld when she was in the third grade. Joan had been obsessed with whales back then. She read every book about every whale. She painted her room blue and got ocean-printed bedsheets. She hung *Free Willy* posters above her desk. It was the year before her mother met Doug, who had ruined everything with his Bibles and devil talk. Once he moved into the house, Joan stopped feeling passionate toward whales or toward anything. She started struggling in school and missing assignments. When she came home, she wouldn't even open her backpack, unable to focus on anything but sitcoms.

"You used to love this thing. You played with it all the time. You used to bring it everywhere we went. Come hold it."

"Mom, can't you see that I don't give a shit about this crap anymore? Can't you see that I'm a grown-up? Why can't you just move on?"

At this, Joan's mother became someone else. Joan could see by the look in her mother's eyes that she had triggered Dolly's core trauma, whatever it was. Joan stiffened when Dolly first threw the stuffed whale at Joan, which landed softly against her chest. Unsatisfied, Dolly picked up a nearby Barbie doll and hurled it hard at Joan's face. Joan ducked and felt it whoosh by, like George W. Bush dodging a reporter's shoe. It crashed into the wall behind her.

"What the hell is your problem? That could have hit me in the head!"

Her mother sat, silently indignant. "I'm just asking for your help," she said.

"I'm going back to Austin," Joan said, desperate to escape. "But I can help for an hour."

This seemed to leave Dolly both breathless and speechless, like she'd been punched in the gut. "You just got here."

"I know, but I've been out of town awhile, I was in Dallas before. I need to go home and try to get my life together. I'm the director of a school, you know. The whole campus depends on my example."

"Unbelievable," her mother said.

"What? I said I'd help for an hour."

"I'm just out of words." Her mother lit a cigarette. She was stone-faced. Joan stood there, waiting. "Pack your shit now."

"What?"

"If you want to leave, you should just leave now. There's no use waiting. I'm tired of putting up with this. You just take and take. You're a bloodsucking vulture."

Joan went into her room and began packing her things. She was shaking. Every cell of her body felt like it might die. Her mother stood in the doorway and briefly watched her pack, shaking her head in disapproval before going back to her bedroom.

When Joan's bags were packed, she loaded them into her car while her mother watched from the doorway. As Joan sat in her BMW with the engine running, Dolly came outside. Joan rolled down the window.

"I can't believe you're just going to leave me here like this," her mother said, tears in her eyes.

"You told me to leave."

"I didn't mean that."

Joan exhaled heavily and turned off the ignition. She went back inside with her bag.

"Are you still seeing that therapist?" Joan asked. "The one who talked about boundaries?" She sat in her grandmother's brown recliner and turned on her mom's favorite crime drama, settling in for the evening.

"Yeah," Dolly said. She moved the whale stuffed animals and lay down on the sofa. "Why?"

"Think she could fit us in tomorrow before I go?" Joan asked.

34.

NONE OF THIS IS JOAN'S FAULT

The next morning, Joan sat in an oversized armchair in Dolly's therapist's home office, while Dolly, in a matching chair, went on and on about how selfish Joan was. Dolly's therapist wore a scarf on her head because she'd just completed chemo, and didn't seem to be listening to Dolly, who was talking about how Joan spent *two whole weeks* in Dallas with her dad recently. "Two weeks!" she said. And then she spent only *one day* with her.

"Joan didn't grow up with him like she did with you," the therapist told her. "Maybe she's making up for lost time."

Joan had never considered this to be the reason why she preferred being around her dad. That she hadn't gotten enough of him as a child. It was an interesting theory. She'd always thought she preferred Randy because he was more honest, more self-deprecating, than Dolly. Of course he was a mess, but at least he didn't demand as much from her emotionally. At least he could take a joke. She watched her mother to see her reaction. Dolly didn't seem to hear the therapist and just kept talking about all she gave to Joan. All she had given over the years, and all she gave now. "I just give and I give and I give," Dolly said. For Christmas, she'd spent over two thousand dollars at Nordstrom on work clothes for Joan.

"I didn't ask for the clothes!" Joan said. "She buys me things so she can control me."

"I'm happy to buy her clothes, I only asked for the small favor of helping me go through my storage unit. Nothing I give her is ever reciprocated."

"You're the parent, she is the child," the therapist said to Dolly. "It isn't her job to be the adult and take care of you."

Hearing this surprised Joan. Nobody had ever spoken to Dolly this way. Not in Joan's presence, at least. Was what she said true? Was Dolly expecting Joan to be an adult? How could her mother expect that from her? Joan couldn't even take her own trash out or keep a plant alive. She had never even peeled a clove of garlic. Why would anyone think she could take care of them?

"This is not your fault," the therapist kept saying to Joan while her mother talked. "None of this is your fault."

Driving back from the appointment, Dolly was quiet, and things felt calm, as if something had been broken open and light was beginning to shine through. The words of the bald therapist rang through Joan's head, shaking her foundation. *This isn't your fault. None of this is your fault.*

She was the child. Her mother was the adult. It sounded like common sense but felt revelatory. Especially coming from a third party, someone objective who had a PhD and knew things.

All of a sudden, Joan felt justified in everything she'd ever done. *I'm the child. None of this is my fault. She's the adult.* At the same time, she felt bad for her mother, who had always reminded her of a three-year-old emotionally.

Her mother drove her to Baskin-Robbins, where they ate ice cream cones, and then Barnes & Noble, which Dolly knew was Joan's favorite place to shop. Dolly was sucking up now, in the only way she knew how. For the first time in a while, it seemed, Dolly had lost the battle and was even admitting to losing.

At the bookstore, Joan bought *No Plot? No Problem! A Low-Stress,*

High-Velocity Guide to Writing a Novel in 30 Days. She knew she'd never write a novel that fast, but she liked to read the words of people who pretended it was possible. The writers of these guides had never written any good novels themselves, of course. But somehow people still bought them, including Joan. The guides contained hope, which was the only thing an aspiring writer really needed.

Dolly didn't object to any of Joan's purchases. For herself, Dolly bought Ben Carson's memoir, *Gifted Hands*, about his growing up in the projects and becoming a brain surgeon, the first ever to separate twins conjoined at the head. Joan had read *Gifted Hands* already and thought it was okay.

"You should probably get this one," Dolly said before they left the store. She had a sheepish smile on her face and was holding a self-help book called *Toxic Parents: Overcoming Their Hurtful Legacy and Re-claiming Your Life*.

"No, no," Joan said. "I don't need that." She didn't want to kick her mom while she was already down by buying that book. But she took a mental note of the title and planned to buy it on her own later.

Back at the house, Dolly put the toys back into the bins while Joan sat on the patio reading *No Plot? No Problem!* She would need to leave soon. She had a lot of business to attend to back home, with the campus audit. But Joan was enjoying herself for the first time since arriving to her mother's. It was sixty-seven degrees and sunny. The sky was cloudless and blue. February was one of Houston's nicest months. Her MCAT study guide sat open on the table beside her. She planned on getting to it soon, but she had a couple months before she would need to take the test. Plenty of time. She wasn't worried. Dolly brought Joan an iced tea with lemon and a plate of sliced apples and cheese. She didn't bother her about the toys again, or make her feel guilty for leaving. Dolly was taking care of her. Joan was the child. Dolly was the parent. The dynamic made Joan feel lighter, if only tem-porarily. It made her want to linger.

35.

A MISGUIDED AND DELUSIONAL
SENSE OF PURPOSE

In early March, two weeks before the campus audit, Joan's dad
called her at four in the morning, three times in a row.

Each time, Joan pushed decline. What the hell was he thinking?
AudioPro business could wait. She was in a deep sleep, angry to be
disturbed. The fourth time he called, she answered.

"What?" she said.

"Wyatt killed himself!" Randy shouted.

"No," Joan said. Her heart sank to the floor. "No, he didn't. He
promised he wouldn't."

"Yes, he *did*. He stabbed himself in the chest!"

"How is that even possible?" Joan said. Aside from Elliott Smith,
she had never heard of anybody doing such a thing.

"He's gone." Her dad erupted in tears.

"No, no, I can't live like this," Joan began whimpering. She couldn't
breathe. It felt like she might vomit. A world without Wyatt felt all
wrong.

"You're going to be fine," her dad said. Already calming down.
"Trust me, you'll get through it."

"What am I supposed to do? Do I go to work?"

"No," he said. "Just get to Dallas when the sun comes up, after you
calm down a little."

Joan hung up, then paced around her apartment, her heart beating quickly. She started to deep clean, something she never did without drugs. At this moment it felt urgent. All dirt must go. No more grime in her life. Without thinking much about it, she opened her bottle of Adderall, dumped her remaining pills into the toilet, and flushed. It was what Wyatt would have wanted for her to do. To feel alive. She didn't flush her weed or her pain medicines, though, which she still might need. Then, realizing that no drug she took could alleviate the way she was feeling, she collapsed onto her floor and cried for twenty minutes.

Afterward, she stood at the sink washing dishes, staring at the black TV screen as if it were playing a movie instead of nothing. *He promised*, she thought, feeling betrayed. *He promised me he would stay. He was supposed to live here.* She washed a knife, examining its sharp blade under the stream of water. She pictured Wyatt stabbing himself, like some kind of samurai or disgraced Spartan soldier. What had been going through his mind? Was he trying to preserve his honor? *I will never look at a knife the same way again*, she thought.

She called Henry, who told her he still hadn't even cried. He sounded confused. He didn't think it had hit him yet. Because all he could feel right then was anger. "Isn't that one of the stages of grief?" he asked. "Anger?"

"I think so." Joan was also confused. She was straightening a picture on the wall. Then wiping tiny spots off the mirror in her bathroom. Adrenaline was coursing through her veins and she could not stay still. It was such a big bathroom, and such a big mirror. She would never get all the spots.

"I'm so mad at Wyatt," Henry said. "Like, all I want is to punch him in the face once I get to Dallas, but I can't. That is such a weird feeling."

"I don't know how I'm going to handle this," Joan said. "How am I going to run the school? We're getting audited soon. And I was supposed to take the MCAT next month."

"You can't let this get in the way of your responsibilities," said Henry. Joan knew that he would just throw himself even harder into his work now. The way he had after Wyatt's first suicide attempt in his apartment. Henry would probably graduate at the top of his class

251

at Booth, start making six figures right out of the gate, working eighty hours a week. This was how he'd always avoided pain ever since he was a teenager—overperforming.

"Have you really thought about it?" Henry asked. "I'm just starting to realize what this means. Wyatt is nothing but a memory now. We'll never see him get any older. Isn't that weird? He'll never have kids. He only exists in our minds now, however we remember him."

This concept was far too devastating for Joan to grasp. She hung up with Henry and started texting all her cousins, Claire, and her favorite ex, whom she'd dated in Miami: the one she had hurt the most, whom she had cheated on multiple times, who had moved across the country explicitly to get away from her. An only child with no father, he had PTSD from when his mother died slowly of cancer. Joan asked him how one ever got over a thing like this.

It's not something you get over, he wrote. *It's just something you learn to live with.*

It didn't cross Joan's mind that the two losses were different. Instead, she took the speed of his reply as a sign that he was still in love with her, hung her hat on it, and moved on.

She threw some clothes into a duffel bag and drove to Dallas with a misguided and delusional sense of purpose. Her body was abuzz with an organically manic energy she'd never felt before. She must tell Wyatt's story now. This was a sign from the universe. It was time to wake up. The reason her writing all sucked was that she'd been focusing on the wrong subject—herself—all along.

She tried to remember things about Wyatt, poignant moments of revelation between the two of them, but everything ran together in a blur. All she had now was her memories, and she could feel them slipping away.

She cursed herself for not visiting him in the hospital or the halfway house more. If only she'd known then what she knew now. The last time she'd spoken to him, he sounded utterly hopeless. Maybe if she'd called him more, she could have convinced him that the struggle was worth it. That there was a light at the end of the tunnel he was in.

But she knew she was ill-equipped to deal with Wyatt's profound despair. She pretty much hated her own life, felt incompetent in her own unique way. What on earth could she have said or done that would have helped?

When she walked through the front door of her dad's house, he came out into the dining room, hunched over the grand piano, and started to weep like a woman. "He was just here," Randy said. "He played 'Walking in Memphis' on this piano and he sounded *so good.* It was the first time I've ever heard him sing a whole song from beginning to end. It was incredible."

Her dad went over to his laptop, scrolled through his music, found "Walking in Memphis," and hit play. Marc Cohn's soulful voice boomed through his state-of-the-art sound system and echoed against the Spanish tiles and stucco walls.

"Oh, this is terrible!" her dad wailed. Joan walked over and hugged him. They were now both crying, embracing in a brief moment of intimacy uncharacteristic of them both. Eventually, her dad pulled away and said, "Great song, isn't it?" For him, the rush of emotion seemed to have passed like any other bodily function—a sneeze, a coughing fit, an orgasm. He turned up the volume to an uncomfortable level and the song became viscerally painful to listen to. Joan wiped her eyes and went to lie on the couch with Skipper, who buried his head underneath a pillow to shield his ears from the sound. She stroked his fur until the music finally stopped. Then Joan sat with her dad in the living room, where they drank black coffee and talked.

It turned out that Randy was the last person in the family to see Wyatt alive. He'd been trying to help Wyatt maintain his sobriety, taking him to AA meetings around town every week, talking to him about God and the twelve steps. Wyatt couldn't get past step two, he said. The "Hope Step," is what they called it. *Came to believe that a power greater than ourselves could restore us to sanity.* When Randy would try to talk about step two with Wyatt, he'd just shake his head, look at the floor, and say, "No, not me."

Her dad had picked Wyatt up yesterday and taken him to lunch. Wyatt was acting real weird, not fully engaging in conversation, looking around the room a lot, muttering things under his breath. Her dad called Aunt Charlene afterward, saying again he thought Wyatt needed a shrink, something more than the twelve steps and prayer. There was something deeply wrong with him.

"He's just playing you," Charlene had said. "Haven't you learned that by now? The world is his stage, you are just his audience."

When her dad told her this, Joan became livid. From that point, she began blaming Wyatt's death solely on her aunt and the rest of Wyatt's immediate family. This made her feel better about the situation somehow.

Henry and Dolly flew in that afternoon, and the next morning they all met Charlene, Grace, and the rest of Wyatt's family at a megachurch outside of Dallas, where they gathered on the porch and drank iced tea, planning the funeral. Charlene and her husband sat at the head of the table with a frog-faced pastor Joan had never seen before in her life. He had a buzz cut. Joan distrusted him immediately. *Wyatt probably never even went to this church*, she thought, looking around.

Joan, Henry, and their parents sat down and learned the upsetting details about Wyatt's death from Charlene. Joan started stringing every scene together in her mind, creating a film she would replay, over and over again, probably forever. First, he got a steak knife from the Miracle House kitchen and hid it between the pages of a Bible. Then he snuck the knife upstairs to the bathroom, where he stabbed himself four times in the chest. The first two wounds were only superficial, the knife's blade being caught mostly by his muscle and bone. It was one of his second two stab wounds that ended up being fatal. Those two he thrust upward, underneath his rib cage, piercing the side of his heart.

"Jesus," Joan said.

"He must have been in so much pain," Mama said.

"He just wanted to stop hurting," said Grace, turning to Steve and burying her face in his chest.

Joan figured this wound would have resulted in a quick death, but it had not. Something about the side of the heart Wyatt pierced was significant, Charlene explained. She'd been a surgical assistant in the military in her twenties and spoke of the medical details of Wyatt's death with an off-putting formality. Wyatt was still able to walk and talk for at least an hour, Charlene continued. After bleeding out for a good while, he stood up, went to his bedroom, and told his room-mate, "I didn't mean to do this, can you help me?" He lived long enough for the counselors and the other clients of the halfway house to wrap his body in blankets and drive him in the van to the hospital. "Please don't let me die, I don't want to die," he said to them the whole way there. He was still alive and begging for his life when they got him onto a hospital gurney and wheeled him into surgery, where he died on the operating table. According to one of the nurses, the last words he spoke were, "I'm a dead man."

Joan hated thinking about Wyatt's final moments. That he regret-ted his actions made it so much worse somehow. She wanted to crawl into a hole forever. The entire thing sounded dramatic, cinematic even. As unbelievably painful as it was, it fit with everything she knew about Wyatt, and his final words were exactly what she would have pictured him saying right before dying. "I'm a dead man" sounded like a line from a cheesy nineties action movie. During their eventless summers at the ranch, they'd spent hours watching and acting out battle scenes from these ridiculous movies. Joan had seen Wyatt fake-die many times.

"Hindsight is always twenty-twenty," the pastor said. "This is not any-body's fault. Nobody at this table is responsible for what happened to Wyatt."

People nodded solemnly, but Joan knew that the only reason he would say this was because everyone at the table was at least partially responsible for what happened to Wyatt. He had an obvious mental illness that went mistreated for years. The path to his suicide had been absolutely littered with red flags. Why hadn't anybody stopped it? Why hadn't she?

"He changed his mind," Charlene said, starting to cry, her tough façade crumbling. "He did it and then wanted to take it back."

"Oh, how awful," Mama said, and started crying too.

Papa patted her on the back. He was chewing on a toothpick, eyes glazed over in disbelief. "He really showed us, didn't he?" he said.

"He *showed* us?" Randy scoffed. "What the hell is that supposed to mean? Yeah, poor us."

Joan felt relieved that her father seemed to be angry too. The family had become fractured like never before.

The pastor confidently assured everyone that even though Wyatt killed himself, he was in heaven. Everyone sullenly agreed, but Joan could tell they were all doubtful. She saw right through the charade. In her family's brand of Christianity, could there be a sin more egregious than playing God and extracting yourself from this fallen world?

Then they started talking about catering, music, how to design the brochures. Feeling powerless, Joan, Randy, and Henry took a firm stand on something that was probably none of their business: the picture of Wyatt they would print on the funeral programs. Charlene had chosen a picture of him from high school that Joan, Henry, and her dad did not like. In the photo, Wyatt was wearing a powder blue button-down shirt, smiling with rosy cheeks in front of an emerald green backdrop. Joan's dad pulled up a much better option on his phone. He'd taken it at an AA meeting. It was the last photograph taken of Wyatt, alive. His head was shaved, and he was staring desperately into the camera, looking gaunt and tragic and sad. This is how he was, Joan's dad insisted. This is the truth. This is how we should see him now. The rest of the family conceded reluctantly.

Henry sent Joan a text message from across the table.

Wyatt would be laughing at all this.

Joan agreed. That they were fighting over what picture to print on Wyatt's funeral program was Wyatt's brand of absurd. She looked up at Henry and saw that he was crying, for the first time since he got the news. She got up and moved to his side of the table, where she sat next to him and placed her head on his shoulder.

They wanted four people to give eulogies. His mother, Charlene; his sister, Grace; and Chet had all agreed to do one.

"What about one of the cousins?" Charlene said. "Joan?"

Suddenly everyone was looking at her, jarring her out of her daze.

"What about Henry?" Joan said. "He's a better speaker. They were like brothers."

"I think you should do it," Henry said. "Y'all were closer in age. You grew up together."

"Fine," she said. "Of course, sure, anything for Wyatt."

36.

THE REAL DEAL

Y ou know, we don't have to go to all this planning shit," Randy
said in the car on the way home. "Charlene and them, they'll
handle all this. We don't have to be so involved."

"It's important to show up," Dolly said.

"What else do we have to do?" Joan asked. She was overcome with
a desire to control and oversee Wyatt's funeral planning. She wasn't
sure why. Perhaps she was just relieved not to have to think about
AudioPro for a few days, or her impending compliance audit.

"I dunno," Randy said. "Nothing, I guess."

Henry stared quietly out the window. "I can't believe they didn't
take him to a psychiatrist," he said. "I told Charlene, when he did this
at my apartment, he was stone-cold sober."

"No use dwelling on that now," Randy said. "It's over. You have to
just forgive and move on."

They got stuck in horrible DFW rush-hour traffic. There was
nothing but cars and more cars as far as the eye could see. Randy
became incensed.

"Look at this shit! Do you see this? Look at all these cars. This shit
is so unsustainable. You know, I think Wyatt was onto something . . .
he got out just in time, man. Just checked out. He's the smartest one
in the family."

"Randy," Dolly hissed.

"What? There's no way this is going to last much longer."

He started talking about his plans again, for when the world ended. He was going to install a safe underneath his RV in which he would keep his AK-47s, a sawed-off shotgun, gold, and ten thousand dollars in cash.

"What makes you think that gold will be worth anything once the world is ending?" Henry asked.

"What do you mean?" Randy yelled. "That's all we'll have is gold!"

"Yeah, but it has no inherent value. Money is only worth what society has agreed upon. In chaos, gold would be literally worthless."

Their dad drove silently, mulling this over.

"It's all about fuel," he said. "All we'll need is enough fuel to make it out to Breckenridge. Papa's getting windmills, we could get water from Gonzalez Creek. We could raise pigs and goats. Cattle might be difficult, on a small scale."

"That's what you want, isn't it?" Joan said.

"What?"

"For the world to fall apart. For everyone to start looting for resources. For total anarchy and destruction. You just want an excuse to use your AK-47."

"Yeah," Randy said. "I love it when shit hits the fan."

When they got back to the house, Joan privately asked Dolly for some Vicodin. She had run out of her own and had a headache from crying.

"I don't have any," Dolly said. "How about some Tylenol?"

"What do you mean? You always have Vicodin."

"I don't have them," Dolly said firmly. "I threw them out. And you should probably do the same with whatever it is you've been taking."

"I don't know what you're talking about," Joan grumbled, before she went upstairs to start working on her eulogy. She wanted to do right by Wyatt, so it needed to be great, which stressed her out. How could she have been so careless, flushing her Adderall back in Austin? She felt like an idiot. She googled "how to write a eulogy." Online, it said there was no way to make a mistake in a eulogy, as long as it was honest and true. This sounded like writing advice from Hemingway. *Write one true sentence. Write the truest sentence that you know.*

Joan wrote: *They never took him to a psychiatrist.*

She crossed it out.

She regretted agreeing to write a eulogy and considered backing out. She asked herself why. Why was she the cousin chosen? The family thought she was a writer, that she had some special bond with Wyatt. Each of these its own kind of myth. She was not a real writer. She had never written anything complete or publishable. And Wyatt had a special bond with pretty much anyone he spent any significant amount of time with. He was like a dog in that way, excited and grateful for whatever company he had. Unlike Joan, who hated almost everyone including herself, Wyatt could bring out the best in people and make them feel they were at the center of his world.

She wrote *Wyatt was like a dog* in her notebook. She scratched it out.

She recalled a day in her dad's kitchen when Wyatt told her: "I don't think I'm normal. I don't need to be around people. If I were stranded on a desert island by myself for the rest of my life, I think I'd be just as happy as I am now. I can entertain myself."

Joan had envied him so much in that moment. It had always been her dream to be completely alone, isolated and happy, but for some reason, no matter how hard she tried to stay away from people, she always went out looking for some form of twisted love.

She wrote *Wyatt didn't need people* in her notebook, and then scratched it out. It didn't sound good or communicate what she was trying to express. Nothing did.

Joan considered what Paul had taught her about good writing in Miami. No clichés. Don't tell but show, etc. She remembered sitting in his Creative Writing 101 class as he urged her and her classmates to come up with interesting ways to say "Johnny was a good guy" without actually saying it. He shot people down one after the other as they talked about saving puppies, doing charity work, and helping old people. Those are too expected, he said. Those are boring. Stop boring me. Joan raised her hand and offered, "Johnny wears the same shoes every day."

"Yes!" Paul had said. "That's exactly what I'm talking about. Johnny wears the same shoes every day. You tell me this and I know in my heart that Johnny is a good guy. I don't know why, I don't even know what it means about Johnny, but I can *feel it.*"

She wrote *Wyatt wore the same shoes every day* in her notebook.

She went downstairs and sat with her family in the living room, to elicit their help. Henry said to talk about his courage. "Remember that time when he gave us all names as if we were superheroes? He named himself the God of Courage, he named you Goddess of Wisdom, I can't remember what he named me," Henry said. "That was such a weird night."

"Integrity," Joan said, remembering. "I think he called you Lord of Integrity, or something."

Wyatt had been speaking in a strange accent, with an air of intensity, as if they were characters in an epic fantasy, tasked with saving humanity, when really they were just home for Thanksgiving break.

Henry talked about what a shame it was, losing someone like Wyatt who had so much potential. "He really was a comedic genius too," Henry said. "Hard to put into words, though. Like, with all his jokes, you had to be there."

"Say he was fun," Dolly said. "Every family needs someone fun. At least one. All the fun ones in my family are dead."

"Oh! I've got something," her dad said. "Write that he was one of those people who had *it.* In all my years in the music business, there were people who crossed your path, once in a blue moon, who just had *it.* They had something that set them apart from everyone else."

"You either have it or you don't," Dolly agreed. She had been with Randy all through the seventies, when he ran his first recording studio out of a ranch in the Hill Country. Joan had found pictures of her mother posing in a field of marijuana they'd grown together there. Dolly had been angelically beautiful then.

"Exactly," Randy said. "You either have it or you don't."

"Yeah, but how would Joan say that in a speech?" Henry asked. "Isn't it better to show, not tell? Isn't that like the cardinal rule of writing?"

"It depends," Joan said.

"He was the real deal," her dad said, louder this time. "He had IT."

Joan wrote *Wyatt had IT* in her notebook.

Her mother lit a cigarette and sat on the hearth of the fireplace. She looked at Joan, seeming uneasy, fearful of Joan's grief and where it could lead. "Whatever you write is going to be fine," her mother said. "Don't drive yourself crazy over it."

It became clear to Joan that her family was only making it harder to write. She needed to get away from the house. "I'll be back soon," she said, and slipped out while Randy, Dolly, and Henry were watching Fox News and arguing about politics. Her parents were in lock-step and were accusing Henry of being a Democrat, which he was vehemently denying. Randy was shouting something about globalists when Joan snuck out the front door.

She drove down the street to her dad's neighborhood country club, which was less nice than his other club at the Four Seasons, but Joan preferred this one because it felt more homey and had better ranch dressing. She and Wyatt had eaten there constantly when they lived with her dad. They were both completely broke and charged all the food to Randy's account. She sat at the bar, opened her notebook, and ordered a dirty martini to help with her writer's block. As time passed, she ordered a few more martinis and sat watching an NBA game on the TV. She remembered watching sports with Wyatt. When the Mavericks made it to the finals against the Heat, he stood up to watch the games, jumping around the room as if he were on the team. He did the same thing with *The Lord of the Rings*, and *Gladiator*, and seemingly every nineties action film. For Wyatt, movies and television opened a portal to a new world. While Joan used television to numb out, he seemed to experience it fully. He could watch the same film on an endless loop for weeks, never growing tired of it, until he had every scene memorized. Maybe this was a detail Joan could put in the eulogy. Maybe this had been a red flag.

She wrote: *Wyatt stood up while watching TV. He watched the same movies over and over again. He wore the same shoes every day. He was like a dog. He was a good guy.*

Joan knew how terrible the eulogy was so far. She thought about her creative writing classes again. She tried to think about Wyatt as if he were a character in a short story instead of a real person. "What does this character want?" Carlos would always ask when she turned her sloppy, hastily written stories in. Joan never knew the answer. Her character was always based on herself, and she didn't know what she wanted.

"To die?" she'd answered once. Carlos sighed and said, "If your character wants to die, then she needs to take concrete actions to try to make that happen. Observing interesting things doesn't make a character interesting. Your narrator has to make decisions that impact her life. And by the end of the story, how does she change?"

Joan looked at Carlos and shrugged.

At the top of a blank page, she wrote: *What did Wyatt want?*

> *Wyatt wanted to join the marines. He wanted to be a country singer. He wanted to be a cowboy. He wanted a bigger penis (he lamented this often). Wyatt wanted a woman to love him as much as he loved her. He wanted to be normal. He wanted to go to sleep at night and work during the day. He wanted to stop drinking and smoking weed and pay off his credit card debt. He wanted to pay back our grandparents, his mom, my dad, and his brother-in-law. He wanted to pay back the IRS and Target and Best Buy. He wanted to move into my apartment in Austin. He wanted to move in with our grandparents out in the country. He wanted to move to Central America and surf every day. He wanted to start over somewhere, anywhere.*

And then a memory came to her. She wrote it down.

> *I remember surfing with Wyatt in Costa Rica. We would go to the beach every day, swim out, and get pummeled by the waves. It was rare that we would catch one. Even rarer for us to stand up on the board. Mostly, the ocean had her way with us. The salt water pounded us into the sand, jetted through our noses and eyes, and we spun in circles like socks in a washing machine. Afterward, we would lie on the shore and bemoan our lack of power. Wyatt talked about the ocean as if it were a woman, breaking his heart. She's a cruel bitch, he would say. She doesn't care how we feel. We're nothing to her. She's so gorgeous and I love her, and she doesn't even care if I live or die.*

Writing this memory, thinking about Wyatt, trying to put him into words, it was all too much for Joan. The surfing scene wouldn't make any sense in a eulogy. It had no underlying point that she could articulate. She stopped writing and had a beer. Then took a few shots.

Maybe a change of scenery would inspire her to finish. Joan left her car in the parking lot and walked back to her dad's in the dark, along the golf course cart path, ascending steep, tedious hills. Her legs grew tired. Her mind grew tired. The liquor was hitting her now; she could feel her body shutting down, like it used to in Miami, on the IM fields outside her dorm, after kamikaze night at the Pike house. Only now, out here, there would be no one to drag her home. Suddenly, now that she was numb, ideas for her eulogy started coming in all at once. This was what usually happened. Drought, drought, drought, then a flood. Joan collapsed into a sand trap, planning to write. It was all coming to her now, clearly and beautifully. Why had she ever lost faith in herself?

Joan woke up in the sand to an ant biting her hard and sharp on the face. She slapped her cheek and rubbed vigorously. Her notebook was open in front of her. There was a circle and some wavy lines drawn on a blank page. She had no idea what the symbol was supposed to mean. Was it the sun? What time was it? She felt urgently thirsty, walking the rest of the way home on the dewy and deserted golf course. Her mother was sitting awake in the living room, in the blue glow of *The O'Reilly Factor*. Joan filled a glass with water and sat on the shag rug to watch while she rehydrated. Bill was one of the few hosts on Fox that Joan could actually tolerate. She appreciated his dickishness.

"Where have you been?" Dolly asked sharply. "I was worried sick."

"I was in the backyard working on the eulogy," Joan said, trying to keep her cool.

"You were not in the backyard. Where is your car?" Dolly spoke in a harsh whisper.

"At the country club," Joan admitted. She hung her head. "I'm sorry."

Joan began to cry, and Dolly lowered herself onto the carpet and embraced her. "I know this is hard for you," she said. "I know you loved him."

Joan allowed herself to cry in her mother's arms. She couldn't believe she'd written nothing, and it was only two days until the funeral. She washed her face, hoping to sober herself up and continue working. Lying in bed with her notebook, she felt useless. She set the notebook to the side and closed her eyes, but she was having trouble sleeping. She kept imagining Wyatt stabbing himself, the way the blade felt and sounded, piercing his skin and cartilage and muscle. Joan snuck into her dad's bathroom and found his bottle of Oxy from his shoulder surgery. This was one of her favorite medications, but she took it sparingly. It felt so good that she didn't even try to get a prescription of her own. She couldn't trust herself with it. She knew from Dr. Drew that mixing benzos and opiates was how everyone died. She didn't want to die. Not yet, anyway. Her mother came upstairs and sat on the edge of Joan's bed, running her fingernails over her back and along her arms and through her hair while she fell asleep.

"My sweet angel. I wanted you, you know," Dolly said.

"I know," Joan said. "You've told me."

"The doctors all said I shouldn't get pregnant again after I had cancer. Something to do with the hormones. But I didn't listen."

Usually, when her mother told her this, Joan became unreasonably angry. She heard: I wanted you, therefore I own you. I wanted you, therefore you must do as I say. But her mother's affection didn't bother Joan right now, as the Oxy was kicking in. She did not bristle. She simply wanted to feel the tickle of her mother's nails forever. She melted into the bed like syrup.

37.

SHE HAD HER DEMONS

The next day at the wake, Joan was extremely hungover. All the adrenaline from her initial shock had disappeared. At first, she refused to enter the room where they'd put Wyatt's embalmed body on display. Her stomach was too upset. Instead, she lingered by the punch bowl, constantly refilling her plastic cup. When Joan was younger, all she needed was an Advil and a Gatorade after a night of drinking and she felt fine. Now, since she was nearly twenty-five, her hangovers were getting powerful. The only cure for Joan's current condition was hydration, electrolytes, and time. If only she could have any influence on the passage of time. Perhaps she would rewind, back to the beginning, to experience Wyatt all over again. Or perhaps she would fast-forward all the way to the end, as Wyatt had. To her final moment, when she would learn everything there was to know. Which was quite possibly nothing at all.

Joan watched a group of young men she didn't recognize moving around the wake looking confused, like shell-shocked war veterans. Those are the Miracle House guys, Grace told her. The ones who were living with Wyatt, who rode with him to the hospital. She pointed out the roommate, who looked much worse than the rest of them—tired, pale, dark circles under his eyes, walking around as if he himself were dead. "I feel so bad for him," another one of Joan's cousins said. "Think of how traumatic that must have been."

But Joan felt jealous of him. She wished she could have been with Wyatt in his final moments. There was so much she wished she could have told him. Did he even know what he meant to her? Tears formed in her eyes as she walked toward a tray of cookies, where she began eating them greedily, one after the other.

She began to worry about the eulogy she still hadn't written. She took her Moleskine notebook out of her purse and carried it toward the casket room with a pen. Perhaps she could sketch him. Perhaps seeing Wyatt might give her some profound insight into his death and her grief, which she might use in her eulogy.

"It won't," her dad said when she told him what she was up to. He told her looking at Wyatt's body wouldn't help her with anything. It had no meaning. It was just a shell that Wyatt's spirit used to be inside.

Joan decided to go look at his shell anyway.

When she reached Wyatt, the first thing she did was touch his fingertips. He had long and slender piano-playing fingers. She pressed against the hardened calluses on his left hand, formed from over a decade of playing guitar. Before he had even touched a piano, he had been one of the best country pickers anyone had ever seen. She imagined how things might be different if he'd pursued a different path— a wholesome country music path. If he'd never lived with Chet and never worked at Rick's and started putting gel in his hair and wearing black skinny jeans. Perhaps he would have been better off. But probably not. His girlfriend, Mabel, was in the room watching the casket from a chair against the wall, as if she were on guard. She was quietly pretty, with long, shiny hair, but not striking like Ruby, who was also in there, lurking around the casket while Mabel stared. Ruby approached Joan, took her hands, and started whispering, gossiping about Mabel's unfair treatment of her. Her jealousy. She didn't own Wyatt. Joan agreed and instinctively took Ruby's side. She didn't trust Mabel. Then she recognized the absurdity of being caught up in a love triangle where one of the points was dead. It would have made Wyatt laugh, Joan realized, which made her start crying.

In bed that night, she read more instructions online about how to write eulogies. The articles said things like "Consider the audience" and "Stay positive." If you're going to say something negative about someone, keep it vague. For example: "He had his demons, but . . ."

> He had his demons, but he wore the same shoes every day.
> He was in thousands of dollars of debt, but he knew his
> creditors by name. He crashed his brother-in-law's car on
> purpose, but they were all just fender benders. He was
> arrested, but they let him off for mental health reasons.

After the wake, Joan, along with her dad and brother and Dolly, hired a professional bagpipe player behind everyone else's back. Their dad paid him in cash. They decided together that this was something Wyatt would have wanted, since it evoked the funeral scene from one of his all-time favorite films, *Backdraft*, about heroic firefighters, scored by Hans Zimmer.

When Joan got to the funeral the next day and saw the bagpipe player, she laughed to herself at how ironic he looked, walking around the lobby of the culturally vapid nondenominational megachurch in his kilt, Scottish dirges echoing from the walls. She hoped that the music annoyed Charlene, Grace, her grandparents, and especially the phony pastor.

Hundreds of people showed up. People from Wyatt's high school, middle school, and elementary school. People from all around Fort Worth, who'd seen him play at Rick's, or at house parties with his burgeoning indie band, or at Guitar Center for fun. Former neighbors showed up. Former coworkers from all Wyatt's odd jobs. Joan waited with her family in a quiet, dark room full of tissues, pitchers of ice water, and cookies while church staff hurried to move all the flower arrangements onto the big stage in the stadium-like auditorium from the smaller room they had planned to use. You can never predict these things, the pastor said, explaining the delayed start time. *Wyatt was famous*, Joan thought, walking in a line into the main chapel. And by extension, so was the entire West family. Just for today, they were the stars of the show. Everyone stared as they filed in and took their seats in the first two rows.

Aunt Charlene was the first to stand up and speak. She read scripture that she said she had turned to back when Wyatt was in North Carolina, when he went to his first mental hospital. It was all Jesus this, Jesus that. Charlene was wearing an elegant black hat, a black satin dress, and a large bejeweled cross around her neck. Her husband and remaining children stood behind her, off to the sides, like embarrassed wives of philandering politicians.

"He was a tortured artist," she said through tears. "As Wyatt said to the Miracle House guys, 'I have a bad heart.' So he stabbed it, as his final performance on this earth. But he didn't mean to die. What he meant as another stunt, another gotcha, Jesus said, 'Nuh-uh, Wyatt, I gotcha.' Jesus took my baby on that operating table. He needed another angel. Now Wyatt is playing piano for Jesus, hallelujah."

Grace went up next. First, she played her song "Baby Brother" on the electric harp. She'd written the song a few months after Wyatt's first suicide attempt in Durham. While Wyatt was in rehab, Grace had recorded the song at AudioPro and created a lyric music video, with encouraging words scrolling over images of glistening ponds, open fields, and majestic clouds, which was posted to YouTube.

In her speech, Grace compared Wyatt to a shooting star that had just burned out. He was too brilliant and bright for this world. Joan was okay with this analogy.

"My prayer for all of you today is that if you don't know Jesus, you will seek and find Him," Grace said. There it was again. Were they trying to turn Wyatt's funeral into a tent revival? In this family, it always came back to Jesus. Everything began and ended and was always run through with Jesus, Jesus, Jesus. In that moment, Joan hated Jesus. What the fuck had Jesus done for Wyatt? What had Jesus done for her?

After Chet gave another vague and uplifting eulogy, Joan stood up and approached the stage with her notebook, her hands shaking. There was almost nothing written on the pages that hadn't been scratched out. She looked at the page with the circle and the squiggly lines she'd drawn while blacked out on the golf course. Then she faced the large auditorium, squinting into the bright stage lights, which blinded her and felt warm against her skin. She scanned the blur of hundreds of faces staring back at her, waiting to be moved.

"My cousin Wyatt was a good guy," Joan began. "He had his demons, but he wore the same shoes every day. Black high-tops, untied. He loved people. He was kind of like a dog." She heard someone clear their throat. She saw someone whisper into someone's ear. She saw people shifting in their seats. She saw Charlene, dabbing her face with a tissue. She started to panic, looking at the notes, then at the sea of faces. What else was she supposed to say? She closed the notebook and thought about what Wyatt would want her to say, if he was lingering around the auditorium, watching them all as a ghost. She wasn't sure what he'd want, so she said the first thing that came to her mind.

"You know, there's been all this talk about Jesus today. I thought you should know that Wyatt changed his mind about Christianity right before he died," she said. "I'm the only person Wyatt ever told about this. He made that clear. He called me only a few days before killing himself."

She had decided to lie. Something to hurt her family, the way she felt they had hurt Wyatt. Joan tried not to look up, to see the faces of Charlene and Grace and her grandparents.

"That day, he told me he'd committed his life to Satan, the fallen angel, the original rebel. He told me that was who he always connected to the most. So, if Wyatt is playing piano anywhere right now, it's not in the happy clouds of the heaven you all want to believe in. He's playing in the flames of hell. And he's happy about it. He told me last night during my séance, when I conjured his spirit. Because I don't know if you knew this, but I'm a witch now."

A loud gasp broke the silence of the auditorium. A mother's shriek. Joan's family stared in horror. The pastor began walking toward Joan, toward the microphone. "Hail Satan!" Joan said before exiting the stage quickly and taking her seat, where she began crying.

"All right," the pastor said, clearing his throat. "Emotions are running high, which is understandable." He loosened his collar, looking around nervously as a choir filed onto the stage. "Let's all stand for a rendition of 'Amazing Grace.'"

Joan didn't expect her family to ever forgive her for what she'd just done. She didn't care. She was tired of platitudes. Tired of pretending there was a happy place that only some people were allowed into after all this. Life was hard for everyone. Why shouldn't we all get the same punishment or reward? It all sounded like bullshit to her. A way for the elites to take advantage of the masses and manipulate their behavior.

At the reception, most people avoided making eye contact with Joan. She didn't mind, because she hated everybody too. It was their fault that Wyatt had died, and she didn't see the point of talking to them ever again. While sipping on punch, Joan overheard one of her cousins complaining that Wyatt didn't look as good today as he had at the wake. He looked bloated and gray, she said with disappointment, like his body was spoiled food.

"Well yeah, what do you expect?" Joan interjected. "It's a dead body that's been decomposing for an entire extra day."

"Are you feeling okay?" Henry asked.

"Are you mad?"

"That was fucking insane, Joan," Henry said.

"I know," she said. "I should have had something prepared. I don't know what came over me."

"I think it will blow over, in time. People have other things on their minds besides your speech. You're not the center of everyone's universe, you know."

"Thanks for the reminder."

Joan went over to talk to Chet and the rest of Wyatt's childhood friends. They thought what she had done was hilarious, that Wyatt would have laughed if he were alive. They understood what Joan was getting at. They shared his avant-garde humor and could take a joke. When Wyatt was alive, he always wanted to say the one thing that would make everyone in the room uncomfortable, and Joan had done just that.

One of his friends, Tucker, was wearing an expensive-looking suit with a purple silk handkerchief in his front pocket. He looked Joan up and down and asked if she'd lost weight. She had, she said. Well, you look good, Tucker said. The other guys in the group rolled their eyes in disbelief and laughed, and one said, are you fucking kidding me, Tucker? Joan felt flattered. She felt suddenly frail and sexy and tragic in her grief.

"Are you coming to the burial?" Joan asked. Tucker and Chet nodded.

"Nice," she said.

Joan rode with her dad, mom, and brother out to the family plot in Breckenridge, near their grandparents' ranch. Wyatt had been born around here somewhere. His mother had been at the ranch when she went into labor.

"I wish I had brought something to bury with him," Henry said.

"Like what?" their dad asked, annoyed. "Should I pull over at this gas station? Do you want to stop and get him a snack?"

"I don't know, just something meaningful."

"What for?" their dad shouted, irritated yet excited by another opportunity to criticize the practice of burial, which he found archaic and primitive. "Who wants to just let themselves rot in the ground? It's fucking gross! Don't people know that you just explode down there? Don't people realize how disgusting that is? What is wrong with people?"

"Randy, that's enough," Dolly said.

"We get it, Dad," Joan said. "You want to be cremated. You don't have to go on another diatribe."

"A what?" he said. "What about a tribe?"

"Yeah," said Henry. "We get the point, we will burn you."

"Good," their dad said. "You can put my ashes in a coffee can.

Remember that movie where they did that? What movie is that from again? That was hilarious."

This was where Wyatt would have wanted to be, Joan heard Charlene say at the graveyard. Out in the country. She still wouldn't even look in Joan's direction. Joan agreed with Charlene on some level, that this was where Wyatt belonged. She thought of all the time she'd spent with Wyatt out here, following him around, looking for animals to shoot, carving spears, making bonfires.

They all stood together under a green tent and cried while the pastor spouted out another bullshit sermon. Joan glanced in Tucker's direction a few times. He looked brawny and mature, grieving in his suit. Joan and Ruby had their arms around each other. Half Chinese and half Mexican, she was just his type, with eyes so brown they looked black. He'd only ever gone for girls like that. Not white. Not evangelical. He thought blue eyes were overrated. Blondes boring. He wanted something different; Joan understood that. She had always wanted somebody different too. A way to sever herself from her family, her roots. A way to become somebody new. Joan was small, but Ruby was tiny, shaking gently in Joan's embrace as she whimpered. When the pastor sent everyone out to find a rock that symbolized their relationship with Wyatt, Joan followed Ruby, mesmerized by her. Joan found a rock that was smooth, simple, and round. Ruby picked a rock shaped like a penis.

Back in the tent, the pastor had everyone place their rocks on top of Wyatt's casket one at a time, while saying a word out loud that represented what he meant to them. The exercise felt stupid, but Joan partook anyway. Ruby pocketed her penis rock, which Joan respected.

The entire drive back home, Joan's dad complained about the family's religion.

"They act like they know everything!" he kept saying. "They don't know shit!"

274

Joan watched the rocky western landscape, remembering all the stories her dad used to tell her when she was little, about the Comanches attacking settlers in wagon trains. About the tribes kidnapping some of the children, raising them as their own. Joan lived for those stories. Back then, she wished some tribe would kidnap her.

"I'm gonna start my own religion. It's gonna be called We Don't Know Shit, and we're all gonna sit in a circle around a room and take turns shrugging and saying, 'I don't know shit.'"

"Sounds like a pretty good religion to me," Joan said. Henry and Dolly agreed.

That night, Joan went out drinking in Fort Worth with Ruby and Wyatt's childhood friends—Chet and Tucker and some others. They walked from bar to bar; there were only a handful to choose from in Fort Worth, all on one small strip downtown. When they got drunk enough, they decided to go to Rick's Dueling Piano Bar, in honor of Wyatt. This proved to be too much for Joan and Ruby, who broke down crying in the street, hugging each other and collapsing into a large potted plant. It was the same place where Wyatt used to sit and play his Casio.

Back at Chet's apartment, Ruby started crying again when she saw Wyatt's Casio set up in the dining room where he used to sleep, with all the flowers from the funeral piled on top. It looked like a shrine. Joan's tears were tapped out, and she wanted nothing more than to get high, go to sleep, and dream she was someone else.

Chet went into his room and came out with a tray of his blunt-rolling supplies, and the four of them sat together and smoked in the living room. Joan was sitting next to Tucker on the love seat. Ruby sat with Chet. Joan looked at the larger-than-life-size decal of Tony Romo adhered to the wall next to the television. Romo held a football next to his face, ready to make a pass, but he was covered in holes. There was a hole in his forehead, his neck, his chest. They were stab marks from the billboard incident, Chet explained, passing her the blunt, which tasted musty and dirty. Joan got up and inspected the holes.

Chet got out his laptop and set it on top of his entrepreneurial books on the coffee table. He started playing all the songs Wyatt had recorded since moving in with him. They were mostly upbeat and poppy and sounded like the Killers. There was nothing country, like many of the songs he'd written around Joan. None of them had the same brilliance or universal appeal as "Conquistador." When Chet reached the end of the playlist, he said he had been convinced Wyatt was going to hit it big someday. He had been so proud of him, he said with a glazed, dreamy expression on his face. He'd been doing so good. Chet said that he never saw Wyatt happier than he was onstage at Rick's, performing in front of all those people.

"Obviously he wasn't *that* happy," said Tucker.

Joan looked at Tucker in a new way after he said this. She saw him as a straight shooter. She decided she wanted him near her.

Ruby slept in Chet's bed, and Joan slept out in the living room with Tucker, who kept whispering in and licking her ear and trying to finger her. Eventually, she let him. In the light of the moon, shining through the vertical blinds, Joan saw that he was covered in stupid tattoos, the most egregious being his last name across his back, written in large Old English letters. A year later, Tucker would get a big tattoo of Wyatt on his shoulder that would look nothing like Wyatt, or any other human. *RIP 1986–2012* it would say underneath, in a banner over black roses.

The next morning, Chet gave Joan a cooler full of Wyatt's writing—notebooks and loose-leaf papers accumulated over the years. Wyatt would have wanted you to have it, Chet said. Because you are a writer. Joan took it home to Austin, opened it up. Inside, she found his stand-up routines; movie ideas; lyrics to love songs about Ruby; prayers and pleas to God, whom Wyatt called his heavenly father, his only father. Joan read long journal entries that Wyatt wrote about wishing he could find a wife who loved him, about not being able to make it in this world, about not being able to hold down a job or stick to a routine, not being able to stay sober more than two days at a time or pay off his credit card debt. It was all so overwhelming. While some of it was lighthearted, his thoughts were like a loop at the end, repeating the same despair over and over again. Joan didn't know what to do with the material. None of the pages were dated. Many of the entries lacked specifics. There were barely any mentions of her or their time together. Disappointed, she put the journals away, zipped up the cooler, and buried it in her hall closet, under bags of unwanted clothes and Halloween decorations. She would deal with it later, after the audit, when she had more time to herself. Someday, she would be ready to write a novel about Wyatt, and she would revisit these journals. She wasn't ready to write it today, but when she was ready, it would be one of the best books ever written.

38.

JOAN V. TEXAS

When Joan first saw the blue and red lights flashing in her rearview mirror, she considered running. It was Monday, the night before the big ACCSC campus audit, and she needed to go home. Her apartment was only a few blocks east. If she were still driving her BMW, perhaps she would have had a chance. But she had totaled her BMW shortly after Wyatt's funeral. Now she was stuck driving her dad's spare car—the bright yellow Jeep Wrangler, lifted, with a roll cage, covered in bumper stickers. Driving this car was like asking to be arrested, she thought, pulling over next to the sidewalk, in front of Urban Outfitters.

I am innocent. I am sober. I am composed, she said to herself.

Joan didn't believe in affirmations but had heard of their efficacy from her therapist, who had assigned her the overwhelming and impossible task of staring into her eyes in the mirror while saying things like "I love you," or "I am beautiful," or "I have a sparkling personality."

The cop was standing outside her window and tapping on the glass with the end of his long flashlight. Joan laboriously cranked the Jeep window down with the plastic lever.

"Any idea why I pulled you over tonight?" the cop asked. He was young, Hispanic, and handsome.

"No. Why?"

Instead of answering Joan's question, the cop retorted with another. Classic. "Where are you headed?"

"Home," said Joan.

"Where have you been all night?"

This was a leading question. It was only nine. A completely normal time for someone to drive home on a Monday.

"The W," she said, adding, "I was there for work."

This wasn't exactly a lie. Joan had been at Vince's concert, and Vince was a graduate of the school. Maybe if the cop knew she had an important job, he would let her go. He would see that she wasn't a drain on the system, like so many others. She paid taxes!

"You work at the W?" the cop said, confused.

"No," Joan said. "I'm the director of a school and I have this big audit tomorrow. Tonight, I was investigating student success stories. For marketing purposes. There was a concert there. . . ."

"You were investigating a concert?"

Joan had said too much. Giving the cop any information at all had been a huge mistake. She braced herself. She'd been coached by her representative, Allen, on how to get out of any DWI.

"Have you had anything to drink tonight?" the cop asked finally.

It was Joan v. the State of Texas now. Every word Joan spoke, every single utterance, could and would be used as evidence against her later. The most important thing was to be polite, but also to give as little information as possible.

"I'm sorry, sir. Under the advice of my lawyer, I can't answer any more questions."

The cop's face betrayed mild surprise, then frustration. "License and registration," he said.

Joan's hands shook slightly as she fumbled through her purse. She hadn't eaten all day. While her Adderall prescription seemed to help her prepare the campus for the audit, it made doing things with her hands much harder. She located her ID and handed it to the cop. He used his flashlight and stood squinting at it for a while. Joan stared straight ahead.

"I'll be right back," the cop said, patting her car with his hand. He retreated to his cruiser, which still had its lights flashing, like a beacon.

Joan sat in the Jeep, waiting. *I am a woman of dignity and grace.*

She hadn't had that much to drink at the W. Not enough to be a danger to the community. One of Joan's few talents was driving home drunk. She reflected on all the times she'd gotten home masterfully in a blackout. And tonight, stone-cold sober, she was pulled over. So ironic. She hadn't had any more than three glasses of chardonnay. Though they had been heaping and consumed in rapid succession. It was possible she'd had four. Maybe she was a little tipsy, but not drunk. Vince had been buying the drinks for her. He'd been wearing his suede hat, his vest.

"I got a haircut," Vince said, removing his hat to reveal a fresh trim. "Not that you'd notice."

"Looks good," Joan said, and gulped a mouthful of wine.

"Congratulations on your new job, you modern woman," he joked.

"Ha, thanks."

"Sorry to hear about your cousin. I saw your posts."

"Thanks," Joan said. She'd been posting incessantly about her grief on Facebook, trying to spread her pain widely and indiscriminately. Eliciting sympathy was now a full-time job for her. The idea that people wouldn't know how much she was suffering, how close she was with Wyatt, bothered her deeply. She'd already changed her profile picture multiple times, alternating between different pictures of Wyatt and her together at different points in their lives. Currently, the photo was of Wyatt and Joan, ages eleven and ten, wearing head-to-toe camouflage, ready to go dove hunting.

"Do you want some advice?" Vince asked.

"Sure," Joan said.

"I lost a buddy once, in college. One of my frat brothers disappeared in South America. They finally found his body at the bottom of a cliff. It was so fucked up." He took a sip of whiskey. "What I learned then is that grieving is something best done alone. It's internal. There's really no use talking about it because nobody else is going to understand the pain or care how you feel. Not because they're bad people. They just won't get it. The best way to deal with a death is just to try to forget about it and move on."

"Yeah," Joan said. "I think you're right."

"I kind of miss you," Vince said, and smiled. "Okay fine, I really miss you."

Joan froze and said nothing. His vulnerability felt like an attack. She hadn't seen Vince since last summer, after the road trip, long before Wyatt's death, which felt now like another era. She had needed help shaving to prepare for a laser hair removal appointment. She could never reach the spots they were lasering (anus and inner labia), and Vince had enthusiastically agreed to help. She recalled lying face down in his tub as she felt him spread her cheeks and glide the razor so gently against her delicate skin. He had treated the area with such care, and such love, that the whole thing felt wildly erotic. But she couldn't bring herself to tell Vince how she felt. She'd always been so embarrassed to love him. That night, they slept beside each other in silence, Joan filled with unexpressed longing as she watched his broad back moving with each breath.

The cop returned with Joan's license. "How much have you had to drink tonight?" he said, trying to catch her off guard. Unfortunately for him, Joan was very on guard, more on guard than she'd ever been in her life. For the first time, Joan felt adequately prepared for something. She was much more prepared for this than she was the ACCSC audit tomorrow.

"I'm sorry," she said. "Under the advice of my lawyer, I can't answer any more questions."

"Step out of the vehicle," the cop ordered.

Joan pushed the large plastic button on the door handle, and the Jeep door creaked as it opened. She hopped to the pavement, trying to project daintiness and ease of motion in her leopard-print high heels. There was a camera on the cop's dashboard, she knew, capturing these movements. *I am sober and I am elegant and full of dignity and grace.*

Joan stood on the sidewalk in front of Urban Outfitters as the cop shined his bright light right into her eyes, the way they do. "I just want you to follow my finger with your eyes, ma'am," he said, holding up his pointer finger, moving it slowly around.

He must have thought Joan was born yesterday. She squinted, looked away. Joan had learned in college that 30 to 40 percent of *sober* people "failed" field sobriety tests. They were subjective and unfair, like everything else in this cursed world.

"I'm sorry, but under the advice of my lawyer, I don't consent to any tests," she said.

"This is standard procedure," he said. "I just need to confirm that you aren't intoxicated, so you can go home."

"I'm sorry, I cannot consent to any tests," Joan said.

"You cannot, or you will not?" the officer said, challenging her.

"I will not. I was advised not to by my lawyer."

"If you haven't done anything wrong, why do you need your lawyer so bad?" The cop was getting agitated, desperate. He had a weak case and they both knew it.

"I'm sorry, I can't answer that question," Joan said.

The cop put Joan in handcuffs and left her standing on the sidewalk alone. He sat in his cruiser for what seemed like forever, doing God knows what. The horrible possibility of being seen by Vince entered her mind. He would be leaving the W around now. What if he saw her out here? Handcuffed, like some loser. Joan pushed the thought away. That negativity would not serve her. *I am not ashamed,* she told herself. *Because I am innocent. I am a woman of dignity and grace. I have a sparkling personality.*

Joan was getting tired of standing. As the minutes dragged on, she wished she could sit or lie down, rest her body and legs. It was likely what the cop wanted her to do. She was still on camera, and if she tried to sit while handcuffed, she would appear uncoordinated, and it would give him evidence for his case. Joan straightened her posture and stood in front of Urban Outfitters like a soldier. She began to think of herself as a hero, a prisoner of war.

When they took her mug shot at the station, Joan tried hard to strike a balance between several emotions she thought she should be feeling as an innocent person—confusion, fear, sadness, but also serenity. Confused as to why she'd been arrested. Afraid to be in such a dirty place with such dangerous people. Still, she worked hard to maintain an air of serenity, which only the innocent could possess. It was a difficult balance, and it happened so fast. In the end, Joan mostly focused on making sure her jawline looked good, the way her cousin from LA who worked for Paris Hilton had taught her. She pressed her tongue fiercely against the roof of her mouth, looked into the camera, and tilted her chin down. Months later, Joan would spend eight hundred dollars to remove the photo from internet search engine results, even though it had turned out surprisingly flattering.

After they took her fingerprints, Joan's ankle was handcuffed to a metal bench in the corner. She watched the officers of the State, wearing tan uniforms with Texas patches on their arms and shiny badges on their chests, as they tackled their administrative busywork.

One by one, throughout the evening, officers came over to Joan to talk, each employing different tactics, until it seemed like the entire staff had tried their hand at breaking her. She had become an office challenge, of sorts, and she heard them muttering among themselves, referring to Joan as "the Total Refusal." "Hey, Jim," one of them said. "You get a chance with the Total Refusal yet?"

If Joan hadn't had anything to drink, why was she slurring her speech? Was that how she normally talked? Was Joan on any prescription medications? Was Joan on any controlled substances? Was Joan sure she didn't have anything to drink? Why were her eyes so red and glazed over? Why did Joan smell like alcohol? Why was she repeating the same thing over and over again? Was Joan in her right mind? She sounded like a robot. Was Joan a robot?

With every question, Joan's resistance only grew. She imagined herself as an armadillo, coiling into a ball of impenetrable shell. She would not be broken by the State. She knew her rights.

"I'm sorry, Officer, but I can't answer any questions without my lawyer present," she repeated.

Finally, a gruff woman sat down next to her with some forms.

"Are you thinking of harming yourself or others?" the woman asked.

Joan looked at the woman. "I'm sorry, I can't answer any questions without my lawyer present."

"I'm not a cop. I'm just processing you. All that's over." She motioned to her left, as if the past were contained there.

This was just another trick, Joan felt certain of it. She'd seen enough cop shows to know they lied with impunity. She said nothing.

"Ma'am, if you don't answer this one question, I will have to assume your answer is yes."

"I'm sorry—" Joan began, but the woman stopped her short.

"I'm trying to help you, here," she said, her voice low and intense. "Listen to me. If you refuse to answer this one question, you waive your right to a phone call. Do you understand? We will have to take you downstairs. We will take all of your clothes. You'll be in jail ten times as long as you need to be."

"I'm sorry," Joan said. "I can't answer any questions or perform any tests without my lawyer."

39.

NO PENS. NO FORKS. NO SPOONS. NO STRAWS.

Down in the basement, everything became colder and brighter. Two lady guards led Joan down a long white hallway lined with minty green doors. It must've been past midnight. The ACCSC would be at the campus in less than nine hours to meet her. She needed to get ahold of her lawyer fast if she wanted to be there in time.

Joan's cell was at the very end of the hallway, next to a small desk, across from another cell that had a big white magnet on its door that read *FEMALE* in black letters. Joan peered into the window but saw no one. Inside her own cell, Joan was told to strip. One of the women held a brown paper bag open, and Joan removed her black sheer top and dark jeans, dropping them both inside. She removed her mood ring, which was almost black due to the cold, and black feather earrings, and dropped them into a plastic baggie that the second woman held. Joan stood facing the guards in her bra and underwear.

"Everything off," barked one of the guards. She had a ponytail slicked back and shining under the light.

"Even my underwear?" Joan said.

"Everything."

"Why?"

"You're on suicide watch. It's a hazard."

Joan unsnapped her sweat-stained beige bra and dropped it in the bag, her breasts drooping and pointy. "I'm not going to kill myself with my underwear," she said.

"Everything off and in the bag, ma'am," the woman said. Joan complied, gently removing her panties, which had a small, soiled panty liner in the crotch. She was on her period and felt appalled showing the guards her brown blood. These were soulless, vile women. This is what the State did to people. It robbed them of their humanity. Joan stood naked under the fluorescent light.

"Put out your arms," one of them said, and slipped a baby-blue backless gown onto Joan, as if she were a young child. The gown had no ties or closures.

"See that window?" the woman said, crumpling the paper bag closed. Joan looked. The window was small—about the size of a cinder block—and located at the top right corner of her cell, looking out onto the lower half of a bush.

"You get to watch the sun come up through there," the woman said. And with that, the door was closed and locked, and the agents of the State were gone. Joan, finally alone in her cell, felt a strange sense of relief. The interrogation was over, and her cell was surprisingly spacious, large enough for her to pace back and forth, trying to generate warmth in her body.

She had everything she needed for the next few hours. Beneath the window, there was a large cement slab, which was her "bed." There was a metallic toilet in one corner, with a small sink attached to the top. In another corner, next to the door, hung a small unbreakable mirror, made of a shiny metal. Joan stared into her fuzzy reflection. She didn't look as bad as she thought she would; her eye makeup was still intact. She could take the bus straight to campus from here for the audit if she needed to.

Bored, Joan stood at the door and looked into the hallway. Down the hall, a man appeared in the window of his own cell and made eye contact with Joan. He smiled and put his tongue through his two fingers, licking them sensuously. Joan quickly stepped away from the window and hid.

Joan didn't belong down here. She wasn't dangerous like that man clearly was. The only time she'd tried to hurt herself was during a fight with her Miami boyfriend. She was drunk and wanted to show him how much he was hurting her. Joan held a knife against the soft skin of her arm, scratching at it while she cried. But she didn't have the guts to draw any real blood. She was too squeamish and sensitive.

Joan needed to get some rest before work. She needed to appear competent, enthusiastic, and alert when the auditors showed up to the school.

Joan sat on the cement slab and curled into a ball. She began shivering violently. It was freezing. She tried to cover as much of her body as she could using the small blue gown, which was hardly better than being naked. The corner was the warmest place. Curled up on the slab, she pressed her body against the cold walls to feel more covered, more secure. There were words and messages scratched into the walls. What tools people had used, Joan didn't know. She hoped to find something profound here, to communicate with her predecessors, but only found short, to-the-point messages, like *bitch, cunt,* and *hell.*

While she was trying to sleep, her soiled tampon slid farther down her vaginal canal with every breath. She practiced her Kegels, gently clenching her pelvic floor muscles while her bare butt cheeks rested on the cold cement. Joan would hold the soiled tampon inside her as long as she could. If she lost it, then she would truly have nothing.

The fluorescent lights remained aggressively bright. Joan squeezed her eyelids shut, tried to block everything out, and rested her forehead against the glossy painted cinder blocks. If she could fall asleep, she'd be out of here before she knew it. She'd wake up and be released in time for work and no one at the office would ever know what happened.

Joan wanted to be good at her job, she really did. During her tenure, she'd read a dozen books about management, networked with industry professionals around Austin, attended the conference in California, and taken online courses through the ACCSC, the TWC, the Department of Education, and the other regulatory bodies, where she learned all about government compliance. She had the certificates framed on the wall, as well as copies placed in her compliance binders. The binders were all the feds and the state cared about. The main thing she'd learned, and was beginning to understand, was that the regulators didn't care about real life, they only cared about what documents you had. You could have the most beautifully furnished school, with the best equipment in the world, the most experienced teachers, and all the regulators would care about was documents.

"They want a whole report typed up if we decide to change brands of toilet paper," her dad would often complain.

Being the campus director was hard. It required managing men twice her age and dealing with her dad's explosive temper. Any time Joan would relay a concern to him from one of his employees, he would yell at her for a half hour straight. If she complained about the yelling, he'd only get louder and say that it was her job to listen to him yell. There was no changing his mind about anything, so she stopped calling.

But the worst part of the job, by far, was dealing with the problem students. As the campus director, it was Joan's primary responsibility to make sure they stayed in school and graduated. Especially the Pell Grant students, who'd gotten federal money to come. She was expected to monitor them, counsel them, and keep them on track and on top of their schoolwork. If a certain percentage of the students didn't stay in school, graduate, and eventually get jobs in the field, the campus would be shut down and her dad could be prosecuted. Something he reminded her of often.

Joan was terrible at exuding this "mother hen" energy, filling this role for the floundering young men at the school. There were one or two female students in each class, but it was mostly men, mostly boys she had to schedule meetings with. Men and boys who were not "cut out" for four-year college. Who were not easily encouraged. Boys with drug habits, babies, baby mamas. Boys who grew up on federal assistance and wanted to make beats. Boys who had gone to Iraq or Afghanistan and had PTSD, who threatened and frightened the other students with their emotional outbursts. Boys who were disappointments to their rich parents, paralyzed by ADHD, who had never liked school before and were not about to start liking it now. These boys wanted to make it big, sing emo songs, play in metal bands. They wanted to work alongside their heroes. The dream would come true for a handful of the students, surely, but not the ones Joan had to intervene with. Some were completely unemployable. Every couple of weeks, one of the teachers—music industry professionals who were expected to prime these students for meaningful and lasting careers in the music industry—would come to her and complain about a large percentage of the students. He would beg for entrance exams. *Please. At the very least a test that makes sure they can read.* These were hardened men, smart and cunning, wily hustlers who had fought for their careers. Joan sympathized, but her hands were tied. Every time she would call her dad and ask about entrance exams, he would yell at her about how the school would go broke if they did that.

One of the students was a legally blind albino who somehow still drove to school every day. She didn't ask questions. One of the students had fluid in his brain, and he would wave to Joan every day, coming and going. He would stand in her office doorway often, smiling while he retold her the story of his oxygen being cut off at birth. He'd almost died, he'd say in a soft whisper. One of the students who'd been in Afghanistan had stood up for their entire meeting about his missing homework assignments, yelling and crying at Joan about having killed Afghani toddlers while she sat stunned.

Suddenly, a banging noise. Plastic against cement, echoing throughout the hall of cells. Joan was jolted out of her daze. She tried to ignore the sound and close her eyes tighter. Then the plastic banging stopped. A temporary reprieve, before a woman started shrieking at the top of her lungs and begging someone to kill her. "Please!" she wailed. "Just kill me. Somebody, please just kill meeeeee." The woman sounded so desperate, Joan felt killing her would be the only humane thing to do. When the screaming persisted, Joan gave up on sleep and stood at the window of her cell, watching. The noise seemed to be coming from the *FEMALE* cell across from hers. There was nothing visible through the window. Taped onto the door was a piece of white computer paper, which read *NO SHARP OBJECTS. NO PENS. NO FORKS. NO SPOONS. NO STRAWS.* in orange Sharpie. Joan grew frustrated, hearing and not seeing. It was like being at the zoo's most exotic exhibit while the animal was hiding in a cave.

But then a woman's face appeared at the window. When she saw Joan, she stopped screaming and stared. The woman had blond and graying frizzy hair. She looked haggard and red-faced, like she'd lived outside for a while. Staring back, Joan was reminded of the look in Wyatt's eyes, through the window of the police car, after the billboard incident. This woman looked to be in her midforties. They both stood there for several moments, locking eyes, before Joan became uncomfortable and returned to her slab.

She found herself thinking about the grim reality of how Wyatt had spent his final days—what it might have been like for him, living in constant terror of being killed by some mysterious force taking the shape of his own family members. How isolating and horrifying that must have been. She thought of all the red flags that she'd ignored along with her family. She had been too focused on her own writing to intervene, too excited about the song Wyatt wrote for her. She hadn't spoken up. She hadn't even visited him in the mental hospital. She was just as bad, just as guilty as any of the people she blamed.

Soon, the screaming began again. And then a banging noise, not plastic, but something heftier and more solid. Joan stood up again at the window. It was the woman. She was running headfirst into the door of the cell repeatedly. She was trying to either break herself out or bludgeon herself to death.

Three male guards appeared wheeling an empty gray chair covered with straps. Swiftly, they entered her cell with the chair, and she began to shriek even louder, shrill and constant, like an alarm. As the men strapped the woman to the chair, a female officer cooed at her like she was a little kid.

"Now, Pammy," she said. "This is what happens when you throw your Coke bottles and try to hurt yourself with them. Soon we won't be able to give you soda anymore. Is that what you want, Pammy? Do you want us to stop giving you soda?"

Pammy didn't even seem to register the guard's kindness. She treated the guards like demons who were trying to drag her off to hell. "Somebody please just kill me!" she cried again. Eventually, she grew tired of screaming and started to sob.

"Just like we had to do with your radio," the female guard continued. "Do you remember your radio? Do you remember how much fun it was to listen to the radio? Remember how we had to take it away from you when you kept using it to hurt yourself?"

Joan would have killed for Pammy's radio, or her soda; both items were visible to her, just sitting there, on a shelf right above the desk outside her cell.

When Pammy had finally grown relatively quiet, the guards stood in a cluster, discussing how long to keep her strapped to the chair. They were concerned about being humane. She'll get tired eventually, someone said. Pammy sighed and moaned in the background. "Excuse me," Joan said through the window while the guards talked. They didn't seem to notice.

"Excuse me," she said, louder.

"What?" the guard barked at her. She put her hand up to her ear. "I can't hear you."

"Could I have some of her Coke?" Joan asked, pressed up against the thick door. "I'm so thirsty. I'm dying. I won't throw it, I promise."

"No!" the woman said. "Drink from your sink!" She was so gruff, so hateful. She'd been so nice to Pammy. What had Joan done to deserve that kind of treatment? She looked at the sink, which was attached to the top of the toilet. Even though her tongue was dry, Joan didn't want to put her mouth near a jail toilet. Gross. Who knew what had been there?

Pammy continued to scream sporadically through the night. Every time it would get silent and Joan would begin to drift, Pammy seemed to sense it and would continue her desperate screeching. Eventually, Joan accepted that she'd never fall asleep here. Instead, she stood on her slab and put her face against the tiny window, watching for subtle color changes in the sky. She had never been so in tune with the passage of time. At home, she always drowned every moment out with conservative talk radio, reality TV, booze, weed, or pills, or some combination of them all. She hated being aware of herself like this. Was this what Wyatt meant by "feeling alive"? As the sky began to grow lighter, Joan began to lose hope of ever getting out and making it to campus in time for the audit. She still hadn't called her lawyer. Nobody knew she was here. She could be here forever.

What would happen at nine when the ACCSC people showed up and she wasn't there? She was the director of the school. She was *important*. She set the tone for the entire company. What would be her excuse? They couldn't know the truth.

Breakfast came, slid through the slot in her cell door by a male guard. "Excuse me," she said through the slot, "it's very important that I call my work. I'm going to be late for my job, and today is very important." The guard told her that she would get no phone call until she went in front of the judge.

"When will I go in front of the judge?" she asked.

"When it's your turn," the guard said, and walked away.

Joan sat on the slab and opened the paper sack. Inside, a bologna sandwich and a grainy apple. Joan ate the apple slowly, savoring the aftertaste. On the outside, she never would have eaten this apple. She liked them firm, tart. But the apple was a sweet luxury in a place like this. She didn't open the sandwich. She could feel her tampon sliding farther down. Barely hanging on.

40.

WHEN WILL YOU STOP?

An hour later, a woman wearing scrubs was traveling from cell to cell, holding a clipboard, asking questions and writing things down. She was different from the guards, softer. Her top was a bright floral pattern and her pants brown. She moved from cell to cell like a bee to flowers.

When she was outside Pammy's cell, Joan could hear the things she was saying. She could not hear Pammy's responses, only the woman's questions.

Do you remember why you came here?

Do you know when that happened?

You came here on December seventeenth. Do you remember that?

You tattooed "Lucifer" on your arm, and you carved a cross into your forehead. Do you remember that?

Do you remember setting your apartment on fire?

Do you think you'll ever stop hurting yourself?

When will you stop?

Pammy had been locked up for months. Joan couldn't comprehend spending that much time here, in this freezing white box, or the effects it would have on her psyche. She would try to bludgeon herself to death too. She had the uncomfortable thought that this was where

Wyatt may have ended up, had he survived into his forties like Pammy. She tried not to think that perhaps it was for the best that Wyatt was gone. That he had made the right call. She tried not to think about any of this. It was too painful and confusing.

Joan stood by the door and eagerly waited for her turn to talk to the woman in scrubs. When the therapist approached, she felt a wave of relief and anticipation. Finally, someone was there to ask about *her*. How *she* was doing. Finally, somebody cared about Joan, and not just Pammy.

"Are you on any medications?" the woman asked. Joan listed her medications, leaving out the opiates and uppers that might make her look bad.

"Lexapro and Lamictal," she said.

The woman wrote them down. "How are you doing without them? Are you feeling all right? How is your mood?"

"I'm just really stressed about my job. I'm the director of a school and I need to call them, so they know what's going on. We have a big audit today."

The woman looked at Joan. "You seem very stressed."

Joan nodded. "I'm so stressed."

"What I'm gleaning from our conversation is that you would feel much more relaxed if somebody called your work for you."

"Yes, I would feel much more relaxed then."

Joan gave the woman the phone number of the Dallas campus, which she had memorized since childhood, and told her to ask for Tanya. She also told the woman the name of her lawyer, to give to Tanya. The therapist wrote it all down, seeming pleased to have a concrete way to help someone. This was probably rare for her. She left and returned about an hour later, saying she had made the call. Joan became euphoric, certain she would be out in no time. Perhaps she could meet the auditors after all, just slightly late.

But Joan was not out in no time. The hours dragged on, and the morning came and went. The light outside changed through Joan's tiny window, and she knew the auditors were there, assessing her campus without her.

The guards changed shifts. The new one was young, with a crew cut and an earpiece attached to a coiled cord that led down to a device on his belt. The departing guard briefed the new guy on Pammy. She showed him where she had put Pammy's Coke and radio, which Pammy was not allowed to have today. It had been one of her bad days. The new guard listened attentively and, after the old one left, sat down at the desk to go through paperwork. Periodically, he put his hand up to his ear, listening to something on the other end. With his pants tucked in and his rigid posture, he reminded Joan of Wyatt when he dressed like a Target employee. The guard appeared so fresh, so pleasant, that she began to cry. The guard turned and looked at Joan, noticing her there for the first time.

"Let me out!" Joan wailed. "Please just let me go to work."

He put his papers down and stood up from the desk. He opened the door of Joan's cell and stepped inside. Joan sat on her slab, astonished. This was the closest any of the guards had come to her since she'd been locked in the cell.

"You've never been to jail before, have you?" he said, looking Joan up and down.

"No," Joan said. "I've been here so long. I need to go to work. I'm the director of a school." She started to cry again.

"I understand that you're at sort of a low point right now. But instead of getting sad, you could look at this as an opportunity. Maybe you could hang on to this moment and reassess your lifestyle. Look around at who you're hanging out with, try to find some new friends. This could be a new start for you, if you choose it."

Joan continued to cry. "I'm so cold," she said. "I'm so uncomfortable. I haven't even been given a mat."

"We can't give you things like that down here," he said. "We're looking out for your safety, do you understand? You'd be amazed what people can use to hurt themselves."

"I'm just so cold and so bored," she whimpered.

"There are no guarantees," he said, "but my guess is, you'll probably get out of here in another four to six hours. Do you think you can make it till then?"

Joan nodded, feeling calmer for being spoken to so nicely. "I think so."

She noticed how smooth his skin was. She wondered about his homelife. He probably had a wife and a new baby. He seemed like someone with a baby that he liked to toss in the air. His wife had probably been his high school sweetheart. She'd probably even gotten a little fat from the baby, but he seemed like someone who would still love her anyway. He existed in a realm so foreign to Joan.

"How about some socks. Do you want me to go get you some socks?" he said.

Joan nodded again. "Yes, please, anything."

When he left, Joan thought about what the guard had said about starting over. She thought of her friends. She didn't have a "crowd" of friends. She had Claire, who had seemed to be drifting away ever since getting engaged to Luke and being accepted to a PhD program in Vermont. Luke had proposed to her in the Hill Country, at the top of Enchanted Rock, which made Joan feel deeply sorry for herself. Claire's life was moving forward and evolving, while Joan's seemed stuck. She also had her new roommate, Claire's friend Bianca, who worked long hours in tech and whom Joan couldn't stop stealing drugs from.

Then she had all her guys. Kyle, gone all the time, working on the Ted Cruz campaign, which was going surprisingly well. Cruz had received enough votes to instigate a runoff with David Dewhurst, and whoever won the Republican nomination in July would be the senator. There were Thad, her dealer, and the sandwich cart guys across the street. There were her employees and the students. Other than that, she couldn't think of anyone she considered a friend. Her world had grown so small.

The guard came back with socks, and she was so grateful. "Thank you," she said, sliding them over her prickly, splotchy, bruised legs.

"Can I ask you something?" the guard said before leaving Joan's cell.

"Sure," said Joan.

"Why did you want to kill yourself?" He looked hurt by it, as if it were personal for him.

"Oh, I didn't really want to hurt myself. It was all a misunderstanding."

"Then why did you say it? Why are you down here?"

"I don't know," Joan said. "I wanted to build the best case possible, I guess."

"Well, just be grateful that you're getting out so soon. That's more than a lot of people down here can say."

"Yes, sir," Joan said, even though he looked like he'd just gotten out of high school. She could tell by his thin frame, his smooth baby skin, his short hair, gelled and spiked unstylishly. Mostly, though, she knew he was young because he wasted his time talking to her. He still thought he could make a difference through this job.

Six hours later, Joan was released, just like the guard had predicted. She walked through the hallway with a guard, a new one whom she hadn't seen before. She glanced through Pammy's door on her way out. Pammy was still lying on her chair, her wrists strapped down, her head over to the side, resigned. The guard handed Joan the paper bag with her clothes. She changed in a bathroom, unguarded, unmonitored for the first time.

Outside, it was warm and sunny; the fresh air felt like a mother's kiss. There were cars all over; it must have been the end of the workday. She turned on her phone, which was nearly dead. It was past five in the afternoon. She had missed the audit altogether. The ACCSC people had come and gone, and she hadn't been there.

First, she called Kyle. She hoped he'd be close by, because he lived downtown, like her. She asked him for a ride home. Waiting for Kyle to arrive, she called her dad.

"I know what happened," her dad said when he answered.

"You do?"

"Yeah. Tanya told me." He paused. Joan watched homeless people lounging, carefree, in the park outside the jail. Two of them seemed to make a drug deal in the gazebo.

"How did the audit go?" she asked. "Did we pass?"

Her dad sighed. "We don't know yet. We should get the report in a few days."

"Oh," Joan said, feeling a sinking in her chest.

"You're a lot like me, you know. Like I used to be."

"Yeah," said Joan. She always told herself her parents, their addictions, were much worse than hers, but perhaps he was right. He told her he would drive down from Dallas the next day, take her to get the Jeep from the impound, so she could get to the school by nine tomorrow.

"What did you tell them about today?"

"Tanya told everyone you were sick," he said.

Joan knew nobody would believe that, not even for a second. But at the same time, she wasn't sure how much it mattered. She was the highest-ranking employee at the Austin campus. What were her employees going to say? She was part owner of the school. Perhaps there wasn't anything to worry about after all.

When Kyle pulled up in his Ford sedan, he was smiling broadly—the way people do when they catch you doing something you shouldn't. "Well look at you," he said. "You don't look worse for the wear."

Joan got in the car, flipped down the visor mirror, and saw that he was right. With her work outfit back on, her makeup still intact, her hair not yet oily or matted, she looked okay.

The sun was low in the sky, and traffic moved slowly. Cars were lined up. Everyone, including Joan, was going home after a long day to relax. Everything felt peaceful and orderly. The entire world was open and vast.

When she got back to her apartment, she was gleeful. She had traveled so far and she was free. She was free! Bianca was in the elevator, wearing her work clothes. What were the odds that they would be in the same elevator? Joan laughed, elated to see her. She looked right into her eyes, feeling so connected to her, to everything. "Where were you? I was so worried," Bianca said, and Joan just laughed and laughed, until tears came into her eyes.

41.

COMPLIANCE

Randy came to Austin early the next morning to pick Joan up and take her to the impound lot, where they retrieved the Jeep. The tow truck had damaged the canvas top, and there was a big, gaping hole in it. A long string of numbers was written on the windshield in shoe polish.

Joan drove the Jeep and followed Randy's Suburban back to the new campus, which he toured for the first time since the move. "I'd recognize that handwriting anywhere," Joan's studio manager said to her, and winked, referring to the numbers on her windshield, which must have been written by the police officer. Joan rolled her eyes and said nothing. The rest of the staff and faculty and students watched with interest as Joan walked Randy through the building, showing off the classrooms and offices and library she'd decorated and furnished. She showed him a custom sign she'd ordered, the parking lot she'd recently had repaved and painted to accommodate more vehicles. She showed him her office, where she kept all the files and had her framed certificates hung on the walls. She showed him the empty warehouse space, where he promised he would build her a theater and a new studio, just like he'd built in Encinitas. Together, they taped off the floor, planning the new spaces. Joan couldn't wait. Once they had their own nice facilities, students wouldn't come complaining to her so much, and her job would be much easier. Randy seemed proud of Joan. She was doing a good job. He thought the new campus looked great. He returned to Dallas, with plans to go back to Encinitas the following week.

Three days later, Joan was sitting at her desk when her dad called. The ACCSC report had come back, he said.

"And?" she said.

"The campus passed," he said. "You did a good job getting everything put together."

"That's great," Joan said, but Randy was silent on the other end. "Right?"

"There's just one problem."

Randy explained that the auditors had flagged Joan as unfit for her role. During their interviews, they uncovered a host of shocking and inappropriate behavior that had transpired between Joan and several AudioPro students. In the report, the auditors had written that Joan had gone to strip clubs repeatedly with one student and even bought drugs from another. They also found out, probably through public records, that Joan had been incarcerated during the audit. Unfortunately, she would need to resign, he said. They needed to hire a new director.

"Oh," Joan said, somewhat stunned. The auditors had been very thorough. Joan wondered who had ratted her out.

"I need to know something," Randy said.

"What?"

"You aren't taking speed again, are you? The report said something about buying drugs from students?"

Joan lied and promised Randy that she wasn't on pills. "That was just weed," she said. "I swear."

"Okay," he said, sounding relieved. "That's what I figured, I just had to ask."

Before they got off the phone, Randy offered to keep Joan on in another capacity. She could be marketing director again. Or a spy. Or whatever she wanted to call herself. She would still be in charge, just unofficially. After all, she was still part owner. This was still her inheritance.

"You know how it is. Just typical government bureaucrats. You don't look good enough on paper for them."

Joan told him she would think about it. But she knew immediately that she would decline the opportunity. Running the school was too time-consuming and overwhelming. She was in too much physical pain to sit at a desk all day anymore. She had legal problems to handle now. She had a very important book about Wyatt to write.

"Neither of my kids care about the family business, I guess," Randy would complain when she told him the following day. "I guess I'll have to cut you both out of the will."

"I guess so," Joan said. She told him she was sorry that it didn't work out, and she was. She had genuinely wanted to please Randy by being a good manager, a good business owner, and a good daughter.

42.

HIGHER SELF

Finally free of her suffocating nine-to-five schedule, Joan spent the next couple of months working on her brand-new novel. She set aside her previous writing projects—all of which seemed so trivial in the face of such tragedy. Joan saw even more clearly now that Wyatt was the one who had led a loud and beautiful life, not her. He was the person who deserved a book, not her. But every time Joan sat down to write about him, she was blocked. Her mind was bombarded with images, memories, sounds, feelings, but she could not articulate them artfully. She didn't know where to begin Wyatt's story, she only knew how it ended. The harder she tried to write about Wyatt's life, the more difficult and frustrating the task became. Nobody would ever understand what had been lost when he died. No matter what she wrote, it wouldn't do him justice. This was incredibly depressing for Joan to realize, day after day.

To unwind, Joan went out most nights, to drink and talk about her novel to anyone who would listen. Claire had moved to Vermont for graduate school, and Bianca didn't seem to care much about Joan's novel. She was in sales and mostly wanted to talk about office politics, as well as a European coworker whom she wanted to sleep with. So Joan would often go out drinking alone with her notebook. She would sit on barstools, order straight whiskey or tequila, and unload her new novel idea on whichever man made the mistake of trying to come on to her.

What was the novel about? the men would ask, intrigued. Depending on how drunk Joan was, she would give slightly different answers.

"It's a *Behind the Music*—esque look at a young man who could have been a famous piano player but died tragically instead."

"It's a contemporary western tale in which a young man rescues his girlfriend from a life of stripping. They move out to the country, where they live happily ever after, until he kills himself, tragically."

"It's a psychological supernatural horror thriller about a young man possessed by demons. Eventually, he becomes a demon himself, haunting his entire horrible family until they all become demons too. Then he kills himself."

"It's a dark comedy, kind of like *The Royal Tenenbaums*, but about an oil-monied Texan family with dwindling wealth, whose overzealous religious views lead them to neglect their mentally ill relative and allow him to destroy himself."

The men would nod, assuring her that the idea was great, commercially viable, and deep. But Joan never wrote any of these pitches down. Instead, she woke up every morning not remembering where she'd been or whom she'd talked to, feeling so useless and ashamed that all she could do was start drinking again.

It was one of these mornings, in early June 2012, that her mother showed up unannounced. Joan was terribly hungover, as usual, and not ready for company.

"Please, I'm not feeling well," she said, panicked. "There is trash all over my apartment. Sewage is leaking in my bathroom. You can't stay here."

To Joan's surprise, Dolly didn't get mad. She sounded calm, accepting. She agreed not to come over. She would book a room at the Four Seasons on the river—Joan's favorite hotel. As long as Joan would allow Dolly to pick her up and bring her there. This was uncharacteristic of her mother, who was mostly wildly cheap and always insisted on sleeping on Joan's couch.

After Dolly keyed into their room at the Four Seasons, Joan climbed immediately into the fluffy white queen-sized bed. It was four in the afternoon, and she was ready to sleep again. She nestled her head into the cold feather pillow. She closed her eyes and covered them with her forearm to keep the light out. Joan loved the Four Seasons. It felt so good to be in a nice, immaculate room, no longer surrounded by her own accumulated filth. The beds were like clouds. She curled under the weighty white covers and felt like she was being hugged. She could forget about her loneliness here, temporarily. She could forget about her life, all the laundry and dishes, her broken toilet, her unopened bills. The only downside was that her mother was also there, seated on the other bed, staring at her.

"Could I have a painkiller?" Joan asked. "My head is killing me."

"I told you I don't keep those anymore."

"Oh yeah, I forgot," Joan said, and groaned in self-pity.

"I want to talk about what you're planning to do for a living. Now that your dad let you go. Your rent is really high for someone who's unemployed."

"I've told you. I'm working on a novel about Wyatt."

"You've been saying you were writing a book for over five years now. That's not a job. It's a hobby."

"Books take a long time to write," Joan said. "But fine, I'll get some kind of job, if that's what you want."

Now that Ted Cruz had a real shot at becoming a US senator, Joan intended to ask Kyle to hire her. In May, David Dewhurst had failed to earn over 50 percent of the primary votes, which triggered a runoff in July. It had been a shocking political upset. Perhaps Cruz would actually win the runoff, and Joan could move to DC, far away from her family, and forge a new life for herself. She could answer phones for him, proofread bills, or run his social media or something. But she hadn't gotten around to asking Kyle for a job. He was always busy, in some small town or another. Besides, she was afraid of what his answer might be.

305

"Well, I think you're going to have to sober up to find any kind of job," Dolly said.

"Can we please talk about this later? My head hurts so bad."

Dolly grunted and turned on the TV. She flipped through channels until she found Fox News. She watched *Hannity* while Joan floated in and out of a shallow sleep. Soon, her mother was interacting with the TV, indignantly cursing Obama's socialist policies. In April, Romney had become the presumptive Republican nominee, finally. But the entire process to get there had disturbed Joan. The way he'd been attacked and dubbed a flip-flopper, as if it were a crime to change and grow as a person. As if it were somehow negative that he'd been the governor of a Democratic state and was able to work with members of the other side. Why had it taken her party so long to accept him? Why had he been such a tough pill to swallow? He was a good man, qualified and humble. She resented Sean Hannity and Fox News and the way they represented the conservative movement. His messages were simplistic. Xenophobic. Dumb. It seemed to Joan that nobody wanted to think for themselves anymore. Nobody except for her. She considered her own views, like Mitt Romney's, to be nuanced, sophisticated, and intellectually rigorous.

"Could you please turn that crap off?" Joan said. "I have the worst headache."

Her mother adjusted the volume a notch.

An hour passed. *The Five* came on. Joan's mother began to get restless, pacing around the room. She brushed her blond hair into her signature high ponytail. She tied the scrunchie and began puffing on an e-cigarette, blowing vapor out the side of her mouth. She'd finally quit smoking.

"I'm going outside. I'm not going to sit cooped up in here all night. I quit drinking and drugging so I didn't have to live this way."

Dolly left the room, letting the door slam. Joan lay there, still feeling foggy, her head still pounding, but she felt better than she had before. It felt good to be alone. Squinting slightly, she watched the rest of *The Five*. She didn't have the energy to get up and find the remote to change the channel. Besides, she didn't mind this show as much as she minded *Hannity*. At least *The Five* had Greg Gutfeld, who made a funny joke every once in a while.

Joan texted Bianca, letting her know she would be spending the night at the Four Seasons. She texted Claire, asking about Vermont. Claire responded with a picture of some trees, vibrant and beautiful next to a glistening lake. Joan had never seen a place like that in her life. She felt a wave of hideous jealousy come over her.

Pretty, she wrote back.

The sun began to set outside. The sky turned pink, purple, then black. Eventually, Joan ventured out into the lobby to look for Dolly. It was nine P.M., and her empty stomach was now desperate for sustenance. She hadn't eaten all day. Dolly sat at a cocktail table in the lobby, drinking a Diet Coke, talking on her blue flip phone to someone, probably Randy, obviously about Joan. She could tell because, as she approached, Dolly kept looking at her and speaking in hushed tones, ending the call before Joan sat down. Ever since Wyatt died and Joan lost her job, her parents always seemed to be scheming behind her back, trying to decide what to do. She had become the family's new problem. It was irritating. She just wanted to be left alone.

"I need to eat," said Joan, motioning for a waiter. Her mother was uncharacteristically quiet, chewing on something in her mind.

Joan ordered a basket of French fries. Salt and grease. That was the only thing that sounded edible in her condition. The fries arrived, hot and sprinkled with garlic seasoning. Joan ate them greedily, three at a time, dipping them in a large glob of cold ketchup.

"I came here because I want to talk to you about something," Dolly said.

"What," Joan said.

"Please don't be like that."

"You know I hate when you introduce conversations. Just talk. Don't say you want to talk."

"I'm sorry you don't like the way I communicate."

"Here we go."

"I wish we could just have a conversation without hurting each other's feelings."

"My feelings aren't hurt. Yours are."

Her mother looked out the window and shook her head. Joan expected her to start crying and storm away, to make a dramatic exit and blame Joan for everything, the way she usually did, but she didn't. She composed herself and turned toward Joan again.

"I've been working the twelve steps again," Dolly said.

"What? Why? Did you relapse again?"

"No. I'm working the steps for codependency this time," Dolly explained. "I'm on step nine, and I owe you an amends."

Joan began to squirm, the way she had when her dad made his amends when she was seventeen. Randy had picked her up from her grandmother's house and driven her to his new beach house on Padre Island. On the drive, Randy admitted that he'd been a terrible father. He told her that on the weekends she and Henry would visit, he would be looking at his watch, waiting for them to leave so he could party. He cried, telling her this. Joan had stared out the window the entire time, wishing she could dissolve. Still, the conversation had broken something open for her and her father. They started seeing each other much more after that, and talking about everything. She appreciated hearing the truth.

"What for?" Joan asked.

"I was wrong for bringing Doug into our lives," Dolly said. "I didn't prioritize my children, and I've never acknowledged how that must have affected you. I saw it all as my pain, not yours. But that was selfish. Obviously living with him hurt you too."

"That's okay," Joan said. Her chest felt tight, like she was on the verge of tears.

"I have to ask you a question," Dolly said.

"What?"

"Did he ever touch you?" Dolly's eyes were wet and glistening. "I remember I left you with him a lot."

"No," Joan said. This was a question her therapist asked her repeatedly. It probably could have explained a lot of her issues. "He was bad, but he didn't do anything like that. Not that I can remember, at least."

Dolly sat back in her chair, relieved. "Thank god," she said. "If he had, I don't know if I could live with myself."

Joan didn't know what to say. She continued eating. "Is that all?" she said. It seemed her mother wasn't done talking.

Dolly sighed. "I'm very concerned about your drinking. And the drugs. Especially the drugs. All those pain medicines you've been taking. Those are dangerous. People are dying. I'm not sure what all you're taking, but I've heard that mixing painkillers with benzos is lethal."

"I don't take benzos," Joan said, focused on the fries. "I have a bad arm. You know that." She motioned for the waiter and requested a side of ranch.

Dolly waited for the server to leave the table before speaking again. "This is serious. If you don't slow down with the booze and stop taking the pain pills, there are going to be consequences."

Joan snorted. "What kind of consequences?"

"I'm going to quit paying your rent."

Joan stopped eating. "What is this, an intervention? I thought this was supposed to be an amends!"

Joan knew all about interventions. *Intervention* was her favorite TV show. She liked to watch the junkies who passed out on their front lawns or face down in their cereal bowls. She liked to differentiate herself from those people, who were much worse off than she was.

"I'm trying to help you get off the elevator before it reaches the bottom. I don't know if you've crossed the line yet. You might not be a pickle yet. You might still be a cucumber."

Crossed the line. Get off the elevator. Pickle. Joan knew what it meant when her mother began to talk in metaphors. "I'm not going to AA," she said defiantly.

In high school, after Dolly's divorce and relapse, she had dragged Joan to meetings all around the slums of Lewisville and held big, loser-filled NA pool parties in their backyard.

"I'm not saying you have to be in AA. What I'm saying is, you're going to need to show me that you're working on this problem. You know, addiction is hereditary."

"I know that. You've told me a million times."

"La Hacienda is a nice place. And they have a bed for you."

Joan began to panic. La Hacienda was where her dad went to re-hab when she was seventeen. Afterward, he began talking about God incessantly and crying during movies. He talked nonstop for a year about a spiritual experience he had there, while lying on a pool float. The clouds had parted, he swore, and a voice in the sky had told him that everything was going to be okay. Stevie Ray Vaughan went there too, in the eighties. So did Wyatt, after his first suicide attempt. A lot of good that did.

"I'll have to think about it," Joan said.

"You can sleep on it. But you'll need to decide by tomorrow morning."

"Fine," she said.

"You know, I'm only doing this because I love you and I know what you're going through," Dolly said, placing her hand on Joan's. "I'm trying to help you before you end up like me."

"Mom," Joan said. "That's a depressing thing to say."

"I'm just being honest."

Walking back to the room with Dolly, Joan wondered what she meant by "end up like her." Alone? Miserable? Wrinkled? Joan brushed her teeth while Dolly lay on her bed and watched more Fox News.

"Will you rub my feet?" Dolly said from her bed. "I'll pay you."

"Do I have to?"

"Please."

"Fine. But only if you rub mine too."

"Okay."

Joan lay at the foot of the bed, taking her mother's rough, callused feet into her hands, putting her own soft feet into Dolly's. This was something they did for each other occasionally. One of the only acts of tenderness left between them. A mutual sacrifice, a mutual pleasure. Her mother groaned in ecstasy. Rubbing Dolly's calves, Joan felt the thick hair pushing its way through her skin, rough as sandpaper, the result of many more years of shaving. Someday, her own legs would feel like this. When Dolly fell asleep, Joan gently moved off the bed, slipped the remote from her fingers, and turned off the TV. She crawled into her own bed, opened her laptop, and looked up the rehab facility online.

La Hacienda was on a ranch in Hunt, Texas. She watched promotional videos. Shots of rolling pastures, wildflowers blowing in the gentle breeze. There was a guy who appeared to be in his thirties standing in a Zen garden, talking about loving himself. Like really loving himself. He had gained total acceptance of who he was, he said. He had a good relationship with his parents, his family. He was no longer fearful of being alone. There was a fountain behind him, an arch with climbing vines, benches, a hot tub.

Joan wanted to love herself too. If loving herself was an option. She couldn't envision a life without alcohol or pills, but she couldn't envision a future with them either. After all, she'd had two months to work on her book and had gotten literally nothing done, despite being heavily medicated. The other night, she had woken up mysteriously locked in her building's stairwell after leaving her keys in the front door of her apartment. When she looked at her phone the next morning, she saw that she had called Roberto thirty times. Even worse, she saw that he had answered and talked to her almost half of those times. She didn't want to think about what had been said between them, what embarrassing truths or lies had been spoken. Perhaps at rehab, they would teach her strategies to stop calling Roberto.

She decided she would go. What did she have to lose? She watched her mother sleeping on the other bed, on top of the covers, her neck bent in an awkward, unflattering position. She knew she didn't want to be like her. She didn't want to give up and let herself go. She didn't want to have to make amends to her own grown children, years from now, for marrying a psychopathic, narcissistic sex addict. Like Wyatt, Joan decided she just wanted to be normal, healthy, and happy. She wanted to sleep at night and write during the day. She wanted to keep her apartment clean, cook her own meals. She wanted to be a woman worth loving.

43.

BYE-BYE BOOKS

December 2012, six months later

Joan woke to the sound of cows mooing outside her window. Her cat lay at the foot of the bed, on a patchwork quilt that had been sewn by her grandmother in the late seventies—the hideous mix of pink, mint, and forest green, neon orange and brown, was almost beautiful. Joan rolled off the bed, careful not to disturb the sleeping cat. She kneeled on the shaggy brown carpet and said her morning prayer.

The prayer was nothing special. All she had to say was "help." The important thing was that she was relinquishing control of her day to her Higher Power. Her Higher Power, which she was told could be anything besides herself. At first, her Higher Power was Wyatt. It felt easy, praying to his ghost. But over the months it had morphed and expanded into something else, something more mysterious and dynamic. It didn't only *contain* qualities she associated with Wyatt—unrestrained creativity, innocence, and love. It *was* those qualities she prayed to.

She walked into the kitchen and got a sugar-free Monster from the fridge—a tall, bright blue can. She cracked it open, took a sip, and carried it outside for her morning walk.

She didn't check the news. She didn't listen to a podcast. Instead, she put in her earphones and listened to a Hans Zimmer soundtrack. At the advice of her sponsor, she had let go of politics, for now. All politics could do was divide her further from her fellow humans, which was the opposite of what she needed. It was just as well. The election had been depressing for her. Mitt Romney had been treated dreadfully by the press, chastised for the smallest things, like saying corporations were people (they were), talking about having binders full of female job candidates (a good thing), and strapping the family dog to the roof of his car for vacation (the dog loved it). Obama had won reelection handily. Watching the map turn blue, Joan tried not to worry about the grim direction her beloved country was headed. If it was God's will that she live in a socialist dystopia with Obama at the helm, she would need to learn to accept that and be happy anyway.

Joan followed the familiar red gravel path, through the cedar-filled brush and past the back barn, through a few pastures full of cows, and all the way to the back tank, where she fed some catfish, watching their gaping mouths open and close. She had moved onto her mother's family's property, Duncan Ranch, over the summer, shortly after graduating from rehab. The reason was dual purpose: It allowed her to escape the temptations of her downtown apartment as well as make financial amends to her mother, whom she had been extracting money from for so long. Here, she could watch the property for the family in exchange for a dwelling. Here, she could be useful. It was never good to leave a house untended to. The pipes could burst. Animals could invade. Leaves could collect on the roof and catch fire.

Some days were good. The prayers seemed like they were doing something, and she could enjoy the nature and the peace. Other days, she felt numb and didn't feel God's presence at all. Some days were just bad. She felt terrible and wished she could be dead, like Wyatt, so she wouldn't have to feel anything. "This too shall pass," her sponsor would say. "In sobriety, you can wear your emotions like a loose garment, let the good and bad feelings come and go through your body like weather patterns." Joan was trying. She had been sober from drugs and alcohol for over six months.

Joan sat on a large rock to rest. She set her Monster on the gravel and reached into her pocket for her vape pen, a habit she'd picked up at La Hacienda. She puffed on the vape, watching the large steam clouds floating against the bright blue sky. She planned to quit soon. Once she hit her year mark. But now, she would indulge. As she sat on the rock, a haiku formed in her mind. She pocketed the vape pen and pulled out a small Moleskine and pen to write:

> Cedar trees, my only friends
> Shaped like green teardrops
> Between red dirt and blue sky.

She knew the poem wasn't great. Nothing she wrote really was. Being great wasn't the point for her anymore. Being present was. Joan had written hundreds of haikus since moving to the ranch, out of sheer boredom. Each day sober at the ranch felt like an entire week. In every twenty-four-hour period, she experienced a range of unfamiliar emotions—joy, terror, despair, hope, awe. She tried to capture them all on paper. She tried to embrace feeling "alive," as Wyatt had always encouraged her to do.

Back at the house, she sat down at her desk. Along the shelf above her, she had placed several books to inspire her—self-help books (*Toxic Parents: Healing Their Harmful Legacy and Reclaiming Your Life*; *Your Captivating Heart*; *Women Who Love Too Much*), some writing reference material (*No Plot? No Problem!*; *The Artist's Way*), and a few works of fiction (*One Hundred Years of Solitude*; *The Lone Vaquero*; *A Farewell to Arms*).

After skimming a few pages of *Toxic Parents*, Joan opened her notebook and began her daily writing practice. Each day, she wrote five pages by hand, filling notebooks with messy cursive words. She didn't know what she was writing toward. She didn't know whether her work would ever be published or receive any acclaim. She didn't know if her writing would ever be read by anyone at all. Joan wrote now only to understand—herself, her god, her family of origin, her past and current relationships, her hopes and desires, her fears and shortcomings. Each day, she embraced the unknown. Her sponsor warned her against thinking too much about the future. Life happened in the present, she would say.

Sometimes, Joan wrote letters she would never send, to her parents, to Henry, to Aunt Charlene and Grace, and to any friends she'd wronged, or who she thought had wronged her.

Sometimes, she wrote directly to herself. As if she were writing an instruction manual. *First, get out of Texas*, she'd written once. *Get as far away from your family as you possibly can.*

Sometimes, she wrote about Wyatt. She still had the cooler full of his journals sitting by her desk, which she opened and read through occasionally. She got to know Wyatt better than she'd known him at the time he died. The truth was, they'd grown distant. The truth was, she didn't know what he was going through. She felt she had abandoned him, but at the same time, there wasn't much any of them could have done to save him.

Soon, Joan would be transferring the notebooks to Aunt Charlene and Grace, at their request. Grace and Charlene were collaborating on a screenplay about the billboard incident. They wanted the notebooks for research. That spring, they intended to enter a Christian screenplay contest. Joan wondered how they'd found out about the notebooks, but had agreed to part with them. Charlene and Grace were his immediate family, after all. Who was Joan to be the keeper of all Wyatt's journals in perpetuity? She was only his cousin. In preparation, she scanned every single page onto a thumb drive. It had taken eight hours over several days.

In his notebooks, she saw what it was he really wanted. It wasn't fame or fortune or attention. It wasn't performing. Wyatt dreamed of a simple, humble life. He aspired only to go to sleep at night and wake up in the morning. To work hard and honestly. To support a good woman who loved him. To be a good father, unlike his own. He just wanted to be normal, and he would never have that chance. Joan did have that chance, and she was determined not to squander it.

Sometimes, when it was too painful to write about herself or her family, she simply wrote down what she observed:

The white windowsill is lined with dead insects.
The jet-black cat sleeps on the hideous quilt.
The sun shines through the dirty window, onto the glossy
antique furniture.
The cows rush toward me, thinking I have food.

Sometimes, when it was too painful to think, she filled the pages with affirmations, repeated over and over again.

I am a force of creativity and love. I am a force of creativity and love. I am a prolific writer. I am a prolific writer. I am a prolific writer.

At noon, Joan stopped writing. She drove her Mazda into town for an AA meeting, held in a conference room of a Baptist church. Hearne was what some might call a shit town, so poor that the Walmart had been closed two years before. Mostly old people, the group had become her support system. One woman had a hole in her neck and talked like a frog. One man had a glass eye and was dying of cancer, but he laughed every time he shared. Joan didn't share today. She was usually too shy and still felt she had nothing to offer. But just having somewhere to be, somewhere she would be seen and recognized and acknowledged, was enough to perk her up and get her through the rest of her day. After her meeting, her phone dinged with an email alert. It was from Roberto.

Lady,

Hope this finds you well. Just wanted to let you know I have a book coming out! I'm getting published by some crazy guy out of Portland. The release party is tonight at Bye-Bye Books. Hope you can make it. Would be so great to see you there.

Yrs, R

Joan read the email a few more times, trying to discern its tone. *Hope you can make it. Would be so great to see you there.* She and Roberto were on good terms now. She had made amends to him from rehab, after completing an exercise in which she cradled a small brown pillow that was supposed to represent Roberto as a baby. "I love you," she had whispered to the pillow. "I love you and I forgive you and I release you into the Light."

Joan wondered which book Roberto had finished. Was it the old-lady book? Or perhaps he had returned to and completed *Bitter Texas Honey.* Perhaps that was why he'd reached out, and she would be immortalized in literature after all. Joan allowed herself to marinate in this fantasy as she shaved her legs, got dressed up, and put makeup on for the first time in several weeks.

The drive to Austin was over an hour. On the way, she called her sponsor to tell her she was going to her ex-boyfriend's book launch. Accountability was important in sobriety. There would probably be wine there, and Joan would have to refuse it. Her sponsor recommended making a gratitude list beforehand and ordered her not to be alone with Roberto. Joan agreed. But if Roberto wanted to be alone with her, it would be hard to refuse. She would want to be alone with him too. "I am a sober woman of dignity and grace," she said aloud in the car after hanging up. "I have a sparkling personality."

She arrived at Bye-Bye Books, a shabby shop in Hyde Park that would likely go out of business soon. Inside, Joan purchased Roberto's book, a tiny hardback with a man wearing a sombrero, riding a donkey, and wielding a chain saw on the cover. The title was: *The Very Bloody Uprising of the Most Well-Read Mexicans You've Ever Met.* A vague sense of shame rose within Joan as she stood in a crowd of hipsters waiting to talk to Roberto. When it was finally her turn to be acknowledged, she asked him sheepishly to sign the inside cover of her book. He smiled and bent down to hug her. He was wearing ill-fitting gray slacks, a vest, and a red tie. She'd never seen him dressed this way.

"I'm so happy to see you," he said. "I already signed them all."

"Oh," said Joan. She opened the cover and saw.

"Here, I'll sign yours again," said Roberto, and he wrote something else on the title page, which she didn't read.

"Thanks," she said. "And congratulations."

"Of course. Are you working on anything?" he asked.

"Y-yeah," Joan stammered, surprised he cared. "I'm working on several things. Some poetry. Something about my late cousin. I also just started a novella about my life. It's called *How to Become a Republican*."

"That is a good title," he said.

"Really?"

"Yes. It is very Lorrie Moore."

"Thank you." Joan blushed. She had enjoyed the book *Self-Help*, which she had read a couple of times in rehab. She planned to apply to Vanderbilt's MFA program once she got her life more together, and she fantasized that Lorrie Moore would become her mentor. Perhaps Joan would spend late evenings over at Lorrie Moore's house, drinking herbal tea, somewhere in the rolling Tennessee hills. Perhaps Moore would become like a second mother to her.

Joan took her seat, watching Roberto continue to mingle. He had so many friends now. Stylish, artsy people she had never seen. When Roberto stood in front of the room at the microphone, everyone went silent.

"This microphone stand perfectly represents the book I published," he said. Everybody laughed. The stand was falling apart, covered with duct tape. "I'm in a room full of the most creative people I know," he said.

The crowd seemed to swell with pride. Joan thought: *Who the fuck are these people?*

"I'd like to thank everyone from the Michener Center," he said, "who have taken me in and shown me so much, and opened so many doors."

Joan wondered when in the past two years Roberto had cozied up to the MFA program that he used to talk so much shit about.

"Finally, I owe this all to my beautiful fiancée," Roberto said. "Without her, none of this would be possible."

He began to read from his book, and Joan scanned the crowd.

His beautiful fiancée.

His beautiful fiancée.

His beautiful fiancée.

Was it that skinny girl over there? Her gaze fell upon a petite strawberry blonde with a Euro mullet. Weird cheekbones, though. Joan had gained at least fifteen pounds since getting sober. Maybe more like twenty. She'd stopped weighing herself at the advice of her sponsor. She adjusted the top of her jeans and sat up straighter in her seat, sucking in. Her neck suddenly felt hot, and her chest buzzed with anxiety.

He didn't have the kind of penis I like anyway, she repeated to herself as he read. Long and thin, like a snake in the desert. Who wanted a lifetime of that?

After the reading, Roberto thanked the room, which erupted in applause. Joan didn't say goodbye. She got the fuck out of Bye-Bye Books and into her dirty Mazda hatchback, still loaded full of her belongings. She saw no point in unpacking it all at the ranch, as it was a temporary living situation. She suddenly became overwhelmed with the feeling that she had nothing figured out. Her life was in shambles. She often complained about this to her sponsor, who kept telling her she was growing, and that Rome wasn't built in a day.

Joan drove down Cesar Chavez, past the freeway, to the Whole Foods in the nice part of town, near the Amtrak station, where she bought a container of presliced mango. A luxury she couldn't dream of getting back in Hearne.

Sitting outside, eating the slimy, sweet fruit, Joan opened Roberto's book and began reading, but she couldn't concentrate on the words. Instead, she imagined Roberto's homelife. First thing tomorrow he would probably be sitting at his typewriter, already working on his next book while his waifish fiancée stood in the kitchen, cooking something organic and hearty. Fattening him up and curling up on the sofa with him afterward. Perhaps they read important hefty books together while his sad cattle dog (happy now?) slept at their feet. Full of despair, Joan opened her notebook and wrote a haiku:

I am fat and hideous.
A talentless hack.
Rome wasn't built in a day.

Joan was looking over her work when she was approached by a short man in gym clothes—a bright blue shirt and black basketball shorts. She closed her notebook. He asked her for her name and if she wanted to get a drink sometime.

"I don't drink," she said.

He told her he was new to town, from New Zealand. "Are you a writer?" he asked, motioning toward the notebook.

"Yes," she said. "Sort of."

His eyes lit up. "I'm a writer too!"

"Really?"

"Well, a copywriter. Mostly web content."

"Oh." Joan took a puff off her vape pen and looked back at her notebook. He asked her what she was writing about.

"It's a dark comedy," Joan said, exhaling a cloud of vapor. "Kind of like *The Royal Tenenbaums*, but about an oil-monied Texan family with dwindling wealth, whose overzealous religious views lead them to neglect their mentally ill relative and allow him to destroy himself."

The man from New Zealand nodded. "Sounds interesting," he said. He told her it was cool that she didn't drink. He was really into fitness, so he didn't drink very much either. Joan found everything about him repulsive—his sensible job, his healthy habits, his earnest gaze. She gave him her phone number and left.

She drove the familiar roads back to Hearne, minding the speed traps. Her Mazda wasn't as nice as her BMW had been, but it was good enough. It would last much longer and cost much less money. She missed her BMW, though. Its speed and power, the responsiveness of its steering wheel. Driving it had felt like flying a jet.

She got back to the ranch past nine. It was eerily quiet. The stars were loud and bright in the black sky. When she got inside, her cat was yowling with hunger; she had forgotten to feed her dinner before leaving. "I'm so sorry, my baby," she cooed, petting the black cat. "I love you very much." She'd taken the cat back as part of her living amends, to her mother and to the animal itself. At times, she liked having a creature to care about, a being relying on her. But sometimes, she felt bringing the animal home had been a huge mistake. It had been Wyatt's idea originally. The first time he ever saw her apartment in Austin, all her furniture and décor and artwork, he'd looked around in awe and said, "You know what this place needs? A black cat."

Joan had adopted a black kitten the following day. An accessory. A decoration. Never could she have imagined that the kitten would outlive Wyatt. She thought about this, lying in bed, stroking the cat, who began drooling on her chest. Before she turned off her cowboy-boot-shaped lamp, she checked her phone. The guy from New Zealand had already messaged her.

Nice to meet you tonight. ☺ *I hope we can talk more about writing soon.*

Joan didn't respond. The text didn't hook her, so she would leave him in suspense, perhaps reply a few days later. Maybe she would wait an entire week, she thought, looking at the water-stained tiles on the ceiling. She turned off the lamp and said her nighttime prayer, a simple "Thanks." Meaning, thanks for keeping her sober. Thanks for dragging her through another day without incident. While she was drifting off, she thought of Roberto's reading, and then the short man from New Zealand. She wondered where he might take her for their first date. Perhaps, the second time she saw him, he would look better. Perhaps, when she got to know him, his height wouldn't be such a big deal. Maybe with him, she would find a real, lasting love, deeper and more wholesome than any love she'd had before. A haiku began to take shape in her mind, but she was too tired to write it down. She would probably forget it by morning, but she didn't care; she was practicing a mindset of abundance. If the haiku was meant to be in the world, it would come back to her later. She didn't have to control it. She didn't need to struggle. She drifted to sleep, reciting the poem:

> *Copywriter from New Zea-*
> *Land. Solid, like earth,*
> *Perhaps you are a real man.*

ACKNOWLEDGMENTS

Thank you, Jin Auh, for taking me on when I had nothing but a few linked stories and a dream. Without your vision and advocacy, this book would not exist.

Pilar Garcia-Brown, thank you for bringing your whole heart to this project, and for going above and beyond. This book is so much better (and funnier) now thanks to you.

Thank you to everyone at Dutton, Penguin Random House, and the Wylie Agency who had a hand in turning this Word document into a book—Ella Kurki, Abram Scharf, John Parsley, Sarah Thegeby, Amanda Walker, Nicole Jarvis, Stephanie Cooper, Alice Dalrymple, Aja Pollock, Ariel Harari, and Alison Cnockaert.

A young writer is a fragile thing. I am fortunate to have had many wonderful teachers along the way. Thank you especially to Benjamin Alsup, for first showing me what fiction could be. Thank you for reading some of my most half-baked work with gusto and encouraging me no matter what. Thank you to Oscar Casares for your patience, sage advice, and your belief in my work over the years.

Thank you to S. Kirk Walsh, who is so much more than a mentor. Your empathy and generosity have made me a much better writer (and person). Thanks also to all my "Kirkshop" homies in Austin for your careful attention to my work over the years.

ACKNOWLEDGMENTS

I am indebted to the Helen Zell Writers' Program at the University of Michigan, where things got real. I am grateful to nearly all my professors there, especially Peter Ho Davies, whose mentorship was invaluable. Eileen Pollack, thank you for teaching me what a story is and what a story is not. Michael Byers, thank you for your enthusiasm. Thank you as well to Claire Vaye Watkins, Laura Kasischke, Dan Shere, and Amy Sara Carroll.

Thank you as well to my Michigan fiction cohort—Yasin, Abdul-Muqit, Austin Blaze, Rebecca Fortes, Sam Jensen, Bryce Pope, Kristen Roupenian, and Clarisse Baleja Saidi—for being amazing and for putting up with Joan's antics for so long.

Kristen Roupenian, Emily Chew, YoungEun Yook, Dena Afrasiabi, Charlotte Mark, Diana Gomez Cook, Lauren Pinkerton, thank you for your early reads, wise counsel, and continued friendship. I am eagerly waiting for all of your books too, so please get to work.

A (very) short version of this book appeared in *Tin House* magazine back in 2018. Thank you, Michelle Wildgen, for giving me a boost by publishing "Canon." That was a great highlight of my life. Thank you as well to the Ragdale Foundation for supporting this project in 2019.

Thank you, Julia Fierro, for your help with my MFA application. Thank you, Dori Ostermiller and Writers in Progress, for giving me a safe, delightful space to explore new material.

Thank you, Rebecca Cook, for keeping me young and explaining social media to me.

Thank you to my parents, for always supporting me, encouraging my creative pursuits, and never being boring. I am who I am because of you both. Thank you to my brother for always being there, solid like earth. Thank you to the rest of my extended family for experiencing this bizarre life alongside me. My soul chose you all, and like it or not we're stuck together.

Finally, to my loves, Garrett, Arthur, and Elliot, thank you for sharing your home and your hearts with me.

ABOUT THE AUTHOR

ASHLEY WHITAKER is a writer from Texas. She received an MFA from the Helen Zell Writers' Program at the University of Michigan. Her fiction has appeared in *Tin House* and *StoryQuarterly*, and has received support from the Ragdale Foundation. She lives in Austin with her family. *Bitter Texas Honey* is her first novel.